OASIS

TOSH MCINTOSH

Aviator
Writer
Press

PUBLISHERS NOTE

**Published in the
United States of America by
Aviator Writer Press**

Digital Edition (v1.3)
ISBN-13: 978-0-9840489-7-7

Print Edition (v1.3)
ISBN-13: 978-0-9840489-6-0

DEDICATION

To my father, may he rest in peace, who wrote short stories and kept the carbon copies in loose-leaf binders on the bookshelves in my childhood home in Dallas, Texas. I never saw the originals. They disappeared into envelopes addressed to many of the popular magazines of the day. To the best of my knowledge, none of his stories ever made it into print to be read by the public.

And that matters not, because I have never forgotten the experience of turning those flimsy pages and reading the words my father wrote. As for so many other things, I owe him a lifelong debt for unlocking my imagination and instilling in me a passionate love of storytelling.

"Being a pilot is like having an incurable blood disease, Toby. All you can do is treat it with more flying. And once you've flown a fighter on the deck at five hundred knots, or docked a shuttle on Oasis, you're hooked for life. It's the ultimate video game, and the universe is yours to do with as you please. And don't forget, if you want to wear these wings, you have to be the best. Nothing less will do."

— Captain Brett Larsen, United States
Space Command Pilot

AUTHOR'S FOREWORD

Oasis is a novel of the alternative past that begins approximately 30 years prior to present day, based on three questions.

What if the 1984 NASA Space Station *Freedom* project had not been transformed into the *International Space Station* in 1993?

And what if chaos born of overpopulation, environmental pollution, unceasing warfare, climate change, and a series of increasingly virulent pandemics had put Earth on an unalterable 30-year collision course toward a final global apocalypse?

How might these events might have changed history?

In the real historical timeline, the space race is born in the 1950s as an extension of the cold war between the United States and the Soviet Union.

After an impressive string of "firsts" for the Soviets in the early '60s, the Americans solidify their technological supremacy through the Apollo program and plant a U.S. flag on the moon on July 20, 1969. The Soviets are unable to respond in kind.

The next step for the U.S. is development of a space shuttle designed to supply *Freedom*, both unrealized technological leaps. Budgetary cuts, design changes and ballooning costs halt any significant advances in the *Freedom* program while space shuttle development continues. With the collaboration of Russia, Japan, Europe and Canada, the *Freedom* project becomes the *International Space Station*.

In the alternative history of *Oasis*, squabbling among *ISS* members, Russian budgetary constraints, and a series of technological problems cause Russia to drop out. The *ISS* project is terminated.

Loss of the *ISS* and increasingly dire predictions for the future of mankind remove any US government hesitancy with regard to accelerating completion of *Freedom* and implementing changes in the space shuttle program with the following objectives: increase payloads; add the capability to leave low Earth orbit for travel to the Moon; utilize powered flight after returning from space; reduce turnaround time for the next launch; and incorporate the latest developments in military aviation technology as defense against any attempts by foreign governments to interfere with America's dominance in space and controlling access to Moon Colony #1.

These space shuttle improvements accelerate construction of *Freedom*, which becomes operational with full-time crew member presence, followed by the first successful space shuttle departure from Earth orbit, trip to the Moon, and entry into Lunar orbit.

Construction of *Oasis* begins. Shortly after the space station receives its first permanent crew member contingent, the Lunar Landing Module transfer of construction materials and supplies for Moon Colony #1 further solidifies and accelerates progress.

In July, 2012, The United States Space Command successfully proves viability of each individual element of the project to the point at which shuttle missions provide a steady stream of supplies in sufficient quantity to support *Oasis* and the Moon Colony #1 project, and the Top Secret Lunar Defense Project delivers its first Spacefighter to Oasis.

As the story begins in April, 2017, might not the world look like this?

The United States has been relatively successful in stemming the tide of self-destruction by aggressively adopting measures to reverse the trends. It has clean water, food production capability meeting its needs, and a stable population. Other industrialized nations are for the most part attempting to do the same, but with varying degrees of success. For the underdeveloped countries, however, the prognosis is not good, with starvation, disease, war, and pestilence exacting a grim toll. It is this widening gulf of disparity which has created the current quintessential have and have-not dichotomy of the world.

Traditional military and border patrol functions have been combined to provide the necessary protection from illegal immigration, but the task is becoming increasingly more difficult. It is a defensive posture of dubious longevity.

Construction of Moon Colony #1, an infinitely sustainable human habitat in space, is publicly dedicated to developing and testing the feasibility of totally recycling all consumable resources, but is privately considered to be the key to survival of the species Homo Sapiens.

U.S. Space Station Oasis is a massive spin-gravity structure, home to about 3000 crew members and their families, all of whom volunteered for an indefinite period of duty with the understanding that they may never be allowed to return to Earth.

Thirteen-year-old Toby Williams, the only human ever conceived and born in space, lives with his parents on *Oasis*. He has never been fully accepted by the other kids, all of whom migrated to the space station when they were between three to five years old. Ostracized and excluded, Toby has developed an independent, adventurous spirit fueled by a loner mentality.

As the novel opens, Toby is also dealing with the internalized, never-revealed fear that the other kids might be right, and he indeed is a freak. For the last couple of years, he has become increasingly aware that he can extend his ability to sense audio, spatial, and heat anomalies beyond his immediate surroundings.

Little does he know how vitally important these unique gifts will soon become.

1

DAY ONE

Toby Williams woke up in his family's tiny apartment on U.S. Space Station Oasis with plans that replaced going to school with two of his favorite adventure-diversions. He put on his exoskeleton undergarment, pants, shirt, and gripper shoes, and paused with his hand on doorknob as he closed his eyes to let his special abilities make sure the corridor was clear. Detecting no sounds, shapes or heat blooms indicative of human presence, he eased open the door and visually checked both ways before stepping into the corridor and closing the door with a barely audible *snick*. Then he hurried toward the nearest entrance into the radial and cross chute system.

About 15 feet from the entrance, Toby began running at the ladder in the wall below the hatch and performed his well-practiced leap maneuver. In the lower gravity of the living quarters, it vaulted him high enough to grab the top rung. He wedged a leg between the wall and the ladder and yanked the handle to open the hatch cover. A quick pull to haul himself headfirst into the chute and a tug on the inside cover handle with a toe of a gripper shoe to close it returned the corridor to its original state.

After securing the latch, which required advancing into the chute far enough to turn around at an intersection of a radial and cross chute, Toby took less than 10 minutes to reach the exit hatch near one of the main access doors into the trash compactor room.

Peering out of the partially opened hatch, Toby watched a man with a tool kit walk by and disappear around a corner. Sensing no other activity in the vicinity, he scrambled out of the chute, closed the hatch cover, dropped into the corridor and ran down the empty hallway in the opposite direction to the compactor room door.

Toby's gripper shoes skidded slightly as he came to a stop. The amount of stick to the floor was computer-controlled and could be adjusted. This new pair needed fine-tuning for Toby's active lifestyle. After quick glances in each direction, he jabbed the "OPEN" button on the control panel and anxiously watched the door begin to move.

Come on . . . *finally!* Toby squeezed through the narrow opening, punched "CLOSE" on the interior panel and held his breath. Sometimes the doors jammed when he reversed the direction without waiting for the door to open completely, but this time it worked as the shaft of light streaming in from the corridor slowly disappeared and returned the compactor room to near total darkness.

Toby stood very still. Compactor rooms collected non-organic trash and processed it for recycling. He was perched on a narrow ledge designed for maintenance workers to walk the circumference of the room and free up frequent jams. To move from the ledge was dangerous until he could verify the trash level in the compactor tube. Depending on the time of day and the amount of trash generated, the top of the pile could be anywhere.

When his eyes had adjusted to the faint ambient light, Toby leaned over and peered down. The trash level was only one floor below him. Using handholds and footholds along the walls, he lowered himself to the top of the heap. Compactor rooms usually offered up interesting stuff, especially on Tuesdays before compaction on Wednesdays, and he loved rummaging around for things to show his one and only friend Rooster.

After spending a few minutes digging into the pile, Toby spotted a piece of wood, one of his favorite things. He had never been to Earth and seen a real tree, much less touched one. Supplies from Earth were occasionally crated in wood, and he checked the compactor rooms frequently looking for some.

The piece he wanted was jammed in tight. Toby sat down and put his feet out to brace himself as he pulled hard. It wouldn't budge. He stared with longing at the stubborn treasure until he heard something.

Toby looked up and gasped. A robodog stood on the ledge two floors up, staring at him. The things were used to patrol the more inaccessible sections of the station, and particularly areas off-limits to the general population.

The top of the trash was only a foot or two below the door onto level three. Toby glanced at the control panel to gauge the distance. When he looked back up at the dog, his heart rate went into high gear. The dog was moving and probably coming for him.

Toby scrambled over the trash to the control panel and punched the "OPEN" button repeatedly, even though he knew it wouldn't make the door open faster.

Head rolled back, he stared up at the robodog. It was running around the ledge as if looking for a way down. Toby was pretty sure it couldn't use the ladder, so he might have time to—*what's it doing?*

The dog had stopped and was staring at Toby. The door was almost open enough for him to squeeze through when the robodog suddenly jumped off the ledge. Toby shoved his body at the slowly widening doorway, pushed through and ran. Although he knew better than to look back, he couldn't help it. The robodog burst into the hallway and never hesitated. Legs a blur of motion, it accelerated down the hallway in pursuit.

Toby sprinted toward the radial chute near the number three elevator, motivated by the sound of the robodog's gripper pads on the floor as the beast gained on him. Gasping for breath, Toby veered to his left to avoid a maintenance man working in the corridor and tripped over the guy's toolbox. His gripper shoes came free from the floor, and momentum launched him head over heels down the hallway. He sailed for about 15 feet in the reduced gravity and bounced off the wall. As he landed on his stomach and skidded to a stop, the robodog caught up with him.

The chute entrance was only a few feet down the hall. Toby rolled onto his back, kicking at the dog as he scooted himself toward the chute. Ignoring the blows, the animal grabbed Toby's jeans at the ankle.

Toby could almost touch the ladder to the chute entrance. With his free foot, he kicked the robodog's head as hard as he could. It didn't even flinch. But when Toby lifted his foot to kick the dog again, the animal growled.

Toby froze. He didn't know robodogs did that. Was this a real dog from Earth? He stared at the dog's teeth, worried the animal might hurt him. Then the elevator chimed, and he glanced up as two Oasis police officers stepped into the hallway and walked toward him. Toby's heart sank. He'd been caught by them more than once doing something that violated one of the many "No Fun Allowed" rules that seemed to be directed specifically at him.

The big one, a sergeant named Cadogan, walked up smiling. "Well now, did the bad doggie catch you being naughty again?"

Toby really didn't like the sergeant. He *always* showed up at the wrong time. "Make it let go! I wasn't doing anything wrong."

Cadogan leaned over Toby. "Save the 'I didn't do it' routine. The dog's video proves you were in the compactor room."

Toby didn't know robodogs had video, either. The critters were full of surprises. With denial as his only defense, Toby protested his guilt again. "It's not my fault. This dog has a chip missing. I didn't—"

"To me, Snooper," said Corporal Bishop. The robodog immediately released its grip on Toby's jeans and heeled at the corporal's left leg.

Toby stood up as Cadogan loomed over him. "You may think you've got other people around here fooled, but I—"

Another elevator chime sounded as Toby's father stepped into the corridor and walked toward them. Toby knew well what the look on his face meant, and that this might be one broken rule too far.

Cadogan said, "Thanks for responding so quickly, Mr. Williams. I was just telling your son that he's not going to lie his way out of this one, and—"

"Lying? I doubt that, Sergeant Cadogan. Toby's been taught to tell the truth."

"Really? Then how do you explain him saying he didn't do anything wrong, and I have video that proves he did?"

Toby busied himself with tucking in his shirt, avoiding his father's stern gaze.

"Toby?"

"Yessir."

"Want to tell me about it?"

"It wasn't my fault, Dad. The robodog came after me for no reason."

The corporal commanded the robodog to stay and stepped forward. "We received an alarm from the compactor room when Snooper entered the pursuit mode, Mr. Williams. Your son *was* inside the compactor room."

Toby had good reason to pay attention to the conversation, but he was fascinated with the robodog. Snooper looked so real. His father's voice startled him back to the moment.

"Listen up, Toby. Were you in there?"

"Uh . . . well, yessir. But only for a minute."

"We'll discuss this later. Is Toby free to go, Corporal Bishop?"

"Hold up," said Cadogan, as he stepped between the corporal and Toby's father. "I'm in charge here."

After a moment of silence, Toby's father acknowledged with a nod. "Is Toby free to go, *Sergeant* Cadogan?"

"Hell, yeah. It's not like he killed somebody. But a day in a cell would be good for him. He'd be a damned sight easier to raise with a little less sand in him."

Toby's father took a deep breath and let it out, which usually indicated to Toby that he was trying to calm himself down. "You may be in charge, but that doesn't give you leave to offer advice on how to raise my son. And you should watch your language around the children. Using profanity sets a bad example."

Cadogan smiled. "Well, Mr. Williams, it seems to me you got this whole thing backwards. Your little ruffian doesn't act the way he does because of my example."

Toby noticed his father's jaw twitch at the word "ruffian," whatever that meant. It was time to leave. "Dad, can we go now?"

"In a minute, son." His father stepped up close to Cadogan. "Perhaps you'd like to tell me how I have it backwards."

"Glad to. You're giving that lecture about setting an example to the wrong person. Try it again in front of a mirror. That clear enough?"

It got very quiet in the hallway. Toby had never seen his father so angry. He squeezed between the two men. "Dad, let's go. We can—"

"It's time to be quiet, Toby," said his father, then to Cadogan, "And that goes for you too."

As he followed his father to the elevator, Toby was sure he could feel the sergeant's eye-daggers stabbing him in the back, but that was nothing compared to waiting for his dad to say something. While standing in line for the elevator, the silence became unbearable.

"Can I explain, Dad?"

"This evening. I'm pretty sure your mother will be especially interested. In the meantime, you need to hurry or be late for school."

With a shouted, "I'll make it before the bell!" over his shoulder, Toby sprinted down the corridor to begin his second planned adventure-diversion of the day.

Toby used the chutes to reach a hatch near the squadron flight operations room, confirmed the corridor was clear, climbed out without being seen, hurried to the entrance and peered at the flight scheduling board, visible through the glass insert in the door.

He'd learned how to read it on the class field trip when he met Brett and got "bitten by the flying bug" as the pilot put it. Shuttle schedules and fighter training sorties were listed. He searched for the name LARSEN and found it, noting an early morning departure and an arrival time about an hour ago.

Toby had also learned about the Brett's typical flying-day routine and remembered a comment about hating early flights. He usually didn't sleep well the night before, and he really enjoyed a short "power nap and eyelid leak check" afterward. Brett also mentioned that his internal clock had never adjusted to spending so much time on Oasis. Toby asked why, and learned about circadian rhythm, a natural, internal process that regulates the sleep-wake cycle by responding to alternating periods of light and darkness, and on Earth, which repeats roughly every 24 hours. Living on Oasis for all of his thirteen years, experiencing 8 sunrises and sunsets every day was for Toby as natural as breathing, and he had never questioned the fact that Oasis used a 24-hour clock and an Earth calendar.

Exiting the chutes near Brett's apartment about 10 minutes later, Toby's excitement had peaked. He enjoyed being with Brett because their time together was so different than his usual boring life with parents or kids his age. Having a Space Command pilot as a grown-up friend was like a dream come true. Toby could talk about flying with his very own hero, who never seemed eager to rush off and do something else. Sometimes he could remember those conversations almost word for word, and over the past month or so Toby had become convinced this was the one thing he wanted to do more than anything else.

But Toby knew he might never be good enough to become a military pilot. And how could he leave his parents? Just the thought of doing that made him sad, but his intense desire to see Earth for himself and get the opportunity to be a pilot helped him concentrate on how to overcome their objections. He had the time to approach them gradually about his plan and obtain their support. If he could do that and return to Earth in the next two or three years, he'd be able to pursue his dream.

For now, Brett was the only person he could talk to, and the only one with the knowledge to advise him on the best way to go about it. Rushing around the last corner prior to Brett's apartment, Toby ran into someone. He lost his footing and fell backwards. Just before he hit the floor, strong hands grabbed and held him. Glancing up, he saw his idol grinning at him.

"Howdy, partner. You okay?"

Between deep breaths, Toby said, "I've been looking all over for you, Brett."

"It's nice to see you, Toby, but shouldn't you be in school?"

"I have an excuse. And I need to ask you something."

Brett put a hand on Toby's shoulder. "You wouldn't lie to a buddy, would you?" When Toby shook his head, Brett said, "Okay. I was headed to get a bite to eat. How about I buy you a snack and we can talk for a bit?"

"Great. I missed breakfast."

They walked a short distance to a self-serve refreshment station. Brett ordered a full breakfast with orange juice and coffee. When Toby chose a slice of chocolate cake and a glass of milk, Brett said, "Breakfast of Champions, Toby?"

"What?"

Brett began buttering his toast. "Back in the day, it was a slogan for a breakfast cereal. What did you want to ask me?"

All the moisture in Toby's mouth had dried up. He didn't expect Brett not to take him seriously, but he also knew his friend wouldn't lie to him. The answer might be more realistic than he wanted. He swallowed hard and fought to keep his voice steady. "Ever since you told me about how you learned to fly I've wanted to ask you what I should do."

"About what?"

Toby reached for Brett's water glass, took a long drink, and blurted, "I want to be a pilot. Just like you. I know I can do it. And you can help me, right? I mean when I get bigger. I'll be your copilot. We can—"

"Whoa, partner." Brett looked away for a moment, appeared to be lost in thought, searching for the words. "I . . . I don't know any other way to say this, and we're buddies, right? We tell it like it is?"

"Sure. You're my best friend, except for Rooster, maybe. But he's—"

"You can't learn to fly on a space station."

The words punched Toby in the center of his chest. All his breath seemed to be knocked out of him, just like space could drain the air out of *Oasis*, so fast you couldn't stop it. He breathed deep to fight the dizziness. "But that's the only thing I want to do when I grow up. Why can't—?"

"We don't teach people to fly up here. We teach them how to fly *in space*. I know that's confusing, but all the pilots in Space Command have proven themselves in basic, primary, and advanced training on

Earth. They have years of experience in operational squadrons and a few thousand hours of flying time."

Toby heard the words without believing them. "But I've been reading about how the four forces affect an airplane, how lift is produced only in Earth's atmosphere and spacecraft don't really fly. And because shuttles operate in space and on Earth, their control responses in space are the same as when flying on Earth so it looks the same and makes going back and forth easier. Why can't I just start here?"

The question seemed to hang above the table, begging for an answer. Toby desperately wanted to say more, but he waited.

Brett put down his fork. "It's just not possible, Toby. You can't buck a system that's been in place for years and trains pilots in the most cost-effective way. I'm sorry, but you need to think about what else you might want to do on *Oasis* for a career. There are plenty of exciting—"

Toby shook his head. "Uh-uh. No way. I've never seen Earth except out the window, and it's not fair. All the other kids have. They never let me forget it. My parents feel guilty about that, and I'm gonna convince them to let me go to Earth and live with my aunt and uncle. I'll learn to fly early like you did, earn a pilot-training slot and be a Space Command pilot."

Brett sat motionless, with a blank expression, then smiled. "That's the kind of dedication you'll need to be successful."

"And you'll help me, right?"

"Uh . . . sure, if I can."

"You can, I just know it. Mom will be the tough one, but my dad always wanted to be a pilot. His eyesight wasn't good enough. He thinks you're great. We'll convince him and then gang up on her. I was thinking—"

Brett looked over Toby's shoulder as the cafeteria door opened with a whoosh. "Hello, Dr. Williams."

Toby turned and watched his father approach the table. *Busted.* "Hi, Dad. Captain Larsen and I were just talking about flying. We've got this idea—"

"Be quiet, son, and wait for me in the hall."

Toby stood and picked up his tray. "Thanks for the food, Brett. Maybe we can talk some more soon."

"Sure, Toby. I'll—"

"Excuse me, Captain Larsen. Toby, wait for me in the hall."

With a heavy heart, Toby put away his tray and walked out of the cafeteria. Leaning against the wall, he lowered his head, overwhelmed by disappointment at his dream being halted by a system that just wasn't fair.

TOBY'S FATHER OPENED THE DOOR TO THE APARTMENT, STEPPED aside and pointed to the dining table. "Sit."

As Toby did that, he got the feeling that this time, the consequences of pushing his parents' boundaries might have crossed the line into being grounded. He watched his dad knock on the door to the home office where his mom worked as an IT specialist, and then listened to their conversation.

"Got a minute?" said his dad.

"What's up?"

"It's Toby . . . again."

"Will I read about it in the morning paper?"

"You might find it in the police report."

"What are you talking about?"

"He went into the compactor room again and got caught by one of the robodogs. I—"

"I thought they were used only for external security."

"Yes and no. Colonel Thomas decided to reprogram a few for interior patrol."

"That's dangerous. Those dogs can kill a grown man, and Thomas is turning them loose to hunt children?"

"Robodogs can be programmed in more than one mode, Lisa. Thomas just wants to discourage people from going where they aren't supposed to."

"In case you hadn't noticed, they didn't keep Toby out of a compactor room."

After a moment of silence, his mom said, "I'll never agree with you about the dogs, Jason, but what did our son do?"

"Let's find out."

As his parents sat down, the feeling of being under close scrutiny, became especially intense.

His father said, "Tell your mother what happened."

Make this good. "I was looking for Rooster. Sometimes he goes into the compactor room to look for stuff for that shuttle model he's building. When I opened the door a dog came at me. I got scared and ran."

"But Sergeant Cadogan said the dog found you *in* the compactor room."

"That is always trying to pin something on me I didn't do."

"He mentioned a video. It—"

"That's enough," said his mom. "Forget the video. Were you in the compactor room?"

She *always* asked the tough questions. Toby lowered his gaze to his lap. "Yes, ma'am."

"You knew it could be dangerous, and if you were caught you'd be punished. But you went in anyway. Why?"

Toby didn't want to reveal the real reason, and the *partial* fib came to him without planning it. "It's where they put the used packing crates. I was looking for a piece of wood. I got the idea from the videos of Paw-Paw carving the nameplate for Dad's tree house, and I wanted to surprise you with one for our door." He glanced up at his parents. *Are they buying this?*

"Your father and I appreciate the fact that you wanted to surprise us. It was a sweet thing to do. But I'm not going to tell you again. Your habit of going in off-limits areas will stop."

"Yes ma'am." Toby slid his chair back and started to get up.

"Where do you think you're going?"

"I've got homework."

"But you haven't been to school today. How do you know?"

"Uh . . . well, I—"

"Oh, I get it," said his Mom. "You must mean *yesterday's* assignment."

Busted, again. Toby knew better than to say anything.

After a moment, his dad said, "Do you really think we don't keep in touch with your teachers? What's the *matter* with you?"

His mother followed with, "Your *overdue* homework assignment is on your desk. Bring it to me when you're done."

Toby nodded, went into to his room, closed the door, and hoped this would be the end of it.

I can't afford to get grounded now.

As Toby closed the door to his room, Jason said, "There's more to the story than what happened in the compactor room."

Lisa shook her head. "I can't wait to hear this."

"I found him in a cafeteria near Brett Larsen's apartment."

"What was he doing there?"

"Talking about flying, of course." As Jason related a synopsis of his conversation with Brett, Lisa listened without comment, but her body language signaled that she was going to have something to say when he finished.

"So what you're really telling me is that our son wanted to talk with Brett about a lot more than just flying?"

"Well, yes, but—"

"You know, the really important parts about Toby's wanting to be a pilot and not being able to because he's here and not on Earth?"

"And it's not just a casual interest. He's feeling threatened by the realization he may not get the chance to try it."

Lisa didn't respond for a moment, and Jason detected a growing agitation in her manner, a usual precursor to his being on the receiving end of Lisa's displeasure.

"And you just had a nice friendly discussion with Brett about our son's reaction to what you think is more than a casual interest?"

"Well, yeah, it certainly wasn't an argument, and I guess you could call it friendly. He's—"

"I can't believe you just chatted with the guy about his part in all this. Our son has changed significantly in a short period of time, Jason. It's almost like he's a different person. You seem to understand that well enough, but aren't willing to take the next step and get to the source of this change to do something about it.

"This hot-shot fighter pilot, always walking around the station with that air of superiority and 'Look-at-me, I-fly-jets' attitude, is so wrapped up in his own world that he never for a moment considered the impact he'd have on Toby."

"But he admitted he might have said the wrong things and set this up to some degree."

"That's a nice way to dance around the issue. How about all three hundred and sixty degrees of it? That's pilot talk, isn't it?"

Jason could see where this was headed, but he was also getting irritated at his wife's sudden attack. "Since I'm going to get blamed for this anyway, why don't you just let me know what's on your mind and get it over with?"

Lisa's expression turned stone-hard. "Fine. From your description of the conversation, you never confronted Brett about his poor judgment. You let him off the hook by characterizing it as Toby's fault for becoming so intensely interested, and then left the door open for him to keep on making the same mistakes or worse.

"Toby is in this with us come hell or high water. He's been led down the path of fascination with flying by someone who should've realized the bridge was washed out. Toby can't get there from here, and we made that decision for him when we elected to leave Earth and planned or not, had a child. He needs to be guided in his focus on our future here and beyond, not behind us in the world we rejected."

Jason almost responded, but the fire in Lisa's eyes stopped him.

"What I'm most disturbed about is that you had more of a male-bonding talk with Brett than a discussion to help protect our son. I think we should terminate this thing quickly before it gets any worse by forbidding Toby to see Brett and make certain they both know it. You gave him the option to decide what he talks to Toby about, and he's used such poor judgment so far that I'm unwilling to leave it at that."

Jason listened to this with a mixture of anger and guilt. Lisa could drive her opinion home with a directness and power that he both feared and admired. And as he thought about it, the nagging feeling grew that he had avoided a confrontation with Brett because he admired him, envied his prowess in a world of excitement and danger, and that Lisa was right. He'd been thinking more of himself than what might be best for Toby.

"I hear you. It just seemed better to let Brett help us in the process of easing Toby away from his goal."

"I disagree. We don't need to enlist the aid of anyone outside this family, particularly an egotistical fighter pilot who's already demonstrated his inability to get outside his own world and think about someone else. I realize you like him, and that's up to you. But as far as I'm concerned, I don't want him discussing anything with Toby. I hope that's clear enough."

Lisa stood, walked into her office, and closed the door a little harder than necessary, another signal to Jason that he needed to tread lightly.

ALONE AT THE KITCHEN TABLE, WITH HIS WIFE AND SON physically close but emotionally distant, Jason reflected on the time when he and Lisa were considering their careers, having children, and how best to plan for the dreams they both had.

So much had changed, and all for the worse. Scientists were predicting a doomsday scenario in which mankind's ability to sustain life on Earth would be jeopardized by the cumulative, synergistic effects of environmental pollution, overpopulation, global warfare, and climate change.

Jason remembered the long sessions at the kitchen table in which his father and grandfather had discussed the future. For hours over coffee, or sometimes late into the evening with cold beers and maybe some W. L. Weller bourbon his granddad kept deep in the pantry, Jason would listen to the adults debate the pressing questions of the time.

In his father's opinion, Earth was fast approaching a period of war that would make conflicts over oil and minerals seem like minor squabbles. He quoted statistics indicating the inexorable march toward the day when a combination of factors would create the ultimate in "have" and "have-not" nation-states.

Reaching adulthood, Jason realized this scenario might be played out in his lifetime. The United States had implemented strict pollution control standards, spent billions for environmental cleanup, and achieved near-zero population growth. It was only a matter of time until the US would have to defend its borders against the masses looking for food and water.

Following the collapse of the Soviet Union and end of the cold war, the US and Russia cooperated in a joint effort for construction of the International Space Station. Launched into low Earth orbit and designed as a microgravity and space environment research laboratory, the ISS proved invaluable as a test bed for learning how to minimize the negative effects of long-term exposure to low-gravity environments. Eventually, the US decided to extend the benefits of this research with plans to construct a space station orbiting the moon and a biosphere on the lunar surface. The project remained underfunded for many years, and was in danger of cancellation when everything abruptly changed.

The US reversed the decision to cut back on the space station and moon colony projects. Budgetary constraints disappeared. NASA urgently needed volunteers, but with drastically altered conditions for employment. All volunteers had to sign up for an indefinite period, with return to Earth only possible at NASA's discretion.

Immersed in a wonderful period of personal and collective discovery, Jason and Lisa paid little attention to current events or the future of the world. They were effectively isolated within a cocoon of their own making when the announcements had been made.

His father's reaction to the news was especially intense, and he offered his theory on the policy change.

"The idiots have finally realized we have the only escape route off the planet. We'll have to close the borders completely, and fight a defensive war to protect our food and water. And we'll lose. There are too many of them, so few of us. It'll be like a plague of locusts, devouring anything that maintains life. We'll have to leave, and we're the only ones who can."

Jason shuddered at the memory. He and Lisa had stayed up until dawn the next morning talking about his father's opinions. A couple of days later their world did collapse, but not in a way they ever expected.

With the wedding only a week away and preparations in full swing, Jason was shining his wedding shoes, smiling at the memory of his father's patient attempts to show him how, and especially his insistence that Jason never fail to use a toothbrush to apply polish to the welt stitching. When the phone rang, he expected to hear Lisa's voice bubbling over with some question about one of the many wedding details, but it wasn't quite like that.

A police officer informed him that the body had been found in a ditch. The widower David Williams had been brutally murdered for the few dollars in his pocket and an old pickup. The oldest of the assailants was not yet seventeen, the youngest not much older than Toby was now. They followed Jason's father from a quick-stop market, ran him off the road, dragged him out of the car and beat him to death with a tire iron.

In the months following the tragedy, Jason struggled with the pain, anger, and frustration as feelings of helplessness and despair flooded over him. They finally held the postponed wedding in a quiet ceremony with a few close friends. The young couple took their honeymoon in the high Sierras on a backpacking trip.

In the solitude of the mountains, late one evening gazing at the explosion of stars above them, Jason and Lisa made their decision. Looking back, he could easily characterize it as running away. But at the time it seemed their only choice: sell his father's farm, volunteer for the space station, and leave the chaos and approaching anarchy behind to seek a new destiny.

Personnel were chosen for their expertise in various fields, and to create a balanced society in space. Families with children were important for the long-term goals of the station, but the population would have to be strictly managed, and birth control was a mandatory requirement.

Jason and Lisa's decision to volunteer for space duty was in part motivated by the possibility of bringing up a child in a new society they were helping to create, free from the evils destroying their dreams on Earth. As a couple without children, they would not be allowed to have a child without permission. Unsure if they would ever want a family, they decided to cross that bridge when they came to it, and it arrived sooner than expected.

Cruiser shuttles could be configured to carry cargo or passengers but usually didn't combine both on the same flight. During initial manning of *Oasis*, cargo always took priority due to the constant demand for supplies to support construction of the moon colony. Once trained and ready to depart, new employees went into a standby status. When sufficient personnel were available, NASA scheduled an all-passenger flight.

Anxious to get started on their new life, Jason and Lisa sold all of their household goods and took only a small amount of personal possessions with them to the departure point. The call came in the middle of the night at a most inopportune time during passionate lovemaking. Laughing about NASA's lousy timing, and after a flurry of last-minute packing activity, they arrived for the flight full of excitement at meeting their new neighbors.

But they were traveling by themselves. A specialist in Jason's field had been injured and missed his flight the week before. With the next personnel shuttle months away, pressing operational requirements demanded an immediate replacement.

Being alone had its advantages. Riding a phenomenal emotional high and drunk with excitement, Jason and Lisa huddled together in a spare crew sleeping room. Once into the cruise portion they shared their feelings at the beginning of this great adventure. During a lull in the conversation, that private signal passed between them.

Although NASA doctors had given Lisa special birth control pills, she hadn't begun taking them. She expected months of delay before a flight would be available, and her regular prescription had been working fine. Maybe it was the emotion, or the interrupted nature of the act, or the micro-gravity of space, but something unexpected happened. The proud parents-to-be successfully petitioned NASA for a waiver. Tobias David Williams was born nine months later and became forever identified as the only person conceived and born in space.

And over decade later, Jason had known immediately that their son had changed the day he came home from his class visit to the flying squadron. The look in his eyes as he spoke of the things he saw. His fascination with the fighter pilot who was their guide. Being told after a session at the controls of the space fighter simulator that he was a natural. And how the intense interest he expressed in reading anything he could find on the subject of aviation announced to the world that he was going to be a pilot.

Jason leaned back in his chair and thought about his father's collection of videos that provided a detailed record of life on Earth with the Williams family. To help maintain their own memories over the long years ahead, Jason and Lisa had brought the entire collection to *Oasis*. For about five years after Toby's birth, they struggled with increasing guilt over their decision to volunteer for duty in space. They had a choice, and he did not. Deciding that sharing the videos would help connect him to a past family life denied to him in the future, they began weekly movie nights.

Over the past few years, Jason had begun to doubt the wisdom of that decision. If anything, the videos only intensified Toby's craving to experience Earth for himself. To run barefoot in the grass. To swim in a lake. Or to play in a treehouse built for your dad by your grandad, an especially powerful thread connecting three generations.

But today, over the course of one morning playing hooky from school, Toby had ignored rules established for his own safety and was detained by the station police. A few hours later, Jason called the school and discovered that his son had lied about going to homeroom and sought out his pilot friend. Fascination with aviation was one thing, but premeditated lying?

TOBY LAY IN BED, STRUGGLING WITH HAVING LIED TO HIS parents, but he had to. It wasn't just a matter of videos and family pictures depicting a life he had never known, or even the jokes and harassment from the other kids. More than anything else, his friendship with Brett had struck the spark that lit the flame and fueled his dream to leave *Oasis* and go to Earth.

Toby approached Brett one afternoon and blurted out the question that none of his research adequately answered. Everything he'd read was so dry, just words on paper, and he wanted to know what flying was *really* like. Brett's answer planted the seed of a dream.

"Being a pilot is like having an incurable blood disease, Toby. All you can do is treat it with more flying. And once you've flown a fighter on the deck at five hundred knots, or docked a shuttle on Oasis, you're hooked for life. It's the ultimate video game, and the universe is yours to do with as you please. And don't forget, if you want to wear these wings, you have to be the best. Nothing less will do."

This conversation had been the point of decision. He had to return to Earth, begin flying lessons early like Brett did, and enter the military as a pilot. But how was he going to do that?

Brett will know. I'll convince him to help because he understands what it means to want to be a pilot more than anything.

Toby began to feel better immediately. A plan was always more effective than sitting around waiting for things to happen, and he knew what he had to do.

2

DAY TWO EARLY MORNING

With the finest fightercraft in the universe strapped around him, Captain Brett Larsen, United States Space Command Senior Pilot, established his ship in a station-keeping position on U.S. Space Station Oasis, orbiting the moon at an altitude of 100 miles and a velocity of 3,600 mph.

Today's mission objective was to train his wingman, a First Lieutenant named Carson, in the procedures and techniques required to operate his fightercraft in low altitude lunar orbit. Viper Two had just aborted his launch for a minor systems malfunction and would be exiting the Sector 3 dock in a few minutes, so Brett moved his ship about 2 miles away and settled down to wait. The autopilot monitored his position and had made one small velocity correction to zero out his "delta V" and synchronize his speed.

Responsible for every facet of the mission, Brett needed to closely monitor the especially serious business of launching. But with the autopilot operating flawlessly, and the military aviation principle of *Hurry up and wait* firmly in play, Brett had nothing more to do than monitor the radio and think about where his career appeared to be heading.

Serving as a primary aircrew from day one, Brett lived his childhood dream every time he climbed into an airplane or spacecraft. Flying was all he ever wanted to do, and all he wanted to continue doing. At this stage of his career, however, the ominous threat of a despised desk job was becoming more real with each passing day.

Two basic principles governed military career progression: the whole-man concept dictated that officers prove their worth in more than a primary specialty; and the up-or-out policy meant that for any officer failing to be promoted on time, the system was biased toward continuing passovers and involuntary separation from military service.

For years, Brett's strategy involved making himself so indispensable to flying squadrons that they couldn't afford to put him behind a desk. Recently it hadn't been difficult. He was the most experienced instructor assigned to *Oasis*, with more logged flight hours in both shuttles and fighters of any pilot in the wing, and he was currently carrying the majority of the load in training the latest group of young pilots. Brett had been flying almost every day for the past few months, but even with fatigue nibbling at his concentration, he wasn't about to remove himself from the flying schedule.

Carson had flown seven previous training sorties with other instructors since arriving on Oasis, about halfway through the required syllabus. There were no two-seat space fighter models, and all training had to be accomplished in two-ship formations with the instructor flying chase on the student. Just like back in WWII, actually, which seemed strangely regressive to Brett.

"Viper One, Oasis Launch Control."

"Control, Viper One, go ahead."

"Viper Two is initiating launch."

"Roger that, Control." Brett eased in a little right rudder and released it. Yaw thrusters fired a short burst to rotate the fightercraft slowly around the vertical axis. When Brett could see the space station easily out the front windscreen, he initiated an opposing burn with the left rudder and terminated the yawing motion.

Sector 3 loading dock had just completed derotation, a procedure in which the massive clutch mechanism connecting the rotating space station with the dock was released and the dock braked to a halt. Positioned at the center of rotation, the stationary dock was now ready for launch. Its enormous door had opened wide with the tiny fightercraft resting on the launch platform.

Since the dawn of aviation, close-proximity flight involving military aircraft had produced almost 85% of all mid-air collisions. So far, no collisions between spacecraft had occurred, and the potential for a disastrous incident involving Oasis demanded that the launch procedure be especially unhurried.

Radio transmissions between Viper Two and Launch Control indicated a textbook sequence as the fighter slowly lifted free from contact with the platform and edged forward into the bright sunshine. Launches could also be performed during dark-side orbital periods, but Carson would have to qualify in that maneuver as well. Brett watched closely as Viper Two maneuvered free of Oasis with thrusters, then fired a short burst from his descent engine to reduce speed and establish a small negative velocity relative to the station.

With no atmosphere encircling the moon, and therefore no way to produce aerodynamic lifting force, all flight in proximity to the lunar surface was orbital, with two counteracting forces in play. The force created by the speed of the object tries to sling it out into space, and the gravitational force of the moon tries to pull it closer. When speed is in balance with gravity, equilibrium is reached, and the object's flight path is effectively bent into a circle.

To join up with Brett, Carson was now performing the same maneuver Brett had used earlier. With a combination of main-engine and thruster burns, Viper Two adjusted his speed to move away from Oasis and assume his own station-keeping position. The young pilot performed the maneuver without wasting time and fuel, and seemed to have a solid grasp of his machine and the technique of small orbital transfers. Brett smoothly positioned his fightercraft in a chase position on Viper Two. Now for the real stuff.

"Oasis Control, Viper Flight ready for descent." Even though the wingman was in front, Brett was still the leader and controlled all aspects of the mission.

"Roger that, Viper. Cleared for descent departure. Have a good flight."

"Viper, roger. Viper, button two go."

"Two."

Brett changed the radio to channel two for the tactical portion of the mission and gave his wingman a few more seconds before calling for the check-in. "Viper check."

"Two."

At this point in the mission, Brett and Carson had done nothing more than separate from the space station and take up station-keeping. Although there was much yet to come, most of the actions required to complete the mission had already been performed as the pilots adjusted their positions relative to Oasis and each other. There would, however, soon be a major difference in the matter of degree, and an enormous increase in the consequences of "inattention to detail, incapacity, or neglect," as the common aviation saying went.

As with all pilots, Carson had learned his trade in Earth flight. Prior to entering the Space Command, he would have demonstrated the ability to maneuver his fighter safely in a low altitude environment because it was a basic skill required of all fighter pilots. Brett's task now was to help the young pilot "recalibrate his eyeballs" for performing the same task in a vastly different environment. Carson's previous instructors had established the groundwork, emphasizing the differences, and Brett had hammered them home in his preflight briefing.

The lack of an atmosphere meant that their fightercraft didn't really "fly" in the Earth sense of the term. Aerodynamic lift could not be used to control altitude above ground level (AGL). All constant altitude space flight in relation to the moon was orbital, in which the fightercraft's speed was adjusted to provide the desired terrain clearance. Once established in orbit, speed reduction resulted in a descent, and acceleration was used to climb. If maneuvering in Earth's atmosphere was equivalent to an agile competition ski boat, maneuvering around the moon was like a ponderous battleship.

The space fighter's ability to turn, climb, descend, and change speed was dependent entirely on a computer-controlled system of ascent/descent engines and thrusters, which fired in a precise sequence based on control inputs from the cockpit. In the same way that the turn capability of an airplane on Earth was limited by a combination of airspeed, angle of attack, and available G-force, engine and thruster limitations defined how well a fightercraft could alter its velocity vector. Approaching the moon's surface with a combination of too much dive angle and too little speed always proved fatal.

To help the pilot perform the descent safely, the fighter's systems provided directive guidance via command "bars" and "bugs." The vertical and horizontal bars were displayed on the attitude indicator, and the bugs on the speed indicator. Carson's objective was to program the briefed maneuvers in the flight and navigation computers, and follow the steering commands using both the autopilot and manual controls.

Time to go. Carson glanced over at Brett, received a head nod indicating that Brett was ready, and then initiated departure from high orbit. Smoothly retarding the throttle, Brett fired his descent engine to slow his speed rapidly and maintain the chase position.

"Viper Flight departing, Oasis."

"Roger that, Viper. Have a good flight."

With lunar gravity pulling the fighters toward the surface, Viper Flight fell away from Oasis. Speed controlled rate of descent. The longer the descent engine fired, the more speed was reduced, and the faster the two-ship plunged downward.

Flight computers used to control the fighters could be operated in three modes: economy, normal, and combat. Since all maneuvering required thrust, and therefore expenditure of fuel, the pilots were forced to choose between two competing objectives.

In the economy mode, the computer-directed thruster and engine responses to control applications always reflected the most fuel-efficient profile by sacrificing maneuverability. At the other end of the scale, combat mode ignored fuel considerations, utilizing maximum thrust to generate the fastest possible response to control inputs.

Viper Flight was behind schedule, but not enough to require wasting fuel at this point in the mission. With their speed reduced by about 75 mph, they were descending to the first planned mid-level orbit at about 30,000 feet above the lunar surface. Following the initial descent burn, no additional fuel would be required for speed adjustments until the wingman initiated level off.

Brett had briefed Carson to let "George," the pilot's name for autopilots, control his fighter during the initial portion of the descent. Using the autopilot reduced pilot workload, allowing Carson to watch and learn as the automatic system followed the computerized steering commands. Brett was hand-flying his fighter, although in theory if he matched his velocity exactly with his wingman, the two fighters would remain in the same relative position with no control inputs whatsoever.

Their departure from Oasis had been timed to occur at the start of lunar day, with the two-ship bathed in bright sunlight. This allowed Brett to easily maintain visual contact with his wingman while maintaining the chase position.

About halfway through the descent, Brett directed Carson to disconnect the autopilot and practice hand-flying the fighter. Pilots new to orbital maneuvering tended to over-control the spacecraft by making small but unnecessary adjustments with the throttle and side-stick controller. Against the blackness of space, Brett could easily monitor Carson's thruster and engine use by watching for bright momentary flashes around the fighter. There hadn't been many, which was good. Viper Two's position on the profile remained solid, and without excessive fuel burn.

At this point in the descent, their speed had increased by about 300 mph. Level off required a speed decrease, which "circularized" the orbit and stabilized the two-ship at a constant altitude. Carson had flown two manual mid-orbit insertions on previous missions, and this one was to provide additional practice. Brett divided his attention between his own steering display and flying the chase position to make sure Carson performed the maneuver correctly.

At the lead point for an economy level off, Carson's descent engine fired and thrusters adjusted the fighter's attitude to "keep the pointy end forward," as pilots were fond of saying. With no atmosphere, it made no difference which direction the fighters were pointed so long as thrust was vectored correctly. But since all pilots learned to fly in Earth's atmosphere, spacecraft responses to control inputs were designed to mimic aircraft. Transition from Earth to space flight and back was far easier and safer if familiarity could be maximized.

Locked in the chase position and with their speed slowing to 3,745 mph, Brett watched Carson perform the level off in the new orbit. The kid was doing a fine job. So far so good.

"Viper, ops check."

"Two."

Descending to low orbit was never done haphazardly. Level off at an intermediate altitude and performing an operations check allowed both pilots time to assess their fighters and systems for anything that might cause trouble later on when the environment was even less forgiving. Computerized systems analysis helped, but there was no substitute for crosschecking all the biggies. Brett completed his scan of the cockpit, ran a couple of self-diagnostics he felt particularly appropriate for the situation, and reviewed the planned mission profile.

Carson's training folder contained all the pertinent information Brett needed to evaluate the young pilot's recent performance. The mission Brett had designed contained a combination of learning objectives, including review and practice of previous skills and the addition of new tasks depending on Carson's performance. The most significant learning objective was an especially challenging one for both pilots.

Low altitude training was conducted in a series of building-block steps. Pilots first learned how to maneuver at higher altitudes where the margin for error was greater. Once proficiency was demonstrated and documented in his training folder, a pilot would be scheduled for increasingly difficult training scenarios. The last step in the process was removal of altitude restrictions, putting the fighters in the most unforgiving environment, "down on the deck."

According to his training records, Carson had flown in the lowest block, but not in the vicinity of high terrain, which required the pilot to divide his attention between a number of conflicting requirements. Learning the concept of task prioritization was the objective of this training, how to shift attention to the most important task in a rapidly changing set of task loadings. If Carson handled the first portion of the mission well, Brett had briefed that they would progress to lower altitude and repeat selected maneuvers.

"Viper Two, ops check complete." Carson's voice sounded crisp and professional. Given the time it took his wingman to report ready, Brett figured that he probably had checked his fighter out well. Many young pilots equated speed in accomplishing checklists with proficiency, which was total garbage.

"Viper One, check complete." The mission clock on the instrument panel was approaching one hour elapsed time. Brett took a moment to gaze out the windscreen at the view, and was almost mesmerized by the beauty of it. Viper Flight was approaching lunar sunset. The stark demarcation line between the sunlit surface and the endless shadow of the dark side was rushing headlong at them. The fighters would spend the period in darkness cruising toward lunar sunrise at an altitude well above the highest terrain. Brett triggered the auto-lock feature on his radar, coupled the system to the autopilot, and let George have it. In this mode, his fighter would hold a constant position on Viper Two during the lunar night.

The mission plan called for descent to a lower orbit just as the flight reached the bright half of the lunar surface. This would provide about 45 minutes of daylight for training, at which time they would climb back into a higher orbit for the next period of lunar night to ensure safe separation from the ground. The cycle would be repeated until time for "return-to-base," or RTB.

Brett had plenty to do as they cruised along in the darkness, and lunar dawn always seemed to happen more quickly than he expected. The thin bright line just beginning to appear on the lunar horizon brought his attention back to the nav display, which provided a graphic representation of his position in relation to topographical features of the lunar surface, Oasis, and Moonbeam, the call sign of a specially modified shuttle in orbit diametrically opposed to Oasis. Modeled after the Airborne Warning and Control System, or AWACS, on Earth, Moonbeam extended command and control to cover the entire lunar environment. A system of communication satellites ensured that Viper Flight would be in continuous radio contact with Moonbeam and Oasis regardless of position in orbit. Checking the readouts, Brett reviewed the descent procedure. Time to go to work.

"Moonbeam, Viper flight of two with you button two, radio check."

"Roger that, Viper, Moonbeam reads you loud and clear, how me?"

"Five by, Moonbeam. Departing mid-orbit, low altitude training, over."

"Moonbeam copies. Radar contact, standing by."

Knowing that a big brother was up there watching had always provided Brett a degree of comfort, because he had seen enough combat to appreciate what AWACS could do for the fighter pilot. And although there would be no shooting today, or even practice intercepts, mutual support was a multi-faceted concept, and he believed in it.

"Viper, normal mode, initiate descent, go."

"Two."

Brett selected normal on the flight computer mode control, terminated the radar lock, and disconnected the autopilot. As Carson started down, Brett smoothly retarded the throttle and eased forward on the stick. The descent engine fired with a long burn, shoving him forward in the straps in a more aggressive speed reduction than their previous economy descent. The fighters began a steep, plummeting path toward the moon. When the attitude thrusters rotated his ship nose low, Brett felt his heart rate increase as the bright, stark lunar surface filled his windscreen. He had done this a lot, but the thrill was always the same.

The world of the fighter pilot changes in a fundamental way when descending below the level of the highest terrain. Low altitude flight was serious enough over a flat surface, and Brett had seen his share of fighter-to-ground contact resulting from failure to maintain safe separation from terra firma.

But the level of risk increased dramatically when the terrain rises to meet you. Up and over or around are the only choices, and low altitude training stresses the importance of always looking ahead and having a plan. In Earth's atmosphere, closure rates are generally manageable, so long as the pilot accurately predicts the turn performance of his machine.

Space Command regulations defined low altitude lunar orbit as flight below the level of the highest terrain anywhere on the moon. The Apennine Mountains, at the southeast corner of the Mare Imbrium, rose sharply to about 15,000 feet above the average lunar surface. Brett had planned Viper Flight's first low orbit level off at 10,000 feet AGL, but in an area of relatively flat terrain and rolling hills. Orbital speed would be about 3,755 mph, only 10 mph faster than their speed at 30,000 feet. Carson's understanding of and unwavering appreciation for this fact was Brett's primary learning objective for this mission. Speed control was critical. Small changes resulted in immediate altitude variations. Flight close to the lunar surface required precision, *all* the time.

Although fightercraft systems were designed to assist the pilot with directive guidance for speed control, Brett had briefed that this would be another manual descent, and he was once again impressed with Carson's performance. Viper Two was right on profile, when the majority of young pilots would be over-controlling their machines.

Approaching 10,000 feet, an advisory tone sounded the beginning of the level off. Brett noticed the speed bug decreasing, and responded by easing the throttle aft, and with a little back stick, he fired the descent engine to slow up and settle into orbit with Viper Two. At this speed, many times faster than any low altitude flight above the Earth, the differences became visually overwhelming. Looking down over the canopy rail at the terrain could be a real mistake, because human senses are simply too limited to process the information in any meaningful way. As on Earth, but to a much greater degree here, a pilot had to extend his attention way out in front of his fighter.

Following a period of training and climb back to 30,000 feet for lunar night, the flight again approached sunlight. Viper Two had been doing well, so Brett decided to crank up the training a notch.

"Viper, combat mode, go." After a short pause, Carson's answer filled Brett's headset.

"Two."

Brett considered what he had just heard. Carson's responses up to now had been immediate, crisp, and confident. But his last transmission had a hesitancy to it, although not enough to ring any alarm bells for Brett. He dismissed his concern and cleared Carson to begin the next maneuver.

Viper Two initiated the descent to 5,000 feet AGL. The engine fired long and hard, along with the ascent engine's thrust vectored in the vertical to shove his fighter downward toward the lunar surface at a rate faster than a speed change alone would produce. In keeping with the flight computer's programming, combat mode ignored fuel economy to produce the quickest response to control inputs from the pilot.

Glancing at his fuel state, Brett called for an ops check and noted that Viper Two didn't have much less. The wingman had done a fine job of maintaining profile without excessive fuel use. Carson will make a good fightercraft pilot, and Brett decided to increase mission intensity. He had done that throughout his career as an instructor, but only for students who proved through demonstrated performance that they were good enough for some extra training.

At 5,000 feet AGL, the speed to maintain altitude was only 2 mph faster than that required at 10,000 feet. But in the combat mode, pilots had the option, fuel permitting, of slowing the fighter to less than orbital speed and letting the ascent engine provide continuous vectored thrust downward to oppose lunar gravity trying to pull the ship into the surface. This flight condition allowed more reaction time and reduced the sensitivity of altitude control to speed changes, but also affected the ability to climb out of danger should rising terrain become a factor. Like everything else in aviation, it was a tradeoff, and in the case of low-altitude maneuvering, a potentially lethal one.

Leveling out with the moon's surface flashing by below him, Brett's years of training and experience took over in the same way the automatic pilot had during the descent. The flying itself required no conscious thought as his right hand caressed the side-stick controller and sequenced the flight thrusters to adjust pitch and roll. His feet gently rested on the rudder pedals for the control of yaw. With small adjustments the throttle in his left hand maintained the chase position as his eyes shifted focus in a continuous pattern to feed vital information to his brain.

It was during moments like this that Brett felt a special oneness with the marvelous world of flight. The machine, a creation of man for man, empowered him with the ability to enter what could at times be described as a godlike state of control.

I think, the machine does. It is an extension of my will and nothing can touch me.

Which, of course, wasn't completely true. If Brett over the years hadn't tempered that attitude with common sense, he'd likely never have survived the dangers of training, much less combat.

After a few minutes at very low orbit and with the approach of lunar sunset on the horizon, Brett ordered a climb to terrain-clearance orbit where they would wait for lunar sunrise and another training session. The mission profile called for repeating this sequence until fuel remaining dictated a return to high orbit.

Oasis completed each high orbit in 2:04. Viper flight's low orbits took 1:48 on the average, so their position in relation to Oasis moved ahead by 16 minutes per orbit. At that rate it would take more than 12 hours for the two-ship to catch up with Oasis, but fuel limitations would dictate mission termination prior to that. For this reason, Viper Flight would transfer from low orbit to a holding orbit higher than Oasis and at slower speed, allowing the space station to catch up from behind. The navigation computer continuously calculated the window for departing the lower orbit for rendezvous, enabling Brett to concentrate on mission objectives.

During the third low altitude session, Brett adjusted the flight's orbital plane to fly over the Apennine Escarpment. In very low orbit at 5,000 feet AGL, the flight was closing on the mountains at over 63 miles per minute, and at 10,000 feet below the highest peaks. Avoiding this obstacle would require the fighters to initiate climb at sufficient distance to be above 15,000 feet AGL prior to arriving at the foothills. Carson had been trained to handle similar situations on Earth, but this was a totally different environment.

Low-level lunar flight produced a closure rate on obstacles ten times that on Earth. In addition, the Apennines rose much more steeply from the surrounding terrain than even the eastern edge of the Sierra Nevada above the flatlands of America or the Himalayas above the plains of India and Nepal. Fortunately, fightercraft pilots had a terrain avoidance system.

A laser rangefinder mounted in the nose and aligned with the ship's velocity vector probed the future flight path for obstacles. Tied in with the navigation system and the flight computer, the rangefinder calculated time-to-impact, compared that information with geographical position, and issued directive guidance to avoid the obstacle.

"TERRAIN. TERRAIN." As the first warning sounded in Brett's headset, he had to throttle back hard to avoid overrunning Carson. It meant the kid had received the same announcement and was paying attention, because the first action was to slow and reduce closure rate on the hazard. This move slammed Brett forward in the straps as the descent engine fired, while the ascent engine increased vectored thrust downward to maintain altitude.

Good for him. But watch him close, he should be pulling for altitude by the time we get to the next big crater.

It worked like a script had been written. The bright glow of Viper Two's ascent engine confirmed that Carson had advanced the throttle and hauled back on the stick, which told the flight computer in combat mode to schedule a maximum climb.

Brett followed his wingman up. The ascent engine only had so much thrust, and with most of it vectored down, the fighters couldn't increase speed and climb steeply at the same time. When clear of the mountains, Viper Flight would be too slow. Carson should recover from the situation by allowing lunar gravity to pull the fighters back to lower altitude and vectoring ascent engine thrust to regain proper orbital speed.

As they flashed over the mountain ridge, Brett glanced inside to check his steering displays. In both Earth and lunar flight, pulling out of a descent low to the ground required careful attention. Carson did overshoot, probably about a hundred feet or so, but at this altitude over relatively flat terrain it wasn't critical.

Okay, kid, good job. Brett was checking at his fuel when the fighter's verbal warning system, known to male fighter pilots as the "bitch in the box" because of the computerized female voice, sounded in his headset.

"FUEL   STATE.   FIVE   MINUTES   TO   ASCENT. ACKNOWLEDGE."

"Yeah, yeah, I hear you," said Brett into the microphone. Checking the nav display, Brett confirmed they were approaching the planned orbital transfer point for return to Oasis. This maneuver required a sustained burn to increase speed, which would result in a climb away from the lunar surface and into high approach orbit for the rendezvous.

But they still had enough time and fuel for one more training event.

"Viper Two, go trail."

"Two."

Another pause in Carson's response, but Brett again didn't think anything of it. He had briefed the possibility of some trail work, time and fuel permitting. Brett followed the nav steering direct to the orbital transfer point as Viper Two assumed a trail position.

"Two's in," announced he was there.

Brett initiated mild vertical maneuvering, giving his wingman the opportunity to hand-fly the fighter in formation. Carson hadn't started formation training yet, but it was obvious to Brett that he could handle it. About two minutes out from the transfer point, Brett initiated one last descent, intending to reverse into a climb out of very low orbit and return to base.

As the departure time-to-go readout reached 00:00:00, Brett advanced the throttle and eased back on the stick for climb. When the ascent engine fired, he suddenly realized that he had not directed the flight to select economy mode. They didn't have enough fuel for a combat ascent, and they'd have to wait in approach orbit for Oasis anyway. There was no reason to hurry.

Brett's next decision would be put in the classic fighter pilot category of "brain fart."

"Viper, economy mode, go."

As Carson acknowledged, Brett made the change and glanced back over his shoulder to check on his wingman. The sight shoved his heart up into his throat with horror as he watched Carson's fightercraft swap ends and plunge toward the surface, impact a small peak, and explode in a flash of flame and smoke.

Brett's first instinct was to haul back on the stick and return to the crash site as he initiated search and rescue. But in orbital flight, reversing direction even once would take more fuel than he had remaining. Clamping down hard on his emotions, Brett reported the crash to Moonbeam, put his fighter on autopilot and his brain in automatic as the navigation computer took over for the transfer to approach orbit.

With the fuel-low-level light glowing bright red, he said a silent prayer for Lieutenant Carson.

3
———

DAY TWO MID-MORNING

The morning after being caught playing hooky twice, sneaking into the compactor room, and being told by his parents that he could no longer "pester" Brett about flying, Toby still couldn't resist setting up another adventure.

From the front row of the observation gallery above the empty shuttle docking bay, he stared through the panoramic window and wondered how much later the morning shuttle from Earth would be. His new friend Rooster had reluctantly agreed to skip school to watch his first docking, but the delay was obviously making him nervous.

Toby nudged him with his elbow. "Relax, Rooster. I'll handle Ms. Taylor."

"That's easy for you to say. You've been living up here your whole life."

Toby had found Rooster sitting at Toby's desk in homeroom one morning last month. After persuading the newest kid to arrive from Earth that he needed to move, Toby convinced Rooster that being friends could benefit them both. If Rooster agreed to tell Toby about what it was like living on Earth, Toby would show him all the tricks he had learned about how to make living on a space station exciting and fun.

Rooster kept looking over his shoulder as the gallery filled up behind them. Toby nudged him with his elbow and leaned closer. "Keep that up, you're gonna draw attention to us."

"Oh, sure. As if being the only kids in here isn't doing that. I think—"

A muffled klaxon sounded. Toby pointed to Rooster's harness to remind him to tighten his seat belt and shoulder straps just as a shudder rippled through the observation room. De-rotation braking then shoved them both to the right and kept them pressed shoulder-to-shoulder until a final jerk brought them to a stop.

Toby pointed to Rooster's phone, hanging from a cord around his neck and now floating in front of his body.

Rooster grinned, reached out and with his finger tapped the phone. It floated away until the cord tugged it back. Rooster caught it and wedged it between his hip and the armrest.

Another rumble from deep within the space station shook their seats. Red lights flashed in the bay, and the docking doors began to open on the star-speckled blackness of deep space. A cruiser shuttle, its white exterior bathed in dazzling sunlight, waited motionless in the pre-docking position. Toby had watched a few dockings, but none in this bay, designed to surround the shuttle in a pressurized environment. It was used for spacecraft maintenance and offloading cargo too large to pass through the normal docking ports.

He couldn't see the pilots, but he fantasized about a future shuttle docking with Brett, Toby's adult friend and hero, sitting in the left seat. As a brand-new shuttle copilot, Toby would be at the controls for his first docking. And it would be perfectly executed, because he was going to be the second-best pilot ever to wear the wings of a Space Command.

A typical supply shuttle arriving from Earth weighed about 460,000 pounds, but in space it didn't matter. Thrusters provided the fine maneuvering control required for docking. A timed burn started a movement, which would last until an opposing thruster fired to cancel it.

The shuttle slowly filled the docking bay. Then in unison, multiple pinpoints of light on the upper skin flared and went out. The shuttle settled to the floor. Heavy clunks rocked the observation room as locks clamped the spacecraft into position.

The doors closed and the entire docking bay and observation room initiated re-rotation to establish about half-Earth gravity. After a delay for re-pressurization, the klaxon finally ceased, red lights went out, and the all clear sounded.

Docking-bay personnel swarmed around the shuttle. Toby couldn't see through the cockpit windscreen, but he waved just in case Brett was part of the crew. The loading ramp came into view as it extended from the shuttle. Workers gathered at the foot of the ramp to begin unloading cargo.

"Let's go," said Toby, "This part is like watching grass grow, although I've never—"

Flashes lit up the inside of the shuttle and muted pops echoed within the bay. The crowd ducked in unison and began to scatter. Workers ran, tripped, fell, crawled.

One figure rose from a group of men huddled at the foot of the ramp, his arms extended in a shooter's stance that Toby recognized from videos. The man fired three times, and then edged up the ramp through a rising cloud of gun smoke, his pistol aimed at something out of view.

An emergency alarm sounded, the one all station occupants had been taught to dread.

Rooster raised his voice over the siren and said, "What the heck just happened?"

Toby began unfastening his harness. "I dunno, but let's go find out."

Sergeant Andras Cadogan stepped out of the elevator into a scene of complete chaos on the loading dock. Klaxons sounded, sirens blared, and flashing red lights bathed the massive room in the color of blood. It looked like something out of hell. A shuttle sat docked at the pier with a crowd of people gathered around the cargo ramp. Andras decided it must be the latest arrival from Earth and walked over to see what was going on. He pushed through the crowd and almost couldn't believe it.

A man dressed in black combat clothing lay sprawled out face down on the loading ramp. Standing near the body, a young security force private leaned over with his lunch coming up. Andras glanced at the man's name stenciled on the back of his uniform shirt. "What the hell happened here, Private Foster?"

Foster looked up, his face the color of wood ashes. "He came outa there shooting, Sarge. I d-d-dunno how I hit him before he got me." And then he threw up again, on Andras's spit-shined combat boots and one pants leg.

Andras backed up a step and turned to his partner, Corporal Dan Bishop. "Get some men and secure this area. I want everybody away from that shuttle. Then take Foster to headquarters and put him in an interview room. Go."

Andras watched Dan for any sign of insolence as he set up the crime scene perimeter, helped Foster stand up on wobbly legs, obediently called Police Central, and escorted the private out of the loading bay.

Their previous call on a domestic violence incident had been interrupted by the shooting, as it should have been. But when Dan ran off toward the elevator without waiting for Andras's lead, he made a big mistake, another in an increasingly frequent pattern of near-insubordination.

And an even better example happened last week with that Williams brat, who kept popping up on Andras's radar as a consistent troublemaker. No wonder, with a permissive father, all high and mighty in his lab coat like he's something special, but who can't instill discipline in his own kid. Andras had been handling the situation fine, and he didn't need any help from Dan, especially when he dropped that robodog's leash.

Did anyone really think that a verbal command to stay would always work? No stray electrons running around that might set loose one of those bionic German shepherds? Andras had seen video demonstrations of a robodog's power and ferocity. The most telling lesson to be learned from watching one was the necessity of replacing a heavily padded human target for training the dogs with a titanium-encased robot. *Jesus.*

Demanding respect and instantaneous compliance with orders was the only way to keep subordinates on their toes and under Andras's control. But he wasn't yet sure about Dan. The corporal had a lean, hungry look, and a manner about him that made Andras a little nervous, especially since promotions were few and far between.

He'd had a dream once, with him lying on the floor torn to pieces and Dan explaining to another cop that the dog, its teeth dripping with Andras's blood, must have malfunctioned. Then Dan laughed and said, "Too bad Sergeant Cadogan wasn't a robo*cop!*"

As his partner walked away, Andras had noticed sergeant's stripes on Dan's sleeve.

And now, as he glanced down at his boots and pant leg, the idea of spending the rest of the day with the odor of vomit prompted a call to inform Police Central that he would be leaving the docking bay for his apartment.

Andras stared at the crime scene, the maintenance workers swarming over the docking bay walls looking for gunshot damage, and the police officers standing around waiting for direction. He didn't trust any of them enough to turn them loose in the shuttle. Dan, maybe, but Andras had banished him to escort duty. That left him, which he much preferred, so he told everyone to remain well clear and that he would be back shortly.

SAMAEL HEBER CROUCHED IN DARKNESS AT THE REAR OF THE cargo bay and considered his options. It didn't take long. The sound of gunshots had changed everything.

He knew of the planned diversion, but none of the details. Compartmentalization safeguarded everyone . . . except him, that is, since he was alone, unarmed, and without backup. Why did they put the space station and him at such risk? He pondered that for a moment and decided they didn't. Something had gone very wrong. Deal with it.

Muffled voices, not too far away, faded in and out. Struggling against the effects of four inactive days in the life-support shipping container, he stretched and performed stationary exercises until normal circulation returned and his legs quit shaking. He crept to the end of the cargo stack and paused.

Voices in conversation from outside the shuttle drifted to him, almost loud enough to understand the words. He moved nearer to the cargo door. They were very interested in where the dead guy had been hiding and was he alone? After a few minutes Samael learned they were waiting for someone to arrive before beginning a thorough search.

Light streaming into the shuttle from the loading bay illuminated the empty space between the cargo providing his cover and the next stack. He took a quick peek, noted the scene on the loading ramp and a portion of the bay wall.

A group of uniformed men stood beside a body. An assault rifle lay nearby, spent shell casings glinting in a sphere of overhead floodlight. Men in orange coveralls clung to ladders built into the walls and stood on narrow, elevated walkways. Flashlights in hand, they were examining the structure. The man closest to the cargo door wore a sidearm. Cops. The diversion had a weapon, station security was armed, and Samael had nothing more lethal than his hands, feet, and a knife. Dangerous, certainly, but he'd always thought it unwise not to bring a gun to a gunfight. He felt naked in spite of his combat clothing.

He backtracked through the narrow corridor between the stacked cargo to the rear of the shuttle, slipped on the backpack and picked up the duffle. He walked around the end of the last stack and forward to the break opposite the cargo door. Deeper in shadow and farther from the group of men, he'd have a better chance of darting across without being spotted.

From his tactical vest he removed a small mirror with attached telescoping handle. He slipped the mirror past the edge of the cargo stack and adjusted it to view the cargo door and ramp. None of the cops in the group had a clear view into the cargo bay. The one standing apart did, and he was looking this way. With his other hand gripping the duffle straps, Samael waited.

∾

ABOUT HALFWAY TO POLICE CENTRAL, DAN OVERHEARD Andras's call about leaving for his apartment. He handed Private Foster off to another cop and headed back to the docking bay. Nothing much happened on Oasis that provided the opportunity for real police work, and he wasn't about to stand on the sidelines as a bystander to a shooting investigation.

He approached the crime scene and learned from the other cops that Andras had ordered everyone to hold off searching the shuttle while he interviewed the private involved in the shooting. It was just another example of the sergeant's obsession with doing everything himself and treating Dan like a gofer.

He questioned the advisability of that decision, which generated a comment from another cop. "So what if the dead guy has a partner? Where's he going to go?" Diplomatic chuckles from all the other cops, the typical subservient response to Andras's authority, had made Dan want to puke.

He couldn't complain about the sergeant's experience and knowledge, honed during ten years with the Chicago police. But as Dan's immediate superior and patrol partner, Andras had zero people skills. Escape from his tyranny required an opening due to illness or death, continued expansion of the security force, or doing something to earn a promotion. Like maybe now.

Dan stood apart from the other cops and stared at the open cargo door. It seemed to beckon him, but he knew the attraction came from within himself, the desire to investigate this startling incident and find answers to the many questions it had raised. He stepped carefully through the field of cartridge casings and knelt beside the body. According to eyewitnesses, the guy had appeared in the open cargo door with the assault rifle held at his hip, firing three-shot bursts. And yet even with the element of surprise, within a few seconds a rookie cop with a handgun had put him down.

Dan looked over his shoulder at the damage-control team. Their calm manner and the lack of casualties, other than a few scrapes, bruises, and one broken leg from leaping off the loading ramp, piqued his curiosity. With his flashlight he examined the assault rifle. Stamping on the barrel indicated 9mm Parabellum. He lifted a spent cartridge casing with a pen and checked the head stamp in the beam of his flashlight.

Well, I'll be damned. The guy had been shooting blanks.

Avoiding the bloody wound, Dan pressed on the man's chest. No body armor. The guy either had a death wish or arrived with outdated information.

The recent decision to issue firearms to *Oasis* police had resulted in new ammunition similar to that used by sky marshals. The .40 caliber bullets flattened out on impact and delivered incapacitating, sometimes deadly, shock to the target. The rounds would not, however, penetrate the interior or external walls of the station.

Dan stood and turned toward the damage-control team. "You guys won't find anything. Come on down."

One of the men on a ladder looked over his shoulder. "Thanks, but we'll wait for somebody with more than two stripes to tell us that."

Dan shook his head and turned toward the shuttle. A vague movement deep in the cargo bay caught his attention. "Any of you see that?"

"See what?" chorused back.

Dan walked to the door and peered into the depths of the dark interior. Ramp workers had never made it into the bay to turn on the interior lights. The flight crew had left on the external floods, and he couldn't see more than a foot or two inside.

Laughter from behind him, then the joke he had heard a hundred different ways, always offered in, or disguised as, playful jest. "You go on ahead and check it out, Dan. It's so dark that the bad guy won't be able to see you. Us lily white goodies are gonna stay right here."

Dan waved his hand over his shoulder. "To the brave go the spoils, fellas." He ignored a shouted, "Sergeant Cadogan's gonna have your ass!" from one of the cops, stepped into the bay and waited for his eyes to adjust. To his left a switch panel was mounted on the wall. He flipped one up and a row of fixtures brightened the rear of the bay. The remaining switches flooded the interior.

Cruiser shuttles transported multiple stacks of palletized cargo fastened to the floor in tracks. The top of the cargo had to be over twenty-five feet tall. Overhead lighting did not shine directly into the spaces between the stacks. The cargo hold reminded him of a moonlit urban area with a cluster of buildings separated by narrow, shadowed alleys.

He approached the closest stack and peered into the dark passageway between it and the adjacent one. A familiar apprehension settled in his gut. Years before on Earth a knife-wielding drug dealer had attacked him in an alley not much wider than this.

Standard procedure for *Oasis* cops required that weapons be carried with the chamber empty. Although nobody liked the restriction, most agreed that in space they'd probably never un-holster their weapons, much less use them. Events might be proving them wrong.

Dan drew his sidearm, racked the slide to chamber a round, and walked the length of the first passageway. After a peek around the corner confirmed an empty corridor in both directions, he continued his search. Ten minutes later he stood at the front of the cargo bay. A staircase led to the crew quarters and cockpit module. He'd seen what appeared to be forward movement across the shadowed break in the stacks, toward any number of hiding places. He was already in violation of Andras's orders, so why not?

TIMING WAS EVERYTHING. THE COP HAD SUDDENLY TURNED toward the shuttle when Samael was still exposed to view from the ramp. Now he watched the guy through a small port in the aft crew module bulkhead. The cop stopped at the foot of the ladder, a pistol visible in his hand. Samael tried to send telepathic messages encouraging the fool to come on up. He didn't believe in that shit, but what the hell?

When the cop grabbed the handrail and started climbing, Samael stifled a laugh, decided he might change his mind about psychic phenomena, and retreated into the narrow hallway separating six crew sleeping rooms.

He opened the first door on the right, shoved the backpack under the bottom bunk, and pulled the door almost closed. He opened all the other doors wide and stepped into the first crew sleeping room on the left.

Standing motionless, eyes closed, he zoned his senses into the environment, mentally filtering out the background hum of electrical equipment, cooling fans, a cycling hydraulic pump.

A clunk and whoosh, the bulkhead door opening. Footfalls. A clink of metal on metal. The guy hadn't silenced his gear. Careless amateur. Then another clink, closer.

Samael tensed as he heard breathing, slightly elevated. A sliver of the cop came into view past the door jam, his head turned away toward the open door of the opposite crew sleeping room. The cop shifted the pistol to his left hand and with his right pushed the door fully open. He leaned into the room and reached inside to turn on the overhead light.

Samael stepped into the hallway with his arm cocked and the sap held beside his ear. A blow to the side of the cop's head crumpled him into a heap on the floor. Samael grabbed the pistol and jerked the weapon free.

He handcuffed the cop, hurried to the hatch opening onto the upper staircase landing and dogged the locking handle closed. A search of the cop's many pockets produced little of interest except for a radio, a GPS device, and a blank spent shell casing.

So much information in a small package. Samael released the magazine from the cop's pistol and ejected the chambered round. Digging into the bullet with the point of his knife, he found a rubbery substance that answered the question of how a pistol could be fired on a space station without causing catastrophic damage.

What a stroke of luck, to be gifted with a weapon delivered on a platter.

He looked down at the cop's nametag and mouthed, *Thank you, Corporal Bishop.*

∽

RETURNING TO POLICE HEADQUARTERS AFTER CHANGING HIS uniform cargo pants and cleaning spots of Foster's lunch off his boots, Andras checked the interview room to see if the private had been brought back for questioning. Finding the room empty, he walked past the Central Communications room to the break area and found Jack Carter sitting at the duty desk.

"Carter?"

"Yo!"

Why can't I ever get some respect around here? "Has Dan returned from the scene yet?"

"Haven't seen him, Sarge."

"Has he reported in?"

"Nope."

"Well call him, you nimwit!" Andras poured himself a cup of coffee, which by this time was the color and consistency of used motor oil, and found the last of the doughnuts waiting patiently for him. He entered the comm room with powdered sugar trailing behind him like a miniature snowstorm.

Carter was trying to raise Bishop on the radio net. "Delta Bravo, Central, how do you read me, over." After a short delay, "Dan, this is Jack on channel two, come in old buddy."

"Call him on guard." This was the emergency frequency monitored by all radios simultaneously.

Carter switched channels. "Delta Bravo, this is Central on guard. If you read me come up channel two." Switching back. Carter monitored channel two for Dan's response.

Andras was pleased to see that Carter was using the standard procedure, which helped maintain a clear emergency communication net by limiting non-critical calls to short messages.

"Keep calling and let him know I'm coming down to the loading dock and to meet me there. If he can only receive for some reason at least he'll get the message." Andras left Comm Central with his anger building at the incompetence around him.

Dan can't follow a simple order, and I'm gonna take a chunk out of his ass for this.

~

AT FIRST THE SAMAEL WASN'T SURE IF HE HEARD SOMETHING, but the second call definitely came from Corporal Bishop's radio. "Who's that?"

"Comm Central. I haven't checked in at the normal interval."

"If you had the radio, and thought there might be another person in the cargo compartment, why didn't you call for backup?"

"It's a long story."

"Well, why—?"

The call interrupted the Samael as the words told of a sergeant coming to the loading dock. Within less than a minute he had the corporal immobilized and concealed in the interior darkness of the crew compartment. He could not allow this to develop into a two-v-one situation.

Come to Papa, Sergeant.

~

ANDRAS ENTERED THE LOADING BAY AND APPROACHED TO THE open cargo compartment door. The area had been cleared, but where was Dan?

"Bishop!" No response.

He walked up the ramp and looked into the shuttle. The interior floods were on, which weren't when he left the dock. If Dan had done that and entered the shuttle, he was in for an ass-chewing. Walking toward the front of the cargo bay, Andras called out a couple more times, getting angrier with each one. As he reached the last of the palletized cargo stacks, he tripped and landed face down on the floor.

"What the fu—?"

Cold steel at the back of his neck sent a shiver through him. A voice whispered, "Do not move."

The attacker removed Andras's weapon, tactical baton, chemical spray, and handcuffs, snapped them on Andras' wrists, pulled him backwards into a kneeling position and stepped around to stand in front of him. After a moment of mutual glaring at each other, the man suddenly reached out to Andras's chest, gripped his nametag, and tilted it up into the beam of a small flashlight. Then he laughed softly and grasped Andras under one arm. "Be very quiet. Get up and come with me."

The man took him forward in the cargo compartment to a bulkhead with stairs attached to the wall. They climbed to the top landing and stepped through a hatch into a dimly lighted narrow passageway lined with individual sleeping berths. Moving toward the front of the shuttle, the man directed Andras to a small room with a table and benches.

When seated at the table, the man asked, "Who are you?"

"Sergeant Andras Cadogan, Oasis Police. Who are you?"

The man looked at him with a cold stare. "What is your service number?"

"Four one two, seven five, two eight three four."

"What is your mother's maiden name?"

Who the hell is this guy? "Falworth."

The man asked Andras a number of questions concerning private information from Andras's past. Apparently satisfied, he changed the subject. "Who else is on the way to the loading bay?"

"No one. The area is off-limits until we get forensics to examine the body. I left another cop to secure the area. I don't know where he is."

"Wait here." The man got up, walked down the passageway, and disappeared through the hatch.

Andras sat at the table trying to make sense of what was happening. Things had been quiet for over a year. He was expecting to be contacted soon, but they hadn't said anything about sending anyone up. *What is this guy doing here? Has the time come?*

The man reappeared in the passageway carrying a duffle bag, definitely not standard issue. As Andras watched him walk into the small room, effortlessly with no wasted motion, confident, in command, he realized that he had been lied to and set up. No way were they going to keep him around with this SOB up here.

The man seemed to sense Andras's confusion. Vacant eyes peering out from the holes in the mask, he said, "Just in case you haven't figured it out, you and I work for the same people. I don't know what they told you and I don't care. I'm here to do a job and I'll do it my way with or without your help. Decide now whether you're in this thing or not."

"But I thought—"

"What you think is of no importance. Forget anything and everything you've been told. You have a decision to make. What'll it be?"

Some choice. To refuse now would be a death sentence.

"Is the deal still the same?"

"I don't know anything about that. Take it up with them. I want an answer."

Talking to this guy was getting nowhere. If Andras didn't protect his own interests no one else would. Same old stuff. "Okay, I'm in."

The man shook his head as he unlocked the handcuffs. He handed over the cuffs and keys, but kept the pistol, spare magazines and the radio. Then he reached into the duffle bag he had brought in from the cargo compartment and pulled out another radio.

"Recognize that?"

The letters "DB" were printed on the radio's call-sign label. "That's Dan Bishop's radio. Where is he?"

"What is it with you cops, asking questions all the time? Shut up and listen. Bring me two extra batteries and a charger. When you leave here, change the master communication controls at Police Central so that channel four is scrambled and available only on these two radios and the one you get to replace yours." The man leaned over close to Andras and pointed his finger in his face, like he was lecturing a disobedient child. "This is very important. Have the batteries and charger ready in an hour. I'll tell you when and where to bring them."

The man picked up the backpack and duffle bag. Standing at the passageway entrance with his back to Andras, he said, "I have work to do, but let me remind you. Do precisely as you are told. Do not try anything on your own. If you start thinking about changing your mind, take time to consider the consequences."

Andras watched the man disappear into the dark passageway, a mixture of anger and fear alternating with thoughts of what he had gotten himself into.

It had seemed like such a good idea, a way out, an escape from the hell his life had become on Earth. But now what? See it through, or back out? Either choice would be played out in the shadow of this black-clad figure, and assuming that Dan had been taken captive, both options opened the door to revealing Andras's treachery.

He gathered his gear and left the small room. Exiting the shuttle into the loading bay and contemplating his next move, Andras dreaded the thought that he would be putting into motion a series of events that would threaten to destroy more than he could ever imagine.

Andras hurried to avoid being found with no radio, sidearm, or extra magazines as he made his way back to his office and entered the rear door. He had just slipped spares into his belt carrier when Carter called to him from the front desk.

"Hey, Sarge! Is that you?"

"Who else has the key to the back door, you idiot?"

"Well, I may be the idiot, but you're the one who hasn't answered the radio with the boss looking for you."

"What's he want?"

"How should I know? I'm only a private."

Andras was in no mood for banter with this moron. "I'm telling you this for the last time, Carter. Whenever Colonel Thomas or one of his staff wants to see me, you damn well better find out what it is they want." Glaring at Carter over the desk, Andras shook his head and turned to face two patrolmen that had just entered. "You guys lost?"

"No. We came to tell you the guy who nailed that shooter is in interview room one."

The other cop grinned. "He sure looks like vomit. It really got to him."

Andras turned on the second cop and got right in his face. "Let me ask you something, son. You ever shoot a man?"

Backing up a bit from Andras's intimidating presence, the cop answered, "No, but I—"

"No, Sergeant, is the correct answer. You ever draw a weapon except to shoot it at the range or clean it?

"No, Sergeant."

"Okay, then. The young private you describe as 'vomit looking' has a hell of a lot more experience with this line of work than you do. He's seen death in the face and stared it down. He stood his ground and made sure that bastard never made it off the ramp. You better hope the first time it happens to you that you'll do half as good."

It was very quiet in the room until the phone rang and Carter answered. After a few "okay's" he hung up.

"Private Foster is in the interrogation room, Sergeant," he said. "The colonel's there too."

Andras nodded at Carter, then turned to the two cops. "Both you guys need to understand something. That uniform and the pistol on your hip can give you a false sense of power, and it all goes to hell real fast when the shooting starts. Foster lost his lunch, but he lost it *after* he did his job. Try to remember that next time you feel superior. His reaction isn't a sign of weakness, but being human."

The two cops mumbled apologies as Andras sent them on their way. Turning to Carter, he noticed the man looking at him with what might be described as respect. "What're you gawking at, Carter?"

"Nothing, Sergeant."

As Andras walked back into his office he couldn't help but note a subtle change in Carter's attitude. Calling him "Sergeant" rather than "Sarge" was only part of it. It was also a difference in Carter's manner, how he carried himself.

Andras knew that he was a hard man to work for, but in this line of work you didn't get the job done by winning a personality contest. It was always better if subordinates thought of you as a hard ass, and Andras played that role well enough. A healthy dose of respect mingled with a little fear never hurt anything.

Carter's attitude changed when he saw Andras making a difference with those two cops, helping them survive someday. Whenever Andras was taking a load of crap from his superiors, trying to maintain his cool in the face of such stupidity, he allowed himself to think about how good he was with his men. And even though they'd never admit it, they respected him. He wouldn't ever get the appreciation he deserved from above, but down here in the trenches where it really counts, he did.

The ringing phone brought Andras back to the present as he heard Carter answer. With all the "yes, sirs" and "no, sirs" it had to be Colonel Thomas on the line. Time to get to work.

Five minutes later Andras walked into the interview room. Private Foster sat at the table listening to Colonel Thomas pontificating about some typical nonsense. Andras motioned to the one-way glass along the wall, indicating for one of the cops on the other side to turn on the tape and cameras.

"Good evening, Colonel Thomas. Sorry for keeping you waiting."

The colonel glanced over his shoulder at Andras and motioned to the third chair. "I was just telling Private Foster about the first time I came under fire. It was during a riot situation. Hell, I couldn't have been much over twenty or so—"

"Excuse me, Colonel, but from the looks of this young man, may I suggest we get the preliminaries over with? He'd probably like to get some food, maybe go to bed for some well-deserved rest."

Foster was glancing back and forth between Andras and Colonel Thomas like a spectator at a tennis match. "Thanks, Sergeant. I'm still a little shook up over this."

With the colonel glaring at him, Andras sat down and smoothly took over doing his job.

"Private Foster, first let me thank you for being alert. I don't know how many lives you saved, but you prevented this from turning into a disaster. Our purpose here is to take your statement for the detectives who will come up from Earth to conduct the investigation. We have the personnel to do it ourselves," Andras paused to emphasize this comment on the record and in front of his superior, "but some bureaucrat decided that detectives have to come up here and do it for us."

"Sergeant," said Colonel Thomas, "what have we done about the body?"

"Nothing, sir. We can't really move it until the detectives get here, which is stupid under the circumstances, because—"

"Don't you think these procedures have been thought out by

people one hell of a lot more experienced in the command of a space station than you?"

The rising swell of anger at being talked down to by this pompous asshole caused Andras's big hands to grip the edge of the table to keep from reaching out and throttling the little weasel.

"Excuse me, sir. I didn't mean any disrespect for my superiors. But nobody thought much about the practical aspects of dealing with this sort of death."

"What sort of death?"

What an imbecile. "Death by gunshot, sir. If someone dies a natural death, the hospital takes care of the paperwork and disposition of the body. With no evidence of wrongful death, that'd be the end of it until the body can be disposed of. But no one considered what would happen if somebody was murdered or killed in self-defense. Criminal investigations using people days away make no sense. We have personnel trained to do it."

And I can do it as well as any detective.

Colonel Thomas appeared to be listening, which caught Andras off-guard. Foster looked confused, probably wondering what any of this had to do with him.

Clearing his throat with a characteristic preparation to wax eloquent on something he knew absolutely nothing about, Colonel Thomas pushed his chair back from the table, folded his arms and said, "Speaking of bodies, how do we . . . preserve, so to speak, the evidence?"

Doesn't this guy know anything? "It's a simple matter, sir. We cool the loading bay down, but that just emphasizes my point about delaying the investigation. Forensics can't do as good a job when we wait this long."

Andras was running a scam here. The cause of death or the circumstances surrounding it weren't a mystery. Forensic evidence wasn't critical to anything. But when it got down to finding out who this guy was, good detective work might uncover a lot.

Andras wanted a chance to examine the body. If he discovered something crucial, it might prove to idiots like Thomas that Andras was capable of running a complete law enforcement operation. It would reinforce his position that they didn't need some snot-nosed detective from Earth taking a trip in space to further his own career while a real cop wasted away in a dead-end job.

"What do you suggest, Sergeant, since you seem to think no one else has any good ideas but you?"

Finally, the right question. "Let me start things rolling with the Medical Examiner. It may not stop them from sending detectives up. But if they get delayed, I bet I can find out all they need to know before they arrive." Andras already knew more than anyone else on the station about what had happened, but he wasn't about to share that secret.

Colonel Thomas leaned back in his chair and looked up at the ceiling, putting on a big show of deep thought about serious matters. Andras knew this colonel was like all the others, looking for any chance to take somebody else's good idea and claim it as his own.

"You know," said Colonel Thomas, "now that you mention it, I identified that problem during my last inspection. This would be a good opportunity to address the issue with NASA. In the meantime, let the M.E. know what I want and be ready to move on it."

Bingo. Andras stood as Colonel Thomas got up to leave only because military courtesy required it.

Here was a man who had risen to a position of command and authority in the service of the United States without being able to lead the way out of a paper bag. The colonel was as predictable as the movement of the sun. Manipulating him was child's play.

Continuing with what he should have been doing in the first place, Andras questioned the private about the events in the loading dock. As he went through the motions, he was careful not to appear in a hurry. He didn't have much time to implement a plan to solve his unexpected personal problem, but two cops and a recording device were monitoring the session.

If he played his cards right, Andras knew with one move he might be able to earn a promotion and terminate a clandestine alliance with the devil that was rapidly turning sour.

DAN REGAINED CONSCIOUSNESS PLAGUED WITH A SPLITTING headache. Cold, hard steel pressed into his cheek. Tape covered his mouth. Handcuffs circled both wrists. He eased his eyes open, squinting in bright light from above. He was lying on the floor in the galley of the shuttle's crew compartment.

The blurry figure of a man slowly came into focus, dressed in black from boots to full head mask. Dan fought to quell the rising bile in his throat as the man rolled him over and lifted him to a sitting position, back resting against the wall, legs stretched out in front.

Dan's personal gear lay nearby, including his empty holster and ammo pouch with extra magazines, along with a backpack and a duffle bag.

The man knelt. "You're looking around too much. Do not make a sound." He removed the tape from Dan's mouth.

Dan tried to lick his lips, but couldn't find any moisture. "May I please have some water?"

The man reached in the backpack and pulled out a plastic bottle. He helped Dan drink and rinse out his mouth. Dan noticed the distinct taste of Earth water.

The man grasped Dan's arms. "Get up. Lean back against the wall if you feel dizzy. Move from here and I'll kill you."

Standing on wobbly legs, Dan struggled to accept the harsh reality that his stupidity had provided this guy with a weapon.

The man reached underneath a corner of a small dining table, pulled a lever, gripped the edge of the table and lifted. A hinged section of the floor attached to the table legs rotated ninety degrees, revealing a hatch. The man knelt, grabbed a handle, and grunted with effort as he turned it and pulled the cover open.

The sound and feel of rushing air filled the small room. Dan stared at the dark opening, an entrance to a radial chute. From his initial orientation briefings, he remembered that with the shuttle in the docking position, the crew could abandon ship in the event of a problem.

The man stood in front of Dan. "We need to move. If you falter or try anything to hinder me, I'll hurt you."

Dan nodded. "That's clear enough."

The man described how a rope would be used to control Dan's movement within the chute while leaving his hands free to climb and descend the ladders. He fastened the backpack to Dan's waist, told him to kneel down, and drew his knife from a sheath inside the top of his right boot. With the blade resting against Dan's throat, the man unlocked the cuffs from one wrist and told him to refasten them with his arms in front of his body. "I'll handle the duffle. Go."

Dan descended into the narrow confines and semi-darkness of the chute accompanied by a sense of doom. Claustrophobia gripped him, but the real demon clutching his heart was the underlying reality. If he had only followed orders, none of this would be happening.

Hounded by a headache, Dan followed his captor's directions through an endless maze of pipes. The man paused frequently to consult a diagram, and on one occasion ordered him to back up and retrace their route.

Dan sensed the gravity lessening. They were moving higher toward the central core. When they came to a dead end with Dan in the lead, the man said, "You know what to do."

Dan opened the hatch cover, stuck his head out. His spirits sank to a new low.

The central core housed the myriad of systems necessary for survival in space. Banks of machinery packed in the massive room created a maze of narrow hallways. Spotlights in the ceiling provided dim lighting. Automatic functioning of the equipment almost eliminated the need for maintenance. Most problems could be handled from the environmental control facility. Personnel seldom ventured here, and it was the perfect place to hide.

At the foot of the ladder, the man immobilized Dan and disappeared with the duffle. After a half hour, he reappeared and lowered the bag to the floor. Dan couldn't help but notice that it wasn't as full as before.

The man sat down and crossed his legs. "What happened in the loading bay?"

Wondering why the man was asking him, Dan replied, "I wasn't there. Witnesses said a guy walked out of the shuttle and began shooting. A cop killed him."

"Tell me about this." The man reached behind his back and pulled Dan's pistol from inside his waistband. "I thought Oasis cops didn't carry weapons."

"That changed about a year ago." Dan thought about telling the man it was because they knew he was coming, but decided it wouldn't be a good idea.

"Do all station weapons use this cartridge?"

Dan looked at the man's gloved hand, holding a case and separated bullet. "It was developed for use here."

"What kinds of weapons and how many?"

Dan hesitated, unsure whether anything he had said so far would be considered treason. After a moment, he shook his head.

The man drew his knife and laid the gleaming point just below Dan's left eye. "Let me remind you that your usefulness to me is key to your continued good health."

The thought of that blade taking his eye sent a shudder through Dan's bowels. "Sidearms only," he blurted. "Forty-caliber Smiths, one per officer, plus extras in the Captain's office."

"Ammo?"

"Three magazines per man, eleven rounds each. More in storage."

"Nothing else?"

"No. They're planning for assault rifles, but haven't decided on the caliber."

The man moved in closer, eyes boring deep. "I'll know if you're lying."

"I'm a traitor, not a liar."

The man grinned through the mouth hole in the mask, sheathed the knife and stood up to stretch his back. "Don't be so hard on yourself. Anyone can be made to talk. The only question is how much suffering it takes. You could be lying there in pain like you've never imagined, minus an eye and spilling your guts. I'd have the information either way.

"I didn't anticipate firearms but it doesn't change anything. And now I know what to expect from you. A real hard case would be too much trouble. But you have an instinct for self-preservation."

"What are you doing up here and what do you want with me?"

"Don't go stupid on me, corporal."

Dan watched his captor disappear into a shadowed corridor and pondered what was niggling at him about the guy. After a moment, he realized what it was.

New arrivals usually appeared uncoordinated as they adjusted to the gripper shoes and exoskeleton under-suits, designed to resist the wearer's movements and simulate the effect of Earth gravity.

This guy had been on Oasis no more than a few hours, yet he moved with efficiency and confidence in the low-gravity environment of the central core. He had to be wearing both the suit and the shoes, which he must have brought with him, pre-fitted and programmed to join the Oasis LAN. Not only that, he displayed none of the newbie expressions of awe and wonderment at being in space. He'd either been here before, or he was superbly trained.

Dan leaned his head against the wall and closed his eyes. His only choice was to wait for a mistake and hope the bastard in black didn't find out he'd lied about the shotguns until it was too late.

4

DAY TWO EARLY AFTERNOON

Toby's plan to find out more about what had happened in the loading dock had to wait almost three hours because of the shelter-in-place order. When the all clear finally sounded, he and Rooster pushed their way past a group of adults and rushed out of the observation room. A steady stream of people in the corridor almost ran them over. Toby had never felt energy like this. The space station seemed to hum with it.

"We need to get back," said Rooster.

"No way, Earthie. This is big stuff."

"It's also a good reason not to be here without an excuse."

Toby grabbed Rooster's sleeve and hauled him around a corner to one of the gyms located throughout the station. It was deserted. He punched his personal code into the door lock, waited for the click, pulled the door open and shoved Rooster inside.

Rooster held his hands out to his side and shook them. "This is not a good time for bench presses, Space-O."

"You wanted to see the chutes, right?"

"Sure, but—"

"It's perfect. With all this excitement, the adults won't pay any attention to us. And I wanna know what happened. The chutes let us stay out of sight and go where we want."

"Where are we going?"

"You'll find out. Trust me. It'll be an adventure."

"I was afraid of that."

"Swallow your fear and follow me."

Toby led Rooster toward the nearest entry hatch. On the way, he explained that the chute system was a network of ventilation/emergency escape pipes with airlocks connecting environmental zones. Radial chutes extended from the central core to the outer rings of the space station. Cross chutes formed a series of concentric rings. "With a diagram, your GPS and the intersection locator signs, you can go anywhere."

"But you aren't supposed to be in there, right?"

"Who cares? They've never had to use them. And it's fun."

They were walking along a corridor forming one of the innermost rings. The curve of the floor was much sharper here than further out. Toby didn't see the hatch until they were almost there. He glanced in each direction. No adults. He punched Rooster in the arm. "Betcha can't do this."

He performed another leap and sailed far enough to grab the ladder and plant his feet on a rung.

Rooster stared at him, grinning. He raised a clenched fist with a thumbs-up sign.

Toby waved a hand in a hurry-up signal. "Start your leap just before you get to that extinguisher."

Rooster did that but planted his foot wrong. He bounced off the padded wall, grabbed for the ladder, missed, and landed on the floor. He looked up at Toby. "How'd I do?"

"Not bad for a newbie Earthie. Get up here." Toby opened the hatch, climbed in and crawled about five feet into the chute. When Rooster's head appeared in the opening, Toby reminded him to use his foot to close the hatch without trying to reverse position in the narrow tube. He led the way to the first intersection, the only places in the system with enough room to turn around.

When he faced Rooster, Toby knew something wasn't right. Beads of sweat covered his friend's face. Shivers rippled through his body.

"What's wrong?"

"I . . . I'm really nervous. This tube is too small. And dark."

"But you'll get used to it. And there are lights at every intersection."

Rooster shook his head. "Maybe next time. I want out."

"Okay, okay. C'mon to the intersection and turn around." Rooster did that and Toby followed him back to the closed hatch. He told him how to push it open against the air pressure, check both ways for adults, then climb out, close the hatch, and drop to the floor. "Do it fast. If anyone sees you, they'll report you to the cops."

"What'll they do to me?"

"First offense? Cut off one of your thumbs."

Rooster glanced over his shoulder, a little more relaxed now. Traces of a smile tugged at his mouth. "But you've still got both of yours."

"Of course. No one catches Toby Williams, phantom of the chutes."

Rooster fist-bumped Toby and climbed out. Toby backed up to the intersection, planned the shortest route to the docking bay and scrambled forward in the dimly lit tube.

A FEW YEARS AGO, TOBY HAD DISCOVERED THAT BY CLOSING HIS eyes and forcing himself to relax, after a moment or two his senses would sharpen. The first time it happened he was lying in bed when he heard things that couldn't be from his own apartment, or from the ones on either side. Oasis designers had soundproofed the walls between units well enough to ensure that one of the most common irritants of close-quarters living on Earth would not be a factor.

During the next few weeks, Toby listened carefully in the late evening or early morning, but nothing happened. Concluding that it was probably just a dream, he forgot all about it. That's all it took.

Lying in bed one morning he heard voices again, this time an argument with shouts, furniture crashing, and glass breaking. The violence of it startled him bolt upright, confused, frightened, and wondering if something was wrong with him.

The next morning at the breakfast table, his dad was reading the paper on his tablet and put it down to get another cup of coffee. Toby noticed the headline, "Early Morning Disturbance Ends In Arrest." Curiosity aroused, he checked it out on his tablet and read about a domestic disturbance call that sent police to an apartment about two Oasis blocks from his own. He had heard the incident as it happened.

By now Toby knew that employing his special ability wasn't a matter of chance, and he could *control* it. Once he detected a sound, he could change what he was hearing by directing his attention to the left, right, up, or down, like using a remote control to adjust the target for a listening device.

At this moment he paused to catch his breath and check the chute diagram to confirm that he had almost reached his target hatch with a view into the docking bay. He closed his eyes and audio-searched for the sounds he knew from a school field trip would be filling the bay after a shuttle arrival. Nothing yet. He crawled forward to the next radial/cross chute intersection and tried again. Still nothing, so he remained stationary to adjust his search and finally detected something to his left. Faint, probably near the max range of his abilities, but unmistakably from the docking bay. To better confirm results of the audio-search, Toby tried another ability he had discovered just last year.

Late for class and crawling fast in the chutes, he arrived at the hatch nearest the high school and reached for the handle when a strange sensation warned him to stop. He waited for his rapid breathing to subside and audio-searched the corridor for evidence of people, adults in particular, and detected nothing.

But the sensation wouldn't go away and time was running out, so he very carefully rotated the handle and eased open the hatch a little bit. And standing right below, a hall monitor who had never given Toby a single break, waiting quietly to pounce. Over the course of the next few days, Toby found out what had happened.

In addition to enhanced audio ability, he had also been gifted with augmented spatial sense. Crawling in the chutes, surrounded by round, smooth contours, he was able to detect intersections where radial and cross chutes met before he could see them. It had also worked with objects, like a maintenance guy's forgotten tool bag.

Detecting a shuttle ought to be really easy, so Toby closed his eyes and began a spatial search when a totally different sensation returned. He instantly forgot the shuttle as an undefined fear took hold. He turned his head to focus his sensory attention behind him. Relaxing, letting it work, he waited.

Normal chute sounds, air movement, but something else too. A rustling, like cloth on metal, and every once in a while a soft clink. There was also a faint, rhythmic sound, evenly spaced with short periods of silence . . . kind of like . . . breathing. Without even thinking about it, Toby's attention shifted from audio to object and space search. Immediately the sensation changed.

Smoothness in the chutes was interrupted by an obstruction. Not something small, like the tool bag. Much bigger, rounded in shape, although not consistently. The shape was changing, from mostly round, or maybe oblong, to having extensions sticking out from it. He tried to picture what the object might be when he became aware of yet another sensation.

Heat. The temperature in the station was kept relatively cool, and the chutes were even colder. But this object radiated enough heat to stand out in sharp contrast to the background.

Toby struggled to interpret the sensation barrage coming at him. Without understanding how, he was correlating the information from different sources into a coherent image whose shape, sound, and temperature slowly became that of a human, crawling in the chute, arms and legs extending alternately, breathing softly and coming closer.

Who the heck is this?

Suddenly it felt like all of his abilities broadcasted simultaneous warnings. He opened his eyes and the sight sent his heart to his throat and most of the air out of his lungs.

A head, covered in black, with small holes for the mouth and eyes, which stared at Toby, unwavering, menacing, deadly.

Without warning, the head surged into the chute behind Toby, followed by the shoulders, arms, and upper body of a man.

Toby turned to escape, intense panic gripping him as he scrambled for his life.

Sounds of pursuit gained on Toby as he approached the next intersection. A fresh burst of adrenaline hit his bloodstream at the thought of being caught by this black apparition, and his mind instantly evaluated three options.

He could go straight ahead along the cross chute; up a radial chute against artificial gravity, or down with it. Toby dove headfirst into the radial chute and streamlined his body like a diver. He felt a slight tug at his feet as the man made a futile grab to hold him, followed by rapid acceleration. Unimpeded, he would hit the bottom where this chute ended far below, and hard enough to seriously injure or kill him.

But he'd learned a trick. Pointing his toes outward, Toby widened his legs until his toes made contact with the walls of the chute. Applying pressure, he used the friction to slow his descent and control it, momentarily releasing the "brake" as he passed cross chutes.

Toby knew the man couldn't have followed him through the maneuver, so after falling about five floors, he increased pressure on his toes and then used his elbows to help decrease his speed even more.

After coming to a stop a few feet lower than he wanted, he reached back to pull himself into the cross chute feet first. He rolled onto his back and peered up into the radial chute.

Far above him, barely visible in the dim light, a black shape descended on the ladder. Toby stared up in fascination as the shape passed the brighter illumination at one of the intersections and clearly saw the man pause, look down between his feet, and—*is that a smile? Move, you fool* . . . Toby scrambled along the cross chute and thought about what he should do next.

He'd never seen another grown-up in the chutes and knew of only a few other kids who had ever ventured more than a few feet inside. That's the way he liked it, his own private place where he could come and go as he pleased.

And then, in spite of the danger involved with being pursued by a guy wearing a mask, Toby became angry at this invasion and decided to show him who *owned* the chutes.

For the next half hour, Toby alternated swift movement with periods of rest, calling up at will his heightened senses to determine the man's location. Using audio was most gratifying. What had been the slow, rhythmic sound of breathing was now a rapid, rasping series of gasps.

Getting tired? Can't find me? Here I am.

Toby used sounds to put the man into immediate pursuit in one direction, then he backtracked or circled around to start the process over again. What fun this was!

He was beginning to tire of the game when he made a mistake.

His abilities were extremely directional. He couldn't hear or sense all the area around him simultaneously, but the experience gained today was helping him refine the techniques to focus his attention in a sweeping pattern until he picked up the target.

As he tried for an audio pick up in the direction he thought the man would be, he came up with nothing. Adjusting his attention left, then right, and finally up and down still brought no contact.

Thinking he may have misjudged how far away the man was, Toby extended his audio search in range and immediately detected something. Using slight adjustments, he zeroed in on what he identified as the sound of breathing. But it was slow and rhythmic, nothing like the out-of-breath sounds from the man.

Toby listened more intently, and decided that's what it had to be. He'd found another person, or the man had recovered from the exertion of the chase.

But how could this be another person? Toby considered where he was in the chute system. His positional awareness had proven surprisingly accurate during his previous travels, but the rapid movement and excitement of the last half hour had confused him. Tracing the memory of his route, Toby figured he was audio searching a relatively small area of the chutes that bordered on the central core.

The core was about five stories tall, and the chute system ran through it in a more complicated pattern than in the rest of the station. Some of the chutes dead-ended at a ceiling or floor, providing more access from the core into the chutes. Toby thought he'd probably gone past one or more of the core levels in his rapid maneuvering.

Traveling the chutes was one thing, but the core had long been a place of mystery. Even though usually deserted, it would be more likely to have activity than the chutes. The equipment was designed to work without having to mess with it, but his dad often talked about sending engineers in to fix problems.

As he listened to the sound, Toby tried to judge the actual distance but couldn't determine how to do that. He could easily extend or retract his reception in relation to the sound. And although the difference in volume and clarity was significant, it served only to help him narrow the search directionally closer to the exact source. *Is this coming from the chutes or inside the core?*

Then he got an idea, and searched his immediate area first, just to make sure. After a few moments he decided the man was still too far away and posed no immediate threat.

Knowing exactly what the background noise of the chutes sounded like, Toby figured that if he moved his audio search off the breathing sound, he might be able to confirm that the breathing was coming from within the chutes.

But if the background noises in the immediate vicinity of the sound were different, he wouldn't know for sure where it was, only where it wasn't.

Concentrating on precise control, Toby began to adjust his point of focus when he felt an immediate, gut-wrenching sense of panic. It was like a dream, and something horrible pursued him, but his legs were mired in some thick, sucking substance that wouldn't let him flee.

Tearing his mind free of the audio search seemed to take forever. As he became aware of his immediate surroundings, he clearly heard the rapid rustling of cloth on metal, superimposed on the heavy breathing of a man under extreme exertion.

Toby struggled against fear-driven paralysis. Movement defied him. His hands and knees seemed glued to the smooth surface of the chute. When he finally turned enough to look behind him, the black-clad figure was emerging from the darkness cloaking the midpoint between two intersections. Crawling like a monstrous insect, he was at full speed and closing fast, the overhead light illuminating the man's masked face and pumping arms.

The sight filled Toby with renewed energy and will to escape. He scrambled to the next radial chute and decided to go up rather than down, which his pursuer would probably expect him to do again. Reaching the intersection, Toby started climbing, arms and legs moving as fast as he could make them go. Looking high above, he almost couldn't believe it.

Trapped!

It wasn't an intersection, but the termination point of the radial chute as it emptied into the ceiling of the central core. Toby had no choice but to go for it and hope he could open the hatch before the man got to him.

As he reached the hatch and gripped the handle, Toby couldn't resist looking past his own feet and focusing on the chute below.

The sight froze him: the demon, scrambling up the ladder, head bent back and eyes watching him with the look of triumph, his approaching success accentuated by a low sound of guttural laughter.

"Game's over, you little shit."

The voice did it. Toby had never heard anything like it. It was so menacing, so powerful with implied threat, that it broke through his dazed state and demanded action. Toby pulled on the hatch handle with all his strength. It didn't budge.

The man slowed down and seemed to be enjoying this. "Well, well, partner. You took me on quite a ride, didn't you? Played with me, having fun." The man climbed one more rung and paused. "What about now? Is this fun? How do you like being trapped like a rat in a hole?"

Toby couldn't understand why the man didn't immediately climb the final distance to the top of the chute. Then it dawned on him.

Maybe it's too dark up here for him see the hatch.

Toby gripped the handle. He had to get it to move. Would talking to the man slow him up? "What're you gonna do to me?"

"Well, I'll be. A rat that talks. In that case I might make you a pet and take you around to circuses."

Just keep talking, mister.

Toby twisted harder but still couldn't move the handle. The panic swelled again as he realized that if the hatch really was stuck, he had no way out.

"What's the matter? No more talk? You aren't much good to me now, are you?"

Looking down, Toby watched the man take another step up the rungs and knew this was it, but not without resisting till the bitter end.

Toby turned his back to the threat, which allowed him to use both hands to grip the handle. He took a deep breath, held it, yanked as hard as he could.

He'd been turning it the wrong way. This time it swung open effortlessly and so suddenly that Toby almost lost his grip on the handle as he fell headlong out of the chute into the central core.

CORPORAL DAN BISHOP HAD BEEN A PRISONER FOR ONLY ABOUT twenty-four hours, and he was already having trouble maintaining his sanity. The man continued to care for him with the same contradictory mix of ruthless efficiency and compassion. At least he wasn't using the blindfold, gag, and earplugs. That was the worst, being robbed of most sensation except his own pain and dealing with the inability to move freely.

And the restraints weren't as tight. Dan was able to change his position enough to sit up. He also found he could kneel to relieve some of the aches and pains of being immobilized.

He couldn't figure out a pattern to the man's schedule. He came and went randomly, sometimes returning only after a short time and then disappearing for an hour or two. He never spoke except to give instructions, and Dan had long since stopped trying to engage him in conversation.

And the curiosity was unbearable. *What is the man doing here? What will happen to me?*

Now Dan's right leg was numb. As he moved to change positions, he felt a popping sensation in his ears with a pressure change in the core and heard a whooshing sound of air accompanied by a scream.

Turning toward the noise, Dan saw a boy hanging by one arm from an open radial chute hatch cover in the ceiling. He stared in amazement as the kid grabbed onto the rungs of the ladder, scrambled down and sprinted down the narrow passageway between the banks of machinery directly toward Dan. It was Toby Williams. Dan knew Toby hadn't seen him lying on the floor, and would run over him in a matter of seconds.

"Watch out!"

Toby made a valiant effort to stop, but ended up tripping over Dan's legs. Crashing to the floor on his stomach, Toby rolled over on his back and stared at Dan. His expression went from astonishment to fear as his gaze shifted, looking past Dan down the passageway and toward the chute.

Dan turned to see the man with the mask grab the hatch cover handle, pull himself head first out of the chute, flip his body upright, let go and land on his feet. The man reached back into the small of his back, pulled out a handgun and extended it into the palm of his other hand in a shooter's combat stance.

It happened so fast. The horror Dan felt, the simultaneous decision to do something, and the screamed, "NO!" as he lunged out to block the shot.

The bullet hit Dan in the upper chest and spun him around to the limits of his restraints. He hit the floor on his back, and lost consciousness as the black blur of the man leapt over him.

TOBY WAS RUNNING FOR HIS LIFE WHEN THE DEAFENING SOUND of a gunshot echoed in the closed spaces of the core. With ears ringing, unable to hear his own footsteps, Toby sprinted to the next intersection and turned the corner. Hoping for an emergency exit sign, he slowed up at the next intersection, looked both ways for the closest chute hatch and didn't find one.

He continued down the passageway, checked the next intersection and saw it, barely visible in the dim light, a glowing red sign. Racing toward it, Toby glanced down an intersecting corridor and caught a glimpse of the man running along the parallel adjacent passageway. just before he disappeared from view.

If he catches me out here I'm dead.

With only one more intersection to go before this passageway ended at the wall below the chute hatch, Toby was gasping for breath as he pushed himself to the limit. Passing the intersection, in his peripheral vision he saw the man running toward him, and he was close. The man had outrun him and used that advantage to catch up without being seen.

Toby focused on the ladder straight ahead. Without slowing his stride and well out from the wall, he leapt up and reached the top of the ladder. He hit the wall hard, grabbed the top rung at the same time he gripped the hatch cover handle and yanked it with all his strength. As the hatch opened and swung down from the ceiling and away from the wall, Toby hauled himself into the chute, pushing with his feet on a rung.

The sound of another three shots punched the air in the core as the rounds smashed into the hatch cover, stunning Toby's hand gripping the handle.

He pulled the cover shut, yanked the inside handle to the closed position and held it there, gasping for breath.

Will the demon stop chasing me? Toby closed his eyes to search for the threat.

Nothing . . . then the pounding of shoes on the ladder, a pause, and then an unseen force trying to yank the handle out of his hand.

Toby wedged his feet against the wall of the chute and pulled with both hands. In spite of his effort the handle began to move. Filled with mounting panic, he shoved against the wall of the chute with his legs and pulled as hard as he could.

But the handle continued to move slowly toward the unlocked position.

Then the sudden release of the opening force caused Toby's legs to extend to a full locked-knee position. His back and head slammed into the chute wall. Stunned and dazed, he needed no enhanced power to hear the man's voice, screaming obscenities, punctuated by the sound of metal banging on metal.

The handle was fully closed, no pressure from the other side of the hatch, and Toby was suddenly free of fear with no sense of impending danger.

He relaxed his grip and let his legs go limp as he slumped down and buried his head in his hands.

With no attempt to stop it, Toby began to cry, great big racking sobs and tears enough to soak the front of his shirt.

DESCENDING THE LADDER TO THE FLOOR, SAMAEL'S LEGS SHOOK. He couldn't believe how things had gone sour so quickly. He never expected to find anyone else in the chutes and was caught completely off guard as he casually made his way on an exploratory trip.

His initial reaction to discovering the kid was completely wrong. He'd assumed the kid was trapped in a dead-end portion of the chutes. Seeing him stuffed up there was so satisfying that he made a classic error, worthy of some inexperienced punk. He paused to enjoy the moment, to savor finally catching him, and to taunt the little pest, actions reminiscent of amateur hour in prime time. He went for him halfheartedly, feeling more annoyance at having to take care of an unexpected problem than concern about not being able to capture him.

Samael couldn't figure out how the kid did it. He obviously knew his way around in the chutes, but there was something else. The way the kid played with him. The well-timed and positioned noises Samael thought indicated carelessness. He didn't even begin to realize what was going on until near the end.

Luck played a part, too, like with those damned hatch covers. One pops open and deposits the prey right in the middle of Samael's own den. Then another cover swings down and blocks three shots, all right on top of the handle mechanism. The kid gets away, but he's not far, still within reach.

And then, for the first time in his professional career, Samael had allowed his frustration and anger to cause a dangerous loss of emotional control as a result of missing another opportunity to cancel this kid's ticket for good.

He could feel the kid's strength weakening on the hatch handle, and knew he could outlast him. But rather than having the patience to wait, Samael had ended up holding a broken hatch handle, damaged by impacts from his own bullets.

Catching his breath now at the bottom of the ladder, he considered how being discovered in the chutes jeopardized his mission.

Beginning with the shooter's diversion, the initial plan was to provide enough time for Samael to maneuver freely within the chute system and create the leverage necessary to hold station authorities at bay. But now, after the kid ran to mommy and complained about the bad man who scared him, Samael's timeline would be screwed all the way to Earth and back.

In spite of this possibility, he couldn't shake a nagging question: *How did that kid do it?* And immediately after that, a promise to himself: *I will find the answer.*

Samael hurried to where he'd temporarily stashed the cop, who was lying on his side. Expecting that the shot to his upper chest had probably been fatal, Samael knelt down, rolled him face up, and stared at what appeared to be a blob of molten substance now cooled. Samael pressed a finger into the substance and almost shit himself when the cop groaned, moved, and said, "Hurts!"

I'll bet it does. But Samael's curiosity about the new ammo would have to wait until he relocated his hostage from the open area of the core to a more secure location. He helped the cop to his feet and supported him with one arm until he could stand on his own, then picked up his gear with the other hand and approached one of the doors into the nuclear reactor room.

Located in the center section of the core, the small, cramped, dark interior spaces of the room offered better cover, and very few people would enter the room if they didn't have to. The ominous warning signs, especially the yellow and black nuclear radiation hazard symbols, made the cop stiffen. Samael was counting on exactly the same reaction from anyone who might come in here looking for him.

He motioned for the cop to sit down with his back against the wall. Examining the electronic lock, he noticed with satisfaction that it was exactly as he'd been briefed. He punched in the access code. The door opened with a solid click, and when he peered inside he knew it was perfect.

The stuff of nightmares in there, enough hazard signs and warning notices visible in the semi-darkness to make anyone nervous. There was something especially insidious about radiation. Unlike many dangerous things that could make an area lethal, it didn't warn you by sight or smell. It just reached out and killed. Good.

After securing the cop deep within the recesses of the reactor room, Samael offered him water and a pain pill. It didn't take long for the cop to fall asleep, and as Samael examined the impact point of the bullet and found no blood, he wondered why the shooter had been killed and the cop only incapacitated temporarily. He decided to check it out, and found yet another example of his failure to be as careful as he needed to be.

The cop was wearing the thinnest, lightest ballistic vest Samael had ever seen.

Ten minutes later, wearing the vest and thanking the cop once again for his assistance by providing Samael with critical equipment, he left the reactor room to shift this operation out of first gear and put the real pressure on.

FOLLOWING A MAD-DASH CRAWLING EFFORT TO PUT AS MUCH distance as possible between him and the man, Toby had been curled up deep within the chute system for what seemed like forever, jittery, nervous, shivering and sweating at the same time, with a rapid heart rate and breathing.

Finally recovered enough to move, he confirmed his location and mapped out a route to find the only adult he trusted with sharing this incident. Unfortunately, it took much longer than normal to exit the chute system. Every time Toby cracked a hatch, the corridors looked like Rooster's ant farm. Once he finally made it out, he approached the entrance to flight operations with the determined manner of someone who had business there. When a Space Command officer hurried by, Toby said, "Excuse me, sir? Lieutenant? A word, please?" He'd heard that in a movie and it sounded really adult.

The lieutenant entered a code in the door lock and gripped the handle. "Yes?"

"Do you know where Captain Larsen is?"

The lieutenant's eyes shifted from Toby toward the ceiling for a few seconds, then back. "He's real busy right now, kid. You better run along." He opened the door and disappeared into the ops room.

The door swung shut, silencing the buzz of multiple conversations, raised voices, intense activity in the room. Toby peered through the glass insert in the door. Turmoil reigned inside. He searched the scheduling board, found the name LARSEN in the lead position of a two-ship fighter mission. The wingman's name didn't mean anything, but the words in the remarks section did, a red OUT OF SERVICE for Brett's ship and OVERDUE for the wingman's.

Toby stepped closer to the door and noted that the departure and arrival times shown for Brett's ship indicated that the mission had ended more than three hours ago. Brett would probably just now be finishing up with his post-flight routine. That meant—someone tapped him on the shoulder. Toby turned around.

A Space Command major said, "If you're planning on setting down roots, do it someplace else."

"Could you help me, sir? I need to find—"

"I'll help you get where you belong. What's your name?"

"Never mind," Toby mumbled.

With all the activity in the corridors, no one paid much attention as he hurried toward the Personal Equipment room. He rounded the last corner and skidded to a stop.

Two Space Command officers were blocking the hallway. They stared at Toby. He stared back, turned around and hurried away, pursued by a shouted, "Hey, kid! Why aren't you in school?"

He ran to the next intersection and looked for a chute entrance, found a red sign on the wall in the adjoining corridor and sprinted to it. After waiting for a group of adults to pass, he climbed the ladder, popped the hatch open, and pulled himself in.

It only took a few minutes of breathless crawling and scrambling up and down ladders before he saw the numbers he was looking for. Once in the corridor, he trotted to the Pilots' Personal Equipment room door and yanked on the handle. An alarm sounded, not a good way to remain inconspicuous.

He ran to the next intersection, slowed, turned the corner, saw two adults approaching. They appeared to be interested in the alarm. Toby pointed behind him. "It's the personal equipment room. There might have been a break-in." Ignoring their suspicious looks, Toby hurried past them and decided it was time to disappear again.

Exiting the chutes near Brett's apartment about 10 minutes later, Toby's concern about the remarks on the scheduling board had peaked. He rushed around the last corner prior to Brett's apartment and pulled up short. Two men were standing near the door. Both were wearing the uniform of officers in the Space Command. Neither wore the wings of a pilot, but one had some sort of insignia pinned over his left shirt pocket. It was a weird looking thing Toby had never seen before.

As Toby approached the officers, he fought back against the fear that something had happened to his friend. He decided to greet the officers as casually as possible.

"Hi!"

"Evening," said the one with the insignia. "What can we do for you?"

"Nothing. I'm here to see Captain Larsen."

"He isn't here."

"Oh. Well, he's a friend of mine, and I wanted to ask him a question."

"That's very interesting, but he still isn't here."

Toby leaned against the wall, trying to look like he belonged in the hallway. "Then I'll just wait for him. Know when he'll be back?"

"You better run along," said the other man. "It's past your bedtime, and you don't want to be here anyway."

Bedtime? It's early afternoon. And how does this idiot know what I want? Toby looked at the second man and decided a slightly belligerent stance was appropriate. The officer didn't wear pilot wings, so why should Toby be nice to him?

"My bedtime is my business, and I can wait for Captain Larsen if I want to."

The second officer had also been leaning against the wall, but he uncrossed his legs, pushed himself away from it and turned to face Toby. Before the man could say anything, the first man held his hand up in a "stop" motion. Looking at Toby with that exasperated expression grown-ups so often get, he said, "Listen, kid, nobody's saying you can't wait wherever you want for whoever you want. But under the circumstances it would be better if you came back some other time to see Captain Larsen."

What circumstances? Toby just *knew* something unusual was going on. "Was there an accident?"

"How did you know about that?" said the second officer.

"I went by the flight operations room."

The two officers leaned toward each other and one whispered something.

Why won't they just answer the question? "Is he okay?"

"Take it easy, son, he's fine. But there was a problem on his mission today."

"What kind of problem?"

"We aren't at liberty to talk about that, and it really isn't something a young man of your age should be concerned about anyway."

Toby knew well enough what concerned him, and he didn't need anyone to tell him otherwise. He also knew this wasn't normal, and wanted more than ever to talk to Brett. "I really need to speak to him, sir. Can you tell me where he is now?"

The second officer suddenly turned into a typical grown-up. "Look, kid, we have a job to do, and it doesn't involve explaining to you why we're here, or where Captain Larsen is, or much of anything else except to tell you to get lost. Now I told you before, and I won't do so again. Go on home where you belong and leave us alone."

"You don't have to be so hard on the kid, Frank. He's just concerned about his friend and—"

"I don't give a damn about that. He can be friends with him all he wants, but he's not going to ignore me or give me any backtalk when I tell him to do something. Now quit mothering him and send him on his way."

Toby had made the assumption the nicer man was the one in charge. He didn't know or much care about the difference in rank insignia, except for Brett's silver railroad tracks of a captain. He hadn't noticed until now that one of the men wore gold leaves and the other silver, which seemed to be the ones to have if you wanted to be a jerk. But it didn't matter one way or the other as the nicer one seemed to lose interest in him and quietly told him to go home. Sticking around was sure to cause trouble.

Once out of sight of the two officers, Toby ran to the nearest chute entrance. After five minutes of breathless crawling and scrambling up and down a ladder or two, he exited the chutes and hurried to the cafeteria where he and Brett had talked last week. Toby entered the cafeteria and approached his friend, who was sitting at the same table and had just begun eating his breakfast.

Brett looked up, paused with a fork of scrambled eggs halfway to his mouth, and lowered the fork to his plate. "You shouldn't be here, Toby."

"But—"

"There are no 'but's. Your parents have made it clear that I'm not to feed your obsession with flying. I've agreed, but for what it's worth, I've decided not to discourage you. That's their problem."

Toby fought back tears, but didn't succeed very well.

Brett pulled a napkin from a dispenser and handed it to Toby. "Have a seat for a minute, then you'll have to leave."

Toby wiped his eyes. "There were two guys in Space Command uniforms standing outside your apartment."

"Did you notice their rank? Were they pilots?"

"A captain with pilot wings and a major with insignia I didn't recognize."

Brett's expression changed, as if a shadow passed over his face. "They were probably from the flight safety office."

"What do they want with you?"

Brett took a deep breath and exhaled in a rush. "We lost a fighter. I was involved in the accident and they want to talk to me about it."

Toby's heart rate increased. "Are you in any trouble?"

Brett shrugged and picked up his fork. "They weren't there to congratulate me on a promotion."

A heavy blanket of worry began to settle onto Toby's shoulders. Brett was usually so upbeat. He looked like he'd been ridden hard and put away muddy, as he once described the fatigue following a long mission. "What's gonna happen?"

Brett looked down at the half-eaten plate of food for a moment, then tossed his fork aside. "I don't know that either. But if they find me at fault, I could lose my wings."

"What does that mean?"

"I wouldn't be a military pilot anymore."

Toby's vision of the world around him shattered. He couldn't imagine life without Brett on the station, flying shuttles and space fighters, protecting his home. How could that be? They wouldn't do that to their best pilot, would they? "When will you know?"

"Lots of things have to occur first. I probably shouldn't have even mentioned it. It's nothing you need to be concerned with."

"Darn it, Brett. I'm tired of adults telling me what I should and shouldn't be concerned with. And until now, you've always been on my side." Toby stood and tossed the napkin on the table. He stared at Brett for a moment, then said, "I hope everything works out and you don't lose your wings."

Then he turned and rushed out of the cafeteria, ignoring Brett's shouted, "Wait a minute, Toby!"

Tears streaming down his cheeks, Toby ran hard to distance himself as much as possible from the loss of his dream.

5

DAY TWO EARLY EVENING

Deep in the central core, Samael paused to replenish his body with a high-energy snack and liquid and review his progress.

Objective #1: Escape the confines of the shuttle and disappear into the bowels of the station without being detected. Done, with exception of the corporal tied up in front of him. Maintaining close control was a slight annoyance, but a hostage might give him an advantage. More important, Samael had the radios, two pistols, and extra magazines.

Objective #2: Gain entry into the central core. Done. Concern about the accuracy of his briefings about how to disarm it proved unfounded.

Objective #3: Position and arm the explosive device. Pending. His employers had provided the exact location and arming procedures. They didn't tell him any more than that, and he understood why. Compartmentalized tasks and restricting the information needed to accomplish them enhanced security.

Samael also accepted that the ultimate objective of this operation was none of his business. He was hired to complete certain actions. Normally he would let it go at that, because curiosity was an undesirable and often deadly trait in his line of work.

But a bomb on a space station created a unique self-preservation problem. He could not afford to be less than inquisitive about what his employers were trying to accomplish. With a relatively small device ingeniously hidden deep within the core, the threat of total destruction had to be its purpose, with the ultimate objective being blackmail.

This conclusion was also at the heart of the Samael's current problem. He'd been given no instructions about contacting station authorities, which likely meant that he was relying on his traitorous accomplice, and a dumb one at that.

Having no information about what was supposed to happen after he planted the bomb was the most vulnerable point in the operation for him personally. Once he armed the device, Samael had no way to initiate and control the outcome of the next step. And in the event of a problem, he couldn't keep the plan moving without contacting the spy or his employer directly. His own failure to consider that possibility in advance meant he wasn't ready for it now.

But then there's luck. In the space of an hour the essential tools necessary to continue beyond what he knew at the outset had been dumped in his lap. Two cops would most likely end up being the key to continued success. And for one of them to be his employer's mole among the large population on the station was almost too good to be true. It also meant that Samael's next move would make him especially vulnerable to treachery.

Never trust a cop, especially one who has betrayed his own kind.

WAITING FOR THE MEDICAL EXAMINER TO FINISH UP WITH THE body, Andras anxiously paced the floor of the loading dock. He needed to find evidence of a second stowaway without risking discovery of his own betrayal of the station, the people on it, and his country.

Damn but it's cold. He should've had enough sense to bring his parka. He was also getting impatient with the M.E. "How much longer, Doc?"

"I'd have been through a half hour ago if my hands weren't frozen.

You want me to work in here, you build a fire or wait as long as it takes."

Dr. Frederick P. Morrison was a crusty old man who must have lied about his age to join the station crew and was hired sight unseen. He fit the job of ME perfectly, however, because he looked like death warmed-over all the time.

"I told you that's not my doing," said Andras. I wanted to take him to the morgue hours ago, but procedure is procedure and I had to arm wrestle Colonel Thomas to get you in here as it is."

"You and Thomas arm wrestling? That must have been a sight. Did he try to talk your arm to the table or push it there?"

Andras grinned. The cantankerous old fart was one of his favorite people, partially because he didn't take crap from anyone. "Don't concern yourself with that, Doc. Just get on with it and quit complaining about the cold. You're old and in space, remember?"

"I'm not that old and I am not in space. I'm in a space station in space. Now come here and look at this. You might learn something for a change."

Finally, Andras could get to examine the shooter. He slipped under the crime scene tape and knelt beside Morrison. "Show me."

"This's the first time I've examined wounds caused by the new ammo. I've never seen anything like it."

Andras bent over for a closer look. Standard big bore ammo usually created a relatively small entrance hole. Depending on the bullet characteristics, a much larger exit wound resulted as the bullet expanded and caused massive tissue damage. Bullets didn't always make it through the body, but this looked like it was an exit wound.

"But Private Foster said he fired as the guy faced him, and the bullets hit him in the chest. This looks like he was shot in the back."

"Yeah, being nothing but a dumb cop, you might think that. See this? The flesh distinctly shows that the bullet entered here, but look at the size of it. The lead, or whatever it is, expands so rapidly that it reaches maximum size and stops before it has a chance to penetrate very far. The impact must be horrendous."

"Are you sure there isn't an entrance wound on the other side?"

"Positive. Help me turn him over and see for yourself."

They did that and found no evidence of a wound of any size on the man's back. Andras shook his head. "Hard to believe, but those bullets didn't penetrate more than an inch."

"If that. I'll know more when I get him on the table, but this guy was killed by the shock of impact." The old man closed his medical bag, which looked like it would fall apart any second now. "I'm through here. When you finish, call Central and have them send some medics over for the body."

"Right. Thanks."

"You're welcome."

After the doctor left, Andras searched the body for evidence and found nothing. The guy had been sanitized, scrubbed of any clues about his origin.

Andras stepped back away from the body and felt something under the heel of his left boot, a shell casing from the man's weapon, flattened out slightly by his weight. *Real fine, Sergeant. That's a good way to impress the detectives.* He picked it up and considered what the incident meant in terms of firearms use on a space station.

The issue had been a contentious one, ultimately settled with development of the new ammo. Although tested extensively on Earth, none of the police on Oasis had ever fired it for real. For most cops it was hard to imagine a situation in which that would be necessary.

Events were proving them wrong. The new ammo worked very well, but it wasn't necessary. The new stuff hadn't been developed for the rifle the bad guy was using. There was a lot of brass lying around, and if standard rounds were so dangerous up here, where was the damage? Andras looked closer at the deformed casing.

Of course. Andras didn't tell them about the weapons, and they sent this guy up here with blanks.

Andras laughed. He could use this as evidence of the second stowaway without revealing his complicity. *How cool is—?"*

A solid clunk that vibrated the floor and a whoosh of air announced arrival of the medics. He put the shell casing in his pocket and radioed Carter to send someone to gather up the remaining casings and secure the rifle. He was watching the medics unzip a body bag when his earpiece filled his head with that voice, the one he had learned in so short a time to fear, the one calling him to his self-created and now dangerously perilous destiny.

"Are you there, Cadogan?"

TO SET IN MOTION THE NEXT STEP, SAMAEL HAD ENTERED THE chutes from the central core and navigated to a location he'd never need to use later. He turned on the radio, confirmed a full charge on the battery, and made the call.

As usual, Cadogan delayed his reply as if that would somehow prove to himself that he wasn't just a flunky. "Yeah?"

"Did you get the stuff I want?"

"Had it ready for hours. Where do you want to meet me?"

"Put the stuff in a soft-sided bag with some cushioning and take it to the intersection of corridors 'A' and ten. Make certain you aren't followed. Call me from there."

No answer.

"If these instructions are too difficult for you I'll repeat them."

Silence, then, "I'll take care of it."

Samael turned off his radio and hurried to put some distance between him and the call location before pausing to spread out his diagram of the radial and cross chute network. He planned out his route to an exit hatch close to the intersection he wanted, but not easily visible from there.

At this point in the operation, he needed to avoid all physical contact with Oasis personnel. To meet the cop for direct physical transfer of the crucial radio equipment would potentially expose Samael to being hunted like a mole being pursued by a weasel. He'd decided to have Cadogan drop the bag into a radial chute, where it would fall into a net of some kind at a lower cross chute, where Samael would be waiting to grab it and scramble to relative safety before anyone could figure out where he was.

Once secure communications were guaranteed, with the ability to charge one radio while using the other, he could continue with the next step. Satisfied that this was the best he could do, Samael folded the diagram and set out to make it happen.

Here he was again, somebody else calling the shots. Andras had almost dropped his coffee when the earpiece piped up. He tried to keep calm as he walked into the shuttle cargo bay to isolate himself from the other cops and use the radio.

And now he had to jump through hoops with this radio crap. He walked back to the loading ramp and exited the shuttle. Two cops were completing the evidence tag on the rifle as he approached them.

"We're just about done here, Sergeant Cadogan. You want us to search the bay?"

"Not on your life. You and your partner are much too clumsy to let loose in there by yourselves."

"What do we do now?"

"Call Central and tell them I want somebody in here ASAP to keep this area secure. Make sure the police line is set up, then you boys go get some food. Move."

"Yes, Sergeant."

Andras left the dock and hustled toward his office. As he approached Police Central, he remembered the padded bag he was supposed to use and detoured into the locker room. He opened his locker and removed his gym bag, hastily throwing the contents into the locker and closing the door. He found a stack of fresh towels near the showers and stuffed some into the bag. Anxious to avoid being seen, he left the locker room by taking a shortcut to his private entrance that opened directly into his office.

He locked both doors and opened the small personal safe in the cabinet behind his desk. Removing the radio and charger, he wrapped them carefully in the towels and put them in the bag. Then he went to the station map on the wall opposite his desk and planned the best way to approach the intersection he was told to find.

Reaching the intersection about ten minutes later, he paused to make sure he was alone. With mounting apprehension he took out his radio, selected the secure comm channel, and called the man.

SAMAEL HAD MOVED SWIFTLY THROUGH THE CHUTES, MORE confident from the previous experience and better able to maintain his directional sense. Reaching the first radial chute exit, he eased open the hatch and confirmed he could observe the intersection.

After referring to the diagram again, he navigated to the hatch he would instruct Cadogan to use and checked it in the same manner. Then he descended to the cross chute two levels below the hatch and removed the rope from his waist. It took about ten minutes to weave a grid between the ladder rungs closest to the opening at the intersection of the two chutes. When certain it would do the job, Samael retraced his route to the first hatch and settled down to wait.

Approaching footsteps alerted him. Peering through a thin sliver of open hatch, he saw Cadogan approach the intersection and stop. Samael watched for a moment, looking for anything that might warn him of a hidden agenda. Sensing nothing, he eased the hatch closed and waited for the cop to call him. It didn't take long.

"Yo, do you read me?" The radio sounded loud in the close confines of the chute.

"Go back the way you came. Take the elevator to the next floor up. Turn right to the emergency hatch numbered seven twelve. Open the hatch cover and drop the bag in. Return to your normal routine and wait for further instructions."

Without waiting for a reply, Samael turned off the radio and made his way to the cross chute that intersected with the radial chute where he'd placed the net. About five minutes later, a sudden change of pressure in the chute signaled the opening of a nearby hatch. Alert and prepared for immediate escape, he heard the sound of something hitting the sides of the radial chute above him. The bag landed in the net directly in front of him.

As Samael grabbed the bag and backed into the cross chute, it occurred to him that he shouldn't leave any physical evidence that proved he was ever there. He dismantled the net, wrapped the rope around his waist, and hurried back to the relative safety of the central core, where he checked the two batteries and their charger.

Satisfied, he reviewed his next moves: take care of the prisoner and secure him for the night; sleep for a few hours; then contact station authorities.

That should be very interesting. Some military puke with a brain irreparably damaged by years of blindly obeying orders will play the tough-guy role, try to delay, maybe even try to track Samael down.

How predictable, and how totally futile.

6

DAY THREE EARLY MORNING

Dan woke up to face only one bit of good news. His headache had abated. He was stiff and sore from sleeping on the floor, although his restraints allowed him to move around and stretch a bit to work out the kinks. With physical activity limited and his mind racing with possibilities, Dan pondered the question of how he fit into all of this.

He doubted that his captor had planned in advance to take a police officer hostage. Dan was being allowed to live because it served the man's immediate purpose. And although he didn't appear to be a cold-blooded killer, Dan knew that his own survival hung in the balance as the product of two unknowns. Did the man really plant a bomb, and what actually went down in the cargo bay?

The possibility that Andras had crossed paths with the guy was too persistent to ignore, which meant one of two things. Either Andras was dead and his body hidden in the shuttle somewhere, or he was alive and outside the man's immediate control. Were Andras's actions being forced because Dan was a hostage? Is that why there hadn't been any alarms, no general alerts, no sign of search activity? He didn't even want to acknowledge a third possibility.

"Get up."

The voice broke into Dan's thoughts with an abruptness that almost caused him to mess his pants. The asshole moved like a damned cat.

For the second time since arriving in the central core, his captor helped Dan with food, water, and elimination. Then he disappeared around a corner for a few minutes, and returned carrying the smaller of two bags Dan had seen in the shuttle cargo bay. They were both made of a dark material, so that the splash of bright color visible inside the top flap of this one immediately caught his attention. Dan watched the man walk into the dim passageway, trying to figure out what it was that reminded him of something. And then it hit him.

Andras had a gym bag that color. *Have the stowaway and Andras made contact?* If the encounter had been by chance, with Andras on duty, he wouldn't have been carrying the bag with him.

Holy shit.

Is Andras working with the guy?

CONFIDENT HE HAD TAKEN ALL REASONABLE PRECAUTIONS, Samael left his hideout and proceeded deeper into the core. He removed the radio equipment from the bag and set it up for transmitting. After checking to make sure all communication would be on the secure channel, he keyed the microphone button. "Cadogan, how do you read me?" Pausing to give him time to respond, Samael glanced at his watch and decided that he would limit the time spent in this location just in case they had found a way to trace his transmissions.

"Cadogan, are you there?"

"Yeah, I'm here, damn it. I can't answer you with people standing around. What?"

Samael detected an increased tone of defiance in Andras's voice, and decided to take him down a notch or two at the next opportunity. He needed unquestioning obedience, and fear did that best. "Did you program the comm computer as instructed?"

"The secure comm channel's in standby status and will transmit and receive when activated by you. What do I do now?"

"Nothing. Turn off your radio's secure function so that no one else can hear what follows. Leave it off for one hour, then call me back. Understood?"

The cop didn't answer right away, and Samael knew what was going on. Stewing in his juices with anger at being locked out of the events, Cadogan was planning to listen in. "Talk to you later."

The only weak link now was the cop. He might decide to betray Samael and help the station police hunt him down. Or he might pursue his own agenda and complicate matters. Eliminating the potential was a tempting solution, but Samael rejected it for two reasons.

First, having an accomplice who could move about the station without suspicion might still be of benefit. The second, less immediate reason might be even more important. Their employer had set up the cop to begin with and might have other plans for him. To get in the middle of that would not be conducive to Samael's continued good health.

Up to this point he had used secure comm only to communicate with Cadogan, a precaution needed to reach the point of having the bomb in place and Samael's presence on the station undiscovered. But he would be using a normal channel to contact station authorities to avoid compromising the existence of secure comm in case it would be needed again.

Normal operations on Oasis utilized one of four channels, changed often to exercise each one on a regular basis. The daily channel was designated as primary for a 24-hour period and monitored by all security personnel, which provided instant communication to all the cops at once.

The three unused channels in standby status could be activated simply by using them. A transmission from a portable radio on a standby channel to the Comm Central would be received there, but would not be heard on other portables. When Central answered, the transmission would be received only on the portable used to activate the channel originally. This feature provided the capability for semi-private communication between Comm Central and a radio at the scene of an incident. The intent was to avoid a situation in which every cop on duty would be listening in on activity that directly concerned only a few.

Samael expected Cadogan to monitor all communications between Samael and station authorities, so he created the impression that secure comm would be used. Cadogan would have to maintain a listening watch with the external speaker on the normal channel for that day, and use the earpiece to monitor the secure channel. If it worked as Samael planned, activation of a standby channel would occur unnoticed, leaving Cadogan in the dark.

It was the best Samael could come up with. But even if it worked only the first time, the caution was worth it. He never trusted anyone, least of all a traitorous cop, and certainly not someone hired by the same employer. His longevity in this business wasn't due to being careless.

And if Cadogan planned to betray him, now was as good a time as any. Being stationary during the period required to contact the station authorities could put him in danger if pursuit had already been organized. They could be on him much too quickly.

With one last check of the radio controls to make sure he was transmitting correctly, Samael keyed the microphone button and made the call.

FOLLOWING ALL THE RADIO BULLSHIT, IT HADN'T TAKEN LONG for Andras to decide the time had come to implement his own plan. Agreeing to help these guys had been a big mistake, and if he sat back while they did whatever it was they were going to do, his predicament would only get worse. His hopes of being included in everything, of being allowed to play a major role and be somebody really important, were forever shattered now. More important, he wouldn't have a single ally on the station once his complicity had been revealed. Labeled a traitor, despised by his fellow crew members, he'd be a man without a country. Unable to escape and forced to engage in further collusion with the SOB in black, his future would be sealed. To survive meant that he had no choice but to separate himself from this new threat and their common employer.

But if he could find a way to stop the takeover and eliminate the hijacker in the process, he might be able to come out of this even better off than before. If he could use the blank ammo as the magic key to convince a few other cops that he had discovered the presence of a second stowaway, he could enlist their help and control the end result. The man would never give up, which would give Andras the opportunity to take justifiable lethal action and make sure there'd be no questions, no answers, and no possibility of being found out.

Among all the uncertainties, the one bothering Andras the most was the fate of Dan Bishop. The duty roster had confirmed the corporal wasn't on duty today, and Andras found out from a neighbor that Dan wasn't home and hadn't been seen since yesterday. Oasis was a big place, and although it was conceivable that Dan could have spent the night with a friend, or gotten drunk and passed out somewhere, none of these possibilities seemed right. With all his faults, Dan would never abandon his post. That meant one of two things. Either he was dead and his body hidden, probably in those damned radial chutes, or he had been taken captive.

The first possibility would be better for Andras. It removed the possibility that Dan could reveal Andras's complicity in the developing crisis. It also meant that when it came time to put the guy down, no trigger fingers would hesitate because of concern about endangering a hostage.

Andras had formed a quick-reaction SWAT team, and arranged for the cops to be special-assigned for the next few days. He emphasized that to protect their chances for success, anything they did needed to be kept confidential. His unrestricted access to the equipment room, and selection of one particular cop who was a communications expert, had allowed him to obtain extra radios and tune them to a frequency unused by any other radio net on the station.

And now he was waiting for the guy to activate the secure channel by using it the first time, with only two other radios capable of monitoring the conversation. Andras was counting on it taking some time for the man to relay his demands. He'd be stationary, transmitting over the radio, less alert than he might be otherwise, and vulnerable to surprise.

Andras would hear the first call and receive the transmissions in un-garbled form, which would tell him exactly what the man wanted, and more importantly, pinpoint his position so that Andras could scramble his team into action.

One of the nagging questions that kept him awake most of the previous night was the location of the guy's hidey-hole. The fact that he had used the radial chutes to obtain the radio equipment pointed to the central core. And although the central core was no small area, access in and out could be easily controlled. All the doors could be locked from Security Central, and with his SWAT team prepositioned, Andras planned to block use of the radial chutes for escape from the trap.

He smiled with anticipation at the thought of entering the core and stalking the bastard as he chatted away on the radio. Andras couldn't wait to see the man's face as he turned to face the cop who outsmarted him, hunted him down, and would now kill him like the dog he was.

And even if the man detected the pursuit, where would he go? Straight for a radial chute. Panic dulling his caution, he'd pop open the hatch and climb into the sights of a SWAT team member. What would he think as saw the dark, twelve-gauge muzzle of a riot shotgun?

Talk about devastating. The new weapons and special ammo will make a handgun wound look like a pinprick.

General Antonio DeSilva, Commander of U.S. Space Station Oasis, stormed into Comm Central feeling like a hungry bear looking for meat. His morning was all planned out, and now he had to deal with a prankster. Who would've ever thought an Oasis crew member would pull a stunt like this? And although he didn't think it was something serious, for the moment he had to treat it as a security threat.

He snatched the microphone from the duty officer's outstretched hand, "To the person who wants to speak with the commander, this is General Antonio DeSilva."

"Well, hello, General. Glad you could join me."

"You're glad, I'm glad, we're all glad. I'm also busy, so let's cut the crap. Who are you and what do you want?"

"You need not concern yourself with who I am. As for what I want, I suggest you either record this, or at the very least copy the information so that there are no mistakes later on. Shall I wait for you to take care of that?"

"Hold on a minute." DeSilva turned to the duty officer. "Everything's automatically recorded, right?"

"Yes, sir."

"Do we have a way to trace the transmission?"

"No, sir, not from Comm Central, anyway."

DeSilva wondered if the police had that capability. He considered making a call to find out but never got the chance.

"Time's up, General. Since I'm sure you're frantically trying to figure out how to do something really sneaky, let's get to the point and give you a task fit for a man of your rank and authority.

"This space station is in danger. I have the power to destroy its ability to survive, along with everyone here, and terminate the moon colony project by eliminating any further support from Earth. I don't expect you to believe that on my word alone, so I will provide a demonstration in a moment to emphasize the truth of what I say.

"In the meantime, I suggest you get started. You will prepare for flight within the next twenty-four hours a shuttle, empty of cargo except for a combat-configured fightercraft loaded in the ferry bay, and both ships with full fuel. I want one pilot, qualified in both shuttles and fighters, ready to depart within one hour of my demand for transportation off this station."

General DeSilva wasn't angry anymore. He was well beyond that, into the realm of obsession with the thought of personally grabbing this bastard by the throat and proceeding with the manual removal of body parts. While he still wanted to believe this was no more than a sick attempt to pull a stunt for the fun of it, the incident in the loading dock yesterday was so bizarre that there must be a connection.

The general began to sweat, beads of perspiration appearing on his forehead and trickling down his face. Concentrating hard on maintaining the look of calm control for all the eyes in Comm Central glued to him, he said, "I copy all that. Is there anything else I can do for you?"

"As a matter of fact, yes. This is probably a good time to remove any lingering doubts you may have about my resolve or the seriousness of your position. You have exactly one minute to evacuate the area adjacent to the intersection Delta Five. There's a small explosive device near that location that will seriously injure or kill anyone standing in the hallway. Do it now. The clock is ticking."

General DeSilva sat motionless, unable to comprehend the last transmission. He'd heard the words, but they didn't register.

The duty officer jarred him back into the present. "Shall I sound the alarm, sir?"

DeSilva nodded. The duty officer stabbed down on a red button labeled "Station Alert," and public address speakers throughout Oasis erupted with the sound of klaxons and his verbal warning.

"ATTENTION ALL PERSONNEL! THIS IS AN EMERGENCY! EVACUATE THE CORRIDOR AREAS ADJACENT TO INTERSECTION DELTA FIVE IMMEDIATELY! DISASTER RESPONSE TEAMS STANDBY FOR INSTRUCTIONS! THIS IS NO DRILL!"

No one in Comm Central moved. As if frozen in position, the duty staff waited for the inevitable. General DeSilva looked down at his watch, and tried to predict which tick of the second hand would coincide with the explosion.

He felt detached from the moment, a disinterested bystander, wishing he'd noted the second the man said, "one minute." Then he'd have a time hack, know just how punctual this guy was, and if twenty-four hours should be considered exactly that.

~

ANDRAS'S SUSPICION LEVEL HAD INCREASED BY THE MINUTE. HE thought the guy was ready to initiate contact with Comm Central, but the secure channel had been quiet. He checked the radio controls to make sure he had the earpiece installed correctly and the channel in the receive mode. Then he decided to run a comm check on the SWAT team net just for something to do.

"Alpha Team, this is Alpha One, comm check, go."

"Two."

"Three."

"Four," and so on until eight had checked in. There were nine men on the net, and Alpha Six hadn't responded. Andras consulted his diagram to check Six's location. Alpha's Two through Eight were assigned fixed positions within the chute system surrounding the central core, with Nine as a roving backup. Communication between the team members was essential. He had to determine the reason for the failure to check in.

"Alpha Six, Alpha One, how do you read, over?" No response. He might be in a blind spot, although Alpha Six still should have heard most if not all of the other Alpha's check in. Or his radio could be malfunctioning, a common event with equipment supplied by the lowest bidder.

"Alpha Five, One."

"Alpha One, this is Five, go ahead."

"Call Six and see if you can raise him." Alpha Five was close to Six's position. Even if his radio was weak, he should be able to hear the transmission. After two calls, Alpha Five reported no contact with Six.

Andras wondered if the target might have detected the trap and managed to take Alpha Six down. Andras had no doubt the man was good enough, but he couldn't understand how he could have found out. Andras had been very careful . . . unless . . . *wait a minute.*

What if the man had found a way to listen in on the new net? Andras thought about that possibility for a moment, then rejected it. His comm man had just installed the electronics for a unique frequency, which couldn't possibly have been compromised so quickly.

But what if the man had taken somebody down and managed to get one of the radios? All communications from that point on would have to be considered compromised. But it was all they had, and he needed an answer.

"Alpha Nine, One"

"Alpha One, Nine, go ahead."

"From your current location how long would it take you to reach Six's position?"

"Probably about ten minutes if you want me to avoid spreading any alarm."

Andras had impressed on the cops the importance of maintaining a low profile and not appearing to be a SWAT team. Armed police were a common enough sight since the introduction of the handguns, but most crew members weren't aware of the shotguns. A group of men rushing down a corridor in riot gear would be hard to ignore. Rumor and panic could be equally devastating on Oasis, and preventing both was essential to safety.

"Alpha Nine, start moving in that direction with the precautions we talked about. Call me when you get there, but do not enter the chute at Six's location without my permission. Do you copy?"

"Roger that, Alpha One. Nine's out."

Andras wanted to avoid any more activity than necessary in the vicinity of the central core. He was concerned that no matter how careful they were, it might be enough to alert the man.

But he couldn't rid himself of the nagging feeling he was being played for the fool. His suspicions were heightened when the emergency klaxons and verbal warning sounded. Was this something unrelated to the man, or caused by him? What the hell was going on? And then it hit him.

Unfolding his station diagram, he searched for the corridor location mentioned in the alert and discovered that Alpha Four was very close to the alert area.

"Alpha Four, this is Alpha One, did you copy the alert, over?" No immediate response, and he had emphasized the importance of prompt replies, being ready to communicate. "Alpha Four, did you hear the alert, over!"

"Uh, sure, Alpha One. Is that location near—"

It was muffled, but unmistakable, the distinctive sound of a high-explosive detonation.

"Alpha Four, how do you read, over?"

"—got a problem here, One." Andras's transmission had covered up the first part of someone else's call, but he couldn't tell whose it was.

"Repeat that last call on Alpha net. One didn't copy."

"One, this is Nine. I'm in the corridor near Delta Five and we've got major damage. Four may have been near the explosion."

"Can you get to his location?"

"Negative. Too much smoke and I think there's a fire. I can hear the sprinklers working."

Andras was torn between the need to help his team member and the desire to maintain the rest of the net in place.

"Alpha Nine, do you see disaster response on the scene?"

"Not yet, Alpha One. It's chaos around here right now. We got people in rooms near the site, and some are evacuating. The hallway is turning into a madhouse."

"Okay, Nine. Take charge of getting those people out of there and keep the corridor clear for the disaster response teams. As soon as you can, find out Alpha Four's status but keep his location secret if possible. If he needs medical attention, get him out of the chute before you bring in the medics. Do you copy?"

"Roger that, One. Alpha Nine copies. Out."

At this point Andras was consumed with doubt. The man and the explosion had to be connected, but why hadn't Andras heard anything over the secure comm net? It didn't seem logical that the guy would wait so long to contact Comm Central.

As Andras looked down to check the portable radio on his belt, he noticed the message light. Someone had tried to call him on the normal comm channel without response. Cursing under his breath at the difficulties of maintaining a listening watch on three channels, he checked the volume control and found it too low.

He was playing tight odds, trying to keep the SWAT team out of the public view and on a discrete channel, hide his knowledge of the second stowaway from everybody, and perform his normal duties so as to avoid suspicion.

"Central, this is Alpha Charlie. Have you been trying to reach me, over?"

The response was immediate and urgent. "Alpha Charlie, that's affirmative. We have a situation here and Colonel Thomas wants you to report forthwith!"

Damn it, this whole thing is going to hell. Stall.

"Uh . . . Central, this is Alpha Charlie, I heard the alert and have a man on the scene. I'm waiting for his report."

As he said it, Andras realized someone might notice he'd obviously been communicating with another cop and none of the traffic had passed through Comm Central. So much for secrecy about his new Alpha net.

"Cadogan, this is Colonel Thomas. The message was I want you here now. We're handling the disaster response, your involvement isn't required. Your presence in Comm Central is, so move your butt on the double!"

Andras acknowledged the order as he ran for the nearest elevator. Reaching the door, he found that it was floors away and not moving. Some idiot was probably holding the door open and chatting away aimlessly. Andras inserted his ID card into a slot near the elevator call button and took control by overriding all other commands.

As he waited, Andras decided contact must have already been made and the explosion had to be connected. Either he'd been fooled about the secure channel, or his radio was inoperative for some reason. He wondered if Alpha Nine could tell whether it was an accident, a malfunction of some sort, or a bomb? He was about to call when the elevator door opened and the occupants inside started in on him with annoyance at having been overridden down when they had wanted to go up.

Andras said nothing as he grabbed the nearest person and bodily removed him from the elevator. The others followed quickly without being told. When the door was closed and the elevator moving he keyed the radio.

"Alpha Nine, One here, how do you read?"

"Weak but readable, One. Go ahead."

"Have you been able to get close to the site?"

The voice over the radio sounded excited, out of breath, adrenaline pumped. "Alpha Nine here. Yeah, I followed the disaster guys in. They got a small fire out. From what I can see this ain't no accident. I don't think there's anything in the ceiling that could explode like that."

I should never have doubted it. "Okay, Nine, copy that. Have you reached Four's location yet?"

"That's a negative, One. Too much crap in the way."

"Roger that, Nine, One copies. Out."

Approaching comm central, Andras steeled himself for what was to come.

He was going to have to manipulate this crisis very carefully to survive it. Leave the Alpha net in place for now. Handle Thomas, that should be easy enough, and find a way to smash this masked bastard in spite of the setbacks.

It's either that, or I'm history.

Entering Comm Central, Andras was startled by the level of activity in the room. He stared at the chaos and noticed Colonel Thomas motioning for him to come over. Making his way through the crowd, he got closer to Thomas and saw General DeSilva sitting at a console. As they turned toward him, Andras noted the looks in their eyes and changed his mind.

Dealing with the demon that had recently possessed his life may not be so easy after all.

7

DAY THREE MID-MORNING

When the preliminary accident board proceedings were adjourned, Brett had walked out of the room without speaking to anyone and headed straight for the bar. Passing the cafeteria, he thought better of the idea and decided to have some coffee. More liquor so soon after last night might just kill him on the spot.

He sat in a corner by himself. People walked in and out, a few friends and acquaintances, but he ignored all activity around him. He felt an immense sadness, unable to comprehend how his life could have taken such a devastating turn in so short a time.

The inquiry had started routinely enough, with the usual questions about his activities during the twenty-four hours prior to the accident. Nothing to uncover there.

The maintenance records of the fighter that crashed were being reviewed, and the investigation teams would comb the accident site for any evidence of mechanical failure. It would take weeks to get the results, but Brett knew there probably was nothing to find there either.

The remainder of the questioning focused entirely on his supervisory control of the mission. Brett was confident that he had done everything required by regulation, and more. He prided himself on knowing his students, their weaknesses and strengths. His mission profiles were the best in the wing, and other instructors came to him for advice on how to teach the most difficult maneuvers. How could there be anything to discover there, either?

He soon found out. A captain on the board seemed to take a particular interest in the recurrent training syllabus. He wanted to know every small detail about how qualification and currency for individual pilots were tracked. The captain quickly focused on how Brett ensured that the mission he designed that day did not violate any regulations. Brett found himself getting pissed, and finally challenged the captain to come up with something other than innuendo. Unfortunately, he did.

Using copies of the dead pilot's training records, the captain sealed Brett's fate. The grade slip Brett used to determine that the pilot was current to fly the mission in fact documented training received by a different pilot. Carson had never flown a space fighter below the terrain-clearance altitude, and had only used the combat mode on one previous mission.

Looking back, Brett remembered with regret his quick dismissal of the hesitation in Carson's replies. The young pilot knew he wasn't current and qualified in the lower altitude block, and probably hesitated as he considered whether to say something to his instructor. Brett also knew that Carson's failure to speak up was rooted in the fighter pilot's undeniable faith in himself: *I can handle this.*

But in the end, none of that mattered. The grade slip had been misfiled, and Brett didn't catch it. Although there was no evidence that his error contributed directly to the accident, Brett briefed and flew an illegal mission as far as the regulations were concerned. As the instructor, the fault became his no matter who put the grade slip in the training folder.

And if Brett hadn't been flying so much to satisfy his own goals, he might have been more careful, taken a little more time, noticed the error and altered mission objectives accordingly. Failure to do that more than likely overloaded the student to the point of making a deadly mistake. Maybe it was something as simple as calling for the change from combat to economy mode as the flight was climbing away from the moon. A small diversion of attention at a critical time is all it takes.

Although the consequences were not necessarily inevitable, Brett's flying status had been put in serious jeopardy. The thought of being permanently grounded felt like a death grip around his throat. He found it hard to breathe every time he allowed himself to think about it. And on top of that, he had been drinking coffee for about an hour. His hands were shaking, for more reasons than one.

When an alarm sounded, Brett listened to the evacuation order and tried to figure out where it was in relation to the cafeteria. Combined with stories about the turmoil in the loading dock yesterday, it struck him that this week might well go down in the history of the station as one of the most unusual on record. A shooting in a loading bay, emergency evacuations, a young pilot splattered all over the moon, and Brett Larsen fighting for his life as a pilot.

Getting up from the table, Brett decided to go back to his apartment and call the squadron from there. He deserved a day off. No one would expect him to come in anyway, and he didn't want to answer any more questions. The grapevine would by now have distributed the results of the investigation throughout the station, and he had no desire to be subjected to any more inquiring minds for the rest of the day.

ANDRAS STOOD BY THE CONSOLE WHERE COLONEL THOMAS AND General DeSilva were sitting. The two officers looked up at him, the tension marking their faces. Colonel Thomas was especially livid with anger, and appeared to be in real danger of exploding. "Where the hell have you been? I've been trying to reach you on the radio for over an hour. Why haven't you been maintaining a listening watch on the frequency like you're supposed to?"

"There must be something wrong with the volume control, sir. I thought it was turned up enough but it must not have been. Sorry about that. What's up with this explosion?"

"What's up? Cadogan, you act like we're discussing a problem with training schedules or something. This thing with the radio isn't over yet, but I don't have time for it now. Sit your ass down in that chair and shut up until I tell you to speak."

Andras had a temper, but he'd also learned how to put a lid on it. Struggling to keep his hands at his sides and away from Colonel Thomas's neck, he sat down and tried to figure out what was going on.

Comm Central was a madhouse. People were running every which way, bumping into one another about half the time, and the radio traffic filled the air with the electronic version of chaos. Activity at the consoles told him the controllers were busy passing information back and forth.

Andras wanted desperately to get back in control of Alpha Team and do something about his problem. But if the explosion and the man were connected and contact had been made, it changed everything for the worse. He couldn't appear to know anything specific about the incident, or his story about the bad radio wouldn't stand up. He had no choice but to sit and wait until Colonel Thomas brought him into the loop. Then it would be a matter of finding a way to follow the colonel's orders and still pursue his own objectives.

The two senior officers were conferring in close quarters. Andras couldn't make out what they were saying, but from the look of things it wasn't good. Then the general stood up suddenly and told the senior duty sergeant to call the Battle Staff together in the War Room.

As Andras followed Colonel Thomas toward the War Room, he realized this was the first time he'd been in it. The room had probably never been used except for exercises and briefings, usually for visiting dignitaries being given the gee-whiz tour.

The War Room was a large conference facility with a long table. Name markers designated seating positions for members of the Battle Staff. Communications gear could be accessed from a recessed area in the center of the table and placed at any of the seating positions.

The room was situated above Comm Central on a raised floor. A wall of glass separated it from the area below. The purpose of this arrangement was to give the senior staff members immediate and continuous access to the big picture, which would be unfolding below them in a vast array of electronic displays.

A staggering amount of information could be presented on the various screens. Each of the consoles on the floor of Comm Central was responsible for a specific screen or set of screens. The controllers manning the positions made sure the data displayed was updated to reflect the most current situation.

Andras looked around for a place to sit and realized he had been checking the small signs around the table for one with his name on it. Sit up there with the big guys, look important. What a joke. He had no idea why he was even here, and had never been told about being on the Battle Staff. Finding a corner that looked out of the line of fire, he pulled over a chair and sat down.

As the room began to fill up, Andras began to feel uneasy at being trapped in here with all this gleaming brass. He didn't recognize more than a handful of the officers, and wondered where they all stayed when they weren't called in here. Probably in dark rooms somewhere like mushrooms, feeding on bullshit and playing officer games.

The armed guard at the entrance to the room got Andras's attention. He was wearing full combat gear, flak vest and all, listening to General DeSilva and nodding as he received his instructions. The officers in the room saw it too, and the background noise of individual conversations dropped to nothing as the guard stepped back into the hall and closed the door. The click of the electronic lock, sliding security bolts, and illumination of the red alarm light over the door brought a sense of anticipation to the room. They were locked in, everybody else was locked out, and it wasn't a drill.

The general took his place at the head of the table. Checking the faces, he seemed to click them mentally off a list in his head. With a look of satisfaction, he leaned back in his chair. The room was absolutely silent, not even a cough or two. He began with security precautions.

"Gentlemen, before we proceed let me remind you that what happens in this room is top secret. You will sign the attendance roster. At the termination of this meeting, you will sign out, and the procedure will be repeated for any subsequent meetings. I will warn you only once. If there are any leaks, no matter how small, I will have someone's head." The general paused for a moment to look at each person in turn, emphasize the order, and put it on a personal level.

"About an hour ago Comm Central received a call from an individual who wants a shuttle, configured with a fighter in the bay, and a pilot qualified to operate both. He set a deadline of twenty-four hours to comply."

Amidst a few whispered comments among the officers, Andras struggled to maintain his composure. The bastard tricked him, and now he was stuck here. The opportunity to come up with a solution to his personal problem was decreasing by the minute.

General DeSilva referred to notes in front of him. "You probably heard the alert broadcast ordering a local evacuation. This action was in response to a warning from the individual about a bomb. I'm sorry to report that there was an explosion near Delta Five that resulted in considerable damage. There were injuries, number and severity unknown."

The room was alive now, with whispers and murmurs. Andras cursed under his breath. The man was involved in this thing too, and he hadn't been able to stop it.

As the volume level in the room returned close to normal, the general said, "Hold it down, gentlemen. We have work to do and not a lot of time. Emergency response crews are taking care of the casualties and will ensure the damage poses no threat to structural integrity of the station. Our task is to deal with these demands. The purpose of the bomb was to convince us he's serious, and demonstrate the ability to detonate a more powerful bomb that can destroy Oasis and kill everyone on board."

"But he'd be committing suicide!" said Major Fielding, the Administrative Officer. "Does he think we'll believe he has a way to escape when the thing detonates?"

"We've experienced far too many examples of terrorists willing to sacrifice their lives for a cause," said Lieutenant Colonel Parker, a flying squadron commander who had enough combat experience to know about dedication. "Why couldn't this guy be one of those?"

"That's just what we wanted to hear." said Major Fielding. "We have a maniac on board who isn't concerned in the least about his personal safety."

General DeSilva held up his hand. "Hold on a minute. We don't have time to concern ourselves with his motives. There are only two questions of immediate importance. One, can he detonate a bomb, and two, will he?"

"Okay," said Colonel Thomas, "what about the bomb? We know he can plant one and set it off with timers, or by command detonation from a remote location. He's proved the capability well enough."

"That's true," said Major Fielding, "but he could be using the small device to bluff us into thinking he'll use a bigger one. It's one thing to plant a small bomb and leave the area. It's another thing entirely to plant a big one and stick around. Why don't we tell him it's impossible to comply on such short notice? Call his bluff, push him a little?"

The question hung in the air unanswered, as if it were too hot to handle.

General DeSilva broke the silence. "But with the number of lives at stake, can we risk it? One man could probably handle enough explosive and put it in the right place to take this station out."

Major Fielding leaned forward in his chair. "So we're saying that because of the potential for loss of life, we have less than twenty-two hours to comply with his demands? We'll make no attempt to stretch the deadline?"

"When I say something like that everyone in this room will know it. We're here to come up with alternatives, if there are any."

"So how about this?" Lieutenant Colonel Parker said. "We plan for the deadline and prepare the spacecraft. But we don't have to sit on our hands waiting. Let's start a search, try to find the bomb and where the guy's hiding."

"Captain Norton," General DeSilva said, "where might this man put the second bomb, and what do you think our chances are of finding it?"

Andras glanced at a sign that read "Engineering Officer" in front of the captain as he answered.

"One man couldn't bring enough explosives on board to make a bomb powerful enough to cause structural breakup. Oasis is simply too large. But down in the core, with all the environmental equipment packed in a relatively small area, a bomb in any number of places might be able to shut down key elements and render this place uninhabitable within a few hours. As for finding it, we couldn't examine all probable locations before the deadline. And I can't imagine this fellow wouldn't be keeping an eye on it."

"But would it hurt to try?" said Colonel Thomas. "If he discovers our efforts we can back off and we know he's close enough to guard it. To do nothing is just giving him the benefit of *our* doubt. I see it as nothing ventured, nothing gained."

General DeSilva nodded. "Okay. Let's get everything ready with the spacecraft, initiate a search, and in the meantime try to come up with other options."

Andras listened as General DeSilva and Lieutenant Colonel Parker discussed preparing the shuttle and fighter. As the conversation continued, he became uncomfortable when the decision was made to launch a search of the central core.

He had a SWAT team in position and no one else in this room knew it. The search team would run into them sooner or later. With neither one knowing about the other, the consequences could be dangerous. If he told the Battle Staff about the Alpha Team now, there'd be questions to answer and he wasn't sure how he was going to explain his actions without someone finding out the big secret. Then a question asked by Captain Norton made his decision for him.

"Colonel Thomas, do we have any evidence to prove this man is connected to the incident yesterday in the loading dock?"

"No evidence, per se, but I don't believe in coincidence. The two incidents are one and the same. If not, it would mean someone already on Oasis planted the bomb, and they made it from components found here. Or maybe they smuggled explosives aboard, which seems unlikely."

Captain Norton said, "Somebody smuggled in a living, breathing, badass dude with an assault rifle, and maybe a partner. What would be so difficult about some explosives? We've had a problem with contraband for years, and the reality is that you can't lock anything out of anywhere if there are people who want to get it in."

Andras noted the inevitable signs of anger building in his boss. Colonel Thomas was an idiot, but he was fiercely protective of the security force. "Captain Norton, if you're questioning the ability of my people to perform the job of security on Oasis, just come right out and say it so I can hand you your ass in a sling."

"Enough!" General DeSilva had a reputation for being patient, but he never let anyone forget who ran the show. "Theories are only that. Interesting to discuss when time permits, which we don't have."

Andras couldn't wait any longer. "Excuse me, General DeSilva?"

As if on cue, all heads turned to the sound of his voice, and Andras found himself the object of more officer scrutiny than he'd ever known. The general didn't answer right away, and was looking at Andras as if he'd just realized he was in the room.

"Sir, I'm Sergeant Andras Cadogan, Senior Non-Commissioned Officer of Security."

"General," Colonel Thomas said, "I asked Sergeant Cadogan to join us in this meeting. He was personally on the scene of the incident yesterday, and I thought we might need him here."

The general stared at Andras, as if trying to remember something, but spoke to Colonel Thomas. "Good thinking, Arlan, because we just might."

Colonel Thomas seemed to puff up a bit at this pat on the back as the general said to Andras, "Do you have something for us that bears on this discussion, Sergeant Cadogan? Please don't hesitate to participate. All this rank doesn't mean all that much, as I'm sure you've noticed listening in."

Andras glanced around the table and noted the impact of this statement on the faces of every officer in the room. Expressions of pure pain, the agony of having their boss in front of an enlisted man degrade their abilities in the hallowed halls of command. Andras swallowed hard, worried about upstaging any of the officers, but he couldn't waste the opportunity.

"I do have something, sir. The incident in the loading dock yesterday resulted in the death of a man who stowed away on the shuttle. As of yet, we have no information about him."

"I meant to ask you about that, Arlan," said the general. "Aren't we investigating the incident, talking with the authorities on Earth and trying to find out who the dead guy was?"

As Colonel Thomas leaned forward eagerly to respond, Andras knew what was coming. Another good idea credited to the boss rather than to the man who deserved it.

"With everything that's been going on, sir, I haven't had the opportunity to talk with you about this. But I think we should ignore the current restrictions and do just that. We—"

"What restrictions?"

"The restrictions on our initiation of criminal investigations on Oasis. They—"

"I don't remember being briefed on any restrictions of that nature."

The silence that followed was typical of situations in which a senior officer indicated displeasure with something he'd been told by saying he doesn't remember ever being briefed on it. The clear implication was that he might never have been briefed on it.

Andras stifled a smile at the sticky problem for Colonel Thomas, which was to present the information without disparaging the general's memory or admitting that he might have failed to do his job correctly.

"Uh . . . Well, sir . . . I was under the impression my people had included this information as a part of your initial briefings, but I may be mistaken."

Andras paid close attention to the way his boss was going to handle this. The slippery little snake hadn't made it this far without being able to sidestep criticism.

Colonel Thomas continued with, "NASA decided that the primary function of police on Oasis would be security rather than law enforcement, and assigned the responsibility for criminal investigations here to authorities on Earth. We're supposed to secure the area and wait for investigators to arrive and take over."

General DeSilva scoffed. "That's horse shit."

"I couldn't agree more, sir, and I think we ought to be actively looking into this thing now."

As the general seemed to be processing this, Andras took the opportunity of silence to jump in again.

"If I may, sir, I have more information."

"Certainly, Sergeant Cadogan, please continue."

"Following the incident in the loading dock I gave instructions to secure the area for the arrival of the investigation team from Earth. I left a man in charge, but he seems to have disappeared."

"You've checked all the usual locations?"

"Yes, sir. I'm positive he didn't just walk off the scene and leave it unsecured."

"What are you getting at, Sergeant?"

"I think he ran into this man and was either killed or taken captive. I probably should have brought it to the attention of Colonel Thomas, but I took the liberty of doing some checking before I said anything. The explosion delayed me considerably, but I do have some additional information that I wouldn't have had then."

"Like what?"

"While in the loading dock, and prior to the explosion, I found evidence suggesting the dead guy had an accomplice. Until now it was just a hunch, but I think I have a way to pin the guy down and isolate him quickly."

"How the hell are you going to do that?"

"I've formed a SWAT team under my command to evaluate my theory. We've been working on a plan to place my men in position around the central core. I—"

"Really?" General DeSilva's expression warned Andras to proceed with care. "I'm going to want an explanation as to why you launched out on your own, but what do you mean about a way to find him?"

Andras planned on never having to explain anything. Finding the hijacker and killing him would be a great first step to getting through this in one piece. "Sir, the core is a large area. Of all the places to hide on Oasis, it's the best for him and the worst for us. Searching it will be a lot like street situations, with blind corners and being confronted with many good places to hide. I think if we can narrow his position down to a smaller area within the core, we might be able to block his routes out of there."

"That's all well and good, but how do we narrow down his position?"

"With a robodog."

The reply seemed to make time stand still in the room. Andras was sure that none of the officers around the table knew much about the dogs. Their patrols concentrated on the remote areas of Oasis, and they were rarely seen in the more heavily populated work and living spaces. Robodogs were like any security system, mostly in the background, doing their thing, out of sight.

General DeSilva leaned back in his chair and smiled. "Now that's an interesting thought, Sergeant. Please continue."

"With high ceilings and equipment stacked from floor to roof, the core looks like narrow streets hemmed in by tall buildings. It wasn't built for ease of movement, because people seldom go in there except to fix something. I think that works to our advantage rather than against it.

"I'd hate to hunt a guy down in there, with or without help. But he faces the same problem of movement that we do. Lots of blind intersecting corridors, dark shadows from dim lights high above, and risking ambush at every corner. My feeling is he'll bolt for a radial chute at the first sign of pursuit. If we get a hit on a current location with a dog, we can apply pressure and drive him in the direction we want."

The officers seemed to like that, but Captain Norton was shaking his head. "There's one small detail we seem to be forgetting. What about the bomb? Do we still hunt for it? No matter how good the trap is we might lose everything anyway."

General DeSilva got up and began pacing about the room. "At this point we have no idea what he really wants. Is the big bomb just a bluff, and once he leaves here he has what he came for? Is the objective to sell a shuttle and a fighter to somebody? Without the threat of the bomb, our goal would be to get him off the station as soon as possible, then blow him to pieces before he gets to wherever he wants to go."

"And sacrifice the pilot?" asked Major Fielding.

Lieutenant Colonel Parker shook his head. "Hopefully that decision would never be required. But he'll be a volunteer, aware of the risks. It's no different than combat. Hell, it is combat!"

Everyone in the room agreed with that statement. After a short period of discussion, General DeSilva summarized their decisions.

"One. I'll call NASA and get them in the loop.

"Two. Colonel Thomas, do not initiate a search for the bomb yet. Get with your rogue cop over there, and let me know how this plan might work.

"Three. Colonel Parker, I want you to ramrod the shuttle preparations. No tricks for now, everything ready to go prior to the deadline.

"Four. Major Fielding, I need you to be the central point of contact in this room while the crisis is playing out and take reports of developments as they occur.

"Five. Captain Norton, get your experts together and brainstorm the problem of this bomb. Make certain the disaster response team investigating the explosion is hot on finding out as much as they can about the type of bomb it was and the triggering device used. Try to come up with possible locations where he might plant it.

"Six. Sergeant Cadogan, find this missing cop. If he isn't a hostage, or if he's already dead, that's one more complication we don't have to consider.

"All right. You all know what you have to do. Plan to meet back here at fifteen hundred hours unless you hear otherwise. This meeting is—"

"Pardon me for interrupting, General DeSilva," said Andras, "but I do have one other item I think you should be aware of." It was going to be another surprise, and the looks on the officers' faces could easily be read as they turned to the sound of Andras' voice.

"It's about the weapon used in the loading dock incident yesterday, sir. There were no casualties among the workers assembled in the dock area. I've heard nothing about damage in the bay. Space ammo hasn't been manufactured in the caliber of the assault rifle he used. Either the concern about using standard rounds up here is unwarranted and he was a terrible shot, or there's another explanation."

"We can't wait to hear this, Sergeant. Please proceed."

"Yes, sir. He was shooting blanks, acting as a diversion. And if you think about it, assuming the incidents are connected, they must have known you can't blast away with Earth ammo on Oasis."

"So you're saying their information was a little dated. They didn't know about the new ammo, didn't expect security personnel to be armed, and got caught off guard. That didn't apparently stop the second guy from doing his thing."

"But sir," said Colonel Thomas, "it means the guy isn't armed. He wouldn't be carrying around a weapon with blanks in it."

"Why not?" asked Captain Norton. "If they thought we weren't armed why wouldn't they think the threat of a weapon would be useful for their purposes? Point an assault rifle at someone and get all the instant cooperation you need."

"What does he need a weapon for?" asked Major Fielding. "He's got his finger on a big bomb and seems to be using that pretty effectively to hold us at bay."

I've got to keep this conversation focused on the weapon.

"Excuse me, sir," said Andras, "but that's my point. If my suspicion is correct, and he took down a cop, he has a weapon now. We won't be pursuing a defenseless man, bomb or no bomb."

Another silent moment ensued. As usual, the general spoke first.

"That's just dandy. We've focused on the bomb as the one thing that prevents us from going into the core. But hunting for an armed man in those tight spaces, and one who might have a hostage, puts the situation in a very different perspective."

"Yes, sir, but I'm not suggesting it changes the basic plan. We have a good chance to make it work, but I need your authority to instruct my men to shoot to kill on sight."

Andras paused to let this sink in. No one said a word. *Now to drive the point home.*

"We won't get more than one chance. If the element of surprise is lost the problem becomes much more difficult. My guess is he won't settle down to call Comm Central within earshot of the hostage, if he's still alive. And he won't be near the bomb. If we captured him with it, he'd lose all leverage to demand anything. All we'd have to do is disarm the thing, or better yet, send it for a space ride and let the universe handle it."

"But if you kill him, how do we find out where the bomb is?"

"In my opinion, General, we won't find the bomb with any information he gives us anyway. He's a trained professional who won't be broken easily. Everyone has different degrees of tolerance for physical and mental discomfort. There isn't anyone on Oasis who'd be capable of doing what's necessary to get this guy talking. Chemicals might work in the hands of someone with the training to use them, but we don't have access to either.

"That's why I'm suggesting we don't even try to take the man captive, and that we leave discovery of the bomb to our own efforts. I also have another idea that might help with this problem. It's an option I haven't heard discussed."

Andras deliberately paused again to let the general ask him to continue. It made the moment that much more impressive, and he wanted everyone in the room to remember his contributions to the successful conclusion of this crisis.

"Well, Sergeant," said General DeSilva, "don't make us wait any longer. The suspense is dreadful."

"Yes, sir. Robodogs can be programmed to act as 'sniffers' for many different substances. They may be able to recognize the scent of explosives used in the small bomb. I think the software includes many different scents, but you can also have the dog sniff a substance, record the scent in memory, and then program it to hunt for that specific one."

The officers seemed to like this news, displaying grins, nods, turning to look at each other with expressions of smug self-satisfaction that things had finally turned in their favor. It was almost as if they had this thing licked. The only one that really mattered, however, was General DeSilva, and Andras waited for his response.

"Sergeant Cadogan," said the general, "that's another good idea. Those robodogs can be real sneaky, real quiet, and *replaced*, right?"

"Absolutely, sir. We don't yet know if this guy was told about them, but I'm not sure it matters. I recommend we send a dog in to hunt for the man, and program it to run a simultaneous olfactory search for explosives."

General DeSilva was grinning now. "I like it. Make it happen, Sergeant. Now, before we break up, there is one more item.

"Colonel Parker, we need to find a pilot for the shuttle. I'd prefer we ask for volunteers rather than assign it. You might consider approaching individuals rather than the pilots as a group, but I'll leave it up to you as to how you want to handle it."

"Yes, sir. I'll take care of that right away."

"Fine. This meeting of the Battle Staff is adjourned."

Andras got up from the table and stepped to the side as the officers gathered their notes and went to the rear of the room. He anxiously waited for Colonel Thomas to leave, eager to get back into action.

Maybe there was a light at the end of this tunnel, and he just might be able to marshal the resources of the station against the man without revealing his secret. The general never approved his request for the shoot-to-kill order, but he didn't disapprove it, either.

Andras had heard a saying that it was always better to ask for forgiveness than permission. Although he'd already violated that rule, he wouldn't do so again. His Alpha Team would believe him, and obey orders. He'd set the stage by telling the team they were hunting a possible cop killer. With the commander's implied consent, all he had to do was leave it alone.

The men were dedicated, frightened by the threat to them and their families, and primed to shoot first. At this point he couldn't have hoped for a better situation, especially when compared to how close he was to losing it all.

Take this guy out, find that bomb, save the station, and I can write my ticket out of here.

He could hardly wait.

TOBY WAS NOT HAVING ONE OF HIS BEST WEEKS. TWO DAYS AGO he'd been caught playing hooky twice, told that he can't learn to fly while living on Oasis, and prohibited from seeing Brett. Yesterday a masked demon tried to kill him. When he went to tell Brett about it, he learned that Brett might lose his wings, which upset Toby so much he never told him about having to run for his life. Or about the cop handcuffed and shackled in the central core. Lots of unfinished business for such a short period of time.

The morning began sitting in silence at breakfast. His parents hadn't said anything more about all the boundaries he'd violated, but he knew it wasn't over. He rushed through preparations for school and left early just to get out of there.

School wasn't much better. Toby had lied about his homework being done, and his teacher could sense when he wasn't prepared. Unable to answer her questions, he became very embarrassed by her criticism and the snickers of his classmates.

The warning announcement about evacuating a corridor blared into the classroom during math. The teacher continued class as if nothing else was happening. She didn't even hesitate when they felt a slight shudder and heard the distant noise.

In the lunchroom some kids were talking about it. As Toby listened to the conversations, Rooster stepped out of the serving line and looked around for him. Toby waved.

Rooster walked up with his tray, sat down and attacked his sandwich. "Did you hear the warning? It was on the PA and then there's this noise, but it sounded far away."

"Our teacher stopped class. I thought she was gonna let us out early, but she came back in and made us finish."

"Miss Tilson must be deaf. She never even looked up."

They talked about rumors of a bomb as they finished lunch. Leaving the cafeteria, Toby suggested they check out the area mentioned in the warning announcement. This kind of excitement didn't happen very often, and Toby couldn't stand not finding out more about it.

"But we don't have much time before class starts," said Rooster. "Are you sure we can make it there and back in time?"

"Maybe not the normal way. But we can in my private tunnels."

"Oh, no, not me. It's way too creepy."

Toby grabbed Rooster's arm. "Hold on a minute. You asked me to show you the ropes up here, didn't you? How to get around, the tricks I've learned, how to take care of yourself?"

"Yeah, but—"

"That's what I'm doing. No one else uses those chutes. They're always deserted, and you can move around without anyone knowing about it. How're you gonna get the hang of it if you don't go in there with me and find out for yourself?"

Rooster wasn't looking too happy about Toby's insistence on this adventure. "I wanna learn about it, but you gotta promise me you'll stay close and not leave me behind."

"Fine," agreed Toby, taking Rooster's arm and hurrying him along the corridor. "But *you* gotta keep up and do it the way I told you. It's easy once you get the hang of it."

Toby led the way to one of his favorite chute entrances. It was located in an area with little traffic and less risk of discovery going in and out.

Approaching the entrance, Toby looked in both directions. "Follow me," he whispered. "Do it like I do, and do it fast." As Rooster nodded, Toby performed his favorite chute-entry maneuver, looked back and saw his friend just where he was supposed to be. Except he hadn't closed the hatch cover.

"Shut it. Hurry up."

Rooster got it done, but not very quickly. Toby reminded him about how to swing the hatch shut with his foot. Then he led the way to the next intersection and turned around to face Rooster.

"All right. Here we are and you did it. You okay?"

"Sure, but this place still feels strange."

"That's why you need to spend more time in here. I felt the same way at first. The more I tried the easier it got."

"You were scared too?"

"You bet." This wasn't exactly true. He'd been at home in the chutes the very first time, but he didn't reveal that to help Rooster over his doubts. Toby often wondered if being born on the station had anything to do with it.

He got out the diagram of the chute system from his school pack and showed Rooster where they were and where they were going. Then he led the way toward the explosion site. His plan was to drop into a corridor close to the excitement, or find a hatch allowing him to view the scene from above. But he had to check it out first, alone. Rooster wasn't ready for the finer points of quiet, undetected maneuvering in the chutes close to people.

Motioning for Rooster to stay put, Toby removed his backpack and attached it to one of the ladder rungs. He figured that one cross chute over and one level up would put him in a position to view the intersection from a hatch not too far down the hall. It took only five minutes to make the trip. Approaching the objective, he knew something was different.

Normally, he heard only machinery hum and the sound of air moving. But as Toby listened, he detected the distinct sounds of human activity, muffled voices, then a louder shout or two, and banging, like a hammer on metal, and the distinctive whine of power tools.

And it wasn't as dark as usual, and more air was flowing, just not as fast. Toby crawled carefully around the corner to the hatch cover and gripped the handle. He opened the cover slowly and peeked out of the chute.

Whoa. He'd never seen so much activity. People running around, dust and smoke hanging in the air, with stretchers leaning against the walls. He couldn't see far enough down the corridor to tell what people were doing, but debris covered the floor, with some kind of foamy fluid on top.

He was easing the hatch open more to get a better look when two medics in white uniforms came into view, carrying a stretcher with a man on it, a technician wearing a lab coat over civilian clothes, with bloody bandages on his legs and head.

Initially repulsed by the sight, Toby overcame his reluctance to continue. He closed the hatch and referred to the diagram again. If he could reach the hatch further down the corridor, maybe he could see the area where all the people were. Moving swiftly, at home in his private world of the chutes, he approached the next intersection and knew he was closer to the site. It smelled weird, the light much brighter, and as he turned the corner from the cross to radial chute he could see why.

A huge hole gaped at him. Jagged metal edges surrounded a bright, dusty glow from emergency floodlights in the corridor below. Workers were busy repairing damage. Other men were standing by with fire extinguishers. In the background, medics knelt over motionless bodies. He stared, transfixed.

Then something changed, as if he had been tapped on the shoulder.

Caution! You are not alone. Be careful!

Looking behind him, he expected to see something, a threat of some kind, and the thought of being chased again sent a shiver of fear through him.

But it was just an empty chute, with brighter light from the hole fading to dim shadows toward the last intersection. Toby retreated to the closest place he could turn around and make his way back to Rooster. He paused short of the intersection to listen. The increased noise level prevented him from hearing anything in the chute ahead of him, but a strange sensation that Toby had felt a few times in his life grew stronger, usually just before being surprised. Like when he'd been fooling around in a compactor room last year and for no reason he could think of, he knew he had to look up.

Many offices dumped material directly into the compactor rooms. This particular item was small, but heavy, and it could easily have crushed his skull. Toby didn't hear anything to warn him, but that feeling was there when he needed it.

And here it was again. A persistent warning signal, growing more uncomfortable by the second. Toby decided the time for caution had passed. No one could hear him with all the commotion going on, and he needed to get out of here before the feeling got any worse. Moving fast, he came to the intersection and turned the corner to reverse his direction.

He bumped into it before he saw it. He had to back up slightly to focus on what was in his way. In a split second of horror, he recognized it as a face, but not really. The scream that penetrated his brain was his own, generated from deep within as he saw the blood, the empty eye socket, and the teeth visible due to the missing cheek and lips. The face of a seriously injured cop dressed in full combat gear.

Toby backed out of the chute in terror, no thought about what he should do, just arms and legs pumping hard to get him out of there fast. Still screaming, he turned the corner to the chute where Rooster waited for him and never slowed down as he crawled headlong into his friend.

Toby's loss of control became mirrored in Rooster's actions. He began screaming too, asking Toby what was wrong as he backed into an intersection out of Toby's way as he rushed by and went for the hatch, hardly slowing to flip the handle as he pushed it open and climbed out. When Rooster reached the floor, Toby grabbed his arm and pulled him along. Rooster's legs weren't as long as Toby's, and he had to trot beside him just to keep up. "What's wrong?"

"You're not going to believe this. We gotta get out of here now. I'll tell you later."

The two boys broke into a trot. Reaching Rooster's apartment, they decided to get something to drink. Toby was gulping down some orange juice when Rooster asked, "What happened? I've never seen you like that."

"I saw the place where the explosion was, and there's all kind of damage around there, but that's not the big thing. Rooster, there's a man in the chutes with no face!"

"I don't believe you!"

"I wouldn't make up a thing like that. I don't get scared easy, but I ran into him and it was the most horrible thing I've ever seen. I think he was a cop, he had one of those vest things on, and he was bleeding and I could see his teeth, and he had only one eye and—"

"Toby, stop it. You can't mean that."

"I'm telling the truth. I—" Toby noticed a red stain on his right hand, and looking at it closer, he saw another red smear on the cuff of his jacket. "I've got blood on me."

Rooster reached out and took Toby's hand, but let go quickly. "Ugh. Are you hurt?"

Toby examined his hands while Rooster looked him over. "I don't have any injuries, but I must've reached out to push away when I saw him."

"What're we gonna do?"

"We—uh oh. We'll be late for class. But we gotta do something to help that wounded cop."

"Let's just call the emergency number. We can do it from here." Rooster reached for the apartment phone.

"Hold on, Roost. I wanna help, but the police will need to interview us and it'll be hours before we're done. And I can't let my parents find out I was in the chutes again."

"We don't have to give our names."

"But we can't call from here. Let's go find a hall phone."

Toby was moving toward the door when he remembered the bloodstains. "Hold on a minute. I gotta get this blood off."

Rooster followed Toby to the kitchen sink. "But they can trace the call anywhere. What good will a hall phone do?"

Toby washed his hands and did the best he could on the jacket. "They can trace any call they want, but it only tells them where it came from. A phone in a hall somewhere, not to your apartment. This way, they won't know *who* made the call. Come on, we're gonna be late. Where's my—oh no!"

"What's wrong now?"

"I left my backpack with my books and stuff in the chute where you were waiting for me. There's no way I have time to get them now. You and I have to get back to class. We'll use the phone in the park on our way."

Toby and Rooster hurried out of the apartment and ran most of the way to the park. There were only a few people sitting at a picnic table. With Rooster standing lookout, Toby picked up the phone and dialed 911.

BRETT WAS IN HIS APARTMENT HAVING AN EARLY LUNCH WHEN the phone rang. He considered not answering it when the doorbell chimed and someone began pounding on the door. As the answering machine took the call, Lieutenant Colonel Parker began leaving a voicemail. Brett opened the door to find Jake, another pilot in Brett's squadron.

"Quit making all that noise and come on in. Why is it I'm so popular all of a sudden?" Hurrying to the phone, he picked it up in the middle of the colonel's message. "Excuse me, Colonel Parker, this is Captain Larsen, sir. What can I do for you?"

"I'm sorry to bother you at home, Captain, but I need to see you about something, and I'm afraid it can't wait. Can you be in my office within the hour?"

"Yes, sir, I was just finishing some lunch. May I ask what this's all about?"

"I'd rather not discuss it on the phone. I'll expect you no later than thirteen hundred."

"Yes, sir, see you then." Brett hung up and turned to find Jake helping himself to the other half of Brett's sandwich. "You are nothing better than filthy pond scum. That's a work of art you're scarfing down."

Jake stopped chewing only long enough to smile, then continued to finish the sandwich as Brett went to the refrigerator to find something else to eat. His morning wake-me-up was wearing off, and he needed more than half a sandwich.

"Brett," said his friend, "you do in fact make one hell of a sandwich. I especially want to compliment you on this one. My only complaint is that there wasn't more of it. How about another, and use more mustard this time."

Brett ignored him, and with practiced skill proceeded to build another masterpiece. "What's all the ruckus about? You're at my door, Parker's on my phone, and next I suppose the general will want to speak to me."

Jake seemed undeterred by Brett's refusal to consider his request for more food, and joined him in the kitchen to build himself a sandwich. "I don't know about that, but I'll bet you aren't up on all the latest events around here. You hear the evacuation warning a while ago?"

"Yeah, I heard it. Didn't pay much attention. It wasn't anywhere near me."

"And you don't know anything about the meeting of the Battle Staff either, right?"

"Battle Staff? I didn't know they had one." Brett took a seat in the small dining area and quickly began eating the sandwich. He hated eating in a hurry, but he was running a little late and Jake would probably try steal half of it.

Jake joined him at the table and between mouthfuls said, "They haven't assembled the Battle Staff in years, but the regulations specify who's on it. I have it on good authority that they met in the War Room under armed guard within the last hour."

"Oh, I get it. 'Good authority' means some pilot brought it up in the crew room, and you believe anything you hear."

"Not hardly. A buddy of mine works in Comm Central. It wasn't a casual get-together. Something's going on."

"Is this connected to the warning?"

"Appears to be. He told me about a mysterious call to Comm Central that got everybody excited. There was an explosion. No one's been in the area except disaster response teams, but I know there are casualties in the emergency room. I walked by there, and it's anything but condition normal."

Brett listened as Jake told him about all the rumors flying around and the possible connection with the loading dock incident the day before. "Has there been anything official said about this?"

"That's the strange part. Usually we get far more information than we want about all the mundane everyday crap we could care less about. But when it gets interesting we're left in the dark."

Brett got up and put his plate in the sink. "I wish I could stay here and shoot the shit with you about it, but duty calls." Brett hadn't changed out of his uniform yet, so he retrieved his tie from the coffee table and began tying it as Jake put away the food. He heard Jake call to him from the kitchen.

"Hey, buddy, I'm sorry I didn't ask you about this before, running off at the mouth about this other stuff. How'd it go this morning? You going to be okay?"

The question hit Brett like a punch to the gut. Clearing his throat, he said, "We'll have to wait and see."

"All the guys were asking about you, wishing you the best and all. Hope it comes out all right."

"I couldn't agree more." Brett put on his coat and checked his uniform in the mirror for lint and those little threads, called "ropes," that seemed to grow out of the fabric when he wasn't looking.

"What does Parker want to see you about?"

Inspection complete, Brett picked up his hat and went to the door.

"I'm not sure. I can't imagine it's about the inquiry results. No way they're through deliberating, and in any case Parker wouldn't be brought into the loop before I was informed of the findings. Other than that, I really have no idea. You're welcome to stay here if you want. Thanks for the help cleaning up."

"You bet. Bye."

When Brett arrived at the squadron, he noticed a change in the mood. The usual banter was missing. His fellow pilots greeted him tentatively, and seemed not quite sure what to say. They probably knew all about the inquiry and were giving him a wide berth.

Within the world of the fighter pilot, this characteristic distancing was partially due to respect for Brett and concern over what he was going through. But it also derived from a superstitious fear that within aviation, bad things were like infectious diseases, and it wasn't smart to get too close. Brett was feeling like an outcast when Lieutenant Colonel Parker came out of his office and begin talking to his secretary.

Brett walked over to the coffee pot and tilted it slightly to see if there was any left. Squadron custom dictated that whoever took the last cup made the next pot. Grown men, however, even those who could fly the most sophisticated aircraft in the universe, were terrified by having to make a pot of coffee. The last dregs were usually barely distinguishable from Mississippi River bottom sludge. Today was no exception.

As Brett stirred sugar into the dark, thick liquid in his mug, the squadron commander walked up. "Hello, Brett, any of that left?"

"Yes, sir, but I wouldn't recommend it. I've already gone through two spoons just to stir in the sugar. The metal won't last for more than a second or two."

Lieutenant Colonel Parker chuckled as he took the last cup. "Not a problem. I drink mine black. Sitting around here as much as I do gives me plenty of opportunity to train on this stuff. Ready to come see me?"

"Yes, sir."

"Come on in and close the door behind you."

As Brett accepted the colonel's offer to be seated, he noticed the sweat trickling down from his armpits. Pilots won't admit they ever get nervous, but it's all a show.

Lieutenant Colonel Parker sat down on the other side of a huge desk. "Before I get to the main reason I wanted to talk with you, I got a call from the board president a while ago. He didn't get into the details of the testimony, of course, but he thought they'd be done within the week. I know you're anxious to have this all over with. Rest assured the safety folks share that goal. I've asked them to wrap it up as soon as possible consistent with a thorough investigation."

Sure. We'll give him a fair trial and hang him in the morning.

"Thank you, sir. I appreciate your interest."

"New subject. You might not be aware of recent events on the station. There've been two serious incidents in the last twenty-four hours involving what we think are stowaways who came up on the noon shuttle yesterday. Although I can't tell you more than that now, I have a job for you that needs to be taken care of immediately.

"I need a volunteer pilot, current and qualified on both shuttles and fighters. I do not want a hotshot, rogue warrior with any tendency to do his own thing. This is not a job for John Wayne and a six-shooter. Understood?"

"Yes, sir. What's he volunteering for?"

Parker didn't say anything for a moment, looking at the wall as he appeared to consider his response carefully. "I'd like to tell you more, but all of this strictly need-to-know. We aren't sure what might be involved, but I can say it will be dangerous."

"Every pilot up here is dedicated to the job, Colonel. I'd like to think with a line drawn in the sand, they all would cross it eagerly. But if we aren't going to get them all in a room and ask, the process becomes unfairly selective. I'd be worried about the pressure I bring into the deal simply by asking."

"I understand your concern and would like to help you. But if you'd heard the general's warning about secrecy you'd understand my reluctance. The more people who know something . . . well, you know the drill."

"Yes, sir. Why don't I just solve this thing right here and now? I volunteer."

Parker shook his head. "Now I'm in the position you want to avoid. It's the same thing, we've just elevated it up the chain of command."

"Excuse me, sir, but not quite. With all due respect, I'm not trying to impress you. I've proven myself over the years. A younger pilot, struggling to gain the acceptance of his peers and superiors, wouldn't want anyone to think any less of him because he didn't volunteer.

"And I probably wouldn't choose a pilot with a family. I know that's not fair, but that's the way I feel. Most of the younger pilots are single, and most of the experienced guys are married with kids. If you want a cool head under pressure, and with no record of being a hotdog, it pretty well mandates one of the older pilots. I have no family up here. Been a bachelor all my life. And I may not have much to lose anyway."

"What the hell do you mean by that? Are you trying to tell me your life is any less valuable because you don't have a family on Oasis?"

"No, sir. But a pilot died yesterday while under my supervision. If the system finds me at fault I'll be held accountable. It may mean the end of my flying career. If that occurs, my life will have effectively ended anyway."

Parker stared at Brett as if he were from another planet. "I can't believe I'm hearing this, Captain Larsen. And it seems to me you aren't the right pilot for this assignment. The last thing we need is someone who has nothing to lose."

"You'll have to make up your own mind about that, sir. But I can assure you my comments don't indicate a death wish. I'm merely talking about risk, and whether I can in good conscience ask another pilot to do something I'm definitely more qualified and likely more willing to do."

"Welcome to the world of command, Captain. I can guarantee you it won't get any easier through the years. And what about from my perspective? Should I let my senior flight commander and number-one instructor volunteer for something that could be this dangerous when there are other pilots available? It might be considered a waste of talent and experience, don't you think?"

"Maybe some would see it that way, sir. But from where I sit the question is who can do the job best. Leaving the issue of risk out of it, remember that no other pilot on Oasis has as much time flying both shuttles and fighters. If the mission requires that, and skill has any bearing on it, I should be at the top of the list."

Lieutenant Colonel Parker pushed his chair away from the desk and leaned back. After a moment, he said, "I need to think about this more. In the meantime, I want you to make a list of five pilots. We'll approach each one separately, and have the volunteers draw straws to determine who will be given the assignment. I want the list before the end of the day."

"I'll get right on it, sir."

Brett went to his office after obtaining a pilot roster from the admin clerk. He was certain any pilot asked would say yes. It was a given, an essential part of the nature of the beast.

A cursory search of the roster surprised him when he discovered there weren't that many pilots in the wing qualified in both shuttles and fighters. Many of them had flown both at one time or another, but were now current in only one. That narrowed the list considerably. As he reviewed the choices, Brett became even more determined to do this thing himself, whatever it was.

The dual-qualified pilots were also the more experienced members of the wing. All but one were married. He wasn't sure, but he thought most had kids. In more than one case additional family members were among the Oasis crew.

Extended family units were desirable and encouraged by NASA, and that policy had proved valuable in creating an atmosphere of normality in the decidedly abnormal living conditions aboard the space station. But in a crisis situation it could be a disadvantage, like having families living and working in the war zone with the warriors.

Brett created the list because he had been ordered to do so, but with the hope he'd never have to use it. As he leaned back to consider other ways to bias Lieutenant Colonel Parker's decision in his favor, the phone rang in the outer office. When the admin clerk didn't answer by the third ring, Brett picked up the handset and stabbed the flashing line button.

"First Aerospace Fighter Squadron, Captain Larsen speaking. May I help you, sir?"

"Brett? This's Toby."

Twenty minutes after Lieutenant Colonel Parker's admin clerk typed and printed Brett's pilot selection report, he arrived at his apartment and found Toby and his friend Rooster sitting in his living room. "You're sure they believed you when you told them about the police officer?"

"Not at first," said Toby, "but when that sergeant came on the line I think he knew I was telling the truth."

"Okay, back up a minute. Tell me exactly what happened."

Toby began with their entry into the chutes, explaining his curiosity about the explosion and how they wanted to check it out. When he got to the part about running into the cop he began to cry. Brett got up from the armchair and went over to the couch to sit beside him.

"Toby, sometimes you amaze me. I can't believe you like going in those chutes. I think they'd be scary even without being surprised like that."

"I agree with you, Brett," said Rooster. "Toby talked me into it so he could help me get used to them, but I don't think I'll ever like it."

"Why do you guys want to get used to it? Why not walk around in the corridors and use the elevators like the rest of us?"

Toby blew his nose on a napkin and then explained to Brett about his living in fear for years of being tormented by one of the older kids, and how he'd been teased and bullied.

"Hold on a minute," said Brett. "Who are those kids? We can put a stop to that."

"No you can't! You grown-ups think you can control things, but there's stuff that goes on you know nothing about. You might punish him, and it'd stop for a while. But he'd get back at me for sure. I've found out the hard way it's better to take care of myself than rely on anybody else."

Brett shook his head and put his hand on Toby's shoulder. "I understand. Every kid has to learn how to take care of the bullies in the playground. But going into the chutes is dangerous business, and you happen to be breaking the law. The rules say they're supposed to be used only for emergencies."

"You think being chased by a kid twice my size isn't an emergency?"

Brett laughed at that, with Toby and Rooster grinning at the joke. "Okay, you got me there. But I still don't think it's a good solution."

"Listen, Brett," said Toby. "I've been using the chutes for years now and I'm really comfortable in there. I know my way around. It's like my private place, and it isn't really dangerous. Are you going to tell my parents?"

Brett felt responsible for Toby's safety, and he worried that by not doing something, he was leaving a kid in jeopardy. On the other hand, Toby trusted him, telling him about a closely guarded secret. To violate that trust didn't seem right either. "I'd like nothing better than to go find this bully and take care of the problem, but you wouldn't tell me who it is anyway, would you?"

Toby shook head.

"I didn't think so. And as for telling your parents, that's the last thing I want to do. I value your friendship, and you probably wouldn't trust me ever again."

Toby didn't answer for a moment. "I trust you. And if you felt you had to tell my mom and dad about this I wouldn't like it, but I'd understand. Grown-ups want to protect us kids, and that's good. But they don't always know what's best. I think you should trust me, too, and believe me when I say I can use the chutes without getting hurt."

The living room was quiet, the only movement being Rooster's eyes darting back and forth from Toby to Brett as he listened to the conversation. Brett was thinking about how reasonable Toby's response seemed, and decided that his friend deserved support.

"That makes sense. But you need to understand that because I care about you, and because adults have to take care of kids as they grow up, I would hate myself if you went out and got hurt roaming around in those chutes.

"So, I'll make a deal with you, and I expect you to keep your part of the bargain. I won't tell your parents. But I want you to promise you won't use the chutes unless absolutely necessary. I don't like it, but it's your business how you want to handle the bully and his threats."

"Deal, and thanks for the help." They shook hands, with Rooster beaming on the sidelines. "But hey, we still don't know about the explosion. Is that what it was?"

"Yes. And before we get back to the duties of the day, there's something I want to say to you both. Some serious things are going on right now, and it's very important that you keep your curiosity in check and avoid adventures like investigating explosion sites. I want a promise. Okay?"

Toby and Rooster nodded agreement. "Brett," said Toby, "can I ask you a question?"

"Sure."

"What happened about the accident thing you told me about?"

Brett paused to consider how much to reveal. "The accident is being investigated and the inquiry this morning was just the first step. It might take months before the final results are out, but don't worry about me. I'll be fine and let you know as soon as I do."

"Okay." Toby looked at the clock on the wall, then at Rooster. "If we get moving, we can make it in time for study hall and we'll have missed only one class."

"Yeah, and I'll call someone about homework. Maybe we can turn it in tomorrow. It might make it go better for us."

"Sounds like a plan. Thanks again, Brett. We've got to get going."

"All right fellas, and do me a favor, okay? Take the stairs!"

They all laughed as the boys gathered their things and left Brett's apartment. Closing the door, Brett thought about what he'd just done.

Toby's call probably saved that cop's life. Even being afraid of the consequences for himself, he came up with a method of alerting the police while maintaining anonymity. Not bad.

But for his own part, Brett was afraid he hadn't made the right decision. Was his concern over loss of Toby's trust justified? Was Toby's use of the chutes serious enough to warrant telling his parents and just let them handle it? Did he have an obligation to them that superseded any relationship with Toby?

Hard questions. Brett's decision wasn't spur of the moment, although he came to it without much thought. Toby's response to Brett's question about trust seemed to be an unusually mature attitude for his age. Although Brett had little experience with children, he honestly believed there was something really special about Toby.

It was a combination of self-confidence, aggressiveness, and logical thought. Toby had been sitting beside another youngster of about the same age, and the contrast in the way the two boys talked, acted, and carried themselves was striking. Nothing against Rooster, he was as normal as could be. The difference was all in Toby, and Brett couldn't help but wonder how there could be so much more of certain qualities in one boy than in the other.

Brett was used to seeing variances in the capabilities of adults. He'd always assumed that it took a number of years for these differences to surface. But Toby seemed to have it all together in everything he did at a very early age. Brett couldn't help but wonder why.

In college he'd studied various theories of human development. The debate over the relative importance of genetics and environment fascinated him. As long-term space colonization became more feasible, adding the variable of a new environment and its unknown effects on the human body complicated the topic.

Toby's birth had been a big deal on the station, and the tantalizing possibility that his origins had something to do with his advanced behavior. Seeing the two boys side by side today rekindled Brett's interest in the question.

But for now, he decided to immerse himself in the familiar ritual of preparing his uniform to meet the public eye. Pride in himself and what the uniform represented would not allow Brett to walk out of the apartment without an inspection. He hated ties, but would never be seen with his carelessly knotted, or loose, or off to one side. He checked off the final items. Was his hat on just right, coat buttoned, insignia positioned exactly according to regulation, and with no lint or those persistent ropes? Satisfied with his appearance, Brett left the apartment.

The time had come to convince Lieutenant Colonel Parker that Captain Brett Larsen was the only pilot for the job.

$\sim$

As the boys left Brett's apartment, Toby pretended to be interested in Rooster's plan to get their homework assignment from a classmate. His friend might as well have been talking to himself, because Toby's attention was currently focused on a more pressing problem.

Toby knew how to manipulate grown-ups. To him it wasn't being devious, just a necessity of life. Listening to parents was like sitting through a sermon, dull, boring, and no fun. Doing exactly what they wanted you to do was even worse.

Teachers were in the same category as parents, but easier to fool. He wasn't worried about handling the problem of the missed class. Doing the homework was a nice touch, but the real key to it was how he handled the next morning when he saw the teacher.

It was all in the attitude. She'd insist on an explanation. If Toby tried to avoid her, or didn't want to talk about the missed class, she'd be much harder to convince that it wasn't all his fault. And that was the secret. Accept some of the blame, but not all of it. Be apologetic and eager to do better. Toby had that all worked out. If he handled it right, his teacher would accept his explanation without talking with his parents.

But the backpack was a different story. His parents would never believe he had lost it and had no idea where it might be. And if they found out he'd been in the chutes, he wouldn't see Brett again for a long time, if *ever*.

Rooster was chatting away as Toby pulled him over by a water fountain. Pretending to get a drink as two adults walked by, he said, "I can't go with you to class now. I've got to get my backpack. Do me a favor. Get the homework stuff and I'll call you tonight."

"Are you nuts? You can't go back. It'll be crawling with cops. Besides that, you promised Brett you wouldn't."

"I promised Brett I wouldn't use the chutes unless it was an emergency, and I rank losing the backpack right up there with being chased by bullies. I can't sell the story that I left it someplace and can't remember where. The best way is to get it now and the question won't come up."

"Toby, I can't believe this. You barely got out of that mess in the chutes and you're ready to jump back into it."

"I'll be in worse trouble if I don't go back. Trust me. It'll be okay."

Rooster shook his head. "Well, I'm your buddy, but I can't stick with you on this one."

"I understand. I wouldn't want you to anyway. I'll see you later."

"Not if I see you first. Bye."

Toby walked quickly to the nearest chute entrance. Checking both ways in the deserted corridor, he jumped on the ladder, popped the hatch, and was inside within seconds.

Toby approached the site of the explosion from a different direction than on his first visit. He was sure the cop would be gone, but there might be other activity to avoid. He stopped to catch his breath and checked out the site. He couldn't see it, but he knew where it was. Willing himself to relax, Toby detected the sounds of repair and voices. Adjusting his attention slightly, he heard a discussion about a patient's blood pressure and something about a bandage. Once satisfied that he was zeroed in on the site, he pulled his attention back and slowly scanned the area between him and the activity.

As the voices and background noise faded out, he detected the familiar sounds of moving air and various machinery noises prevalent in the chutes. It took him about five minutes to complete this audio sweep. Only when satisfied there were no alien sounds in the chutes ahead of him did he move forward.

Toby's enhanced auditory ability worked well as long as there was something to hear and he prepared himself for it. Earlier that day in the chutes he had been surprised because the cop wasn't making any noise. Toby's hearing was focused on the activity below him in the corridor. He'd been alerted that he wasn't alone by what he'd come to believe was an ability to correlate all his senses into a coherent evaluation of the overall threat.

Was it working now or not? Toby advanced, stopped to listen, to sense the environment as best he could, and repeated the cycle until he reached the chute where he'd left his backpack. This time he waited longer.

Nothing. No sounds, no bumps in the smoothness . . . no . . . wait a minute. Something's different.

What is it? Something soft . . . something around the corner to the left? There. It's still, small, about the size of the backpack, and it's cold.

Cold? I don't really know that, just that it's the same temperature as the surrounding area. I wonder what it is, or if it's my imagination. Why not look?

Toby had trusted his senses before, and they weren't any good to him if he remained suspicious. Easing slowly forward, he peeked around the corner and saw a vague shape about halfway down, barely visible in the semi-darkness. It was probably the backpack. He moved forward to enter the chute and retrieve it but stopped and retreated as another thought came to him.

Let's be more careful. Come in from the other side and see if it feels and looks the same.

Toby did that, and was gratified to find the sensations were no different. The backpack was slightly closer to this intersection, and he could see it more clearly and even make out the color.

He entered the chute, climbed to where the backpack was and unhooked it from the rung. Retracing his route, he stopped at the original vantage point and took out the map to confirm his next move. Toby decided to use the chutes to reach a point closer to the school rather than go back the way he came from Brett's apartment. It would save him time. If he hurried he might make his next class. It would, however, take him closer to the site of the explosion.

It took only a few minutes to reach a point from which he could view the damaged cross chute. He stopped out of sight, closed his eyes, and let his senses search the area before he looked around the corner. Almost immediately a sensation was there.

An object, smaller than the backpack, but harder. Much harder, compact, lying in the cross chute ahead.

Toby concentrated on the object, and tried the same technique he used with his hearing. He let his senses wander from the thing to the area around it, and was surprised that as he did so, his sense of the object itself faded, became less clear. Playing with it, he tried returning to the object, then moving off again, and found that the same thing happened. Satisfied that he'd discovered an element of control and that whatever it was posed no threat, he moved to the intersection and looked around the corner.

There it was, a black object about three feet long. Cylindrical in shape, much thinner than it was long, the object was difficult to see in the darkness. As he moved slowly forward the details became clearer.

Toby's heart almost stopped when he saw the pistol grip. He'd never touched a gun, but had seen them in videos. When the station police first began carrying guns, he and Rooster spent an entire afternoon looking for cops and trying to get one to show them his pistol.

But this was no pistol. Toby inched closer and recognized it as a short-barreled shotgun, like the kind used by police and bad guys in action videos. An evil-looking weapon, lying there in ominous silence, exuding the power of death.

Instinct said back away and leave, but curiosity held him fast, trying to figure out how it got there. Then he remembered the cop, his black uniform, wearing what looked like a protective vest. The police had teams for special operations like riots and maybe they carried short weapons like this. Toby didn't know what police units there were on Oasis and the idea of a riot seemed pretty far-fetched, but how else would a shotgun find its way into the chutes?

What now? Should he leave it here and tell someone?

No, that wouldn't work. He'd have to explain why he was in the chutes again.

Leave it here and don't tell anyone? That seemed like a stupid thing to do. Why not take it?

But he couldn't take it with him when he left the chutes. Privacy was tough to find on Oasis, and how could he move a shotgun and hide it from his parents without being discovered? As Toby thought about what to do, the feeling returned. He instantly forgot the shotgun, fear settling in his bowels, and turned his head to concentrate his attention behind him. Relaxing, letting it work, he waited.

And a familiar panic engulfed Toby as a repeat of the threat warning when the man in the black mask had surprised him.

Toby surged ahead in the chute. Reaching the shotgun, he grabbed it in one hand and kept on going until the sense of danger abated completely as he reached the next intersection, turned the corner, and paused.

Searching back the way he had come, he correlated sound, spatial, and heat sensations that remained stationary. The absence of threat warnings tempted him to peek around the corner and into an empty chute. Curiosity aroused, he advanced a few feet at a time and paused to search until he reached the previous intersection, where a quick peek discovered a man in the gray coveralls worn by maintenance technicians. He was repairing the breach in the chute caused by the explosion.

Toby eased backward to an intersection where he could turn around and get away from the site without being detected. Holding the shotgun slowed him down in the chutes, so he stuffed it in his backpack and managed to zip it closed. Then he abandoned all caution to put as much distance as possible between him and the events of the past hour. When he finally reached an exit near his apartment, he paused to catch his breath and consider his latest problem.

The plan to become a pilot would never be anything more than a dream if his parents wouldn't agree to let him return to Earth. Toby knew it was going to be a long process, and he intended to present the idea gradually. But for his parents to be receptive, his relationship with them had to be on good terms. Toby also needed help with how to approach them. He had tried to talk with Brett twice about it and had been unsuccessful both times.

And now he had literally crawled and fallen into the middle of events he did not understand. He couldn't go home without talking with someone about it first. He needed help, and Brett was the only person he could trust. He began to turn around in the chute and suddenly remembered that he still had the shotgun. Common sense told him to get rid of it. Maybe take it to Brett and hand it over. But would he give it to the police? Would Toby have to tell them where he got it? What if his parents found out he had it?

And in the midst of this uncertainty, in spite of all the concern over being good, doing the right thing, and letting things settle down, Toby got angry again. Something in him rose up, demanding attention, and it wouldn't let him walk away. It was as if giving up the shotgun would be a mistake, something he'd regret, like he just knew he'd need it.

What if he hid it in the chutes? He could always turn it in later, or call the police without identifying himself and tell them where it was. What was the harm in that?

Decision made, Toby crawled back to the last intersection and climbed halfway up the chute. Satisfied that the darkness would conceal the weapon well enough, he unhooked the sling and ran it through two of the rungs, then reattached it to the shotgun. He descended to the bottom intersection, and looked up.

Good. Time to get more help from Brett.

~

TOBY EXITED THE CHUTES AND TIMED IT SO THAT HE COULD make it to the door of Brett's apartment before anyone came by. He had used the audio search to make sure the corridor was clear, and counted on the fact that Brett didn't lock his door. He was pouring some juice when Brett burst into his apartment.

"You're not going to tell me this happened in the chutes, are you?"

"Didn't you say I could come to you about anything?"

"Don't avoid a question by asking one. Let's have it. And don't leave anything out."

Toby had decided there was no way he could hide any of this, except maybe the part about the shotgun. He had no idea what was going on down in the core, whether it was connected to the warnings he'd heard, or how much the police knew or didn't know about the man in black and his captive cop. But if he had information they didn't have, it was his duty to tell it.

So he told Brett about going back into the chutes to retrieve the backpack after finding the cop at the explosion site. He also wanted to give Brett the impression that being chased by the masked man had happened at the same time by pure chance, and not as a direct result of his having violated a promise *again*.

As he related the events following the initial encounter, Toby watched Brett's reaction to the story. Toby was good at this, and knew how to adjust both his story and the way he told it to achieve the desired effect. He left out the part about his playing around with the guy, knowing that Brett wouldn't understand why he didn't get out of there at the first opportunity and call the police.

Then Brett interrupted him. "Let me get this straight. You said you know the chutes well. You've been in there lots of times, and can find your way around with no trouble. Certainly you knew the way to the nearest exit."

So much for that omission. "The guy wasn't giving me time. He was too close. If I'd stopped it would've been all over."

"How did he trap you?"

"I ran into a dead end where the chute stopped at the ceiling of the central core."

"So you're caught in a dead end, he's coming for you, and you manage to get the hatch open."

"Yeah. I climbed out onto the ladder and fell to the floor. And Brett, you're not going to believe this, but there was a cop down there, tied up." As Brett stared at him, Toby related the events in the core and how he managed to elude capture. He left out the part about the shooting, trying to minimize the threat to himself and focus Brett's attention on helping him do something about the man and the cop. There was far more important business to talk about, but Brett didn't seem to be buying it.

"How did you keep him from following you in the chute?"

Time to bend the truth. "I was able to lock it before he got there. He may have tried to come after me using another entrance, but I had too much of a head start. He didn't have any chance of catching me."

Brett got up from the chair and excused himself. Toby watched as Brett walked out the door of the apartment. After a minute or so, he came back, sat down, and pulled his chair right up in front of where Toby sat on the couch.

Reaching out with one hand to grip Toby's arm, Brett said, "I've been listening to this, trying to decide whether to believe you. I know kids sometimes come up with tall stories, and at first I found myself thinking you were making this up. But now I know better. You're too old to be telling stories, expecting me to believe something like this. I think you're holding back, not telling me all there is to tell, and that last bit about locking the hatch cover has convinced me I'm right."

"Brett, wait a minute, I—"

"Let me finish. I don't roam around in the chutes, but they aren't as far outside my experience as you might think. With the shuttles docked in the bays, one of our escape routes in case of an emergency is to enter the chute system through a hatch in the floor of the bay. We practice it from time to time, and I don't remember any lock on the cover. I just checked the emergency exit at the end of the hall, and guess what? It doesn't have a lock either. What do you have to say to that?"

Toby decided that this seemed like a good time to come clean.

"Listen, Brett, I need your help. I don't know what's going on in the core with those men, and I don't want to. But I can't ignore what I saw. I have to tell somebody in case the police don't know about it. But I can't get involved. My parents will be really mad. They'll ask all sorts of questions, and I'll be in real trouble."

"So what do you want me to do? Tell the police I was casually cruising through the chutes when a bad man dressed in black chased me into the core?

"I didn't mean that. Just help me come up with a way to tell them and stay out of it. I don't know what to do."

Brett stared at Toby hard for a few seconds. "Let's back up for a minute. Why did you lie to me about locking the hatch cover?"

Toby was out of ideas, so he came clean about the shots fired at him, his attempts to hold the handle closed and what it felt like when he heard the man cursing on the other side. Toby watched Brett closely, and it didn't look good, especially when he shook his head.

"Here's how it shakes out for me, Toby. We had a deal. You hadn't left here more than five minutes when you went back in the chutes. Maybe the encounter with the man happened just like you said it did, pure coincidence as you were getting the backpack. But if you hadn't been in the chutes in the first place you wouldn't have left it there. And if you hadn't gone back, you wouldn't have run into him.

"Your own choices resulted in being involved. You may not like it, but that's the way it is with choices. They have consequences, and you can't avoid it. You come to me again for help, want me to bail you out for the second time in a few hours, and still won't tell me the truth."

"Brett, I thought the part about the shooting would be such a big deal that you'd make me go to the police myself. Once that happens my parents will have to be told."

"I know, you'll be in trouble. Let me tell you something, Toby. You're more concerned about being punished for disobeying your parents than you are about how important it might be for the police to know that some dude is running around loose on the station with a gun. What if you were the first cop into the core trying to find him? Still think it's okay to ignore the consequences of that?"

Toby had never seen Brett angry. The tears came without warning. Brett got up and walked over to the phone, and as Toby heard the words, he knew that his life on Oasis was about to change forever.

"Hello, this is Captain Brett Larsen. May I please speak with the officer in charge?"

8

DAY THREE MID-AFTERNOON

They called it an interview room. But based on the movies Toby had seen, it was a place where wily detectives conducted *interrogations* about serious events. Alone in the room, he sat at a bare table, waiting. He didn't know exactly what he was waiting for, but it couldn't possibly be any good and he was terribly depressed.

After Brett had notified the police, he called Toby's parents. The walk to the police station was a silent one, as if the time for conversation had long since passed. A sense of profound loss, of something precious gone, draped Toby like a heavy overcoat of fear that his relationship with Brett would never be the same.

When they arrived at the station, that big cop Cadogan was waiting and took them into the interrogation room. After the two men left, Toby sat in the chair, resigned to the fact that his future was uncertain at best. He didn't know if he'd broken any laws, or if being a kid they could do anything to him even if he had. But one thing was for sure. He wouldn't be able to hide anything from his parents. They were going to be furious.

Toby couldn't sit still. He got up to wander around the room, just to move, do something. As he paced back and forth, he noticed the glass panel on one wall of the room and walked over to it. In every cop movie he had seen, interrogation rooms had one-way glass.

Then it dawned on him that they could be in there now, watching him, just like in the movies. Maybe he could find out what was on the other side of the wall and no one would know about it.

Returning to his seat, he lowered his head to the table and closed his eyes. It felt so good that he almost forgot what he was here for, and he began to relax. He heard sounds almost immediately, but they weren't focused, and it was a conversation between two people about some experiment they were conducting. Gaining control of the audio search pattern, he concentrated on pulling it back in range and into what he thought was the next room, the one behind the glass. His mother's voice startled him, loud, angry, insistent.

"*—my son. I want to see him and I want to see him now!*"

"*Mrs. Williams,*" it sounded like the big cop's voice, "*I understand you're upset, but we have an investigation to run. There are things going on I can't talk about, and your son has information crucial to how we handle it. I've been a cop a long time and I know how these things work. When kids are reluctant to talk about something they can go either way with parents close by.*"

"*I don't give a damn how whatever things you're talking about work. I get a call from Captain Larsen telling me he's with Toby, asking me to meet them at the police station. I get down here and find the captain, but no Toby. You've got him locked away alone in some room and I'm supposed to sit back and wait until you're through?*"

"*As a matter of fact, that's exactly what I want you to do. If you want to get technical about it, I can hold him as a material witness, and prevent you from seeing him until I say otherwise. I don't want to do that, but I do need to talk with him about this afternoon.*"

"*Fine, talk with him all you want, but let me see him and be there when you do.*"

"*Mrs. Williams, I told you there are things going on that are privileged information. I can't allow you to be present during questioning.*"

"*All right, damn it, but at least let me see him. Captain Larsen said he was hurt, and I want to make sure he's not in any pain. He's my son, for Christ's sake!*"

"Please, Mrs. Williams, listen to me. I don't have a lot of time here and I'm not going to argue with you any longer. Your son is fine, and regardless of what you think of me or the police in general, we don't get any pleasure from seeing anyone in pain. I'm not going to let you see him before questioning because once he's comforted by you he may really clam up and refuse to talk. Some kids do that.

"And besides that, the Captain thinks Toby may be trying to hide information. If it isn't going well, I'll let you see him under the condition that you agree to help me convince him to tell me all he knows. Some kids will open up with parents in the room when they won't say a word to us. Now I want you to have a seat here. There's coffee in the next room if you want some, and I'll be back as soon as I can."

Toby heard no more conversation, just the sound of footsteps, followed by the scraping of a chair on the floor. Suddenly the door opened behind him. Sergeant Cadogan entered the room, smiling. Toby expected to see another cop behind him, who should be frowning. He knew all about the good-cop, bad-cop interrogation technique. He'd seen it in the movies countless times.

But there was only one, and Toby watched Cadogan as he sat down opposite him.

"Hello, Toby, I'm Sergeant Andras Cadogan. Remember me?"

How could I forget, you big bully? "Yes, sir."

"Well, first of all, I'd like to apologize for the way I treated you the other day. I was in a bad mood, what with all the things going on at the time, and I kind of took it out on you."

This has got to be the nice guy part of it. I would've thought this cop would play the other role. "Yes, sir."

"All right. Before we get started I need to go over a few things with you. This interview is being recorded as a matter of standard procedure, nothing special. And I want to make it perfectly clear that you're not being charged with any crime. We don't need to concern ourselves with any lawyers, or anything like that."

Toby was a little disappointed. He wanted Cadogan to read from the little card, tell him all about how he could remain silent, all that stuff. "Yes, sir."

"Good. I've had a long talk with the captain, and he told me about what happened in the core earlier today. We have some serious stuff going on that's strictly police business, and although you seem to be right in the middle of it, your parents don't need to be."

Toby had been sure his mom would be watching this from the other side of the glass, but the cop had told her that she couldn't be present during questioning. Now he was saying he wouldn't tell her anything. This might be the break Toby was looking for. He could tell what he knew to the cops and then modify the version for his parents to minimize the damage.

"Yes, sir, I understand. Kind of like our secret, huh?"

The cop chuckled at that. "That's one way to put it. Now that we've got that settled, why don't you tell me what happened, right from the beginning? And don't leave anything out just because you think it might not be important. Lots of times it's the small details that can make the difference."

Toby related the whole story, beginning with finding the injured cop in the chutes. He wanted Cadogan to know it was his action that alerted them. And when he mentioned the shooting, the sergeant's interest really peaked, showing more concern about that. Cadogan paused to review his notes, then asked, "During your time in the chutes you never saw anything that looked like a short rifle, and you never saw the man with one?"

Why should I tell anyone about the shotgun? "That's right, sir."

"And the officer you saw in the central core, you're sure he was alive?"

"Yes, sir. I remember a bandage on his head, but he looked fine. I did hear him yell just prior to the first shot but I was running hard and never looked back."

"Was the officer between you and the man when he fired?"

"Yes, sir. But he was lying on the floor. That's why I tripped over him."

"Okay. I think that covers it for now, but I need to mention a few more things before we terminate here. First, and this is important. I know your parents aren't going to like it, but that's the way it is. You can't discuss with them or anybody else the stuff about the man, the officer in the core, and being shot at. It's police business, and if you disobey me on this I guarantee that it won't be pleasant. I'll consider that to be a crime, arrest you, toss you in the slammer and throw away the key."

"Yes, sir."

"Now for the second point, and you listen carefully. Stay out of the chutes. They may have been a fun place to play, in violation of station regulations, I might add, but the rules have changed and this is no joke. Do I need to say any more about that?"

"No, sir."

"All right. When we leave here I'm going to turn you over to your mom and you're free to go. If you think of anything more, something you might have forgotten about, you call me."

"Yes, sir."

"Let's go."

Cadogan led Toby out of the room and down a hall into what looked like a visitor's area. As he entered, Toby seemed to be an object of curiosity to all the cops standing around. He was a little embarrassed when his mom hurried over and hugged him, looking him over like she was concerned there were some pieces missing. He felt a strange unity with the policemen, sort of like being a part of the whole thing, an accomplice, in on the secret.

His mom took his hand and started for the door. As they left the police station the tears welled up and cascaded down his cheeks.

It was the longest walk home, ever.

ANDRAS MADE THE CALLS TO ASSEMBLE THE ALPHA TEAM. HE now knew for sure the hijacker was holed up in the core. And although he had probably moved since the incident with the kid, it was at least a place to start.

Andras had a very simple goal, to kill the bastard before he could implicate him. If he'd been able to keep the existence of the Alpha Team secret, he might have accomplished that before any other command functions were involved. They'd have criticized him for taking independent action, but with the threat to the station eliminated, the punishment would have been mild, a slap on the wrist, while they congratulated him for the good work.

But now he had to work within the orders of his commander. His plan was to flush the man into a trap, but the hostage complicated things. Andras knew the other men in the team would be primed to protect a fellow cop, and facing an adversary of this caliber, any hesitation would probably be fatal.

Andras had made up his mind that if Dan were still alive and it came down to it, personal survival was his number-one priority. So the answer was to leave the Alpha Team out of the direct confrontation if at all possible, for two reasons.

First, he wanted to eliminate the possibility of interrogation; and second, ensure there were no witnesses. If putting the hijacker down required application of deadly force outside departmental guidelines, Andras wouldn't be challenged later by anything other than circumstantial evidence. Any investigation would more than likely find the shooting righteous and justified.

When Andras got back to his office, he told the duty sergeant to hold any calls except from his boss or the commander and sat down at his desk with a diagram of the core and the chute system surrounding it.

Andras used the boy's story to determine the general location where Dan had been. It didn't take long to realize there were dead ends in some of the chutes, and that this could work both to his advantage and against it. If he could drive the man into one of these traps, it would be all over.

Andras also had to make sure that all members of the Alpha Team avoided them. Once the man became aware of pursuit he'd be on the move quickly, with escape routes thought out well in advance. The noose would have to be drawn tight with no knots in the wrong places. As he studied the diagram looking for the best way to arrange his team, a knock at the door interrupted his concentration.

"Enter."

The door opened and the duty sergeant stuck his head in. "Excuse me Sergeant, but a Corporal Phillips is here and said you'd want to see him. He has some officers with him."

"Send them in, please, and bring some coffee."

"Yes, Sergeant."

When the Alpha Team had gathered around the desk with steaming mugs of hot coffee in their hands, Andras said, "Okay, gents, plan 'A' is toast. Here's plan 'B.'"

Corporal Doug Phillips was Andras's second-in-command of the Alpha Team, and used the call sign Alpha Nine while filling the position of roving team member. He stepped forward as Andras took a seat at his desk.

"We think the guy's got to be in the core area. With only so many ways out, we should be able to cover them all. The trick is to get him moving, especially if we can make him feel threatened and rushed. Looking back over his shoulder increases his vulnerability from the front. Covering the main exit points is easy, but he probably won't enter the station proper, especially while under pursuit. So we're going to block all the chute exits and try to flush him with a robodog."

As Andras listened to Doug brief the team, he became more and more convinced that the plan had a better than even chance of success. Following the briefing and a few questions and answers, Andras decided it was time to emphasize an important point.

"When we move up no further in each corridor than the last intersection before the central core, he'll have no place to go. If he tries to advance out from the center, he won't be able to make it to any of the circular corridors, and retreat's his only option. And since we'll be holding position rather than moving closer in, we won't be faced with running into each other. Once we stop, any movement between us and the core is the target."

"What happens," asked a private, "if we get the net closed down and he isn't moving? Seems to me we end up with a stalemate, nothing happening. Why don't we just start moving up and use that to flush him from cover?"

"No," said Andras. "Let's get this straight. What we want is to create a static line surrounding him, each of you stationary and hunkered down. Then when he bolts, he's the only one in there on the move, and one of *you* is going to be presented with a target. You damn well better be ready."

Andras liked what he saw. The men were eager to get on with it, and he could almost feel their desire to smash this guy like the insect he was. The time had come to add some personal control over their collective mentality and make sure they'd do what he wanted them to.

"Before we break up here, I want you all to listen very carefully to me." Eyes locked onto each of the cops in turn, Andras asserted his authority and command as forcefully as he could. "Without going into the details of what this guy is doing here, it should be obvious to you the situation is as serious as it gets. The only thing between him and his objective is us, and I guarantee you he'll be absolutely ruthless.

"Our chance of success depends largely on being just as ruthless in our determination to stop him. Each and every one of you needs to make up your mind right now you'll do whatever's required when the time comes. If you have any doubts about the caliber of your opponent and the sophistication of his scheme, just keep in mind what he's accomplished so far. There's not a man among us who could've done it."

Andras paused to emphasize the point that the man was better than any of them individually. He wanted to instill fear, the idea that teamwork was essential to their success, and create a mindset among them that as members of the team that they owed it to each other to do exactly what he told them to do.

"Take my word for it, and consider this an order. Anything less than deadly force will not work. Once he realizes he's being trapped, things will happen quickly. When the opportunity presents itself you must act immediately. Shoot on sight and shoot to kill. I want to know right now if any of you have a problem with that. Don't keep silent here and then let your buddies down later. Are we clear on this?"

Andras paused again. It was a way of obtaining an unspoken but powerful individual commitment from them, one cop to another, and was essential for the next step. After looking around the table and being convinced every man had agreed, Andras tossed in the grenade to see if anyone would dive for cover.

"Okay, that's settled. Before I dismiss you, there's one more thing to cover, and it's not an easy subject to bring up. How many of you know Corporal Dan Bishop?"

Heads nodded, with murmurs of acknowledgment and a smile or two. They appeared to know him and like him. Time to do some manipulating.

"We've determined he may be in the core with this asshole." The cops seemed stunned. Andras waited while the impact took hold, and let each of them reconcile this new information with their earlier commitment to shoot on sight.

One of the privates broke the silence. "But Sergeant, that changes everything. The bastard will certainly keep Dan close to him, use him as a shield, and we'll need a lot more of a clear shot than we're likely to get in the core."

Andras couldn't have written the script better himself. He hadn't said anything about Dan being a *hostage* and the private made that assumption for everyone.

"I know how you feel. But the question now is whether you think endangering the life of one man is worth the safety of the entire station. You must be willing to put yourselves at risk, or you wouldn't be here. If you know Dan, then you know he feels the same. He'd expect you to do what's needed."

Andras was positive no one would back out. The bond between men in dangerous jobs was like a code of honor, sworn to on a bible of arms and sealed in blood. Once there was doubt about how a person would act when the chips were down, it was impossible to erase it completely. No one wanted to be an outsider, distrusted, the weak link. Now for the final touch.

"And here's one more thing for you to think about. No one knows for sure why Corporal Bishop is in there. But we do think this man has an accomplice among the station personnel."

It was very quiet in the room. Andras let the doubt take hold for a moment, then twisted the pressure up a notch.

"I have no evidence that Corporal Bishop is a traitor. But what I'm saying to you is this: *It doesn't matter.* In either case, if you want to save the station you must do as I tell you and be ready to act decisively regardless of what the underlying truth is. We can't sort it out before-hand because we don't have the time."

The phone rang, and every cop in the room jumped, including Andras. He picked up the handset. "Sergeant Cadogan."

It was the duty sergeant. "Sorry to bother you, Sergeant, but Colonel Thomas just called and said for you to report to the War Room."

"Thanks." Andras slammed the receiver down on the cradle. He didn't have the time to screw around with this, and if the Battle Staff got into another marathon session he'd never get anything done.

The men of Alpha Team seemed lost in thought, with expressions of worry, fiddling with equipment, looking at their laps. Andras couldn't do more to ensure their obedience.

"I have to meet with the Battle Staff. Review your assignments, check out all your gear, especially the radios. Doug's your commander for now. Follow his instructions and let's hop to it."

As Andras left the office he paused at the door to watch the men gather around Doug at the table. There was no way to be sure until the time came, but Andras was confident they would follow his shoot-to-kill orders. He closed the door and hurried toward the War Room.

Things were looking up.

SEATED IN THE WAR ROOM, ANDRAS WATCHED AND LISTENED AS the officers discussed the questions raised in the first meeting. It was only the second time in his career that he'd been able to observe the way they interacted among themselves. Colonel Thomas treated Andras like dirt, but he was a sniveling pimp around General DeSilva. Andras figured that subordinates and superiors in organizations everywhere did the same, and for those on the lower end of the totem pole, learning how to use the system to their advantage was an essential skill. His thoughts about how he might be able to benefit from being included in the Battle Staff screeched to a halt when Captain Norton began discussing the bomb.

"It was a common form of plastic explosive, but we don't how it was triggered. As for the second bomb, and assuming that the objective is to render the station uninhabitable, we looked first at the life support systems as being most vulnerable. The conclusion is one bomb wouldn't do it."

"What?" General DeSilva sat up and onto the edge of his chair. "I thought that even a relatively small bomb could disable the life support system and kill everybody."

"That's what we all thought, sir. But the systems are designed in a series of zones that can be isolated in the event of failure. Even in the worst-case scenario, the loss of life could be limited to that zone rather than spreading throughout the entire station."

"Are you telling me the threat of the bomb is overrated and we're reacting to a possibility that doesn't exist?"

"Not at all, sir. The threat is real enough, but not in the area of life support. The main power source is the most critical to survival. A relatively small bomb in the right place could render the nuclear reactor and solar power systems inoperative."

General DeSilva shook his head. "I find it hard to believe this. You mean our security system can't keep a person out of the reactor area?"

"That's outside my area, sir," said Captain Norton. "All I'm saying is that if you wanted to turn Oasis into a ghost town, that would be the easiest way to do it."

Colonel Thomas leaned forward in his chair. Andras cringed at the thought of having to listen to the man's asinine drivel.

"From the security perspective," said Colonel Thomas, "the initial response stopped one guy and missed the second. The question now is whether we can prevent him from accessing key areas."

General DeSilva said, "Have we had any alarms from the reactor area, any malfunctions in the security systems that protect it?"

"Not to my knowledge, sir."

"So . . . He could be in there right now and we don't know it?"

"Well," said Colonel Thomas, "in order to prevent the alarms from activating you'd have to disable them and then hide that fact from the system itself. All the security networks run random self-checks for continuity. A failure would alert us."

Andras loved this stuff. Here he was, sitting right up close to the throne of power, listening to these officers do their thing. The bastard in black is loose in their midst, and they lean back in comfortable chairs talking about possibility this, and possibility that. What they needed to do was get in there and blow the SOB's shit away. It was time to get things moving in the right direction.

"General DeSilva?"

"Yes, Sergeant Cadogan?"

"You asked me to find out about the robodogs, and I may have some information of interest here."

"Go ahead."

Andras confirmed his earlier statements that the dogs can be programmed to search for any scent available while the video is sending back images of the area. "I told them to prepare the dog ASAP. I'm expecting a call any minute now."

General DeSilva smiled. "Good work, Sergeant Cadogan."

Andras had just accumulated some more attaboy points with the general. This was the way to pave the path to advancement, one stone at a time, laid at the feet of the man at the top. Make a smoother road for him, and hitch a ride in his cart on the way up.

The general studied notes in front of him and then looked up at Andras. "What do you have to report on your plan to isolate this guy?"

Andras summarized his work with the Alpha Team, leaving out any mention of Dan, and assured the commander they would be ready to go within the hour.

Colonel Thomas sat forward in his chair, his face livid with a barely subdued anger, probably because he hadn't come up with the idea, or at the very least been able to take credit for it.

"I don't think we should be too hasty, General DeSilva. We still haven't come to a decision on whether to take this guy before we know the location of the bomb or whether it's capable of being remotely activated."

"No one's being hasty here. But if and when we move on him, we have to do everything we can to block his escape. If the robodog finds the bomb, we can either remove it, or at least block his access to it. If he slips the trap, he must not be allowed to get his hands on the bomb again. Remote activation is always a possibility, but we can't be intimidated into inaction because of it."

The room was quiet for a moment. The men seemed to be preoccupied with the idea of a man who would plant a bomb and activate it with no apparent regard for his own safety. Andras took advantage of the silence.

"On another topic, General DeSilva, I think with this man we can't afford to go halfway. The trap will work only if we use the element of surprise and catch him off guard. He won't be vulnerable for long, and I need your authority to issue the shoot-to-kill order. Without it, I'm afraid the net may not be tight enough."

The room was again quiet. With the exception of Colonel Thomas, still visibly seething over being on the sidelines, the other officers seemed lost in the problem at hand.

Killing and death were the business of war and warriors, but up here on Oasis? For many of the volunteers, this was to be an escape from all such cancers of the human existence, a barrier of miles between them and the evils that were helping turn Earth into the hell they left behind.

The general sighed, looked down at the floor between his feet, and seemed lost in thought for a moment. "Sergeant Cadogan has recommended we approach the problem of stopping this guy with the pre-approved use of deadly force. I'm inclined to agree. A small number of innocent people may die if we do, but the chances are good that many more will die if we don't." Turning to face Andras, General DeSilva said, "I approve the use of deadly force. Do what you have to do."

As Andras heard the magic words, he realized that he had obtained the authority before telling the general about Dan. "I'll take care of that, sir. And as for the missing police officer, we have an eyewitness who saw Corporal Dan Bishop in the central core with the second stowaway."

"Somebody's seen this guy for real?"

Andras told a short version of the incident with Toby in the chutes and central core. He watched General DeSilva carefully, concerned that he might think he had been tricked into the shoot-to-kill order before knowing that Dan was confirmed as a hostage. Andras breathed a sigh of relief as the discussion evolved. The life of one man wasn't worth losing the station by not shooting when the chance presented itself, hostage or no hostage. He had a green light.

Halle-frigging-lujah!

The fighter squadron commander presented a report on the status of the shuttle. Andras didn't know Lieutenant Colonel Parker, but was in awe of him because he wore the wings of a pilot. The whole business of flying had always been a mystery to Andras. He really perked up when the discussion turned to problems.

"Are we going to be ready?" asked the general.

"Yes, sir, but it looks like we may have to leave some cargo on board he didn't ask for. Our original plan was to use ship zero four three. But when we pressurized the fuel tanks we found a leak. Rather than take the time to fix it, we decided to go with ship zero five six, the one involved in the loading dock incident yesterday."

Lieutenant Colonel Parker explained how a communications glitch during a shift change resulted in the cargo being left on board when the fighter was loaded. The pallets were trapped behind the fighter, with no way to remove them in time to make the deadline.

"Is that going to cause a problem with this guy?" asked Captain Norton. "If he considers this some sort of trick he might get real upset."

"Well," replied Lieutenant Colonel Parker, "it might. If we leave it on, he can make us remove it and we miss the deadline. If we remove it now, we'll miss the deadline for sure. Either way we'll have to deal with his reaction. My guess is that since he can check the cargo, it's better to leave it."

"Okay," said General DeSilva. " Leave it on there and get the shuttle ready. What about a pilot?"

Andras perked up even more. Ground combat was bad enough, but the thought of being airborne and getting shot at was terrifying. He'd heard pilots felt just the opposite. This situation didn't involve combat, per se, but to sit in the cockpit of a spacecraft with a gun to your head? *No thank you.*

Lieutenant Colonel Parker described the process of finding a pilot. He had assigned the task to a senior captain, who volunteered before any of the other pilots had a chance.

"What's the problem with that?" asked the general. "Why wouldn't you put your best man out there in front, and a volunteer to boot?"

"Two reasons, sir. First, the rest of the guys will feel cheated they haven't been given the opportunity to risk their lives also. Call it the right to compete for glory, or maybe it's just wanting to do it so a buddy won't have to, but it's the way they feel.

"Second, and really more to the point, the pilot in question is the same one involved in the accident yesterday. He said that in addition to him being the most qualified, and there isn't any argument there, he had no family and nothing to lose."

"Bullshit. Nobody thinks their own life is worth nothing."

"Under most circumstances I'd agree with you. But here it has a special meaning."

The general wasn't buying this. "There's got to be more to this than I've heard so far. What are you talking about, 'special meaning'?"

"The initial inquiry for the accident investigation was held this morning. He told me afterward that he might lose his wings if the investigation determines he's at fault. It isn't a farfetched concern."

"Okay," said the general. "You're afraid he might consider this a suicide mission, and end up being a loose cannon out there doing his own thing? Is he the most qualified?"

"Yes."

"Does he have a history of willful violation of directive, hot-shot flying, anything like that?"

"No sir."

"Case closed. I'll talk with him, and I can guarantee when I'm through he'll be the perfect pilot for this mission."

Andras was thinking he would really like to hear that conversation when Captain Norton changed the subject.

"Since there's the threat of a bomb, General DeSilva, I reviewed the contingency plans for evacuation of Oasis, and I suggest we accomplish a complete check on the lifeship system."

The room went into one of its quiet periods for a moment, and Andras wondered if the rest of the Battle Staff was as baffled as he was by the term "lifeship." Apparently so, because Captain Norton was asked to brief the staff.

The lifeship system was designed for emergency evacuation. They were manned and launched individually as they reached full capacity.

Once free of the station, the ships automatically attained and maintained a fixed position relative to Oasis. Pilots were not required. Any occupant could input the necessary commands by following on-screen instructions. On-board life support systems provided sufficient survival time for rescue by shuttles, with automatic recovery and docking.

General DeSilva asked the question everyone else in the room was afraid to ask. "Do we have enough of these things to evacuate everyone?"

"My initial estimate," replied Captain Norton, "is we might have sufficient capacity."

The word "might" was not missed by anyone in the room, and yet another quiet period followed Captain Norton's explanation of why lifeship capacity had not kept up with population increases.

"Wonderful," murmured the general, "simply wonderful. I've got a maniac on board threatening to bomb the place, and now you tell me we'll have to draw straws for seats on the only bus out of town." General DeSilva ordered Captain Norton to complete the survey as soon as possible and determine the current evacuation capacity.

As Captain Norton acknowledged the order, the general turned to his executive officer, Colonel Radcliff, who hadn't spoken a word in either of the Battle Staff meetings.

"Rad, I need to know exactly how many people are on the station at this moment. I also want you to determine what would be considered minimum crew during this crisis, and identify the non-essential population. I have an idea how we can work around the lifeship problem, if there is one."

The general turned to face the other officers. "Everybody listen up. I'm considering a controlled evacuation of the station prior to any crisis point. If we remove enough personnel and reduce the population to no more than can be handled by the lifeships, I'd feel more inclined to issue the abandon-ship order as a preemptive move. The fewer people at risk the better, and I think it might enhance our options as we approach the deadline."

Andras promised himself he would locate the lifeships nearest his office and apartment as a first priority after this meeting ended. He didn't doubt for a second that everyone else in the room had the same thought.

The discussion then turned to the question of retrieving the life-ships. Two different types of shuttles were available. Cruiser models could dock with lifeships and offload occupants, but could not land on the moon. Lunar shuttles could rescue lifeship occupants and transport them to the lunar colony. Neither model was available in sufficient numbers to do the complete job, but cruiser and lunar shuttles could dock and transfer passengers for the trip to the lunar colony.

As a take-charge commander, General DeSilva made the final deci-sion. "We'll use the moon shuttle fleet for the controlled evacuation to the moon colony, and cruiser shuttles for evacuation of the remaining essential personnel if that becomes necessary. Work the numbers with Colonel Radcliff, and let me know how long it'll take."

Although interesting to Andras, the discussion had strayed from his immediate area of interest. His mind had wandered a bit until the subject came home again as General DeSilva related his conversations with NASA about the options available.

"The first question is whether to let this guy get on a shuttle with a pilot and allow him to depart. The second is whether to attempt a capture and risk him detonating the bomb. The third will be whether to go ahead with an evacuation, partial or whatever. I have no answers yet, but the next conference call is in about thirty minutes."

The general worked his way around the room, soliciting comments from the Battle Staff members. The meeting was then dismissed and the officers began signing out and departing the War Room. As Andras waited to go last, General DeSilva walked toward him.

"Sergeant Cadogan, I'd like a word with you please."

"Yes, sir," said Andras, coming to attention.

"At ease, Sergeant, make yourself comfortable. Have a seat."

Andras sat as the general took a chair next to him, leaned closer and lowered his voice. "Have you figured it out yet?"

"Sir?"

"I want to know if you've figured out what's going to happen here."

"Uh, no, sir, I haven't thought much about it. Too much to do."

"Then let me give you a little prediction. NASA is never going to give this man the spacecraft. The ramifications of that are just too hard to comprehend. I think they're more concerned about what he wants to do with the shuttle and the fighter than with the threat to Oasis. Maybe they don't really believe he can damage it sufficiently, I don't know.

"But the what-if's aren't what I wanted to talk with you about. I think that the solution to this crisis may well come down to your ability to take him."

Is this perfect, or what? "We'll be ready to do that, sir."

"All right, then. I predict NASA will approve the decision to evacuate as many personnel as we can to reduce the threat to lives, and then authorize us to take action against this guy rather than let him leave."

"I understand, sir, and my men will also."

"Good. Well, I'll let you get back to it. Keep me informed through Colonel Thomas of your preparations. It may happen sooner than we think."

"Yes, sir." Andras got up as the general rose from the chair and followed him to the rear of the room to sign out. As he exited the War Room he saw Colonel Thomas standing in the hallway, looking just a little short of explosive. Andras steeled himself as he walked up, determined not to get mad and do something stupid. He had the general's ear, Thomas couldn't hurt him so long as he kept that connection solid, and he was convinced more than ever that he could make this work.

Promotion, here I come.

～

GROUNDED. TOBY HATED THAT WORD, ESPECIALLY SINCE deciding he wanted to be a pilot. It brought visions of being bound to the Earth, or in this case his room in their apartment, unable to escape the incessant hold of an unseen force. His parents had terminated all privileges. School was the only approved activity outside the apartment, and his mom or dad escorted him there and back just to make sure.

In addition, Toby had to deal with the reality of what had happened. At first the experience in the chutes was a detached dream, something to discuss with a cop and then keep secret. But now, the impact had come home to roost whenever Toby recalled every detail of that first glimpse of the man's head, eyes peering at him out of the darkness from behind the mask. The fear seemed no less intense now than when it happened, but he managed to deal with it by concentrating on a sense of satisfaction underlying that fear, generated by pride in having fooled the man and beaten him at his own game. Strangely enough, the harrowing experience had allowed Toby to appreciate that he could do something really special.

Toby had never mentioned his special abilities to anyone. He wanted to, but didn't because of being laughed at, or thought of as a freak, or of losing the ability once it wasn't a secret anymore. But all of those doubts had been eliminated once his audio, spacial, and heat differential search abilities had proven themselves. The powers had been there when he *really* needed them, and they had saved his life.

Sitting alone in his room, Toby pondered the impact of recent events on his future. He would have to deal with the grounding as best he could, by concentrating on homework, doing better in school, and proving to his parents that he could be trusted.

But what was he going to do with all his spare time? As he thought about that, Toby glanced at the monitor sitting on the work desk built into the wall. It seemed to be staring at him like some huge single eye, a Cyclops seeing every move he made.

Well, now, there's an idea. He didn't use the computer in his room very much. He had access to one in study hall, and computers were always available at the library. But with all this captive time, why not?

Toby decided to find information on flying. If he put his mind to it, maybe he could get a head start on the process, learn the book stuff early and be ready to start the actual flying as soon as he got the opportunity.

He also had to find a way to talk over his plan with Brett, and the answer sat right there on the desk, right by the computer. The most basic of electronic communication tools, the phone. Forget about *seeing* Brett for a while, but his parents hadn't said anything about restricting his phone privileges. Just call him up.

With that decision made, Toby felt better and was anxious to get started. First things first. Homework. Glancing at the time, he saw that Rooster wouldn't be home yet with the assignment and he could put that chore off for an hour or so.

Next item, call Brett. Too soon, he's probably at work, and it'd be better to call him at home anyway to avoid being interrupted. That left the computer, still staring at him, waiting for instructions. He found a link for "Student Pilot's Manual." Remembering what Brett had said about the requirement for a student pilot's license, this seemed like a good place to start. He downloaded the manual and transferred the first three chapters to his tablet before closing his eyes for the eyelid leak check so popular with fighter pilots.

Although Toby had become more confident of his ability to call up a specific search pattern, he wasn't sure if he needed to be relaxed, or if he could speed up the process. He was also curious about whether it took conscious control, or if it could just occur on its own.

With a shudder he remembered the feeling just before he looked behind him and saw the man's masked face. He had been concentrating on the dark shape in front of him in the chute. And yet something warned him of the threat behind him. It couldn't have been a sound. The background noise level was too high for that. It was as if an internal device had detected danger and tapped him on the shoulder.

And now, before Toby even tried to take control, he heard the steady, rhythmic sound of water dripping. It must be the kitchen sink. His ability to audio search began in the direction he was facing. But from his experience in the chutes he knew it wasn't restricted there. Once the search was activated he could consciously control direction and distance.

For the next half hour Toby played with it, projecting his hearing in specific directions. He searched for the drip a few times and found that to be easy. Then he adjusted the direction and searched for things he knew made noise. His dad had an ancient wind-up alarm clock that had belonged to his grandfather. Toby found that he could focus on the drip in the kitchen sink, then swing to his right and immediately find the clicking of the clock.

He turned to his left on the bed so that the drip was to his right and the clock behind him. This was harder, because the initial extension of his search always seemed to be in the direction he was facing. Once out there it was easy to move left or right. After a bit of practice he was able to rapidly extend his focus, swing it right to the drip, then behind him to the ticking of the clock.

Toby tried the same drill with the space search and discovered that it was much harder. Things were too vague, like being out of focus. The big shapes were easy to distinguish. He could recognize the kitchen as different from the bedroom, but he couldn't find the kitchen faucet or the clock. It was during this practice that he remembered something else.

Given a uniform shape, like the roundness of the chutes or the basic box form of a room, he could detect variations caused by objects inside an area. Facing the living room just on the other side of his bedroom wall, Toby extended his focus and "felt" about the room. Here was the couch, the chair, the lamp, the bookcase, and so on until he had identified all the large objects in the room.

While conducting a space search of his parents' bedroom, he detected an object that stood out vividly from everything else. It seemed to be just beyond the bedroom, and as he extended his focus, the area seemed to shrink and the image of heat became vivid and sharp. Toby was puzzled as he searched around the room trying to determine what it was, and finally got up to go see for himself.

Of course. His parents' bathroom was just beyond their bedroom, and there on the counter by the sink sat his mom's curling iron, red light aglow, hot and ready for business. Toby unplugged the iron, and returned to his room remembering the sensation of heat within the chutes that turned out to be the man who tried to kill him.

Sitting on his bed, Toby reviewed what he'd learned. There were three modes to this ability . . . well, maybe four, counting the warning thing, which might be just a combination of the other modes that tied them all together. But no matter what he called them, they were valuable tools for a kid, especially for one who gets in so much trouble.

The phone rang. It was Brett, and hearing his voice gave Toby a little hope for controlling his own future.

He told Brett about the grounding. They danced around the issue for a few minutes, but finally got around to it. Brett was concerned that Toby might be mad about the way things turned out. But Toby was so glad to be talking with his hero that he didn't want to waste time on apologies.

"It's okay, Brett. My mom and dad have told me that most of what happens to us we bring on ourselves. I got caught, and now I have to pay the price."

Brett asked a few questions about the police interrogation, but Toby wanted to change the subject. This was an opportunity to talk with Brett about flying, and he didn't like wasting time with this other stuff. "I need some advice."

"About what?"

"Becoming a pilot. I know what you're going to say, that I'm too young to worry about this, and I can't learn to be a pilot on a space station, but I have a plan and I need your help with it."

"Toby, listen to me. Face reality for a minute. You live with your parents on Oasis. They're committed to stay and so are you. What kind of plan overcomes that?"

"Mine."

Brett laughed. "With that level of confidence, it just might, and I really wish you the best. I know you look down at Earth and long to see it for yourself, particularly with the notion of becoming a pilot. But it's not nearly as pretty as it looks when you get close, believe me. The future is where you are."

"Sure I want to visit Earth, Brett. I've never seen it except out a window, wondering what it's like. But with your help I can learn what I need to get a head start on being a pilot, like you did. My mom and dad will understand how much this means to me, and I—"

"Toby, if your parents—hold on a minute. I've got another call."

The line went dead, and Toby laid his head back on the pillow to wait. Within a few seconds he heard a voice that sounded just like Brett's. He started to answer when it became clear that his friend wasn't talking to him.

As Toby sat up the phone went dead again. He shook the handset, thinking there must be a bad connection. Placing it back to his ear, he heard only the silence of a line on hold.

Then the voice returned immediately, and Toby suddenly realized he was hearing the other conversation with his own audio search powers and there was nothing wrong with the phone. He quickly moved the handset away from his ear, embarrassed to be listening in.

But then he got curious. This was another way he could use his special abilities, something he hadn't been unaware of. He decided that as long as he was sitting here he might as well use the time to practice. If he'd learned anything today, it was that using his powers of search made them easier to initiate and control.

Toby placing the handset back to his ear, closed his eyes and relaxed. Brett's voice filled the receiver.

"—got another call waiting, sir. Why don't I take a moment to termi-nate that and I'll be right back with you."

"Don't bother, Captain, this won't take long. Lieutenant Colonel Parker tells me you wanted to volunteer for the mission yourself. You want to tell me about that?"

"Yes sir. I'm the best qualified. It's a dangerous undertaking. I have no immediate family stationed on Oasis. With the first day of the accident inquiry out of the way, it appears the system may come after my wings."

"Sounds like you're saying you don't have anything to lose."

"That's one interpretation, sir. But if my mistake contributed to the loss of that young pilot yesterday, there may be a measure of redemption for me personally. I might be able to prevent a disaster and save lives while risking mine alone."

Toby jerked upright on the bed. What does "dangerous undertak-ing" mean? Volunteer for what? Risking Brett's life?

The other voice said, *"Your squadron commander thinks you may bring your own agenda to the party and decide which of our instructions to follow and which ones to ignore."*

"With all due respect to the colonel, sir, that's bullshit. I haven't worn this uniform all these years to dishonor it now."

"Okay. That's a good answer, and what I thought you'd say. I want you

to take this mission. Without going into details now, consider the following to be your instructions.

Toby listened with mounting concern as the other voice told Brett he was now a member the "battle staff;" to get his flight gear ready to go; how serious the situation was with a bomb planted on Oasis; that Brett would be the pilot of the shuttle they were giving to someone; and his instructions could be considered as coming directly from the president.

Toby was near total panic when he heard a click and the sound of Brett's voice.

"Toby? You still here?"

"Uh . . . sure, Brett. What was that all about?"

"Just work stuff. Some things have come up that I need to take care of pretty quick. We'll get a chance to talk more about the flying soon. You asked for advice, so listen up. If you're really serious about this, read that student flight manual. We could get you ready to pass the written exam. You won't be old enough to take it for a while yet, but you can't start too early when you want to be the best."

Toby hardly heard Brett's words. They were finally discussing the one thing he'd been wanting to talk with him about, but it didn't mean anything. Brett was putting on a show for Toby's benefit. If he heard what he thought he heard, Brett was in for some very dangerous business.

"Toby? Did you hear me?"

"Yeah, sorry. Can I ask you a question?"

"At any other time, but I really do have to go now. We'll talk again soon."

Toby stared at a dead phone, stunned by the rapid turn of events. Within the last hour he'd seen his new plan for the future take shape and then come apart in the space of a few minutes. Being temporarily grounded was one thing, because he had a way to make that work to his advantage in the long run. But how was he going to prepare for becoming a pilot if Brett wasn't around to help him?

And what about the danger to Brett? Was it as bad as it appeared? Toby's imagination filled with visions of his friend sent off on some futile mission filled with danger, helpless in the hands of the same man who'd tried to kill him.

It's just not fair! Send someone else to do it!

Then he began to consider an option that scared him even before he acknowledged it.

He was convinced that Brett was the best pilot in the world, and that their friendship was one of a kind, worth doing anything to preserve no matter what. But from what he knew of the situation, being a good pilot might have less to do with survival than having a friend with the ability to extend his senses beyond the usual limits.

And what if the other voice was right? Somebody named Parker was worried Brett might take matters into his own hands and do something that wasn't authorized. Combine that with having nothing to lose and no family, along with a bomb that could make the station unfit to live on, and the picture forming in Toby's mind quickly became unbearable.

He had only one choice, to help Brett in any way he could. Some people might think that was a pretty bold decision for a kid, but he didn't look at it that way.

He'd already met the man who was causing all the trouble. In spite of the close calls, Toby had come out of it alive, and even better than that. He beat the guy at his own game and he could do it again because he knew what he was up against. There would be no playing around this time, nothing but the business of doing whatever it took to defeat him.

And if Brett really was planning to do something drastic and risk his own life, Toby could just get in the way. Brett might sacrifice himself if he had to, but he'd never put a kid in danger.

And so, armed with nothing other than the decision to do something, Toby went to the computer and found an annual issue on guns and ammunition dedicated to all the new products for the current year. He selected it for viewing and eventually found an image of a combat assault pump action 12 Ga. shotgun that looked like the one he had in the chute. It had the same short pistol grip, gaping wide muzzle, and was all black. Toby had no idea whether the gun he'd hidden in the chute was this specific weapon, or even what "12 Ga."

meant, but he knew one thing. He had a weapon if he needed one, and he was going to know how to use it. Time to find some operating instructions, an owner's manual, or something like that.

He found the owner's manual for the shotgun and downloaded it to his tablet. He opened the manual and began reading when so suddenly that he felt his bowels loosen, there was a knock at his bedroom door and his mother said, "Toby?"

As the door to his room opened, Toby wished he'd remembered to lock it. He turned enough to hide the tablet in his hand. "Hi, Mom, What's up?"

"I was going to ask you the same thing."

"I just downloaded some information about flying. When I was talking to Brett the other day he told me this was the first thing you learn when you start training. I just wanted to read about it."

His mom shook her head. "Your father and I have told you how we feel about that. Under the circumstances I thought you'd be smart enough not to provoke us by wasting your time with it."

"But I don't have my homework assignments yet. Rooster's not back from practice and won't be for an hour or more. I figured with the extra time I'll have being on restriction I can use the computer to get into some different subjects. Flying's just one of them. You ought to see all the stuff they have in there."

"I am not interested in other stuff. Here," she said, handing a piece of notepaper to him. "I went to school and apologized to your teachers for you. This's your homework for tomorrow, and I want you to concentrate on it until it's complete. The extra time, as you put it, had better be spent doing some quality schoolwork or this could be a real ordeal for you. Am I making myself clear?"

"Yes, ma'am. I would have done it first, Mom, if I'd known what the assignments were."

"That's good to hear. You would've known what the assignments were if you'd been even remotely involved with school today and not running around like some hooligan. Now put that other stuff down, start on your homework, and from now on you'll show it to your dad or me when you're through. If it doesn't meet with our approval, you'll do it over until it does."

"Yes, ma'am."

As his mom left the room, Toby breathed a huge sigh of relief. Studying the homework assignments, Toby realized he was going to have to do some reading. With the underlying tension of his secret plan competing for attention, he opened his backpack and removed his schoolbooks for what he hoped would be a short excursion into the relatively dull world of academics. There was a lot left to do tonight, and he'd never get to it unless this was done. Resigned to his fate, Toby read the first assignment and waded in.

9

DAY THREE EARLY EVENING

When Andras got back to his office, his blood pressure had almost returned to normal. Colonel Thomas had stopped him outside the War Room and reamed him out about exceeding his authority, going behind his back and trying to make him look bad in front of the general, blah, blah, blah. Andras was proud of himself for staying as calm as he did. The experience in the Battle Staff meetings had taught him something.

Power is relative. He'd always thought of it as absolute, but that was a fool's view. On a day-to-day basis, Andras answered only to Colonel Thomas. There were other police officers who outranked Andras, but he almost never saw them, either by his own design, or because Thomas had cut them all out of the loop and came to him directly.

But in the War Room, Colonel Thomas was a bootlicker around the general. As soon as Andras had gotten over his initial fear of being noticed, he was able to see that General DeSilva knew the difference between true competence and a smoke screen. Andras could read men, and he saw it happen. He watched the general as he listened to what was said and sifted through the information.

He also knew he'd made a name for himself in that room,

surrounded by all that rank and privilege, and he could use that to his advantage. Andras could extend his own power by infusing it with the implicit approval he received from the man who sat at the top of the Oasis command structure.

And yet that man, all-powerful in his immediate surroundings, undoubtedly said "sir" into the phone on a regular basis. And in the current situation, the general was unable to act on his own authority without specific approval from some nameless voice passing down a decision from some other nameless voice.

Power was where you found it. And for now, Andras had enough to meet his immediate goals. He instructed the duty sergeant to contact Doug and get an update on the Alpha Team. Then he called the engineering section and asked for a technician named Chip. Andras had assigned him the task of programming a robodog to be used in searching for the bomb.

Andras was waiting for Chip to answer the phone when the duty officer informed him he had a visitor. Thinking Chip must still be at the site of the explosion, he hung up and heard a voice say, "Sit, Noser."

Looking out the door, Andras saw a man in a white lab coat. His hair looked as if he'd stuck his finger in a light socket. There were at least a dozen pencils and pens sticking out of a breast pocket in one of those plastic protectors. A robodog sat by his left leg. Andras got up from the desk and walked to the door.

"Let me guess. You have got to be Chip, am I right?"

"Yes, Sergeant. You asked for assistance with a robodog?"

"I sure did." Andras stepped forward to shake Chip's hand.

The dog's reaction stopped him in his tracks. It was a classic attack-dog response to threat, and the growl sounded so real that Andras doubted for a moment whether this animal could possibly be a robot.

"Down, Noser," said Chip. The dog settled down beside Chip's feet. Noser's mouth was open, breathing like any dog, and its eyes were closed as Chip leaned over and scratched its head. "Sorry about that, Sergeant, but he's still got the attack program installed. He'll protect the owner of the voice he's been told to obey. That's me for now, so don't make any sudden moves."

Andras never liked working around Dan's robodog Snooper, and he didn't like this any better. Backing away, he said, "Fine with me. You and the dog come on in the office. Noser?"

"Heel," ordered Chip as he followed Andras. "Yeah, it seemed like an appropriate moniker at the time. I gave him a sensitive one to do the job, and I think it'll work well."

Andras sat at his desk while Chip took a chair and Noser curled at his feet. "So, what can you tell me about using the dog to find an explosive?"

"It was quite easy, really. After you called I went to the K-Nine section and checked this one out of the kennels."

Give me a break here. "The kennels?"

"What else would handlers call the storage facility for the dogs? Anyway, I went through the manuals and discovered how to set up the olfactory search program, which is a combination of two factors, the characteristics of the target odor itself, and the sensitivity you want to program into the detection circuits. I used debris from the explosion site for the target scent and ran some tests. Noser was able to alert on trace amounts. But it's only a guess as to how successful a search will be in a real situation."

"Why's that? If the dog can find a small amount he should be able to find a bunch of the stuff, right?"

"Not necessarily. The odor used as the target is from the residue of an explosion and not the explosive itself. The difference is significant because of the changes the original material goes through in creating an explosion. It might be that the dog will alert only on residue and ignore the explosive."

Andras took a moment to digest this information. One of his concerns was using a dog to conduct a useless search of the core and alerting the man to the impending pursuit. "Is it worth even trying?"

Chip nodded his head. "You bet. From the technical perspective, that is. There may be mitigating operational considerations, but I wanted you to know the realistic chances of success with the dogs."

"Okay," said Andras. "Is the dog ready to go?"

"With one exception. If you want someone other than me to initiate the search commands we'll have to program the dog to accept his voice. That's another area of specific programming, and it's required to keep the dogs under the tight control of only one person. If you've seen the dogs in action, you know why."

No shit. Andras got up from his desk to shake Chip's hand when he remembered the dog's reaction the first time. From behind the desk and with his hands behind his back, Andras said, "Thanks for all your good work."

Chip nodded and told the dog to heel. Andras watched as the animal, or rather the robot, got up off the floor and assumed a position locked to Chip's left leg. The dog's movements were so lifelike that it really was difficult to think of it as an it.

Andras sat down at his desk and remembered he'd taken off his equipment belt and removed the earpiece for the radio tuned to the man's frequency. He didn't expect the guy to be calling him, but he put the earpiece back in anyway and was greeted with the familiar sound of that voice.

"Cadogan, where the hell are you? Do you read me?"

FOLLOWING THE INCIDENT WITH THE KID, SAMAEL HAD SECURED the cop in the reactor room and decided to take care of the bomb. He retrieved the bag of explosives, found the targeted spot, and carefully went through the process of assembling the device and positioning it correctly. When the device was ready, he unfolded the diagrams of the power core and studied them. He'd been told only what they wanted him to know about the bomb and its purpose, but he knew enough to come to his own conclusion about the ultimate objective.

The threat to the station had to be real, or at least perceived as such, or there'd be no leverage. If obtaining a shuttle and a fighter was the goal, it wouldn't matter what the bomb did or didn't do. It could be nothing more than a bluff and still have served its purpose.

But the device he'd just assembled was no bluff. This much explosive detonating close to a nuclear reactor would be deadly serious. His employer more than likely wanted more than to run off with a couple of spacecraft and a personal pilot.

The most sophisticated security network on Oasis protected the nuclear reactor, but Samael didn't have to disable it. He was given an access code to open any of the doors into the area with the keypad entry system. The system had been reprogrammed to accept this code without creating a record of the entry. That was the best kind of security breach, an invisible one.

So if the code had worked as advertised, they wouldn't know he'd been inside the reactor room. And in the absence of any alarms or alerts, they might not consider the possibility he had been there, or that the bomb might be hidden inside. This charade would only have to work until he was on his way, providing him with a period of time to maneuver and accomplish his objectives.

Samael reached into the bag and took out one of the remote detonating devices. He had one for each entrance into the reactor area plus two spares. They were capable of detonating the bomb on demand, but he had absolutely no interest in that option. The detonators could also be set to activate at a specific time, or after a preset elapsed time.

His instructions were to attach one device to each of the doors, and hide the other two so they could not be found easily. Just prior to departure, he was to activate the last one and exit the reactor room, which would now be closed off from station personnel. Opening any door would trigger one of the devices, initiating a short delay. If the proper code was not entered within that time, bomb detonation would occur at termination of the timer.

But why? Samael had been hired to take control of a shuttle and get it back to Earth, but not until he put the station in jeopardy. Maybe the shuttle and its cargo were the only objectives, but he didn't think so.

With the nuclear core off-limits to authorities, and the threat of destruction hanging over their heads, they would be rendered helpless whether he was there or not. Why would his employer then give up such a powerful weapon? There had to be something else to this, and the only objective that made any sense was to take control of Oasis.

After attaching and activating the devices, he took a tour and looked for places to hide the two backups. He positioned one, but returned the last device to the bag. Instinct told him to have in his possession a remote link to the bomb. Once out of the relative safety of the central core and on the move toward the loading dock, the device might make the difference. Would they rush or shoot at a man holding a remote detonating device? He didn't think so, and regardless of his instructions to the contrary, he kept one.

Samael got the radio tuned to the secure frequency and walked to the opposite side of the reactor area. The time had come to call the cop again and stir things up a little.

"Cadogan, this is you know who. How do you read me?"

No answer. The shit bird was never there when you needed him.

"Cadogan, where the hell are you? Do you read me?"

THE SOUND OF THE VOICE IN THE EARPIECE STARTLED ANDRAS. It sent a chill down his spine and the fear that he was going to end up trapped on Oasis with nothing but enemies for company and no way out. All the preparations, enthusiasm and optimism of the past few hours disappeared in an instant.

"Cadogan! I'm talking to you!"

Walking into the corner of his office away from the door, Andras put the radio close to his lips and softly spoke into the microphone. "What do you want?"

"You're a hard man to get hold of."

Working both sides of the middle was proving to be harder than Andras thought, especially with the double-cross in the works. "Sorry. I took the earpiece out and forgot to turn up the volume."

Andras waited for what seemed like a long time, and began to think that the radio might have quit when the voice said, "What's going on with the police? Will they try to stop the shuttle?"

"No signs of that. They're scared shitless of the bomb."

After a pause the man responded. "If that changes, convince them that would be a mistake, and that if they aren't immobilized by the bomb, they haven't thought it through well enough."

Andras was thinking on his feet now, looking for ways to put the guy at ease and off guard. "You've got nothing to worry about. I've been reminding them how difficult it would be to find the bomb, and that mounting a search would be useless and could get us all killed."

"Good. Let me know if that changes. They'll tell you, maybe ask you to plan it, right? Being a sergeant and all."

"Right." *What the hell else can I say?* "You'll be the first to know."

"Next subject. I'm curious to know if a kid reported anything to the police about a problem in the chutes."

"He sure did. We've had trouble with him before about going into off-limits areas, but I think that's over for good. He's so scared he won't go near the chutes again."

"Anybody else know about it?"

"There may be one other, a pilot the kid went to right after it happened. He was the one who called us to report it."

"But as soon as he tells his parents what happened it'll be all over the station."

"No. I took care of that by making the kid think he was part of a secret police operation. I told him if he mentioned it to anyone I'd throw his ass in jail. I had him alone in the interrogation room. He isn't going to tell anyone."

"So they don't know I'm in the chutes?"

"They may suspect it. There's only so many places you can hide, but the whole chute and central core area is large enough that you don't have to worry about that, and definitely not because of the kid."

There was a long pause before the man replied. "Okay. That's all for now. And don't forget to monitor the radio."

Andras didn't bother to acknowledge. This fence-sitting was about to end. Once he realized he was being played for the fool and decided to change loyalties again, he became committed to his plan. And if DeSilva told him to go ahead with it, Andras would be staking his own life on the outcome.

Success meant redemption, basking in glory as savior of the station, a chance for promotion, all the goodies. Failure equated to living with the uncertainty of a certain fate.

Uncertain, in that the guy might not come back. Andras had always assumed he would, being led to believe when the shuttle returned to Oasis it would bring a new order of business and a radically different mission.

But what if they neutralized the bomb threat and the military got involved once the shuttle departed? Or if the real objective was just to take the spacecraft? In either case, life on Oasis might end up almost back to normal, same old shit, but with the possibility someone on both sides might know of Andras's treachery.

That possibility read like a real long shot, however. He couldn't imagine all this trouble for two spacecraft, which led to the realization that his life wasn't worth much. They'd come back, take over, and without hesitation exact their revenge. Andras shuddered at the thought of being hunted down with no place to hide, no way to escape the inevitable.

Andras got up from the desk knowing that he could do all the preparation he wanted, obtain the shoot-to-kill order, and convince the men to do that without hesitation. But in the end he could trust only one person to pull the trigger. Time was running out, and it didn't matter what the president, or whoever in hell it would be, told them to do. The Alpha Team would follow his orders. If it meant a wildcat action, so be it. It was his only chance to control the outcome.

He grabbed his hat off the couch and opened the door between his office and the front desk area where the duty officer sat. "Find Doug and have him call me with his current location. If Colonel Thomas calls tell him I'm off the radio for a short time, but find out what he wants and call me ASAP." Without waiting for a reply, Andras turned to close the door and leave the back way when the voice of the duty officer stopped him.

"Sergeant Cadogan? Colonel Thomas just called, and you're wanted in the War Room."

Shit! Every time he had something important to do they called a Battle Staff meeting.

"Tell them I'm on my way." Although Andras was frustrated at the interruption, he was also thankful to be included in the decision-making process. At least he had the opportunity to show the general what he could do and accomplish some manipulating of his own.

Encouraged by that thought, Andras hurried to the War Room,

anxious to be there early and not miss anything. This might even be the moment he'd been waiting for, the official approval to search for and destroy the man in black.

SAMAEL REPLACED THE RADIO IN THE EQUIPMENT BAG AND smiled. This Cadogan fellow was comedy in action. The fool probably thought they were actually going to keep their part of the bargain. And he could hear it in the cop's voice now, the deception, trying to cover up the fact he knows exactly what's going on and can't reveal it without blowing his double-cross out of the water.

So they're planning something. Samael examined the problem from his opponents' viewpoint as he walked back toward the reactor area and tried to anticipate their moves.

What's the possibility they'd just go along with his demands and let him leave in the shuttle? Slim to zilch. They couldn't stand by while somebody waltzed in and stole a couple of spacecraft. Unless they planned to come after him later without jeopardizing the station. Lots of luck with that.

But what about the bomb? They have to fear it. They could search all they want afterwards. But even if they discovered it, two things would keep them at bay. If they tamper with it the bomb would detonate at a specific time unless they got the disarm code. They couldn't get the code until he gave it to them. They had to let him go, didn't they? But something nagged at him about the plan, a small but important overlooked detail. Approaching the reactor room, Samael suddenly realized what it was.

The doors into the reactor were protected by a security system and unauthorized entrance triggered alarms. But even when station personnel turned the system off to enter, the system recorded the fact. When Samael used the special code, however, the system ignored the entry. This invisible breach was helpful during the initial stages, but it created a problem for later.

The authorities had to believe the bomb existed or it wouldn't force them to do anything. With no evidence of unauthorized entry into the reactor room, why would they believe the bomb was located there? And worse yet, they might not hesitate to go inside and look, which would activate the timers and detonate the bomb. The idea wasn't to blow the place up, but keep people away from the bomb and docile long enough for other things to happen.

Samael concluded that it wasn't good enough to leave the bomb in the reactor room and depart on the shuttle having left only a vague warning that it was hidden somewhere on the station and don't mess with it. His entry into the reactor room was too invisible. He had to have it that way now for a place to hide, but once he was out and on the move, the station authorities needed a reason to fear going in there. Samael decided that when he entered and exited the reactor room for the last time, he wouldn't use the special passcode he'd been given. The resulting single unauthorized entry-exit activity would prove he'd been inside and focus attention of station authorities on the bomb in the reactor room during shuttle departure, the most vulnerable period of the entire operation.

Samael checked on his prisoner and found him sleeping soundly. The pain pills must be some powerful medicine to put him out like that. After making one last security check of the doors into the reactor room, he lay down with his head on the equipment bag and began yet another review of his plan to end up as the victor in this contest of wills between Samael, his employers, station authorities, a treacherous cop, and a kid who couldn't mind his own business and would soon pay the price.

Brett entered the War Room and paused, amazed at the huge conference table, the massive array of communications gear, the view beyond the glass into the Command Post, the amount of activity in progress, and a cop standing just inside the door, decked out in full SWAT gear, holding at the ready the meanest short-barreled shotgun Brett had ever seen. He didn't know they had any weapons like that on Oasis. That big sergeant named Cadogan stood on the other side of the entrance beside a table.

"If you would, Captain Larsen, please read the statement at the top of this page, fill in the form at the bottom, and sign it."

The statement established the security rules governing the meetings of the Battle Staff in the War Room, standard stuff with regard to classified material. Brett signed it and handed it back to the sergeant, who suddenly came to attention and commanded, "OFFICERS! ATTENTION!" The last word was drawn out, and Brett hadn't heard it spoken like that since boot camp. He turned to face the entrance and assumed the position as General DeSilva walked into the room.

Enlisted personnel normally didn't command officers to do anything. But a precedent in military courtesy dictated that when the most superior officer entered a room, the person who saw him first should call the area to attention. On most occasions, an officer arriving with the ranking individual would perform the honors.

But as Brett watched an entourage of rank enter the room behind the general, he noticed that the second officer to enter, who Brett recognized as Colonel Thomas, was glaring at Cadogan with a look that could kill.

At the command "SEATS!" from the general, Brett looked for a place to sit. Junior officers and enlisted personnel always sat the farthest from the head of the table in order of rank, and he ended up at the end opposite the general. Brett sat down, wondering if they were going to issue binoculars and megaphones. It was a *big* table.

As Sergeant Cadogan sat beside Brett and nodded, he noticed a barely suppressed grin. He glanced down the table at Colonel Thomas and knew immediately that the sergeant had planned it to yank the colonel's chain.

The SWAT guy closed the door and activated the security system. Figuring he was here just to observe, Brett settled back and prepared to listen. It was quiet, the general looking at some papers in front of him, and everyone else would sit like this until the ranking officer started things off. They didn't have long to wait.

"This meeting of the Battle Staff is called to order. Our first item is the status of preparations. Colonel Radcliff?"

Brett didn't think he'd ever seen the man. Probably a paper-pushing admin type, or maybe the general's executive officer.

"Yes, sir. You directed me to assess the capability of the available shuttles to conduct a partial evacuation of the station. The factors involved in my analysis were the number of shuttles available, as affected by reduction in operational capability due to maintenance, cargo capacity in numbers of persons that can be carried per load, total number of persons requiring evacuation to reduce station population to minimum essential manning, and the time required to complete the evacuation."

Yup. This guy was definitely one of those types.

"As for shuttle availability—"

"Excuse me, Colonel Radcliff," said the general, "but I think in the interest of time it would be advisable to summarize your findings rather than present the details. Let's save that for questions, if there are any, and stick to the essential question of whether we can do what want in the time available."

A look of disappointment flashed across the man's face. He'd done his homework and wasn't going to be able to strut his stuff. But he recovered nicely, proof he would go a lot farther in this man's military.

"Certainly, sir. The evacuation can be completed prior to the deadline only on the condition that we do not delay the decision and initiate the actions required in a timely manner."

"What does 'timely manner' mean, exactly?"

The colonel glanced at his watch, then at some papers in front of him. "Within two hours from now."

Brett didn't know what had gone on before in the War Room, but this answer obviously made an impression on the men at the table. It was as if they all realized something at the same time. No one said anything for a moment, waiting for the general to do what generals are supposed to do, make the big decisions.

"That means we'd better get on with what we have to do here. NASA agrees, so we'll conduct a partial evacuation of the station as soon as feasible. Colonel Radcliff, do you have the essential personnel list?"

"Yes, sir. We assumed a twelve-on-twelve-off schedule. Evacuating all non-essential personnel, and one-third of the requisite population normally assigned in three eight-hour shifts, we have reduced the number of persons at risk below the maximum capability of the lifeships.

"I don't want to get into Captain Norton's area, but I did coordinate with him to determine how the lifeship testing was going. Projecting a ten to fifteen percent failure rate, no person would be denied escape due to lack of lifeship capability."

Brett was impressed. This paper-pusher really had his act together. After a few minutes of discussion, they decided the standard contingency plan wouldn't work because it assumed a sudden emergency condition.

This would be a selective evacuation, requiring an efficient way to tell people who was staying, who was leaving, and when. They decided on a station-wide announcement, followed by an order for everyone not engaged in essential activities to return to their apartment and monitor the emergency net for instructions.

General DeSilva didn't give anyone time to think about or question this unprecedented step. "Sergeant Cadogan, what do you have to report on the use of robodogs to search for the explosives?"

Brett wasn't sure Cadogan was alive, much less awake, but he perked up.

"A dog has been successfully programmed, sir. The expert who did the programming has offered to serve as the handler for the operation."

"Who normally handles the dogs?"

"Members of the K-Nine unit, sir. Each dog is assigned to one handler, programmed to accept orders only from him."

"You don't say. Is this expert a cop?"

"No, sir. He's a member of the Technical Engineering Unit."

"I like the idea of using volunteers, but I'm not sure I agree with having an engineer involved in the front lines of a dangerous operation like this."

"Excuse me, General, but he won't really be on the front lines. He can direct the dog from a remote location using the dog's video and a transmitter to send voice commands."

Brett had no idea you could do that with a robodog. What fun that would be at a squadron party. Chase that fool Jake away from all the pretty women and leave some foxes available for the rest of the pilots.

"Okay," said the general, "but I want a cop with him if he gets anywhere near the action."

"Will do, sir."

The general addressed the group. "The net will be in place prior to initiating the search for the bomb. Sergeant Cadogan, inform this expert of yours that he'll be the handler, and make certain all preparations are completed so he'll be ready at a moment's notice to begin the search."

"Yes, sir."

"Next subject. Captain Norton, from what Colonel Radcliff said, am I to assume that we've found a ten to fifteen percent failure rate in lifeship self-tests?"

Brett knew stress when he saw it, and Norton had just swallowed a big glass of trouble. But he handled it well, explaining that the self-tests only identified the pass/fail status of systems. To determine specific problems and how to fix them, further diagnostics were required. The effort was way behind schedule.

Silence reigned in the room as everyone else seemed to shrink into their chairs to avoid collateral damage when a four-star general pulled out the big-bore word cannon.

General DeSilva fired the first salvo with, "I find it incomprehensible that a system designed for the evacuation of this station is not only inadequate to begin with, but is also fifteen percent under capacity due to systems failures. But since that's what we're stuck with, I want a plan to ensure all personnel remaining on board will be able to evacuate under emergency conditions at a moment's notice.

"Captain Norton, I want you personally to ensure that every person who remains aboard following the shuttle evacuation is aware of the actions required to get off the station successfully. We can order them to stay, we can put them in danger, but I'll be damned if we'll ask them to commit suicide. Understood?"

"Absolutely, sir."

The depth of planning for this crisis really impressed Brett. He'd always assumed that meetings like this were of no use other than to create confusion among the troops. Pilots had a saying for it: *The key to tactical aviation is flexibility, and the key to flexibility is indecision.* If you never make a decision, no one can ever fault you for making the wrong one.

But this discussion was way different. Evacuate the station? Who would've ever thought it?

General DeSilva asked Sergeant Cadogan about the Alpha radio net. The sergeant said it was a go, and explained that when the hijacker communicated again with Comm Central, the SWAT team would be in place, ready to move in as the search narrowed down the man's location. The objective was to block his access to the bomb, and capture him if possible. NASA had agreed on one attempt, but only if they had a reasonable chance of success. General DeSilva got to define reasonable.

The general paused, looking around the table at the men staring at him. Brett noticed that most of the others seemed puzzled, and he was wondering why when General DeSilva held up his hands. "I know, you're all wondering about the bomb. How do we know if we've isolated him from it and what about the remote device?

As multiple heads around the table nodded, in a communal visual reply to the effect of, *Yessir, you got that right,* the general said, "Engineering has determined that the most logical place for the bomb is in the reactor room. But we've detected no access within the last twenty-four to thirty-six hours, so one of our enterprising command post controllers ran a self-test of the security system and found indication of a code problem in the keypad lock to the main door.

"We're going to send in a robodog to have a look-see. If we can do that without alerting this guy and find evidence to confirm there is a bomb and its location, the problem becomes much simpler. We confirm that he isn't in the reactor room, send in the team to block him from reentering the area, then take him if we can."

Now that Brett was getting up to speed, the general's comment about a remote device made some sense, but only if they could block the guy from just pressing a button and boom we're all dead.

General DeSilva addressed that possibility next. "For this defensive tactic to have any chance of working, we have to determine whether the bomb can, and more importantly, will be remote detonated. According to NASA, the possibility is slight. They believe the goal has to be more than stealing a shuttle or two. These guys want the station, and destruction isn't part of the plan.

"If that assessment is faulty, the next factor is how far away the remote can be used to trigger the bomb. All remote devices have a limited range, but we have no way of knowing what it is. So, we take a chance. And that's the reason we have to be ready to abandon ship quickly."

Lieutenant Colonel Parker leaned forward and motioned toward Brett. "Captain Larsen is the newest member of the Battle Staff, and we included him in these discussions because he'll pilot the shuttle in the event this situation gets to that point. I asked him to monitor the shuttle preparations and will let him bring us up to date. Captain Larsen?"

Talk about reacting quickly. Brett has just taken the hot seat, with all eyes focused on him. "Yes, sir. When I left the loading dock for this meeting, the estimated time to repair a couple of items and have the shuttle ready for launch was between nine and eleven hours." Brett summarized the status of the fighter computer problem, tie-down fitting repair, and what was being done to complete preparations. "The chief tells me he'll have the shuttle ready to go."

The general nodded. "Captain Larsen, when and if you leave here with the man in the shuttle, anything could happen. We don't know what else he wants, how long it will take, nothing. Speculation is fine for planning purposes, but in the end neither of us will know what the other is doing. So how do we assess the effects of our independent actions on the other?"

"Bottom line is we can't. Once you leave here I must insist that you consider the bomb to be the single most important factor defining your decisions. The hijacker tells you to do something, I want you to do it, period. I hope that's clear."

"Understood sir. I also have a suggestion to provide us flexibility, and maybe change the ground rules at a later date."

The general smiled, then chuckled softly and shook his head. "Change the ground rules? You fighter pilots are all alike. You want to own the ballpark, both teams, the ball and bat, and run the scoreboard too. Perhaps you should expand on this proposed change before I agree to it."

"Yes, sir. Let's assume we can't keep this guy from taking the shuttle, and the bomb is a continuing threat at the time of departure. Then after he's gone you neutralize it or find out it's a bluff. If I knew that, why couldn't I be authorized to take independent action?"

"Communication will be the key. I'll work with the avionics techs and splice a discrete radio channel into my headset. You find out something I need to know, put the information on that frequency and transmit it in a continuous loop. If I don't have the helmet on, the information will be there when I put it on the next time. The hijacker will never know the difference."

General DeSilva nodded. "That's a damned fine idea, captain. I don't suppose you have a plan in mind to regain control of the shuttle?"

"Not really, sir. But if this man has weaknesses, maybe I can exploit them. And the one advantage I have, no matter how well he's trained, or how elaborate the preparations were to send him up here, is that he has to rely on me to pilot the spacecraft."

"Very well. I accept your assurance that in the absence of new information to the contrary, you'll do what the man tells you."

General DeSilva turned his attention to the group. "Gentlemen, we're approaching a turning point in our dilemma. If you believe the history books, great leaders always seem to come up with something inspiring and motivational to say on the eve of a great battle. I guess I won't be recorded as a great leader, because I don't have much else to say.

"Each of you knows what is required of you and the importance of what we seek to accomplish. If there are no further comments, this meeting of the Battle Staff will stand adjourned."

The senior officer's departure from a room demanded the same courtesy as his arrival. Brett stood at attention until Colonel Thomas gave the "AS YOU WERE!" command, then waited until everyone else had left. Alone with only the silence surrounding him, Brett walked over to the observation window and watched the activity in the command post. Staring at notations on the status board tracking shuttle preparations, he once again acknowledged to himself that the hijacker would never succeed because Captain Brett Larsen, United States Space Command, would do whatever necessary to prevent it.

DINNER HAD BEEN A SUBDUED AFFAIR. AFTER TOBY FINISHED rinsing the dishes and filling the dishwasher, he mumbled to his parents about doing his homework and went to his room, closed the door, and sat down at the computer.

His homework was typically easy, which allowed him to resume his research into flying. He started reading about the forces acting on an airplane in flight when the public address system suddenly came to life and a voice filled the room ordering everyone to stand by for an announcement from the commander.

After a short pause, a voice of authority flowed out of the PA speaker in the ceiling.

"Good evening. This is General DeSilva. I ask you to stop what-ever you're doing and listen carefully.

"Yesterday two unauthorized passengers arrived on the noon shut-tle. One individual began firing at officers and was killed. An accom-plice escaped and is hiding, whereabouts unknown. This person has presented demands and threatens to damage the station if we don't comply. He also claims responsibility for the explosion that occurred yesterday afternoon.

"As a result of these developments, I have ordered a partial evacua-tion of the station to the moon colony. Following this announcement, a list of personnel currently manning essential positions will be posted on the central bulletin board and announced over the PA. If you are currently on duty in one of these positions, remain where you are for further instructions. Do not leave your post.

"All other personnel return to your apartment without delay. Refer to your emergency checklist and follow the instructions. Remain in your apartment and monitor the emergency net for evacuation instruction.

"This evacuation is precautionary in nature. There is no immediate danger to the station or its personnel and no reason for undue haste that violates normal safety standards. Remain calm, follow instructions, and let's get this done in the same spirit of excellence we use every day on Oasis. Thank you for your attention. DeSilva out."

Toby sat immobile at his small desk, stunned by the realization that evacuation to the moon colony would eliminate any chance of helping Brett. As the PA announced a long list of duty positions, he got up to talk with his parents about what this meant.

Then the monitor on his desk come to life. Every computer on Oasis was connected to the same network, and commands could be sent from a central mainframe to every terminal. The first item was a repeat of the general's speech, followed by a list of essential duty positions being read over the PA. The list ended with a notice to standby for further announcements. Then it appeared.

To: Jason Theodore Williams
Lisa Ashley Williams
Tobias David Williams

From: Oasis Command Central, Emergency Communications Division
Re: Station Evacuation, Special Order No. 54-12

IAW with referenced Special Order you are directed to complete preparations for evacuation to Lunar Colony Base #1. In the absence of further instructions to the contrary, you will remain in your apartment until such time as necessary to arrive for processing and departure at the time and place indicated below.

Date: 24 May, Oasis Year 0021
Time: 0300 hours
Place: Sector Four Loading Dock, Level One Entrance

End Transmission

Toby stared at the screen. He read it again, but it said the same thing. And although he had closeup and personal knowledge of events leading to this moment, the shock was almost too much to handle.

He sat down at the desk, trying desperately to come up with something to make the impending deadline go away. But it stared back at him, and he had less than six hours to decide what he should do.

If he went to the moon colony with his parents, the crisis might be quickly resolved. Then he could return to the normal routine of life on Oasis. But the conversation Toby overheard between Brett and the other man indicated the station might be abandoned. How long would it take to get back? Would he ever get back? The time had come to decide his very next, immediate course of action.

Toby loved his parents, and understood his place was with them. But if by leaving them now he could figure out a way to help Brett and be a part of solving their common problem, then he might be able to have it all.

"Toby? Would you come in here for a minute please?"

"Yes ma'am." Then without a moment's hesitation, he selected the message and deleted it. The later his parents knew about the evacuation, the more time he'd have to put his plan into motion.

He found his parents talking softly in the living room and noticed they were smiling.

Sit down for a minute, Toby," said his mom. "We need to talk to you about something."

"You heard the general's announcement, right?" asked his father.

"Yes, sir, most of it. I was working on my homework. Does it mean we have to leave Oasis?"

"It appears that way at the moment. Your mom and I won't be included on the essential personnel list, so we can expect to be evacuated earlier rather than later. I know this is all confusing to you, but we don't want you to worry about it. We'll be together, and this thing will be cleared up in no time.

"There's an emergency checklist in the center drawer of the computer desk. Look on page twelve for the list of personal items to pack. Leave them out for your mother or me to check before you pack them in that big bag on the top shelf of your closet. Call us when you get that done, and then you can go to bed."

"Yes, sir." Toby went to his room. He packed a change of clothes in the backpack, along with some packaged food he had stored away for when he missed dinner. Then he realized he'd need a better way to hide the shotgun.

He found a laundry bag in his closet that looked large enough to cover the weapon. He put it in his backpack, along with the pilot's manual and the shotgun information, and concealed it under some dirty clothes in his closet.

Using the checklist, Toby assembled the items listed and got the big duffle out of the closet. Once satisfied the effort would pass inspection, he went into the living room to find his parents. They weren't there, and the door to their bedroom was closed. He went into the kitchen to pour some juice and sat down at the table. Closing his eyes, he relaxed just a bit and almost immediately began to extend his audio search into the next room where his parents were.

He heard snatches of a conversation, but lost it quickly as the sounds of a dishwasher filled his ears. Must have gone too far, into the kitchen of the adjacent apartment. Concentrating on bringing the search back toward him, Toby heard his dad's voice.

"—*serious business going on, and it doesn't matter if Toby's trouble had anything to do with the current crisis or not. The family issue is whether he should be allowed to keep something from us. He says he can't tell us because the cop told him not to. You don't accept that, fine, I understand. But that issue needs to wait while we deal with the current crisis. Doesn't that sound reasonable?*"

"*Of course, Jason. I just can't get the thought out of my head that Toby has been involved with this. Scares the squat out of me, to be perfectly frank about it.*"

"*I feel the same way. The evacuation is frightening, but at least it means we're out of immediate danger. It will also prevent any further involvement by Toby in the crisis.*"

Toby lost interest in this conversation, canceled the audio search, and suddenly realized that he'd made up his mind: he could not afford to be isolated on the moon colony. Everything he had ever dreamed of doing would be left in the hands of someone else. Finishing the juice, he told his parents he was ready. His mom looked at his clothes and they packed the duffle bag together.

When they were done, his mom pulled him close to her and said, "I want you to get to bed as soon as you can. We don't know when our evacuation order will arrive, and it may be a while before we get a good night's sleep. Okay?"

Toby nodded and his mom kissed him, hugged him for a moment, and left the room. He got ready for bed, turned out the light and climbed in. Lying there thinking about his future, he felt a strange combination of fear and excitement, enough so that he knew it would be impossible to sleep.

But he was wrong. Sleep did come, and dreams of flying airplanes soared in his head.

Sweat trickled down Andras's face and into his eyes. Nervous tension always made him perspire, along with the extra clothing and vest he wore. He listened as Doug directed the deployment of the Alpha Team.

Andras was proud of the men and the way they had taken to this assignment. He deliberately kept them in the dark about some things, however. This was no time to be thinking about anything other than the job he wanted them to do. He was confident that when he gave the command to go, the men would respond without hesitation. If things went bad they could always defend themselves truthfully. They were simply following orders. If things went well, Andras would gladly take any heat from above. After a short period of criticism for having exceeded his authority, he would assume his rightful position as hero of the hour.

"Sergeant Cadogan?"

"Yo, Doug. What's up?"

"We got a problem with Alpha Two's radio. I'm sending him a replacement. As soon as he gets it and we check the net again we'll be ready."

"Okay. Get it done. The general is waiting for word."

"It's on the way, Sergeant."

A commotion at the back of the room got Andras's attention. He turned to see Chip and one of the robodogs enter the room. The dogs looked so real, even when you knew they weren't. "We ready?"

Chip nodded. "Yes, Sergeant. Noser is all primed and eager to get on with it. We ran some more tests and I think my concern over residue versus original material was too pessimistic."

"Good news," said Andras. "Come on over to the diagram and let's talk this over one more time. Have you decided how to insert the dog?"

"You can call him Noser. After working with him so much over the past few hours, I have to tell you the guy who designed these was really good. This dog will respond to a scratch behind the ears just like Rover from back home, and when that tongue gives you a lick you'd swear somebody smuggled a real dog up here."

Yeah, sure. "Let's don't get carried away here. You realize we're sending your doggie *friend* into a dangerous situation, right? Might get shot. Killed, even. You ready for that?"

Chip looked hurt and angry at the same time. "I'm not ready for *anything* to get shot, die, or whatever. But you might show a little appreciation that the dog takes the risks so you don't have to."

If you really want the dog to help, teach it—uh—him to shoot a pistol. "Okay, Chip, okay. Have it your way. But back to the question. How do we get *him* in?"

Chip commanded the dog to stay, walked over to the desk and picked up a pencil. He pointed to the diagram. "I figured we could put him in the core about here, have him look around, do a circuit or two, then try the reactor room."

Andras shook his head. "The core's easy. Lots of entry points. But the reactor room doors have to be considered armed. How do you plan to get the dog in there?"

Chip examined the diagram more closely. "It doesn't show here, but I checked out the engineering drawings of the environmental control ducting. Right up here in the ceiling there's a series of panels that can be removed for maintenance."

"Hold it. This's a robotic dog here, a mechanical gadget. How does it open a panel?"

Chip looked at Andras as if he were a dunce. "You just won't give this critter any credit, will you? The panels are opened with a lever. I've trained him to open it. And from the top, inside the duct, the latch sticks up enough for the dog to grab it in his mouth and turn. The panel will swing away and he can drop to the floor without setting off any door alarms."

Andras was speechless for a moment. "How the hell did you come up with that idea?"

"I went to the environmental control engineers, studied the diagrams, and got them to show me a panel. Then I trained Noser to turn the lever and programmed the command in his computer. I say it, he does it. Simple."

There I go, underestimating people again. "That's good work. Then what?"

"Once he's inside I can have him look wherever I want, or put him on auto search, visual, olfactory, whatever. You ought to see him, it's really something."

"I'd like to, believe me. Let's get this thing on the road. You ready?"

"Absolutely. How about it Noser? Want to go to work?"

Chip reached down and the thing raised its snout to lick his hand. The dog really was something. *It's getting so you can't trust anything anymore, and know what's real, or what isn't.*

Andras asked Chip to wait a minute, then got Doug's attention and took him over to the side of the room. "I'm going with the dog and its—uh . . . *his* handler. When the net's in place, call me and I'll inform the general. Remember the announcement may have started the target moving, so be ready to respond if he tries to contact Comm Central. If that happens and he stays in one place long enough, you may be able to pin down a location and avoid the deadline altogether. Understood?"

"Roger that, boss. We'll be ready."

"And do not, under any circumstances, enter the core until you hear from me."

"I've got it, Sergeant."

Andras motioned for Chip to follow him and led the way out of the office to an elevator. Using his preemptive privilege, he commandeered an elevator and took them up toward the core while reviewing with Chip the objectives of the search.

Andras had decided the place to be was close to the core so he could enter it quickly. With the dog's video transmitted to Chip's handheld monitor, Andras might be able to see something to confirm the man's current location. He was more than ready to take control, by launching the team, directing them into blocking positions, and flushing the man into a trap. Snap it shut, done, finished, no talk.

And Andras's favorite mind picture returned: a body, lying in a pool of blood, black mask removed to reveal the face of one dead SOB who thought he could come up here and take over, push Andras around, and do whatever he wanted.

Andras smiled.

Not so fast, shitbird. I'm going to hand you a one-way ticket to hell before this is over.

～

WHEN THE ANNOUNCEMENT ABOUT A PARTIAL EVACUATION blared over the PA, Samael's only concern was whether that changed anything.

The bomb threat would be more effective if it put people in jeopardy rather than just things, even if they were expensive things like space stations and sophisticated spacecraft. Would the authorities act more boldly once they had reduced, or even eliminated the danger to personnel?

Tough call, except for one thing. How many people were there in two shifts' worth of essential personnel? Few enough that it was okay to sacrifice them?

That didn't *feel* right. Americans revered the sanctity of human life, although in an often hypocritical and conflicting fashion. They were probably doing this to reduce risk rather than eliminate it. The leverage still existed, but it might have to be played more closely.

And the stakes didn't just involve things, either. They were far more than that, both in a practical and symbolic sense. The ability to leave Earth was the exclusive domain of the USA. They controlled access to the Moon colony and had the power to deny it to anyone else. No way would they allow that to be taken without a fight.

After checking on his prisoner, Samael left the reactor room and walked to a position from which he could move in a number of directions depending on what happened next.

Time to crank up the pressure a notch . . . or two.

10

DAY THREE LATE EVENING

The elevator door opened to reveal another hectic scene in the loading dock. Brett's ship had moved off to one side to make room for a lunar shuttle in the launch position. He climbed an exterior maintenance ladder and watched through a cockpit side window as Buck and a technician consulted tech manuals, trying to install the discrete comm link in Brett's helmet. A critical task, but way too boring, so he climbed down and walked around his ship to check out evac preparations.

The lunar shuttle looked like a massive living thing being tended by hundreds of workers. A long line of people snaked out from the open cargo door, moving slowly into the huge spacecraft as if being swallowed up.

The processing seemed to be moving along smoothly, and Brett could imagine scenes similar to this one in the other loading bays as the station conducted the first evacuation in its history. He wondered where it would all end.

"Hey! Captain!" It was Buck, calling to him from the landing at the top of the ladder to the crew compartment. "Quit stargazing out there and do us the honor of reporting front and center."

What a guy. Chief Master Sergeant Buck Logan had been Brett's crew chief for years, and their daily interactions seldom reflected the standard officer-enlisted relationship. Brett entered the ship and made his way up to the cockpit. "Okay, Chief. Have you found the solution yet?"

"Of course. This is the first team here. Put the helmet on."

Brett sat down in the left seat and donned the helmet. Buck picked up another helmet plugged into the copilot's console. The technician called from the crew apartment aft of the cockpit for a radio check. "Testing. One, two, three, four, five, five, four, three, two, one. Test out."

Brett keyed the microphone and called the man back. "This is Bravo Lima, read you loud and clear. How me, over?"

There was no response. As Brett wiggled the wiring to check the connections, he glanced to his right and saw Buck staring at him through the visor of the copilot's helmet. A blatantly scornful expression had hijacked his face.

"Are you with me here, Cap'n?"

"Yes, Chief, I hear you. How me?"

"Likewise, sir, but you can quit trying to call the tech. The plan was to splice in reception only, remember? Can you keep that straight until the time comes?"

"I knew that, Buck. It was just a test. You passed."

"Uh huh. And you failed. Don't make that mistake when the time comes."

Buck took off his helmet and told the technician to put things back together. "And don't leave any visible evidence of the work. I don't think this guy's that sharp, but you never know."

"Roger that, Chief."

Brett and Buck left the technician to finish up and took a walk through the cargo bay. "How's the rest of the maintenance doing?"

"Fine, Cap'n. They're buttoning up the fighter now and will have it armed up in an hour or so. By that time the attachment fitting will be in place. We can load it into the bay in another hour, finish up some last minute stuff, and be done with it."

"What do I tell the general?

"Three hours, tops."

"Okay. I'm going to the command post. If anything changes you'll let me know?"

"Hell no! The secret is to keep the brass out of the loop."

"Now I'm a part of the brass? I thought you considered me as one of the guys."

"I was just buttering you up. I get lonely sometimes at night, and like to keep my options open. Come by my place later?"

Buck could carry on this sort of banter indefinitely, and most of the time never crack a smile. It played hell with the new guys who didn't know him.

"Forget it, pilgrim. You're not my style." Brett turned to go, leaving Buck with a sad face, acting crushed at being rejected. But it didn't last long.

"Hey, Cap'n!"

"What? I've got to go!"

"The bathroom's in the other direction."

As Brett turned to acknowledge the joke, Buck locked eyes with him, serious now, no playing around. Brett waited.

"You'll get the best machine we can give you. But we both know that's only part of it. You'll be careful, right?"

"Always. See you." Brett returned the salute offered by the sergeant and left the loading dock. He stopped at a phone and dialed the number for Comm Central. After confirming that the general was not immediately available, he decided to get something to eat. It was a common fighter pilot response to inactivity. Since you never knew when you might miss a meal, never pass up an opportunity to stuff your face.

ANDRAS HAD SPENT THE LAST HOUR WITH CHIP AND NOSER. He'd always thought of the robodogs as relatively useless, something to be played with by people who weren't serious about police work. Andras didn't mind progress, but felt the dogs represented technology just for the sake of it rather than for a clearly defined law enforcement objective. But now as he watched Chip go through preparations for the dog's entry into the core, he was way more than glad to have this creature on his side. He might even hug *him* when this crisis had passed.

NASA had remained secretive about robodogs because there was nothing to gain and plenty to lose by announcing to the world how their security system worked. If the man knew about them, he'd realize the dog was part of an effort to find him. But if he didn't, there'd probably be an initial period of disbelief that dogs were even on the station, much less allowed to roam around by themselves. And Andras was sure the man would never guess he was looking at a robot.

It really was amazing. The look, the movements, the reactions to Chip's commands, all of it totally realistic. Andras had never touched Dan's dog Snooper, although on occasion during routine patrol the dog had brushed up against his leg or tried to lick his hand. It was tough to maintain the strict attitude that Snooper was just a machine when a cold nose and wet tongue touched you.

During the work with Noser, however, Andras deliberately took the opportunity to pat him, scratch his ears, treat him like a dog. It had been years since he'd even seen a real dog, much less touched one. He had to admit if he were blindfolded he would have never known it wasn't real. And from any distance there would be no way to visually tell.

The radio on Andras's belt came to life. "Alpha One, Alpha Nine, over."

Andras moved away from where Chip was adjusting something in the dog's program. "Go ahead, Nine, One here."

"Everything's in place, Sarge. We got the radios up and checked. The team's positioned as you wanted."

"Roger that. Stand by for further instructions, and stay alert. One out."

"Nine out."

Andras returned his attention to the business at hand. He'd never seen work done on a robodog, and he watched with keen interest when Chip commanded Noser to lie down, then with a small tool began opening up an access panel on the dog's side. Andras almost looked away, as if this were going to be a bloody affair, or an invasion of the dog's privacy to watch. Even then, no matter how hard he tried, he had difficulty maintaining a detached view of Noser as nothing but a piece of machinery. The tendency to treat the dog as real always lingered just below the surface, ready to influence his reactions.

Chip finished an adjustment of some kind, closed the access panel, and put Noser through a series of commands. Then he told the dog to sit. Noser barked and wagged his tail. Andras was about to walk over and give Noser a pat when he caught himself. *No time for that doggie shit.*

Then he smiled at the thought of asking Chip if the dogs needed to be picked up after, right before the familiar excitement began to build, with the anticipation of danger, the possibility of death, the uncertainty about the outcome, and the heightened senses that prepared him for combat.

And then it dawned on him. He didn't yet have approval to start the search, but it was as if he had already made up his mind to go in. He thought about that for a moment, and decided, *Why not?* Waiting for some bureaucrat to make a decision was like watching grass grow. With no further thoughts about the consequences, Andras began giving Chip last-minute instructions about how they would do this. But he soon realized that Chip wasn't really listening and seemed concerned about something.

"What's the matter? I need your attention here."

"I'm listening, Sergeant, but I thought we were going to wait for—"

Andras moved as close to Chip as he dared with Noser sitting so close. He wanted to intimidate the technician, but the last thing he needed was to lose a leg. "I'm running this show, Chip. You're here because I don't have time to become *friends* with a robodog. Lots of things will be going on that are none of your business, so just do as I tell you. Understood?"

Chip didn't appear to like it, but after a few seconds he mumbled a quiet, "Okay."

"Get that puppy moving and follow me."

Andras, Chip, and Noser proceeded to a location from which the dog would be introduced into the central core. Approaching the access point, Andras motioned for Chip to remain well clear of the entrance. Andras entered the passcode, drew his pistol and opened the door. After checking the immediate vicinity, he waved for Chip to come forward.

Chip walked up with the dog at heel and pointed to the open door. "Search, Noser." The dog walked into the core and disappeared around a corner. Andras closed the door, holstered his pistol, and looked over Chip's shoulder at the device he was using to monitor and remotely control the dog's progress.

Noser's audio, video, and olfactory sensors transmitted information in real time to the device. Chip had programmed a continuous sweeping search pattern, but he could override it and adjust where the dog "pointed."

A couple of minutes into the search, Chip noticed something lying on the floor. "Stop."

Noser froze, the object partially visible at the right side of the screen.

"Look right. Hold."

Andras leaned closer. It was a small dark shape, but the light was too dim to make out what it was.

"Zoom," said Chip.

The view enlarged until the object filled the screen. Chip adjusted the focus slightly and the two men studied it for a moment.

"What the hell is that?" Chip asked.

Andras had just recognized the object. "It's a handle for one of the radial chute access hatches. Move the video over to the end . . . no, the other direction. I want to see the end that isn't smooth. There, hold that. Can you zoom in closer?"

As Chip made the adjustment, Andras saw the jagged end of the handle where it had broken off. He stared at the handle, trying to determine in the slightly fuzzy video why there was something about it that seemed familiar.

"How do you suppose that happened?" asked Chip.

"I'm not—wait a minute. Can you focus that any better?" With a slightly clearer view Andras recognized the telltale pattern. "That handle was damaged by one of the new rounds. We must be near the location where the kid was shot at. Okay, let's press on."

Chip stared at Andras. "This son of a bitch shot at a kid?"

"Yes, and I want to return the favor. Continue."

The dog moved very quickly through the corridors with nothing more to see than empty space. There were no signs of human activity, movement, or foreign objects. It was time to move on.

Andras told Chip to have Noser search the reactor room, and he couldn't believe his eyes as he watched the video. He could tell immediately when the dog broke into a trot, and from the screen he could visualize the easy stride as Noser turned corners, slowed for crossing corridors to look in each direction, and then accelerated to the next one.

Andras knew that Chip had trained Noser to turn the handles on the environmental duct access panels. The dog found one, but it was up on the ceiling. How the hell was the dog going to get up to it and open the thing? He didn't have to wait long for the answer.

"Noser, jump," said Chip.

The video remained centered on the handle, but there was some unusual side-to-side movement Andras hadn't noticed before. Then, without warning, and with such speed that Andras instinctively felt like closing his eyes, the handle came at the screen in a rush and disappeared off the edge of the video. All that remained was a blurry view of what appeared to be the vented surface of the access panel. Then there was some jerking movement, as if the camera, or the view through the dog's eyes, was rotating to the right.

And just as suddenly the view changed again, creating a falling sensation followed by a sudden stop. Andras concentrated hard on the video, trying to make out what was happening, when another of the same rapid view changes occurred that ended up with the video once again centered on the panel. But this time it was open, hanging down from the ceiling at a right angle, with a dark square indicating the opening into the duct.

Andras was about to ask Chip what was going on when the handler repeated the command and once again the ceiling rushed at the monitor and went almost dark. There was more jerking, then stillness. As the contrast automatically adjusted for the darker surroundings, Andras could make out the rectangular shape of what could only be the inside of the duct.

He couldn't believe it, but there it was. "Did I see what I think I saw?"

Chip laughed. "Hard to believe, huh? We had to work awhile to get the programming we wanted, but it works like a charm." He had a diagram of the ducting system on the floor and was issuing commands for Noser to navigate to the opening he wanted in the ceiling of the reactor room. Andras watched with fascination as the dog crawled through the duct. "How close are you to the reactor?"

"Any moment now, I think. This must be the area just outside the room, and if I go one more section over I should have him in position."

"Hold up a minute."

"Stop," Chip ordered quietly into the microphone.

As the video froze, Andras considered his options. He had seen no evidence of the man or his hostage. The dog made what appeared to be a complete sweep of the corridors in the core. Unless the man was keeping track of Noser's movements somehow and managed to stay out of his view, he wasn't out there for the dog to see. The guy's good, but how in hell would he be able to anticipate the dog's search pattern? Could he see the dog and not be seen?

"Chip?"

"Yo."

"How sensitive is the dog's hearing?"

"Very. A real dog might miss something covered up by the background noise level in the core, machinery, airflow, whatever. But we took audio samples of that, and put in a noise cancellation feature that eliminates it from the dog's audio search system."

"Do you think a man, either alone or with a prisoner, could have been moving in there without being heard?"

"Hard to tell. One man by himself might escape detection if he was really good at it, and had taken care with his clothing. If he's carrying any equipment, it can't squeak, rattle, or rub together. He would have to know about the dog to be that quiet."

Andras considered that for a moment. Here was the decision point that could make or break this thing. If he knew the man was in the reactor room, he might be able to close the net down tighter. Did he want to bring in the Alpha Team now, or stay with his original plan and go in alone? Hard choice.

His thoughts were interrupted when Chip whispered, "Sergeant! I have noises from the reactor room!"

"What kind of noises?"

"Not sure, but definitely not background. My guess is human activity."

"Okay," said Andras, as he drew his pistol, rechecked the chamber to make sure a round was ready for firing, removed the magazine to check that it was fully loaded, and rammed it back home with a distinctive metal-on-metal click. He lowered the pistol to his side and looked at Chip.

"Wait five minutes, then send the dog in as we planned. You have two objectives, but the bomb is primary. If you discover any evidence I want video, as close up as you can, of the device itself and any wires leading to it.

"Do the same with anything else that seems out of place. Pay particular attention to the doors. Remember the existence of a triggering device activated by opening a door is one of the most important bits of information we need. People will be making life-or-death decisions based on this video. I want clear, unobstructed views of whatever there is to see in there. Got it?"

"Yes."

"And make certain the video feed into Comm Central is turned off. The bomb guys aren't there yet anyway, and they can look at it later for information about the bomb."

"It's off."

Andras moved over to the door. "Hack your watch. Five minutes, then go. Understood?"

"Yes, Sergeant."

〜

It was always like this. Andras's senses became super-tuned in to whatever there was to see, hear, smell, feel. It was as if his whole body became a receiver, with the sensitivity control turned up to the max. He had been in the core for almost five minutes and made his way closer to the reactor room by moving in a direct line from where he entered. He was cautious, but from what he'd seen on the video the man was most likely in the reactor area or very close to it.

It also made sense that he would be: better concealment and defensive position in case of an assault, along with direct control over the only item with any chance of holding the police at bay. The man had to know that threatening a hostage would never be enough to force compliance with his demands.

Andras abandoned some of the caution he felt and made sure he was within striking distance of the reactor room when the dog entered. He had two radios, one on the Alpha net, the other tuned to the frequency used by Chip to report the dog's progress. Both were connected to an earpiece so any calls to him would not be heard by anyone else. Andras had no intention of transmitting unless he knew it would make no difference if the man heard him or not.

He was crouched down at an intersection. Although he hadn't looked past the corner, he knew that a short hallway to his right dead-ended into another corridor surrounding the reactor room. There should also be a door into the room visible from this intersection. He was tempted to look, but didn't dare.

The earpiece came to life with Chip's voice as he reported the dog on the move. Andras's heart rate increased as the handler kept up a constant commentary, broken only by pauses when he used the remote control to transmit commands to the dog.

"We're in the duct above the reactor room. I can see the handle to the access door ahead. The door is open. Noser's at the opening, nothing unusual in sight. Noser's in. Random search in progress. Audio and visual circuits show nothing, olfactory beginning to activate slightly. The dog is in olfactory search priority at this time."

The silence seemed to last forever. Andras waited anxiously for the next word from Chip.

"We have an alert. The dog is on point."

From listening to the handler's commands, Andras concluded that Noser had entered the reactor room in random or slow search mode with all the sensors in equal status. The visual scan pattern would have been in a continuous side-to-side sweep, with the audio and olfactory sensors activated while the camera recorded whatever the dog's eyes saw. When Noser smelled something, Chip terminated the random search and commanded the dog into a priority mode in which olfactory sensors became primary to concentrate the dog's attention toward one objective.

"We have the olfactory alert object on video. Zooming in. Looks like a duffel bag, explosive residue positive. I repeat, explosive residue positive."

In spite of Andras's building excitement, he had to move back from the intersection a little to stretch. Advancing age had taken a toll on his ability to remain still in one position for a long time, and his knees ached. He continued to listen as Chip described the action. Noser had found another dark shape that alerted the olfactory sensors off the chart, and there appeared to be wires attached to it. If this was the bomb, the explosive experts might be able to use the video and do something about it.

Suddenly Chip's excited voice filled Andras's earpiece.

"We have a man! He's tied up, lying on the floor, not moving. I'm sending the dog in closer. Jesus Christ! It's the cop—hold on a minute."

Chip began transmitting commands to the dog.

"Noser, stay. Hold it there, boy, hold it. Look left. Slower. That's it. Hold. Back to the right. There, hold. Noser, walk. Now stay. Noser, touch him. Noser! Touch him. Holy shit! The cop moved. He's seen the dog."

Andras listened with a mixture of conflicting feelings as Chip gave Noser commands to get Dan out of the reactor room. Andras wanted to save his partner if he could, but was more concerned about what the hijacker was doing. He needed the dog searching for him.

This was taking too long. The dog had been programmed with as many preset commands as Chip and Andras could come up with based on what they wanted him to do. Although this provided precise actions in response to standard commands and was the preferred method for using robodogs, the actions required now necessitated a different approach.

The dog would also accept a handler's instructions based on its understanding of language, and could be controlled by the handler simply telling it what to do. And while the dog's responses were generally adequate, it usually took longer to get the point across. The specific actions were never as precise as with preset, *pretested* commands, and Andras was growing more impatient by the minute as he listened to Chip search for just the right words to get Noser to remove Dan's restraints.

Then Chip's voice commands changed when it sounded like he was redirecting the dog into a stalking mode. Andras was trying to form a mental image of what was happening when Chip's voice filled Andras's earpiece with,

"ATTACK, NOSER! KILL!"

The hijacker must be in the reactor room and Andras was sitting on his ass out here in a corridor. He was fumbling with the microphone trying to ask Chip where this was happening when the sharp report of a handgun initiated a madhouse of input over the radio as Chip described the action and gave the dog commands at the same time. Andras tried to get up, but his left leg had gone to sleep and he hit the floor hard.

Shaking off the tingling sensation, Andras struggled up and hobbled out into the corridor leading to the reactor room. As he turned the corner he saw that the door into the reactor room was open. The bastard had to be close by, and hopefully distracted by the dog. Running as hard as he could with a leg that didn't want to work, he covered the distance and charged into the dark interior of the reactor room.

SAMAEL HAD THE GENERAL LISTENING TO HIM LIKE A PUPPY DOG, probably along with a host of other idiots all clustered around, while he told them that when he started to move toward the shuttle, the

hostage would be at his side and the bomb detonator in his hand. He'd take a random route, and didn't want to see another soul anywhere near him as he made his way to the bay.

None of it meant anything. He wasn't about to move anywhere on the station with the authorities knowing about it. He'd already told them what they needed to know to comply, and they either were doing it, or they weren't. This charade was just for confusion, but it did have the secondary objective of finding out if there were any plans to take him before the big event.

Corridors formed by circular banks of machinery surrounded the reactor room. The walls forming this central core were vertical at the lower end, but curved into a high domed ceiling. Ladders attached to the walls of the core terminated at the upper end with the rungs hanging down rather than protruding out.

Samael was an experienced rock climber, and this was a piece of cake. He made his way to a position high above the machinery banks, and could see most of the area as he hung there, swaying gently from the straps holding him to the rungs.

When he decided they weren't trying to find him, he left his perch for the relative comfort of his hiding place in the reactor room. He was still talking to the general as he walked up to the door into the reactor room and opened it.

Samael had forgotten all about the radio when he peered around the door to check on his prisoner. What he saw froze him in his tracks.

A dog, a big son of a bitch, stood over the cop. The thing turned its head and looked right at him. Samael felt as if he were in a dream, unable to move. He couldn't take his eyes off the dog's head, which appeared to have turned about one hundred eighty degrees on its axis. Then with incredible speed the animal turned and charged.

Stepping backward, Samael moved behind the open door to put it between him and the advancing dog. He grabbed the door handle with his left hand and pulled it toward him as he drew his pistol with his right hand. The dog hit the door with such tremendous force that it slammed the door into him and knocked him off his feet into the corridor.

Lying on his back, stunned by the speed and power of the dog's attack, Samael held the pistol out at arm's length pointed at the partially open door. He expected the animal to push its way out and into the hallway in pursuit, but the door remained motionless.

Attack dogs were trained to continue pursuit relentlessly, and fight to the death in spite of what faced them. They didn't pause, head fake, break off an attack and reinitiate it from another direction, or crouch behind open doors and wait. What the hell was this one doing?

With his pistol still pointed at the door, Samael got up and retreated into the corridor that encircled the reactor room. Once far enough away that he felt safe to turn his back on the threat, he ran to the next door and used his entry code to open it. With only a moment's hesitation at the thought of what might be waiting on the other side, he peered in to check both directions, then closed the door behind him and moved away from the dog's last known position and into the darkness.

Samael was experienced at this, but he was stalking a dog that was probably stalking him and had already shown evidence of unusual behaviors. Moving slowly and as quietly as he could, he maneuvered to a position where he could see the cop. He peeked around an equipment locker and was surprised to see nothing. Had he navigated through the darkness accurately, or did the cop move?

He backtracked to try another approach, and this time he could see the bonds that had secured Bishop. They were lying on the floor, badly frayed on the ends as if they had been chewed through. What the hell was he dealing with here? The straps were heavy nylon, but the handcuffs and leg shackles were steel. The dog might be some kind of super canine, but he damn sure couldn't bite through those. The cop had to be close by.

Samael turned another corner and heard a strange sound. It was a combination of a clanking noise, like metal on metal, and the periodic grunting of a man under exertion. A quick peek around the next corner produced the picture of the dog, facing away from him and tearing at Bishop's leg shackles with his teeth. The cop was facing in Samael's direction but had his eyes closed, grimacing in pain at the force of the dog's jerking at the metal chain between the two leg shackles. Bishop's hands were behind him, so he must still be handcuffed.

The dog was distracted, the cop still neutralized. Knowing the situation wouldn't get any better by waiting, Samael rounded the corner with the gun leveled.

What the hell? No dog. Bishop was lying there, looking down the next corridor. Samael advanced quickly to cover the cop, who turned to look at him. As he approached, he noticed Bishop's eyes shift to a point behind him, then return to look right in his eyes.

Instinctively Samael began the move, and was immediately aware of a rapid, rhythmic clicking sound. He knew what it was even before he turned around, and the result was probably as much a matter of luck as anything.

The dog was on him, charging at full speed. By the time Samael got his left arm up in a blocking move to ward off the dog's head and snapping jaws, it was airborne. With his left arm coming up, Samael dropped toward the floor to get below the dog's attack and use its momentum against it.

Some attack dogs went for extremities, others for the body, interesting places like the throat or the crotch. This one went high, and Samael's arm caught it in the chest. Although the impact of the collision knocked him down, he was able to drop far enough below the attack to deflect most of the force. The dog skipped off Samael's arm and hit the floor at Bishop's feet.

Samael landed on his back, sliding in the same direction as the dog. He rolled while bringing the pistol past his head and brought the sights in line onto the target.

The dog hit the floor with legs already backpedaling, struggling to stop and turn at the same time. The sound of the pistol shots was deafening in the small space, three rapid-fire hits right on target. The bullets punched the dog down the corridor into a crumpled pile. Samael got to his feet, cursing himself for having forgotten to insert his earplugs.

Standing over the dog, with Bishop cowering on the floor, Samael tried to make sense of what he was seeing. No blood, although the dog was obviously dead. Then he noticed one of the dog's wounds had some wires sticking out of it. Bending down to look, he felt the dog's side, then looked closely at the other two wounds and whistled softly to himself when he realized he had spent the last few minutes fighting a robotic dog.

He was also stationary, and someone had to be reacting to the commotion. Samael went over to the cop. Bending down to remove the leg shackles, he caught a glimpse of movement in the dimness of the corridor to his right.

Samael turned slightly to his left and knelt down by Bishop's feet with his back toward the new threat. Busying himself with the leg shackles, he intentionally made the task last longer than it should have while he watched the cop's eyes.

And there it was. Just a flicker. The cop saw something behind Samael and wasn't able to remain completely passive. The threat was probably in the corridor now, with no cover.

The next move was part skill, part luck, and part doing your homework. Samael assumed the security forces on Oasis had no way to practice marksmanship other than with a special range and weapons modified to use a laser scoring system. He also knew that no one could be proficient with a handgun unless he practiced religiously.

The person behind him knew it too, and would be hesitant to shoot from much distance. He'd try to close the range, and put the first round where he wanted it to reduce the chance for effective return fire.

Samael fumbled with the keys to the shackles, dropped them beside the cop's feet, and reached down to pick them up. His pistol was lying on the floor next to the keys. He felt the cop tense. Glancing up at his face, Samael saw the cop's eyes sending a silent warning down the hall behind him.

Samael tucked his head toward his chest and did a flip onto his back. As his legs left the floor he was able to see an upside down shadowy figure crouched in the dimness of the corridor. His own pistol was on its way up to the target when he saw the bright muzzle flash of the man's pistol and heard the shot.

Samael adjusted his aim to the position of the flash and squeezed the trigger. The other man fired again at almost the same time. Discipline and extensive training notwithstanding, the bullet got Samael's attention as it hit the floor by his ear and ricocheted off down the corridor. Eyes locked on the target, he fired twice more, and after a slight pause a fourth time as he saw the man jerk backward with the impact of at least one of his shots.

Then there was silence, at least as far as he could tell with his ears ringing, and through gun smoke in the dim light, he saw a motionless prone shape lying on the floor. Samael rolled slowly over onto his stomach with his pistol sighted on the shape, ready to shoot again.

He got to his knees, then stood up and advanced toward the downed man. He thought he heard activity outside the reactor room, but ignored it for the moment as he approached and saw the blood.

Two of his bullets had hit the man in the torso and created the familiar splayed-out pattern of impacts on a protective vest. One hit the man's right leg, but the fourth and last did all the damage. The bullet had caught the man in the lower face, probably when he was prone on the floor.

Leaning over the body, Samael placed his pistol to the man's head as he felt a slight pulse. He unfastened the straps holding the vest to the man's chest and pulled the front half away to reveal the uniform shirt of the Oasis police.

And there it was, just above the pocket, a tag imprinted with the name Cadogan. Looking at the destroyed face, Samael saw a little resemblance from what was left, but not enough to be sure. As he walked back toward the other cop, he decided to consider Cadogan as still alive and plan accordingly until he could verify it.

Samael picked up the remains of the straps that had held Bishop and fashioned a loop between Cadogan's feet. Dragging the cop behind him, he hurried to the nearest door, the same one he'd originally entered and probably the one used by Cadogan. After checking the corridor, he set the remote detonator and hauled Cadogan out of the reactor room to the center of the nearest intersection.

With speed being more important than caution when in the open spaces of the core, he ran to the nearest ladder and climbed to the ceiling. If they came in here to get him, he'd be able to see the assault. On previous explorations of the core, Samael had searched the walls and ceiling carefully with binoculars for any evidence of surveillance cameras. The briefings indicated there were none, but he found that hard to believe. You couldn't go anywhere on Earth without being spied upon by a camera. If they installed elaborate systems to catch shoplifters, you would think they'd do at least as much on a space station.

There was always the possibility a cop might look up and spot him hanging in the darkness, but the chance of that was remote. Most men trained in combat search did a good job of protecting a circle around them, leapfrogging in steps so the advancing member was always covered in front and the trailer protected the team's rear. But very few instinctively paid the same attention to what is above them.

Samael's backup in this situation was the chute system. He was within arm's reach of a hatch. It was peaceful up here, and he settled down to wait. If they were going to try something, it wouldn't be long now.

BRETT ARRIVED AT THE WAR ROOM IN TIME TO GET A CUP OF coffee and chat with the duty officer for a few minutes about the status of the evacuation. Things appeared to be on track. Two shuttles had already left and a third was about to launch. As Brett sipped his coffee it occurred to him that the launch of the lunar shuttle in the loading bay with his ship would require all the maintenance personnel to exit the dock for the departure. He mentioned this potential delay to the duty officer and saw General DeSilva enter the War Room.

"Good evening, sir."

"And to you as well, Captain Larsen. Are you ready to go if it comes to that?"

"Yes, sir. The shuttle will be ready sooner than we originally estimated, possibly within the next three hours. And the private comm link to my helmet worked fine. You'll be able to broadcast information to me on that frequency without the hijacker's knowledge."

The general pushed back from the table and crossed his arms, stared at the ceiling, and after a moment of silence looked at Brett. "You know, the more I think about that, the more I like it. We might be able to use it in more ways than one. But I should warn you that with all the other things we've seen this man do, he might think of something like this. You need to be careful, and don't underestimate his abilities."

"I won't, sir."

"I would also—what does *he* want?"

Brett turned to look out the window behind him and saw the Comm Central duty officer frantically waving from his position at the desk. Then a phone at the back of the War Room rang and the general motioned to Brett to answer it.

Brett hurried over and picked up the handset. "Captain Larsen."

"Tell the general the hijacker is on the radio and wants to speak with him."

Brett passed the message. The general walked to the rear of the room where the communications gear was located. "Tell them to transfer that channel up here on radio number one, and remind him to turn off the overhead speakers in Central."

As Brett did that, the general grabbed the microphone. "This is General DeSilva."

"Good evening, General. I just wanted to say I enjoyed your announcement immensely. But I'm confused why you risk making me angry with this sudden move. I don't remember saying anything about evacuation, do you?"

Brett felt a chill when he heard the voice. It was softer than he would have expected for a man threatening to blow up a space station, and it had a quality about it he couldn't identify, except to think *sinister*.

The general glanced at Brett, rolled his eyes and shook his head. "Very perceptive of you, sir, attesting to your exceptional grasp of the facts. I did not then, however, nor do I now, feel it necessary to obtain your permission to act in the best interests of the station and its personnel."

"Very pompous of you, General. But to put our differences aside for the moment, let me remind you that your first priority should be to meet the deadline. You may have some notion of delaying, but such tricks will be futile."

"We're not planning any tricks. Nothing about the evacuation will slow up our preparations. But I'm sure you're aware I won't be the one to make the final decision. NASA has the controls."

"Spare me the speech. Just listen, and take notes if you need to, because I won't say this again."

Brett listened intently as the man began with a repeat of the original demands, followed by instructions about what he expected to see as he moved to the shuttle. Then suddenly in the middle of a sentence the transmission ceased. The duty officer in Comm Central looked up at the War Room, and pointing at the radio with one hand, gave the thumbs-up signal with the other. DeSilva snatched a phone off the table. "What the hell happened?"

General DeSilva spent the next few minutes talking with the duty officer. From the one-way conversation, it appeared to Brett that the Alpha Team had reported shots fired and wanted to enter the core, but was under orders to hold position until they heard from Sergeant Cadogan. General DeSilva questioned why the Alpha Team was even in position and told the duty officer to get Cadogan on the radio. Then suddenly the overhead speakers erupted.

"General DeSilva, the Alpha net reports more shots. They cannot contact Alpha One and want permission to enter the core."

Brett noticed the internal struggle apparent on the general's face. The responsibilities of successful command came right down to this, choosing the right action for the right time, and often without benefit of all the facts.

"Tell them to go," said General DeSilva. "And to be careful."

MOVEMENT BELOW CAUGHT SAMAEL'S ATTENTION. HE WATCHED men enter the core and fan out into the corridors. He couldn't see everything, it was like looking down into a maze from off to one side, but enough to know they had a plan and were executing it perfectly. The men formed a semicircular net and began to shrink it down. Hopefully they'd taken the bomb threat seriously and wouldn't just barge into the reactor room and set the thing off.

The authorities had played this thing so cautiously thus far that the attack by the cop and this team action seemed out of place. He considered whether the cop had coordinated his movements with the team, and concluded he either didn't even try or his plan had failed.

So why now? As he watched the net close down on the reactor room, he began to wonder if the dog had provided them with some information about what was in there. Did it have video? Did it operate independently, or in response to commands? No way to tell for sure, but Samael became concerned they were going to try an assault on the room. That would be disastrous, and he considered ways to prevent it.

He could decoy them away. Let them know he wasn't in there and divert their attention.

No, that wouldn't work. They have to know the cop is in there. They're planning to get him out, and they appeared to be more aggressive. But in case they think busting into the reactor room is a good idea, Samael needed to get them thinking about more explosions.

Samael's instructions called for only two bombs, one demo and one to disable the nuclear reactor, but this was another case of independent planning for his own survival. The doors to the reactor room were the only ways in or out. If he got trapped, he needed a diversion or some method of clearing them out of the way.

He opened a small pouch attached to his belt and removed the remote detonator he'd used on the previous explosion, and which was programmable to a number of frequencies. He turned on the device and selected a surprise he had placed, manufactured from materials he found in a maintenance storage locker and the explosives he had brought.

This one covered the approaches to the primary entrance into the reactor room. With the injured cop lying in plain view, the team was concentrating on him and moving into the open area of the intersection. When he was sure they had taken up positions close enough to the door, he pushed the button.

Two simultaneous detonations created instant pandemonium below him. Scattered gunfire attested to the confusion. As the smoke cleared slightly and the debris settled, Samael could see figures retreating from the door, dragging other team members with them. He was enjoying the results of his work when to his surprise the chute hatch handle beside him began to move.

The hatch swung open and a cop stuck his head out of the chute. The cop hadn't seen Samael yet, and appeared to be watching the scene unfolding below. But before Samael could recover the man turned and looked right at him.

Here again training paid off, and instant action with little thought gave him the advantage. Samael's left hand went for the cop's throat, and his right hit him just under his nose. The suddenness of the attack and the strength of the blow stunned the cop long enough for Samael to pull him about halfway out of the chute before he could grab onto something inside the chute.

With the cop's hands occupied, Samael drew his knife with his right hand and stabbed at the man's chest. When the cop released his handhold to protect himself, Samael let go of his throat with his left hand, gripped the shoulder strap of the cop's protective vest, and pulled the screaming man the rest of the way out of the chute.

Avoiding the cop's frantic attempts to hold onto him, Samael ignored the falling figure and scrambled into the chute as he released the straps holding himself to the ladder. Once inside, he reached behind him with his foot and pulled the hatch cover closed. Air pressure held it there as he crawled to the nearest intersection, turned around, and crawled back to secure the latch. Hopefully none of the cops in the core were looking up as the man fell. By the time they discovered the body, they'd be unable to pinpoint his position.

Seen or not, he had to get away from here, and fast. It wouldn't do for the manhunt to extend into the chutes just yet.

Scrambling forward, Samael crawled into the darkness toward his next objective.

11

DAY FOUR VERY EARLY MORNING

The computer alert tone, obnoxious, insistent, and much too loud, hauled Toby out of his first sound sleep in what felt like forever.

He sat up in bed and stared at the light from the monitor. He had shut it down last night, and wondered if his parents had been in the room since he fell asleep. Concerned that they might have seem the evacuation notice, he climbed out of bed, went over to the desk and checked the screen. That stupid see-all, hear-all nagging-all-the-time central station computer had detected that the monitor was turned off, powered it up and sent the latest notice that demanded a response to the evacuation alert.

Anxious to silence the tone, Toby acknowledged receipt to prevent it from waking his parents before he had a chance to leave. Then he ran a quick audio and spatial search of the apartment to confirm they were still sleeping. Having slept in his clothes, all he had to do was grab his backpack out of the closet and get out of here, but something held him back. Making the decision was one thing, but now was the time to do it. From this point forward he knew the consequences of his actions would be irreversible.

Did he really want to do this? A severe case of second thoughts filled him with doubt. But when he tried to imagine himself on the moon colony, the image of being trapped flooded over him like a tidal wave, leaving him gasping and breathless. He wanted to be a pilot so badly he couldn't conceive of not achieving his goal.

The two fears opposed each other, and the conflict wavered back and forth in a mental war. He was more than ready to call a cease-fire, but persistent uncertainty and indecision seemed to be holding him in place. The computer message alert tone suddenly interrupted his internal debate.

Departure time had been moved up by 30 minutes. The message also demanded acknowledgment, and said if none were received within 15 minutes, an evacuation control official would be sent to the apartment.

Toby debated whether to acknowledge the message, but decided not to. They would check on the family, which would give his mom and dad as much warning as possible under the circumstances.

He opened one of the outside pockets on his backpack and took out an envelope with a letter. He hated that they'd be concerned for his safety, but the letter explained again and in more detail why he had to do this. Maybe it would help them understand how much thought he'd put into the decision and help ease their worry.

He propped the note against the monitor, picked up his backpack, tiptoed across the apartment and stood by the door into the hallway. After an audio and spatial search of the corridor in both directions found nothing, he breathed deeply to settle his churning stomach and disabled the security alarm.

With his hand on the door knob, Toby reaffirmed his conviction that with this move, his life would begin a journey in a totally new and radically different direction. It was one of those crossroads his dad frequently talked about, when you have a choice, and once you make it, the door closes behind you. You can't turn around, go back and make it like it was before. The consequences of what you have done are permanent.

And so, with the realization that this was the most important thing he had ever done, Toby opened the door, checked the hallway in both directions, stepped out, closed the door as quietly as he could, and hurried toward the nearest radial chute entrance and his new destiny.

BRETT STOOD IN A CORNER OF THE WAR ROOM AND WATCHED the third round of chaos he'd seen in Comm Central. Within a few minutes of General DeSilva's order for the Alpha Team to enter the core, reports flooded in of more explosions, shooting, and casualties. When the general became involved with the immediate problem, Brett decided to leave and complete his own final preparations.

He returned to the squadron and found it not much better. With the evacuation in full swing, the activity there was almost as hectic. He entered the personal equipment room, gathered his flight gear, and went to the loading dock.

Activity had significantly decreased since his last visit. The lunar shuttle was gone, and ship 056 had been moved into the launch position. Two technicians were finishing up the fighter-loading checklist, and other men were lying on the floor, probably catching up on lost sleep.

Brett laid his gear on the cargo bay ramp and found the ship's maintenance records. Every discrepancy and preparation action had been entered, signed off, and initialed as checked by Buck. If the lunar shuttle departure had delayed anything, you couldn't tell it from the records. Smiling at the thought of how valuable a good maintenance supervisor was, Brett began the walk-around inspection. The preflight checklist for the shuttle was complicated, and he wanted to perform it carefully.

Everything looked good on the outside, and he entered the cockpit. The interior preflight checklist was usually performed as a crew, so it took Brett longer to accomplish it. He made a few notes regarding items he had to leave for later, and found a discrepancy he wanted to ask Buck about. When satisfied things were in order, he went back into the cargo bay and looked for the loadmaster's checklist.

The usual minimum crew consisted of two pilots and two loadmasters. But a shuttle could be flown single pilot, and that's the way the hijacker wanted it. The loadmasters were required more for loading and unloading than in-flight duties. While in transit they regularly inspected the cargo to make certain everything remained secure, but they weren't essential during normal operations. Brett didn't know whether or not he would be required to do anything with the cargo. But once they left the station it might be up to him to do whatever was required.

He found the checklist in a holder beside the master cargo control panel just to the left of the open bay door. This panel contained all the switches needed for loading and unloading functions, along with the environmental controls that regulated temperature and pressure within the bay. He read through the checklist and familiarized himself with the various controls before he began the inspection. When he got to the rear of the bay he saw the cargo remaining from the last Earth shuttle arrival.

He felt uneasy about the decision to leave the stuff on board, but nobody had asked him. He checked the pallets carefully, and decided to forget about his concerns. The decision was out of his hands, and no purpose would be served to question it now.

Forward of the cargo, radiating a sense of power, speed, and awesome capability, the space fighter had been strapped down for the journey. Bathed in the light of the loading bay streaming through the open cargo door, she was to Brett a beautiful sight, and he felt the old familiar desire to climb in and strap her on.

The thrill of flight in such a machine was almost indescribable. He'd tried often enough. Someone would ask him what it was like, and in spite of intense desire to share his feelings, he'd been unable to capture the essence of it in words. Truth be told, maybe that was the way it should be.

As he walked up and touched the fighter's skin, it was almost an act of love, a caress that meant much more than the mere act of touching. Hard to explain, almost impossible for others to understand, but when a pilot and a machine like this took flight for the first time, life changed.

Brett spent about 15 minutes inspecting the fighter's exterior, opening access panels, checking the ordnance, and ensuring himself she was ready to fly. And in the back of his mind lingered the thought that at some point, this fightercraft might be his ticket out of danger.

He pondered opening the canopy and performing an interior check, but it had been sealed by ordnance personnel following the loading of the weapons and systems checkout. This was standard practice for situations in which a ship was left in launch status for an extended period. He looked at the seal for the signature of the certifying supervisor and chuckled to himself. Of course. Buck always took the extra time required to make certain his pilots had the best machines he could give them. No need to check anything here.

As Brett walked forward and climbed the ladder to the crew level, he wondered whether anyone had thought to restock supplies in the crew apartment. The shuttles were capable of extended space travel, and were designed to accommodate up to three complete crews. The off-duty area wasn't roomy, but it could handle the basic needs of the two additional crews with regard to eating, sleeping, and just hanging out when not actively involved in shuttle operation.

Brett entered the largest of the common crew areas, which served as a combination kitchen, dining room, and lounge. It was dark, so he stopped to let his eyes adjust and suddenly felt a stab of fear. He'd walked through here twice on his way to the cockpit and back, and was sure the light had been on. He felt a little silly, but he didn't want to step into the shadows. As his vision adapted he noticed a dark shape in the middle of the room. Although he was sure it was just the table where crews ate their meals, something wasn't right. Looking to his left, Brett saw the light switch on the wall and reached out to turn it on. The scene created by light flooding the room confused him.

The table had been flipped up on edge, and the hatch cover for the emergency evacuation chute was open. He couldn't remember the last time he had seen that. *Could someone be performing maintenance or preflight—?*

A soft noise, from behind him in the direction of the sleeping quarters. It sounded like a sneeze, kind of muffled as if the person had tried to stifle it. He hadn't seen or heard anyone when he passed through the corridor earlier. What the hell was going on?

"Hello? Is anyone here?"

The lack of an answer puzzled him, and Brett decided it must be someone who probably shouldn't be there. Any of the maintenance personnel would have answered right away, and there certainly wasn't a legitimate reason for casual visitors to be roaming around.

Walking toward the sound, he called out again. "Hello in the shuttle, this is Captain Larsen and I need you to identify yourself. This is an off limits area—"

Something tripped him, and Brett fell flat on his face. Dazed, he began to push himself up when a blow to his back drove him down on the floor and pinned him. He struggled against the unseen assailant until cold steel pressed against his temple and a voice struck fear in his heart.

"Be still, Captain," it whispered. "Be very still."

Brett had been in life-threatening danger many times, but he couldn't stop the panic as hands began to search him. This guy knew exactly what he was doing.

And then Brett noticed an odor. Familiar, but yet from somewhere deep in his past. As the hands finished with the search, Brett remembered.

Gun oil, or cleaning solvent, from the pistol pressed hard into the side of his head. Brett suddenly realized that he had to tell the hijacker he was the shuttle pilot.

"Hey, I'm—"

"Shhhh. Be still and quiet, Captain."

"But you have to—"

The gun slammed against Brett's head and stunned him into silence. Blood trickled down his cheek and to the floor beside his face.

"I have to do nothing. You are not so lucky. Do as I tell you."

Brett lay still, tasting his own blood, and frightened beyond his wildest imagination as the man handcuffed him. The feel of the metal restraints tight against his wrists and the realization of helplessness with his hands pinned behind him created a mounting sense of doom. The old military adage jokingly bantered about seemed to arrive out of nowhere.

Never, repeat, never volunteer for anything.

The man pulled him to his feet, and with a hand gripping the collar of his flight suit, directed Brett toward the open door of the cargo bay. He still hadn't seen his assailant, and a part of him didn't want to. The hand moved him forward, stopped him, then repeated, evidence of extreme caution.

After a longer pause at the door leading out of the crew compartment onto the landing at the top of the ladder, the man pushed Brett out and guided him down the ladder. Once on the floor of the bay, they waited again before moving out from the shadows. Approaching the open cargo door, the man stopped him in front of the loadmaster's panel.

"Put your nose on the switch that closes the door."

Brett complied, and was then pulled back from the opening and pushed face first into the wall of the shuttle. He could tell the man was off to his left slightly, probably looking at the loadmaster's control panel. Then he sensed the man move behind him and felt his minty breath on his neck.

"I question, you answer with a nod or a shake. Got it?"

Vigorous nod.

"That switch closes the door and has to be held in position manually during transit. The closing cycle takes about one minute, and the lights on the panel indicate door status. The cargo bay door open light must be out or the door isn't fully closed and locked. Once the door is locked from the inside, the door controls on the outside are disabled and entry is impossible."

The man had paused between statements, and Brett nodded yes to each. This guy must have memorized the flight manual, with one very important exception. The normal outside door controls were indeed disabled when the door was locked from the inside. But safety considerations dictated that emergency personnel could activate an override feature and gain access to the shuttle's interior. What the man didn't know just might hurt him, and Brett had no intention of pointing out the error.

Once again Brett felt his assailant move to the left, and in his peripheral vision saw the man cautiously peak out the door. The sight of the mask, black clothing, and equipment harness confirmed his fear that this guy was prepared for whatever came his way. During the contingency planning, listening to the other members of the Battle Staff, Brett had never realized it could come down to this. The opinions expressed about the man's invincibility had seemed just so much worrying. But not now, and from his perspective the reality was way more than believable.

The man retreated from the door, then told Brett to lie face down, where he pinned him to the floor with his shin. Although Brett couldn't see much, he guessed the man was using his right hand to activate the cargo-door switch, while he guarded the opening with the gun in his left hand. Activity outside the shuttle, voices, and alarmed shouts told the story.

"Hey! Joe! Wake up!"

"Watch out for that door!"

"What the hell is this? Buck said we had to leave the door open. Hey, you on the shuttle. What do you think—?"

"Holy shit, he's got a gun! Get the hell back, Joe! Move back!"

"Who is that up there?"

"Go ask him if you want. I'm out of here."

More shouting indicated total confusion in the docking bay. The man stayed by the door until it fully closed, then gripped Brett's collar, ordered him to get up, guided him forward to the front of the bay, up the ladder, into the crew quarters, and ordered him to sit down.

"Any coffee on this tub?"

"Try the lower cabinet over there."

While the aroma of the brewing java filled the room, the man removed the handcuffs from one of Brett's wrists and secured the loose end to a steel handhold attached to the wall. When the brew cycle was complete, he poured two cups and handed Brett one.

"Need anything with that?"

"Black's fine." Sipping the coffee, Brett watched as the man searched the crew quarters and appeared to familiarize himself with the layout, contents of the drawers, and the food supplies. He disappeared into the cockpit for a moment, then returned and walked back into the cargo bay. As Brett waited he began to relax a little about his prospects.

The man seemed to be hard enough, but only when he had to

control a situation. With nothing threatening him at the moment, he was almost courteous. A man like that wouldn't kill just for the sake of it, would he?

The man returned from the cargo bay and sat down at the table. During the short period since his capture, Brett had decided their previous assessment of what they were dealing with might be short of the mark. The man exuded confidence in everything he did. And what impressed Brett the most was that being trapped in the shuttle seemed to be the plan rather than an unforeseen development. What kind of man would react to this with so much ease and relaxation? The man's eyes were almost serene, nothing like the threatening, sinister pinpoints of darkness that first glared at him out of the mask.

"Who are you?"

"Captain Brett Larsen."

"Pilot?"

"I'm *your* pilot."

Suspicion glowered at Brett through the holes in the mask. "How do you know that?"

"I've just spent the past twelve hours preparing for a mission involving a terrorist who has demanded a shuttle."

"Just for the record, I'm not a terrorist. Want more coffee?"

Brett handed the man his cup. "Then what are you?"

The man poured two cups and sat down. "What I am is not the question. We were talking about what I'm not. A terrorist is a mindless fool who tries to achieve some goal, usually political, by conducting senseless acts of violence against targets that may or may not have any relationship whatsoever to the objective. Guilt or innocence has no meaning. That's not what I do."

"There are some people in the morgue and hospital who might take exception to that."

The man shrugged. "The difference is both in objective and method. My objective will remain a private matter. As for method, I have to do whatever is required by the objective. It's one thing for me to react with force against an adversary, but a different matter entirely to target innocent people."

"But you've threatened to set off a bomb which could destroy

Oasis, an act that targets innocent people, women and children included."

"Absolutely, although there's a difference. It may be futile to discuss it with a man wearing a uniform, but the terrorist will place the bomb anywhere, the more random the better, and set it off without warning. The *objective* is terror by causing senseless loss of life. That isn't the same as using the threat of the bomb to provide leverage for a demand. The initial casualties were regrettable, but necessary to make the point that I'm not bluffing. Once we get that straight, no one else need be hurt.

"You think of these two situations as the same. Nations, leaders, and anyone supporting those in power always do. But in a world without power there are only two things that count, money and force. These commodities are inextricably interrelated, and no one knows it better than your president. But enough of this. You know who holds the power here, and it's time for the business at hand. What are your orders?"

"Follow your instructions to the letter."

"Really?"

"The authorities on Oasis have every intention of doing what you want."

"Oh come now, Captain. They tried to trap me within the last hour. You call that cooperation?"

"I can't speak for the police, but the aviation contingent has worked their butts off to get this shuttle ready. My commander briefed me personally on the importance of doing what you say. I think they thought I might try something on my own."

"Save the station, maybe?"

"Something like that. But they were wrong. I just want to get out of this alive."

"I bet you do. Just so we understand one another, the only way you can do that and save the station in the bargain is to do exactly what I tell you. Any doubts about that?"

The man was leaning close to Brett, the masked face only inches away. *Can he tell if I'm lying?* "No doubts. Tell me what you want me to do and let's get on with it."

"So we're eager now, is that it? In due time, Captain. But first I have some items to attend to, and you will have to remain here."

The man secured Brett's wrists with the handcuffs through the handhold and disappeared up the ladder into the cockpit. On two occasions the man came out of the cockpit and walked back into the cargo bay, returning after a few minutes, carrying a toolbox.

Brett's chest hurt. The shuttle had been carefully prepared for flight, and this guy is walking around with tools? *What the hell is he doing?*

In a flashback memory from his childhood as modified by current circumstances, Brett saw himself filling a blackboard with: *Never, ever, volunteer for anything.*

TOBY KNELT IN THE CHUTES, EXAMINING HIS DIAGRAM OF THE network. He needed to get to the shuttle, sneak on board, and find a hiding place. Unfortunately, years of experience roaming around in the chutes didn't help, because he hadn't spent much time near the loading docks. They were large open areas with few places to hide, but that's where the shuttle was.

As he studied the diagram, Toby noted something confusing. There appeared to be single chutes extending into the loading docks. Usually the hatches were located in a wall, or maybe a ceiling, but these were in the floor. They were also positioned in the middle of the dock where the shuttles were parked. According to the legend, a symbol by the hatch identified it as an "Aircrew Emergency Shuttle Evacuation Point."

Could this be a way *into* the shuttle? Toby spent about ten minutes trying to answer the question. After studying each of the chute diagrams adjacent to the docks and tracing the evacuation points backward, he decided they must be just what they looked like. How to get over there?

Long route, short route, what were the chances of discovery if he went this way or that? With the evacuation in progress he might be able to leave the chutes, but the risk of discovery far outweighed the advantages.

This morning's evacuation information on the computer had listed multiple flights for every dock except number seven, which meant Brett's shuttle was probably parked there, so Toby decided to try that one. The quickest route would be across the station past the central core and from there to the Sector Seven loading dock. It also would allow him to get the shotgun. Toby finished studying the diagram and headed out.

As he neared the core, the memory of the chase returned with a vengeance. He began to sweat and his legs were shaking. After drinking a half bottle of water and deep breathing helped calm him down, he advanced very slowly, pausing frequently to audio and space search in front of him. He had performed three move-pause-search-move sequences as he neared the central core.

This search pattern took longer because he had to scan such a large area. After about 30 minutes he finally got an audio hit, the sounds vague, too indistinct, probably near the limit of his range. And where were they, exactly?

Toby studied the diagram and realized he hadn't considered the nuclear reactor room. His previous explorations had remained well clear of it, and he wasn't eager to go there now.

He could navigate around it, but what about the sounds? What if the man was in there? Could Toby do something to hurt him and stop this thing before he ever got to the shuttle?

He thought about his options and decided he had to check it out. If nothing else, he could get to his destination faster, and he didn't know how soon the shuttle would be leaving. He advanced again and paused when the audio search resulted in clear reception, which stopped him cold.

Shouts, lots of noise, and cries of what sounded like wounded men sent chills up his spine. Did this mean the man had been captured and it was all over? Toby hurried to the nearest hatch overlooking the core. After audio-space searching the immediate vicinity, he opened it enough to peer out.

Men were everywhere, standing and prone, along with a biting odor he couldn't identify. Toby moved his position twice to get a better view, but everyone was dressed in black clothing, the prone figures all looked alike, and no one appeared to be a captive.

He wanted to give the reactor a wide berth, but time might be running out. Swallowing his uneasiness, Toby entered the chute circumventing the reactor room and advanced faster than he liked until something appeared in the gloom ahead, a darker patch on the floor of the chute. What the heck was that?

Silent and still, Toby searched the area and received no warnings. He moved slowly forward until he could identify it as an open hatch, but not like the normal ones. He studied the diagram and discovered that it was an access port into environmental control ducting within the reactor room. Why a chute would connect with the duct he couldn't imagine, but there it was.

Toby stuck his head into the opening and found that the duct was almost as large a chute. If he could crawl in there, and if the diagrams were correct, he could save time by proceeding across rather than around the reactor room. Toby tried to enter the duct, but his backpack caught on the entrance. He took off the pack and pushed it along the floor of the duct in front of him. Even though he'd been taught that the reactor posed no hazard, he scurried along without pausing.

He was looking behind him when the backpack dropped out of his loose grip. He froze and heard the pack hit the floor below. It had fallen through a square opening in the bottom of the duct. With no idea of the layout, he extended his audio-space search. No hits, but there seemed to be something interfering with his ability. Nuclear power? The radiation, maybe? Or what about the heat? What if he extended his search into the reactor? Would his ability to sense heat allow it to hurt him?

Toby decided not to use any of his search abilities here and crawled forward to look down. The odor hit him immediately, the same one he detected in the core when he was looking in. Extending his head down and into the room, Toby peered in both directions of a more sharply curved corridor than he'd ever seen, and he couldn't see very far.

What to do? Then he heard something. Zeroing in, he searched out in range until he could distinguish the sound of breathing, labored, in distress. Was this the man? Toby felt the panic rise in him and pulled himself back into the duct when the sound of a voice pounded his audio-search-enhanced ears.

"HELLLLP!"

Toby's initial panic quickly subsided when he realized it couldn't be the man. Way different voice, and Toby couldn't imagine him needing help from anyone, much less calling out for it.

He didn't want to go down there, but he couldn't leave the back-pack, and someone needed help. He dropped into the reactor room. Pack in hand, he crept along the corridor toward the voice, listening for other sounds. He hadn't moved very far when he heard it again, close this time, and he slowed up.

A locker stuck out from the wall. With his body concealed behind it, Toby peered out around the curve of the corridor. Ahead in the darkness he could barely make out a shape, crumpled up against the wall on the floor. He audio and space searched it carefully and knew it was a man, breathing heavily. But the person was still, and no warnings occurred from the search. Choking back his fear, Toby stepped out from behind the locker and crept forward.

As he got closer he smelled something else he didn't recognize. A puddle of thick substance covered the floor. Light from the corridor ahead cast a pale glow, and Toby advanced to get a better look. He recognized the imprint of a booted foot in a pool of blood with a broad smear leading away down the corridor.

Toby recoiled from the sight and banged into the open locker door.

"WHO'S THERE! I'M A COP!"

Heart pounding as he hugged the wall, Toby peered around the curve as he advanced. He passed the blood without looking at it and tiptoed forward as the voice continued to ask who was there, then fell silent.

One last short step and Toby saw a cop lying on the floor. Another shape lay nearby, but he couldn't tell what it was. After pausing to search in both directions and detecting no danger, Toby inched closer and saw the robodog just as the cop saw him.

"Damn if you're not a sight for sore eyes! I'm Corporal Dan Bishop. You're Toby Williams?"

Toby nodded and pointed to the pool of blood. What happened back there?"

"There's nothing we can do to help him. Would you come over here, please?"

Toby did that and knelt down. "What can I do?"

The corporal stared at Toby. "Wait a minute. How did you get in here?"

"In a duct that connects with the chutes. I found an open hatch."

"That explains how the dog made it. Could a man crawl through the duct?"

"I don't think so. It's smaller than the chutes, and even with my backpack off I had trouble."

"Okay. I'm not going to ask what you're doing here. This is the second time I've seen you in places I would have never expected to. But the only important thing now is that you get word back to the police for me."

Worried that he might miss the departure of Brett's shuttle, Toby hesitated. He wanted to help, especially since the cop had helped him escape pursuit in the core. But he couldn't go directly to the police. They'd never understand what he *had* to do and he'd be forced to evacuate with everyone else.

"What do you want me to do?"

"First, don't get caught by the guy who was chasing you. He could be back here any minute. Find a policeman and have him tell central where I am, that the reactor room is wired, and there's no way to enter without triggering the bomb. That's very important. Don't try to get in through the doors. Got it?"

"Yes, sir."

"Tell them to put another dog in, and have him bring a set of handcuff keys, a radio, first aid kit, and a weapon. Tell them to use the equipment harness we made up for the dogs, and I need the best explosives man they've got ready on the radio. Can you remember all that?"

"I got it."

"Time is important. If the guy comes back before I'm ready, we're right back where we started. It sounds like they tried an assault and failed. Make absolutely sure they don't try to get in here through those doors."

Toby nodded and told the cop what he'd been able to see in the core. The corporal said the police probably hadn't tried to enter the reactor room but were attempting to set a trap for the man as he came out.

After finding out about the activity outside the reactor room, the cop seemed less concerned about the man returning soon. He questioned Toby about what had been going on, and he was pleased that the evacuation had begun. When he started asking questions about Toby's being in the chutes and when he was scheduled to leave, the time had come to change the subject.

"Is that Snooper?"

"I thought so at first, but it isn't. And before I forget it, have them send in a repair kit for this dog. He may be of use later if I can get him up and running."

Toby nodded and was staring at the prone figure of the dog when the corporal asked, "Have you ever had a dog?"

The question surprised Toby, and he took a moment to answer. "I've always wanted one, but I was born up here. Some of my friends had dogs on Earth before they came to the station. They told me what it was like."

The cop nodded. "Would you like one? Not a real dog up here, but robodogs can be great friends if you let them."

Toby was speechless. How would the cop do that? His silence must have made the corporal think he didn't want one.

"You're probably going to be stuck on the moon colony for a long while. Having a dog of your own might be fun. They may not let you take him with you, but it'd be worth a try."

Then Corporal Bishop said that he sent Snooper back to his apartment rather than the kennels following the incident in the compactor room. His apartment was on the way to the Sector Seven loading dock, and with special commands, Toby would be able to make Snooper stay. Then using the corporal's instructions, he could set the dog's program to respond to the next voice it heard. In this way Toby would become Snooper's handler, so that the animal would ignore commands from anyone else.

"And this is important," warned the cop. "Make absolutely certain you go through the steps to change the program from 'attack' to 'companion.'"

"Yes, sir," said Toby, even though he had no intention of doing that. The possibility of using Snooper to help him on his quest was great news. With the dog as his ally the man wouldn't have a chance.

Assuring Corporal Bishop that he would find a police officer immediately, Toby carefully avoided the blood and retraced his steps to the duct. He discovered a ladder inside a locker and used it to reenter.

Exiting the duct into the chute, he reviewed his map and came up with a route that would allow him to call the police, retrieve the shotgun, pick up Snooper, and proceed to the loading dock.

Once satisfied that he could do it from memory, he struck out with a mounting determination to get his plan off the ground and make it work.

~

GENERAL ANTONIO DESILVA WAS HAVING A VERY BAD DAY. EVERY time it appeared that things couldn't possibly get worse, they did.

The problems began with the evacuation. In spite of all the planning, some of the players knew nothing about the purpose of the operation, much less the small details necessary to avoid confusion.

And once the trouble started, it spread like a contagious disease so fast you couldn't stop it. In a sporting event, this was when the coach called for a timeout, a breather for his team, and to cool off the opposing team's momentum.

DeSilva had always loved that word. It was the key to winning, at least if you listened to sports commentators. He had always wanted to come up with a way to bottle it. Then when a team needed some, the players could take a swig of his product, go back out on the field and kick some ass. He'd just sit back and watch the money roll in.

But in this situation he was the coach, and his team's momentum meter read zero. As General DeSilva poured virtual water on another evacuation brush fire, he received reports of more trouble in the central core. Leaving Colonel Radcliff in charge of dispensing whatever momentum he could find, DeSilva hurried to Comm Central and walked in on a scene he almost couldn't believe.

He'd seen chaos before, but nothing like this: Everybody talking at once, with snatches of conversation that indicated the evacuation was a minor activity compared to events in the core. He listened for a few minutes and decided it was hopeless. He needed *accurate* information.

General DeSilva instructed the major on duty to call the Battle Staff together and then follow him into the War Room. Once inside with the door closed, he sat on the edge of the conference table and pointed to a chair. The major sat down with a heavy sigh and looked up at him with tired eyes. This man was on the edge of collapse.

"You going to make it?"

The major managed a weak smile. "Hopefully. There's a point where you begin to run on reserve power, but I'll make it to the end of my shift."

"Want me to relieve you?"

"Under any other circumstance I would accept in a heartbeat, General. But I think being here since the start of the evacuation allows me to coordinate things better. I can't imagine having to brief a replacement at this point."

"Okay, but make sure you don't hang on too long and let fatigue get the better of you."

"I hear you, sir."

"Good. New subject. What the hell's going on in the core?"

The major shifted in his chair, and grimaced as he uncrossed his legs. He summarized the action based on radio reports. "At this point, it appears that the Alpha Team Commander decided all on his own to put the team in place and send the robodog into the core. The audio and video feeds were not activated at the time, but that only means we didn't get the information as it occurred. The data was captured, stored in the dog's memory bank, and all we had to do was bring it up.

"We got more information than we ever expected. There *is* a bomb in the reactor room, well protected by anti-tampering devices. And we found the cop, the one who disappeared from the loading bay. He was being held captive in the reactor room."

"What do you mean, 'was'?"

"The cop's still in there, but the man isn't."

General DeSilva shook his head. *Why does this kind of stuff always happen on my watch?* "What about the gunshots?"

"We haven't pieced all the events together yet, but apparently the dog was being used to free the cop when the man returned to the reactor room. When the dog attacked him to protect the cop, the man shot him."

"The cop?"

"No, sir, the dog."

"Christ, Major, you had me going there for a minute. You mean he shot *it*."

"Yes, sir."

"Continue."

"The Alpha Team did not respond. Too much confusion, and they'd been told to wait for a go command from Sergeant Cadogan."

"Where is Cadogan now?"

"Don't know. No one's seen him since he left the dog's handler, who told us the sergeant went in the core alone."

"Damn it!" General DeSilva slapped his palm on the table, stood up, and began pacing the room. "People were all concerned about that pilot being a loose cannon, and Cadogan had his own private agenda. Am I mistaken? Did we discuss any contingency in which it would be okay to send someone into the core alone?"

"No, sir," said Colonel Thomas as he entered the room, trailed by a long line of other Battle Staff officers. "It looks like Cadogan issued his own instructions to the Alpha Team, and then kept them in the dark to boot. He went in there solo, and he's been seriously injured."

General DeSilva stood in the corner of the room, digesting what he had just heard and developing an upset stomach in the process. When Colonel Thomas and the other remaining members of the Battle Staff had taken their seats around the table, he began.

"We've got ourselves a real mess here. Let's piece together what we know so far."

The duty officer repeated his report on what happened in the central core, and with the assistance of Colonel Thomas presented the chronology of events. The Battle Staff members sat in silence as the debacle unfolded before them. General DeSilva listened with mounting frustration as he tried to make sense of what had happened.

"So, let's see if we have this straight. The dog is searching the core and reactor room. Alpha Team's in position, waiting for word to move, but they don't even know what Cadogan is up to. The dog finds the bomb and then a cop. The man enters the reactor room and there's a fight. The dog's in pieces. Then we hear more shooting. Probably Cadogan, goes in by himself, gets his face blown away. Alpha team hears the shots, can't raise Cadogan on the radio, asks for permission to go in. The guy's always one step ahead. He sets an ambush, cuts down Alpha with two bombs, and disappears again.

"And where does that put us? Bomb still set, a cop trapped in the reactor room with it, cops dead and wounded lying all over the goddamn place. That about cover it?"

As he sat at the table with the question hanging, General DeSilva's anger-meter fast approached red line, and he struggled to control it. Commanders must present the right example in front of subordinates at all times, and to give vent to his feelings now would be viewed as loss of control.

Would this nightmare never end? He became lost in private thoughts when he realized the entire room was looking at him. Time for more leadership.

DeSilva decided the first order of business was to evaluate the progress of the evacuation. If the bad news kept pouring in, the best thing he could do would be to reduce the risk to as many people as possible.

While listening to a status report from the engineering officer, another brushfire popped up when the overhead speakers came alive with the excited voice of a duty sergeant.

"Excuse me, General DeSilva, but we just received a very important phone call."

The general turned to face the glass partition between the War Room and Comm Central. Motioning to the duty sergeant, he pointed to the speakers and indicated for him to play the call over the intercom. At this point, he didn't care who heard what.

As the speaker crackled to life, General DeSilva held up his hand to quiet the room.

"Comm Central, Sergeant Story speaking, sir."

"Uh . . . I was calling for the police."

"Calls to the police duty desk are being transferred here during the evacuation emergency. Can I help you, son?"

"Can you get a message to the police?"

"The central police function is operating from here, and an officer is on duty. Tell me what it is you want, please. We're very busy."

"This message is from Corporal Dan Bishop. He's the one in the reactor room, you know, the one who was taken hostage?"

The boy's voice was haunting, captivating, and incongruous with the subject matter. It was obvious the speakers in Comm Central were on. Activity beyond the glass came to a standstill.

"Who are you, son? And I need your location. I'll send an officer to where you are."

The boy ignored the question and relayed information from the corporal about sending in another dog, the equipment he needed, and that the bomb was no bluff.

"Listen to me, kid. We need to talk with you about this in person. Tell me your location and I can have an officer there in a few minutes."

"The corporal said to put your best explosives man on the other end of the radio so he can talk to him. Have you got all that?"

"No, son, I don't. Would you repeat the part about the equipment harness?"

The line went dead. It had to be the same kid who was in the chutes and ran into the man the previous day. DeSilva wanted to deal with the question of how the kid got involved, but more pressing matters needed attention. "Colonel Thomas, how long will it take to get the equipment together?"

"Thirty minutes max, sir. And there's another dog standing by. Alpha Team's with the technician as we speak."

"Make sure we have an explosives expert ready to go when the dog enters the core. Maybe with the cop able to move in there we can find a way to disable that bomb and put this bastard *down*. Let's get on it."

Colonel Thomas went to the rear of the War Room to use the phone. DeSilva asked Captain Norton to continue with the evacuation report.

"Yes, sir. But first you might be interested that we have reports of a missing thirteen-year-old boy. He's gotta be the one on the tape."

"When was he reported missing?"

"About an hour ago. His parents never acknowledged the evacuation alert message. We sent an officer to investigate and found them sound asleep. The kid was gone and left a note."

"You mean he ran away from home?"

"It appears so. He's not the only person unaccounted for, and—"

From the overhead speaker again, "General DeSilva?"

With exaggerated slowness he answered, "What is it, Sergeant?"

"Sir, we have reports someone closed the cargo door on the alert shuttle from the inside. Eyewitnesses say it was a man with a gun."

This guy was like a ghost, popping up here, then over there, then behind you, creating havoc wherever he went. "Are police responding?"

"Yes, sir, we're just getting the first information from an officer on the scene now."

DeSilva nodded through the glass at the duty sergeant and turned to Lieutenant Colonel Parker. "I thought we had that place locked down."

"So did I, sir. The loading docks are guarded around the clock, and especially this one."

"How the hell could a man get in there?"

"That's a good question, sir, and I don't have an answer."

"General DeSilva?" said the duty sergeant on the overhead speaker.

"Go ahead."

"Sir, the on-scene commander reports the shuttle is locked down tight. There's no response from the interior, and the outside emergency entry mechanisms have been disabled."

"Anyone else on the shuttle at the time?"

"The man with the gun was standing just inside the opening, and there *might* have been someone on the floor beside him."

DeSilva turned to Lieutenant Colonel Parker. "Do you know where Captain Larsen is?"

"Not for sure, sir, but I told him to stay on top of shuttle preparations."

"That's just dandy. If the hijacker has his own personal pilot, we've lost any chance to stop him."

"Maybe not," said Colonel Thomas. "If we can find a way to disable the bomb with Corporal Bishop's help, and then get word to Captain Larsen over that private comm link, we might still be able to prevent this."

"Prevent what?" asked Captain Norton. "Do we know what his real objective is?"

"No," replied DeSilva, "and it doesn't matter. The bomb gives him the leverage to keep us at bay. I need good news about that effort yesterday, and then we'll figure out how to regain control of the shuttle. Make it happen."

~

AFTER MAKING THE PHONE CALL TO COMM CENTRAL, TOBY retrieved the shotgun. It was just as frightening as he remembered it, but he was able to overcome his reluctance by concentrating on his anger at the man who was causing all this trouble, threatening Toby's family, friends, and home.

When he got to the chute exit closest to the cop's apartment, he went through the usual search routine, dropped into the corridor, and made it to the apartment within without seeing or hearing any signs of activity. Oasis had become a ghost town.

Toby entered the code the cop gave him and paused with his hand on the door handle. As a safety measure, code words were programmed into each dog, allowing the handler to disable all the circuits instantly in the event of a malfunction. The code wasn't dependent on the handler's voice imprint, so it *should* work.

He'd also been told the dog would challenge him without charging, but if Toby attempted to enter the room he would be attacked. Reviewing the code words that would freeze the dog in position,

Toby opened the door *very* slowly, peered in and almost wet his pants.

Snooper crouched motionless in the middle of the room, ears laid back, snarling, mouth open and full of teeth. Toby decided this was not a good idea, and started to back out. Snooper took a step forward. Toby's fear spiked but in a croaking voice he said, "Snooper, big dog, be still."

It worked. *Thank you, Mr. Programmer.*

Reprogramming Snooper was easy. Toby gave the dog a few simple commands, and he obeyed without hesitation. This was great! Toby took a moment to consider the part about changing Snooper from attack to companion program.

If Snooper was going to be the partner Toby needed, the dog would have to do something more helpful than "stay." Something like pursuing the man relentlessly through the station, catching him, and tearing him to pieces. Companion dogs probably don't do that.

So with Snooper the faithful attack dog at his side, Toby left the apartment and reentered the chutes. He'd been worried about how the dog was going to get up to the hatch, but was amazed at the awesome display of power as the animal leapt from the floor to the opening.

With another look at the diagram, Toby decided on his route and started out. Crawling along, he looked back and saw Snooper right behind him, panting softly and looking content. How could he fail with this ally at his side? Brimming with confidence, he pressed forward and soon found himself grinning.

What an adventure this was!

BRETT WOKE UP DISORIENTED AND CONFUSED. HE YAWNED AND tried to concentrate. What had happened?

Oh, yeah. He was in this mess for the duration. The man held all the cards. Why didn't they just leave? The shuttle was ready to go; all they needed was a ground crew. And assuming the bomb was still a factor, no one was going to stand in their way.

Brett sat up, looked around, wondered where the man was. "Hello? Can you hear me?"

From behind him, the man's voice was so close that it startled Brett. "I can hear you fine, Captain. You don't need to shout."

"I'd like to use the restroom, please."

"Certainly. Turn to your left and I'll loosen the cuffs."

The man's cool efficiency with the various tasks required for total physical control over Brett once again impressed him. Even if he knew more than the basics of how to take advantage and try to overpower the man, it didn't appear that he would ever get an opportunity. Whenever Brett's hands were not secured, a weapon of some kind was right there.

Back in the galley with one wrist handcuffed to the nearest table leg, Brett was drinking a hot cup of coffee as he watched the man prepare a meal from the ship's stores. When the food was ready, the man cut it into pieces, placed it in front of him, and handed him a spoon.

With his one free hand, Brett began to eat as the man stepped back from the table and sat on one of the benches. "Won't you be joining me?"

"Later, maybe," the man replied, and never took his eyes off Brett. He probably didn't want to be occupied with anything else while Brett wasn't fully handcuffed. The fact that he was holding an eating utensil may have had something to do with it. Brett wondered if the man knew how to kill another human being with a spoon.

When he finished, Brett asked for another cup of coffee. Returning with two steaming mugs, the man sat down across from him and placed the portable radio between them.

"Are you qualified as a pilot on both the shuttle and the fighter?"

"Yes."

"And you have been ordered to perform this mission?"

"I volunteered for it."

The man raised his eyebrows. "Just for the record, you might have wanted to keep that to yourself. For a man in my position, it raises all sorts of red flags about why. It also creates suspicion as to your intent. The last thing I need is a hero."

"I'm no hero. They wanted the most qualified pilot, and that's what you've got."

The man laughed softly." That may be what *they* wanted. But I just want competence, and that's what I'll expect from you. Before this goes much further, I'll find out whether you're qualified. If you aren't, and are here for any other reason, I'll kill you. Understood?"

Brett could see the man's eyes almost change color as he made the threat. "Yes."

"Good." The man stood up and cleared the remains of Brett's meal. "More coffee?"

"I'll just finish this in a minute."

The man nodded, rinsed and dried his cup, secured it in the galley and sat down at the table. "When we're clear of the station I'll provide you with a destination, which you will program into the navigation computer. Reaching Earth, I want the orbital decay and reentry accomplished so the transition to powered flight will occur at five hundred miles from that point. You will plan for the final four hundred miles to be flown at minimum altitude."

The instructions took Brett by surprise, and he wondered if the man understood the effect of altitude on range. He was about to ask about that when the man picked up the radio and keyed the microphone button. "This call is to Comm Central, for General DeSilva. Do you read?" Then he activated the speaker and placed the radio on the table

Brett could imagine the scene in the War Room. Another chaotic affair, with Battle Staff members scrambling to respond, wondering what the message would be, and always, what additional bad news would be received. The general must have been fairly close, because he answered quickly.

"This is General DeSilva."

"As I'm sure you're aware by now, I have the shuttle, and I caution you against trying to breach it. To emphasize the point, I want someone to say hello."

The man motioned toward the radio.

"General DeSilva, this is Captain Larsen. I—"

The man held up his hand in a "stop" signal and said, "That should

make the point. Thank you for providing me with such a highly qualified pilot, and I hope what he tells me is true. If he doesn't do as I tell
him, the consequences will be severe, which I trust is clear enough to
prevent any more futile events like the attempt earlier tonight.

"And to reiterate, the reactor is protected from intrusion by a
tamper-proof bomb. You have all the evidence you need to realize I
can do what I say, and will without hesitation. Let's avoid any more
violence. Agreed?"

Brett could picture the general sitting in the War Room, hands
clamped down on the arms if his chair, on the verge of a massive coro-
nary. He wasn't used to being told anything, and following instructions
from this bastard must be unbearable.

"Agreed."

"That's settled, then. The captain tells me the shuttle is ready to go.
Plan on an 0800 departure. In the meantime, you probably have a lot
to do on your end."

The man turned off the radio as he stood, and disappeared up the
ladder into the cockpit.

As Brett watched him go, he realized how foolish he'd been to
think he could prevent any of this. In the cockpit of a fighter, he
considered himself nearly invincible. Not bulletproof, but with the
training, skill, and determination to do the job as well or better than
anyone. The ability to perform under fear, remaining effective in spite
of it, made all the difference.

But this was totally different. He knew almost nothing about his
adversary. In combat, he studied the enemy's training methods, the
strategic and tactical doctrine employed, and the capabilities of his
weapons. Then he performed a comparative analysis and developed a
battle plan to maximize his advantages and exploit the enemy's weaknesses. The end results were as often as not more dependent on this
prior preparation than the skill of the warriors.

Without the plan or the skill, isolated from support, and in the
grip of a man who seemed to be as invincible in this environment as
Brett was in his, he knew it was no longer a matter of winning, but of
survival.

Or, maybe he'd have to trade survival for winning. If the bomb could be disarmed and Brett knew it, he'd have the option of taking them both to their deaths, side by side. As Brett thought about that, he wondered if he could do it.

It sounded good sitting here just thinking. He'd seen pilots filled almost to bursting with bravado at the bar. But when the bullets started flying, the true measure of a man rose up for all to see.

Despair settled over Brett like a cloud of dust, seeping into every fold in his flight suit, down the back of his neck, and tasting of grit.

Staring at the table turned on its side and exposing the entrance into the chutes, Brett was suddenly struck by how close escape could appear and yet be so far away. All he'd have to do is get in there and crawl away to safety.

Then it occurred to him that the man had left the hatch unguarded. Brett changed his position as best he could, straining with the handcuffs digging into his wrists until he finally got a better view of the hatch. Open. The black hole stared back at him, beckoning.

He couldn't get to it, but if anyone on the outside realized it was a way into the shuttle, maybe they were at this moment considering that option.

Can I get word to them? As Brett thought about that, a barely detectable movement in the darkness of the chute entrance caught his attention.

Eyes straining, wondering if they were just playing tricks on him, he leaned as far out from the table as he could. He ignored the pain in his wrists and focused on empty space just below the floor.

Then he saw it again and knew he wasn't imagining things. The next few seconds passed in what seemed like slow motion.

A slight movement, something dark and round, the size of a pipe with a hole in the end. It disappeared, then came back again, farther out this time, and Brett's spirits soared when he recognized the muzzle of a shotgun barrel.

They had thought of the evacuation hatch! He glanced over his shoulder at the ladder into the cockpit, and when he turned around again his heart almost jammed in his throat.

Toby's head rose up, but he was looking away from Brett.

A soft "Psssst" from Brett snapped Toby's head around. His eyes widened as he grinned and rose up out of the hatch and—

The sound of boots on the cockpit ladder.

Toby banged his head on the rim of the hatch and dropped the shotgun as he disappeared into the chute.

Brett grabbed his cup off the table and poured the remaining coffee on the floor just before the man appeared at the base of the ladder.

"What's going on, Captain?"

"I spilled my coffee. I'll clean it up if you'll hand me some towels."

The man looked around the room, then went over to the chute entrance and pointed the beam of a flashlight into the darkness.

Brett held his breath until the man returned the table to an upright position, closing the hatch cover. Then he walked into the cargo bay and disappeared. Brett adjusted his position, trying to look further into the darkness, but he couldn't see anything except the occasional glow of the man's flashlight beam as he appeared to be searching the interior.

When the man returned, he said nothing as he wiped up the spill, climbed the ladder and disappeared into the cockpit.

Brett's entire body felt like it was deflating from having the thrill of rescue so close, only to be snatched away. But even in the midst of that emotional letdown, he was so relieved that Toby hadn't run into the hijacker while roaming around in the chutes.

Except for one nagging thought . . . that he couldn't imagine a universe in which Toby Williams would give up on his dream.

12

DAY FOUR EARLY MORNING

Sitting in the cockpit, Samael had just finished with a few modifications. He felt comfortable about the shuttle, the pilot, and the ability to leave the station on schedule. But two doubts lingered.

He had originally intended to leave the reactor room on his own timetable, taking the cop with him at least as far as the shuttle. But now the cop had been left in the room, and Samael still didn't know how the dog got inside.

Then there was the noise from the galley while he'd been up in the cockpit. The pilot had lied to him. The bit about the coffee cup was a good try, but not good enough. Samael was convinced there had been someone in the chute.

But who? The connection between the chute system and the shuttle had been a late addition to the design. With the exception of the pilots, few people probably knew about it. He didn't think it was the cops, but he had to assume it might have been.

Samael inspected the cockpit for anything out of place to alert the pilot, then gathered his tools and descended the ladder. The pill dropped into the pilot's coffee had worked again. He was sound asleep.

Standing by the chute entrance, Samael took a moment to review his immediate objectives.

Leaving the shuttle was a risk, but with calculated benefit. It was a matter of unfinished business. He had to check the reactor room, and he had to find out if it had been the cops in the chute or someone else.

Someone else? Go ahead and say it. Or the kid. The little bastard who stuck his nose into things that didn't concern him, deliberately played at hide and seek, and managed to escape with barely a scratch. The memory of that episode was nagging at Samael like a biting fly and he couldn't shake it. Why did he think it might be the kid now? Because it was the last thing he should expect. The time had come to settle it.

One last check of the shuttle detected nothing amiss and the loading dock appeared deserted. The only way in or out was through the chute hatch, which Samael now opened and silently entered, closing it behind him.

He checked each of the chutes in the immediate area, thinking the kid might have settled down to wait. Finding nothing, he searched the next outer ring of chutes and came up empty. Satisfied there was no immediate threat close to the shuttle, he used the chutes to reach the central core, and changed positions around the top of the dome to check for activity in the corridors surrounding the reactor. He found no evidence of police presence. They were probably wary of additional bombs, but also would never expect him to leave the shuttle and return to the reactor room.

Samael lowered himself down on a line from a hatch on the opposite side of the reactor from where the assault occurred. With weapon drawn, he entered the access code on the keypad and opened the door. He knew something was wrong before his foot passed the threshold.

No warning signal sounded from the anti-tampering device. There should have been a series of beeps, counting down a time delay for entering a code and preventing bomb detonation.

Confident in his care with rigging the bomb, Samael held his ground and fought the impulse to run. No warning meant the countdown was not in progress.

The anti-tampering device must have been disabled. He had to fix the problem, or the bomb threat wouldn't force the authorities to do anything. His destination and objective were determined, the only variable being the method of approach. Sneaking up on someone undetected depended on many factors, some of which he could control, but most of which he could not. Stealthy movement meant nothing if he didn't move in the right direction and have a plan.

In about ten minutes Samael gained a position just short of where he could see the controller for the anti-tampering system. Someone was there. He heard a voice, intentionally softened. He peered around the corner and saw the cop standing on a ladder, facing away from him and staring at the overhead piping where the bomb had been placed.

How the cop had removed the restraints was a question for later. Samael's immediate problem was to stop further tampering. The cop was alone, but others could be moving in, or holding back somewhere. The solution in either case was to do this fast.

The cop said something into a portable radio, then listened to a response and used a small flashlight to inspect the wiring. He was receiving instructions from someone outside the room as he worked to disable the explosives. After listening to a long transmission, the cop put the radio down in front of him on the ladder, picked up a screwdriver, and with the flashlight in his other hand leaned in close.

As Samael left the comparative safety of his hiding place he knew two things: the cop wouldn't need to communicate by radio for instructions if the police had gained access to the reactor room, and it would be relatively easy to surprise him. The cop had no clue what was going on behind him.

Samael was about ten feet away when his peripheral vision picked up something to his left that had been hidden from sight behind the open door to an equipment locker.

His heart pounded so hard he could hear the beats. It was the paw of a dog, and the image came flooding back of the super canine from space as it charged him out of the gloom. Then as Samael shifted his weight to his back foot in retreat, he noticed the dog's paw was laying on its side.

Attack dogs don't sleep on the job, and he couldn't imagine that a robot version would either. Samael trained his pistol on the dog's position, shifted his weight forward, and advanced. As more of the dog became visible, he could feel the tension relax when he saw the wires.

This was the dog he'd shot. It was motionless, and looked as if the cop had been working on it. Electrical parts lay about, a small tool kit open on the floor, and the "wound" site had been enlarged.

The cop remained unaware of the impending threat. Samael relaxed his caution as he took two steps forward, drew back the pistol, and clubbed the cop over the head.

As Samael felt the jarring impact of the pistol striking the cop's head, he detected movement to his left. The cop's body began to crumble off the ladder and the follow-through of the blow turned Samael's body to his left. When he saw what was coming, true fear gripped him.

A second dog, very much "alive," was already airborne. With Samael's momentum to the left, arm swinging past the dog's attack, he had no way to block it. The dog hit him with tremendous impact and struck him dead center in the groin, knocking him backward to the floor. The pain dimmed Samael's vision, but his training and superb physical condition allowed him to react.

Lying on his back with the dog tearing at his groin, Samael reached for the stun gun attached to his equipment harness and ripped it from its holster. He placed the gun on the dog's neck, pressed the trigger, and heard a zapping sound as the electrical charge surged between the two prongs at the top of the device.

The dog spasmed, circuits hopelessly overloaded, and the smell of electric wiring heated to melting filled Samael's nostrils. The dog shuddered violently and then lay still when Samael released the stun gun trigger.

He looked down between his legs. His pants were shredded at the crotch. It hurt like hell, and he was afraid the dog had castrated him. Sitting up, he peered down for a closer look and in spite of what had happened almost laughed.

Samael never went to work without protection. He had no family, but that didn't mean any less interest in protecting his jewels. Since the groin was a common target in hand-to-hand combat, he wore a custom fitted jock strap with a hard cup. Lightweight and extremely strong, it had served its purpose today. He hurt, but he was still in the game, and in more ways than one.

The cop moaned and rolled over. Ignoring his own pain, Samael got up, found the cuffs attached to the cop's belt, and snapped them around the man's wrists. The melted dog wore a harness that must have held the extra equipment. Samael didn't know how they got the dog in here, but it was a damned good idea, except that he now had another radio and a weapon with more ammo. In the end, his adversaries might prove to be his best allies.

Whoever was on the other end of that radio would soon know something had happened. Samael couldn't afford to get trapped in here with the bomb. The controller for the anti-tampering device wasn't damaged, and he quickly reconnected the wiring. With considerable disgust he noted the cuts were in places he had thought would result in triggering the bomb. So much for the expert who briefed him on this circuitry. Nobody did quality work anymore.

When satisfied the bomb was reset, he considered looking for how the dog got in but decided against it. The only reason their plan had worked was because the cop had been locked inside, and once free of the cuffs he could follow instructions.

Dragging the cop's limp form to the nearest door, Samael smiled to himself as he pictured a dog, head cocked to one side like the Dalmatian in the old commercials, listening to the radio and disabling the bomb with a pair of wire snips. The dogs were good, but not that good.

They do, however, have powerful jaws and sharp teeth. He took the time to check the cup in case he had another run-in with one. The cup had a crack, but it didn't appear to have compromised the cup's ability to protect him.

Standing by the door, he considered what to do about the cop. The safest thing was to kill him. It would be quick, clean, and easy. If he had a way out of here without opening a door and exposing himself to capture, he'd just do that and think no more about it.

But he had to leave the way he'd come, and he could achieve the same objective of protecting the bomb by simply depositing the man outside the reactor room and activating the anti-tampering device.

Although he had little aversion to killing, he needed a reason and an objective other than the killing itself.

Decision made, he armed the anti-tampering device and opened the door. He dragged the cop with him to use as a shield in the event of an attack. Reaching the line hanging from a ladder rung, Samael left the cop slumped against the wall, climbed to the chute entrance, pulled the line in after him, and closed the hatch.

Pausing to catch his breath, he smiled with the realization he almost had it made. All he had to do now was make his way back to the shuttle, and maybe arrange a little surprise in the bargain.

The thought of the kid just wouldn't go away. As he crawled off into the darkness, Samael remembered the humiliation he felt as the meddling little runt got away. Something told him it wasn't over, and their paths would cross again. He promised himself the next time would be different.

He also decided he might make an exception to his philosophy about killing, and cancel the kid's ticket just for fun.

TOBY'S HEART TOOK A LONG TIME RETURNING TO NORMAL. AS HE crouched in the dark chute halfway between two intersections, he gripped Snooper's collar and tried to extend his search. He was pretty sure the man had stopped hunting for him, but couldn't afford to be wrong.

The dog had been tough to control, and almost caused trouble by trying to crawl toward their pursuer rather than following Toby. Whispered commands didn't seem very effective. Toby was afraid to speak louder, so he pulled the dog along behind him.

The power of the animal was controllable, but it took time to fully program the dog's receptors to a new voice. Toby had been told to expect some confusion. He assumed the confusion would be Snooper's, but quickly discovered the dog knew exactly what he wanted. It must have something to do with Toby's decision to leave him in the attack mode. In the absence of other instructions, Snooper was going to protect his master as a first priority.

Once satisfied the way was clear, Toby commanded the dog to heel and moved back toward the shuttle. He became more cautious the closer he got, and spent a good deal of time using his audio and spatial search to clear the way ahead of and behind his current position. He was determined never again to be surprised due to his failure to remain alert, and in both directions.

He'd been surprised in the shuttle because he stopped his search in Brett's immediate vicinity rather than going beyond the first contact. Luckily his internal warning mechanism, or whatever it was, protected him again. The sudden surge of impending danger had hit him like a wave of nausea. The lesson was clear. With his search modes shut down or too narrow, danger could be very close without triggering a warning.

Armed with a new confidence in his ability to protect himself, Toby returned to the shuttle. His heart pounded as he detected Brett's breathing pattern in the same location. The breathing was even slower, and Toby wondered how his friend could remain so calm and cool in the face of adversity. It must be his training as a fighter pilot that did it.

Extending the search pattern, Toby conducted a thorough sweep of the shuttle. Finding no danger, shotgun at the ready, and with Snooper frozen in position by a stay command, Toby crawled forward and peered around the corner. He expected to see the shaft of light from the shuttle's interior illuminating the chute directly below the hatch, but he found only darkness ahead.

Backing up, Toby wondered if the hatch could be locked from inside the shuttle? There were no locks on any of the other hatches, but that didn't mean anything. Then it dawned on him that the man could not have left the shuttle and locked the hatch behind him.

Time for a decision. He couldn't stay here, and the only way to find out was to do it. Fear nibbling at his stomach, Toby turned the corner and crawled toward the hatch. Hearing Snooper's soft whine behind him, Toby repeated his whispered command to stay and approached the vertical portion of the chute.

Lying on his back, he inched forward to look up and saw the closed hatch cover. He pulled himself forward and up into the chute just below the hatch. Shotgun in one hand, Toby reached for the handle. He needed to do this quietly, and knew that some of the handles came loose suddenly with a loud clang. Hopefully this one would be an exception.

No such luck. When it finally gave way, the sound reverberated through the chute. Someone could have heard it easily. Toby grabbed the shotgun, swung the hatch open, and stood up into the shuttle's interior and found Brett sound asleep.

Toby climbed in and walked over to the table. Brett was sitting on a bench seat, with his head lying on the table. Both arms were behind his back. When he got closer, Toby saw the handcuffs and the length of additional chain securing Brett to the seat supports.

"Wake up, Brett."

No response. Toby reached out and shook his shoulder.

"Brett! Wake up!"

Still no response. Toby tried a few more times to rouse him. As he considered what to do next, Snooper growled. Toby stepped over to the chute opening, angry with himself for having forgotten about the dog. "Snooper, come!"

The clicking of Snooper's feet on the floor of the chute sent a thrill through Toby that he had such an ally, one who obeyed instantly and without question. When Snooper's head appeared below the chute opening, Toby smiled at him. "Come on, boy."

Snooper crawled up and out of the chute, tail wagging vigorously. As Toby tried to calm the dog down, the all-too-familiar rush of danger hit him.

Toby began to lower himself into the chute when the warning doubled in intensity. Of course! The man wasn't on the shuttle.

Toby started toward the cockpit, but stopped. He had to find a better place to hide. If he hadn't tripped on the shotgun he would have forgotten it. Regaining his balance, he picked it up and ran into a corridor he hoped would take him into the cargo bay.

Snooper's growl stopped him. Looking back, Toby saw the dog crouched by the opening, hair on his back raised and with all the signs of being ready to charge.

"Snooper. Heel."

Snooper stepped back, looked over his shoulder at Toby, then back towards the chute entrance. He seemed to be considering his choices.

Could robodogs think? Toby repeated the command. With a final soft growl, Snooper turned and followed.

The corridor led past a series of doors on either side. Toby opened one. It was a small room, with two bunk beds and a tiny living area that probably served as sleeping quarters for the crew. No place to hide there.

He ran to the end of the passageway and opened a large door. Looking out on a cavernous space, he knew this was his only chance. He climbed down the ladder with Snooper close behind, then sprinted past a fighter strapped down to the floor toward a huge stack of cargo.

With no more time to look and concerned about being caught in the open, Toby used the netting to climb up the side of a pallet. Snooper was still at the bottom, pacing back and forth and looking up at him. Toby leaned over the side and commanded, "Snooper. Come!"

The dog stopped pacing and stood perfectly still for about five seconds, head tilted to one side, looking up at his master. Toby was about to repeat the command when Snooper crouched, paused for a second or two, then jumped.

The dog's incredible strength propelled him almost straight up. Snooper didn't make it to the top, but with his legs grabbing at the netting, he managed to climb to a point where Toby reached a paw and pulled him the rest of the way up.

Toby's internal warning circuit began working overtime. He looked around and noticed one of the containers had a loose top. It was almost empty. Toby climbed inside. Holding the top open with his head, he whispered to Snooper and motioned for the dog to follow. It took a while to settle the dog down. Once Snooper stopped shifting around, he looked at Toby and licked his face. Toby knew Snooper was nothing but a robot, and had seen the wiring to prove it, but it was really hard to accept sometimes.

Toby held the lid up a little for some light to examine the interior. It had two six-packs of water, some energy bars, packets of energy drink powder, a green oxygen bottle with a tube and small face mask attached, and some loose straps lying on a padded floor. He thought about that for a moment. This had to be the 4-day hideout for one of the two stowaways during their trip from Earth.

He'd found the perfect place to wait for an opportunity to show the hijacker the muzzle end of a 12 GA riot shotgun and the unmuzzled teeth of his trusty attack robodog.

Toby smiled as he laid his head on Snooper's chest and fantasized about what that victory would feel like.

SAMAEL PAUSED TO REST HIS KNEES. IF HE HAD REALIZED HOW much crawling this assignment required he would have planned for it. Knee pads, maybe. He could barely reach down and rub them in the confines of the chute, but he did so for a moment and reflected on his current situation.

The decision to return to the reactor room had almost been a disaster. The end result was satisfactory, but being surprised by a dog again troubled him. His crotch still hurt, an effective reminder of how close he had come to some real bad shit. A shudder ran through him as he remembered the power of the attack.

Samael's next objectives were to return to the shuttle, make the final preparations for launch, and get the hell out of here. Pretty simple, except for the little voice in his head warning him about the kid. What bothered him the most was the feeling he had to be careful at all. Against a trained adult adversary, the requirement to be alert and ready was as natural as breathing. But to feel that way about a kid rankled in the extreme.

He couldn't understand how the youngster was able to elude him, or why the kid stayed around when he had numerous opportunities to leave the chutes. You would expect a child to run from danger, but this one seemed attracted to it.

And there was something else. In all but the one instance in the chutes, the little runt had demonstrated an uncanny ability to know when he was threatened and move just in time, and Samael was determined to find out how he did it. Creeping around the corner, he

stopped when he saw the shaft of light from the shuttle interior illuminating the chute. It had been closed when he left.

Cops? Unlikely, unless they had just arrived, and in that case they
would have positioned a guard in the chutes. If it were a trap, they
would have closed the hatch to avoid alerting him. This didn't fit either
possibility.

His move was sudden, practiced. Weapon extended, he popped up
out of the hatch and trained his view along the sight line down the
barrel at the three positions he would have expected a cop to take
cover, moving from the first to the last as he confirmed the absence of
threats, in an empty galley. Except for the pilot, who was barely awake
and leaning on the table. Pulling himself up and onto the floor, Samael
ignored the captain's groggy, questioning stare as he lowered the hatch
cover and secured it. He then proceeded to search the shuttle carefully
from the cockpit to the end of the crew quarters. As he stood in front
of the last of the small sleeping rooms, he noticed that the door was
open. He remembered closing it. A quick look confirmed it was
empty.

Next was the cargo bay. An area this size presented entirely
different problems, but his task was relatively straightforward because
of what he knew had not been done.

Cops would have positioned men inside the shuttle and used a
pursuit team to drive him into the trap. This tactic would combine the
elements of haste, preoccupation with threat from the rear, and
surprise from the front.

None of that had happened. It didn't really matter why, just that
the cops weren't inside now. The open hatch into the shuttle and the
open sleeping quarters door meant someone else had gained access.
Someone who didn't cover his tracks.

Like maybe a kid.

A kid who either had an uncanny ability to survive, or had been
incredibly lucky so far, but who in either case was an amateur dabbling
in serious shit and was now in a world of hurt.

Samael was grinning as he stepped out into the cargo bay.

~

Toby bolted awake from a deep sleep as a sensation of extreme danger came close and then receded. He waited, hand over Snooper's muzzle, and audio-searched the area around the cargo stacks. Nothing.

He wanted to stay where he was in the shipping container because it seemed safe enough, but the darkness was getting to him and he needed some fresh air. Finally he couldn't stand it any longer. He scooted around until he was kneeling with his back against the top of the container and pushed up slowly to lift the top a little. The fresh air felt wonderful. He closed his eyes as he breathed deeply for a few minutes and then looked around the bay. He didn't see anything suspicious. After performing another multi-sensor search of the area, he lowered the lid and thought about his next move.

The man had been close within the last half hour, but he didn't know Toby was hiding in the container. He might still be in the shuttle. Brett was a captive, secured with handcuffs. Would it be better to wait here, or try to get Brett out before the shuttle left? How was he going to get the handcuffs off? Was anyone out there trying to stop this?

Too many questions and no answers. Better stay put for now. Toby wasn't sleepy, but he put his head down and snuggled next to Snooper. Suddenly a maximum warning flooded over him.

A scraping sound, soft clunking at the sides and top of the container, then a thump across the top.

Silence again, followed by the voice, sinister, evil, dripping with a familiar mocking tone.

"Hey kid. It's you know who, and I'll be back!"

Where the hell did all this fog come from? Brett's surroundings seemed hazy, indistinct, out of focus. And he couldn't figure out why his arms wouldn't move. Then out of the dark hole in front of the table a black specter appeared. Brett stared as it went forward and disappeared into the cockpit. He wondered if the thing was preparing to fly the shuttle. Then it reappeared and walked past him toward the cargo bay. Brett tried to ask it something, but his lips wouldn't work.

He was so confused, and all he wanted was to go back to sleep. But when he felt himself becoming agitated, it was as if someone flipped a switch allowing current to flow into his brain.

Drugged. Son of a bitch. Brett had no idea how long he'd been sleeping, but he felt wired now. It was as if he'd been out for hours and was completely rested, with mental and physical energy to spare. Maybe he ought to ask the guy where he got that really good stuff.

The hijacker returned and released Brett's cuffs from one wrist, then from the table and reattached them with his hands behind his back. He pulled him to his feet and led him forward to the ladder and up into the cockpit. He secured Brett into the pilot's seat with a device around his waist that looked like a prisoner's restraint system, then removed the handcuffs, told him to complete launch preparations, and left the cockpit.

Checklist items were arranged so that progression began on one side of the cockpit and moved in sequence to the opposite side. Brett had done this so many times that it didn't require much concentration, and he took the opportunity to consider the task ahead.

Assuming the obvious, that the hijacker had every reason to conceal the shuttle flight's progress to destination, Brett intended to help radar operators track the spacecraft. Although radar energy can detect targets on "skin paint" alone, a transponder allowed more positive detection under a variety of conditions. Civilian transponders operated only in Mode 3, referred to as traffic identity, used for safe separation of aircraft. A newer system had been adopted that used GPS positioning, but shuttles didn't use it because the vast majority of their flight time was well outside the coverage area of an Earth-bound satellite system.

The transponder control panel was relatively insignificant in relation to the vast array of other switches in the cockpit. Hoping the hijacker wouldn't notice, Brett set the Mode 3 transponder code to 7700 and switched the function selector from standby to emergency. These two actions would create the maximum radar target size and trigger alarms at any Earth-based radar console. Tracking the shuttle would be virtually assured. But with the transponder turned off or disabled, NASA didn't have a prayer of tracking this shuttle, which was a military version with stealth technology.

If the hijacker knew about transponders, he'd probably notice the trickery. But he might not know that U.S. military aircraft also utilized Modes 1 and 2, collectively referred to as Identification Friend or Foe/Selective Identification Feature, or IFF/SIF.

Mode 1 was used for security identity, or safe passage, a term referring to the problem of identifying friendly aircraft among a number of radar targets in a combat environment. The safe-passage plan was published daily, providing a list of two-digit codes for all aircraft, and that changed at thirty-minute intervals. The pilot could manually select the codes, or program the ship's computer for automatic operation based on time or geographic position.

Mode 2 provided personal identity, with discrete settings for each individual aircraft, programmed on the ground and therefore fixed for any one flight.

Brett didn't know if anyone had thought of using these modes to help track the shuttle, but he couldn't ignore the possibility. With another quick glance to make sure he was still alone, he selected the last two digits of the shuttle's tail number in the Mode 1 field. He had no idea what the current code plan called for, but at least they'd be able to use Mode 1 to help find and track him.

After completing the preflight checklist, he decided to try again on a minor item that had failed to produce the right indications by generating a tone in the headset. He put on his helmet, and within a few seconds heard the last part of a transmission in his right earpiece.

Was that Colonel Thomas?

After a short delay a looped recording began, in which Colonel Thomas announced that they had disabled the bomb, Brett was free to take independent action, and to acknowledge by flashing the navigation lights.

Clamping down on his emotions, Brett flipped the nav lights switch on and off. They were the smallest of the exterior lights, impossible to see from the cockpit, and they would also be very difficult to observe from any of the small windows in the rear of the shuttle.

Following a delay that seemed to stretch on forever, the announcement quit mid-sentence, and the voice of Colonel Thomas in real time reported that the signal had been observed.

Brett felt like cheering for the home team but managed to resist, and he celebrated with a clandestine fist pump.

With the bomb threat eliminated, once the shuttle departed this contest of wills to determine the winner would be just between the two of them.

He would try to save the ship if he could. But if it came down to it, Brett would never deliver this son of a bitch or his stolen ride to his destination in one piece.

13

DAY FOUR MID-MORNING

General Antonio DeSilva sat in the War Room staring at the blank video screen on the table in front of him. Whenever he thought there might be some good news, the situation had only gotten worse.

The police lost no time in getting the robodog ready and into the reactor room with the equipment the corporal asked for. General DeSilva had watched the dog's video with fascination as the cop followed instructions. He clearly saw the man step out of the darkness and club the corporal down. Everyone in Comm Central thought the dog had gone for the man's crotch, and DeSilva felt an involuntary shiver as he thought about that. The bastard deserved it, but the pain must have been incredible.

They sent a team in to examine the exterior of the reactor room. It was closed up tight and still armed as far as anyone could tell. The cop had been found lying outside the room. He was alive, though injured and in bad shape.

And the man had disappeared again. Was he still in the reactor room? Had he survived the robodog attack and returned to the shuttle? Or was he somewhere else, preparing to cause more misery?

"General DeSilva?" The duty officer's voice through the overhead speaker startled the general back to the present.

"Yes, go ahead."

"Sir, it's the hijacker."

Well, here it is. This is what you've been sitting here waiting for, the next turn of events that will put this whole situation in the toilet.

DeSilva exited the War Room and went to the main console. The duty sergeant handed him the microphone and headset to keep the conversation private.

"This is General DeSilva."

"Good Morning," said the now familiar voice. "The attempt to disable the bomb has failed. Entry into the reactor room will result in detonation. I have control of the shuttle, and you will be unable to prevent my departure. Do we agree?"

General DeSilva listened to the man's words with the resignation of a man who had given up hope. "Yes."

"Good. Have your launch team in place no later than 0800 hours."

"I understand." There was nothing else to say.

DeSilva put down the microphone, handed the headset to the duty sergeant, and ordered him to scramble the shuttle launch crew. Walking back toward the War Room, he noticed Lieutenant Colonel Parker and Colonel Thomas enter by the rear door. They were talking excitedly and smiling for some reason. He couldn't wait to find out what this was about, and was dreading their reactions when he brought them up to date. Smiles were hard enough to find around here without pissing on them.

Thomas smiled. "Morning, General DeSilva. We may have some news to brighten your day."

"Enjoy it while you can. You may not like mine."

Thomas's face clouded over for a second, but he recovered quickly and related how they were looking for a way to contact Captain Larsen over the discrete comm link and found the tech who did the work. "He came up with the idea of taking a radio to the observation deck overlooking the loading dock."

DeSilva began to get an uneasy feeling about where this was going, but was so tired that his reaction to the story was well behind the telling of it.

"And this is the great part," said Parker. "When we arrived the observation deck was dark. We crawled over to where we could look out without being easily seen. Captain Larsen was sitting in the cockpit with his helmet on. I radioed him with the news, and suggested he turn on an exterior light momentarily to acknowledge he heard us. He flashed the navigation lights, the small ones on the wingtips and vertical tail. No way the hijacker could have seen it."

Both officers paused. DeSilva stared at them through the fog of his growing fatigue. "Okay. I've really enjoyed this story about a sneaky comm link with the pilot. Which one of you wants to tell me the only thing of importance, which is what in the hell you told him?"

Thomas and Parker leaned back a little from General DeSilva and made eye contact with quick sideways glances. He couldn't figure out whether they were struck dumb by his inability to grasp what the message was, or by their own failure to include it. But it was obvious that neither one wanted to answer a question loaded with a general's criticism.

As the junior officer, Parker had no choice. "We told him that the bomb was being disarmed and he was free to initiate independent action. That was the purpose of the comm link, and it worked great."

DeSilva gritted his teeth so hard it hurt. Then he stood up abruptly, sending his chair crashing to the floor. "I should have guessed something like this would happen. It gets worse by the minute around here."

Both Parker and Thomas had stepped back, instinctively putting distance between them and DeSilva's explosive temper. Then he shook his head. "Relax, guys. It's not your fault, but the bomb isn't safe, and now Larsen thinks it is. He could come up with any number of ideas that will blow this place all to hell."

The officers stood speechless. Finally Colonel Thomas said, "I'm sorry, General, we didn't know anything about that. I've been monitoring the radio continuously and there was no traffic to warn us."

"This is no time for regrets. You two get the hell out of here and make that magic comm link work again. Keep me informed, and do it fast."

Thomas and Parker hurried out of the War Room, hats in hand and at double-quick time.

As the door closed behind them, DeSilva felt like a deflating balloon.

He didn't doubt for a minute that if Captain Larsen didn't get the word, he would take matters into his own hands.

And that any action he took would be catastrophic for Oasis.

THE HIJACKER SEEMED TO MATERIALIZE IN THE COCKPIT. BRETT never heard him. He was wondering how long it took to learn to move so silently when the man leaned over and appeared to study the switch panels to Brett's left. Although he couldn't tell for sure, Brett sensed the man was moving his attention around the cockpit in the same way the checklist did.

The man finished his scan and sat down on the edge of the copilot's seat. "Are you rested after your little nap?"

What the hell does this guy care? "I'm fine. When are you going to tell me what you want me to do?"

"No sooner than you need to know it. I'll provide instructions, grouped as you need them. I believe the last thing I told you to do was prepare the shuttle for launch."

"I'm ready, but we need to discuss a few details before the sequence begins. You haven't told me where we're going, and I need that information to program the computer."

"Okay, but first, tell me how this thing is launched for departure."

"We can undock whenever we want. That will put us in a parking lunar orbit and establish a station-keeping position on Oasis. Departure has to be timed to slingshot the shuttle out of lunar orbit toward Earth. We rendezvous with the Earth's gravitational field and use it to capture the shuttle into orbit. Then we schedule the deceleration burn for orbital departure depending on our final destination."

The hijacker didn't respond for a moment. "Okay. I told the

commander to be ready for launch this morning at 0800. Set up orbital departure for the next available window. Plan to leave Earth orbit so as to arrive at this location."

The man handed Brett a piece of paper with a set of geographical coordinates. He took it, trying not to appear interested, as if it were of no consequence to him where they went.

As the man left the cockpit for the bay, Brett could barely keep from laughing. This might work out after all. The bastard didn't know the bomb had been disabled, or that "Mother" would know exactly where they were going the moment Brett entered the coordinates in the navigation computer. The transponder trick might not even be necessary. Brett looked at the piece of paper. As he began to enter the coordinates, he became curious as to where this place was.

Although latitude and longitude were always used to define Earth locations for navigation, Brett couldn't associate a specific set of coordinates with a given city, state, or even area of the country. Normally, all he did was enter the abbreviated destination identifier and follow the resulting steering information.

But he did have a generalized knowledge, like knowing the approximate boundaries of the Continental United States. As Brett entered the coordinates, he realized that the numbers were totally unfamiliar, and he had never been anywhere near the place.

Then it dawned to him that it didn't matter, because he had no intention of going there.

GENERAL DeSILVA SAT BEHIND THE DUTY OFFICER, WISHING they could get this over with so he could catch up on some sleep. Comm Central was usually a quiet, laid back place, appearing as if nothing much were going on. Most station functions did fine all by themselves.

But disorder reigned supreme today, wearing a spectacular crown. The launch team chief was waiting for the final report from the loading dock. Thomas and Parker had left to correct their earlier message to the pilot, which in the final analysis might be the key to everything. If the pilot thought the bomb had been disabled, this whole affair could turn ugly fast. Captain Larsen looked, sounded, and acted like a take-charge guy.

The phone on the desk rang. The duty officer stabbed at the illuminated button as he picked up the handset.

"Speak to me . . . Okay . . . tell that wrench monkey I said to get that outer door system up and ready ASAP. I don't want excuses. Call me back when that's done."

Another line began ringing before the duty officer had finished, and he cut off the first line by selecting the second.

"This better be good news . . . WHAT? Say that again . . . Okay. Call the guy back and tell him this shuttle's going to launch within the next thirty minutes. If he's not out of there in time he can kiss his ass goodbye. Remind him how cold it is out there, and ask how long he can hold his breath . . . Yeah, I'll tell him."

The duty officer punched the line dead and turned to DeSilva. "We're just about ready, sir. I should get final confirmation pretty quick now."

"Hard to believe. Have you received any good news since I've been here?"

"You bet, sir, don't let my reactions fool you. These jokers are all good men, but they sometimes try too hard. You know, want to make everything perfect. I have to light the fires, get them humping a little faster."

The phone rang again, and the major answered it with a question. "You're ready, right? . . . Good. I'll tell him."

The major used the earpiece of the handset to deselect the line. "They're ready to go, General."

General DeSilva nodded and forced himself to acknowledge the reality. He was about to hand over a shuttle to a man who, in spite of all the effort and blood expended, had managed to thwart every attempt to stop him. What a way to end a career. He could see it now. A dollar sign followed by more numbers than he could count in the line labeled "Amount Due" on a bill from the U.S. Treasury.

"General?"

"Sorry. Just pondering my future. Where's my radio?"

DeSilva took the radio the major handed to him and paused for a moment to collect his emotions, which were beginning to surface no matter how hard he was clamping down. After checking the volume control, he put the microphone to his lips and called the hijacker.

THE TIME HAD COME FOR BRETT TO PREPARE FOR THE FINAL launch of his career.

Control of the atmosphere within the space station was the foremost concern of every individual on Oasis. Shuttle launches involved actions diametrically opposed to this requirement, and the potential for disaster loomed every time the operation was performed.

The loading docks were massive rooms, capable of handling two shuttles and a couple of fighters at the same time. At any given moment, there might be about a hundred personnel within the dock, performing maintenance, loading cargo, or fueling spaceships.

Coordination of this activity was the responsibility of individual control centers assigned to each loading dock. From an enclosure high above, duty officers for each of the major functions worked under a master coordinator responsible for integrating the separate pieces of the puzzle.

At this point in the launch sequence, all personnel had been removed from the dock area. The launch alarm system maintained a continuous visual and audio warning from the time the master coordinator determined the dock was ready until all the work areas had been cleared.

Brett had locked the shuttle down tight. His current task was to monitor its pressurization system during the lowering of pressure within the dock. His counterpart was the master coordinator, who would be performing the same function for the station. A leak between the dock and the rest of Oasis could be disastrous, especially after the main doors were opened. The vacuum of space could swallow the entire air supply of Oasis in less time than it took to blink. There were secondary lines of defense against such an occurrence, but no one had the slightest interest in checking them out.

The hijacker was still back in the bay somewhere. At this stage it didn't matter, and Brett preferred being alone anyway. During his career he had flown both single-seat and multiple-crew airplanes and spacecraft, but his preference was to be by himself, totally in control and with no requirement to coordinate anything in the cockpit with anyone.

With a twinge of sadness, Brett again thought about never doing this again. He was lost in thought, contemplating the end of his career, and maybe even his life, when a garbled and unreadable transmission crackled in his headset.

Brett started to key his microphone and ask for clarification when the same message repeated, and he realized it had to be coming in over the discrete comm link to his helmet. Whatever they were trying to tell him wasn't getting through. And since it was reception-only comm, he had no way of telling anyone about the problem.

Movement behind him got his attention, and Brett turned to see the hijacker enter the cockpit. The man stood motionless for a moment, then stowed a bag he was carrying. He climbed in the copilot's seat and began to strap himself into the restraints. He lowered his helmet into position and spoke into the microphone before he had completed all the connections. Just like a regular copilot did, as a matter of fact. Brett wondered if the guy had flown shuttles in a past life.

"I did everything you told me to," the man said, "and checked all the environmental controls. The cargo area is ready for launch. What's the status here?"

Brett glanced at the pressurization system's tele-light panel, with switchlights in three colors; green (normal); yellow (caution); and red (warning). "Should be complete within a few minutes. The master launch coordinator will run through the final confirmation checks with us, then open the outer door and initiate derotation. Once that's completed, we're ready to separate from the station and be on our way."

Clamps holding the shuttle securely in the dock would not be released until both the launch coordinator and Brett agreed to separate. Commands from the shuttle and from the coordinator's console were required to release the locks, effectively creating a consent system for every launch. Brett checked the tele-light panel again, and saw the pressure outside the shuttle was indicating the absolute vacuum of space. The coordinator would be confirming the integrity of the seals between the dock and the rest of the station before he opened the outer door. Any problems now could be controlled, and the dock could be re-pressurized rapidly without jeopardizing the station.

"Shuttle Zero Five Six, Launch Control."

"Control, Zero Five Six, go ahead," answered Brett.

"I show the dock evacuated and ready for outer door opening and derotation. Do you concur?"

"Roger that, Control. We're all systems go, pressurization panel's clean, personnel secure, ready when you are."

The coordinator acknowledged and within a few seconds the door began to open. A deep shudder rippled through the shuttle as the clutch disengaged and the brakes began to slow the dock's rotation. It took about five minutes for the door to rise far enough to launch. Brett's arms began to float, signaling resumption of zero gravity. He waited for illumination of the green "door clear" light mounted in the ceiling above the opening, then reported that to the coordinator.

"Roger that, Zero Five Six, You have a go for launch."

Brett turned his attention to the task ahead. Throughout the history of military aviation, airplanes, and now spacecraft, were frequently required to maneuver in close proximity. In spite of all the preparation, procedural attention to detail, and constant practice, mid-air collisions still occurred.

As the ship's commander, Brett was responsible for anything and everything involved with the operation. During a launch, his first priority was to maintain physical control of the shuttle so that safe-separation criteria were never violated. Brett preferred to hand-fly the shuttle during launch. But without a copilot to assist in the event of a malfunction, he chose to let the autopilot do it.

Brett scanned the instrument panel one last time. With his hands resting lightly on the thrust controllers, he engaged the autopilot and felt the slight clunking in the airframe as the system took over. The absence of any warning or caution lights signaled readiness for launch.

"Control, Zero Five Six, prepare for release on my standard command. Ready, ready, now."

Brett triggered auto-launch with his thumb but kept his hands ready. With the solid feel of release, the locks holding the shuttle tight to the floor of the dock opened and the lower vertical thrusters fired to lift the craft clear. As the shuttle rose to its programmed height for exiting the dock, the upper vertical thrusters fired to stop the movement and center the ship in the dock.

At this point the autopilot's function was to maintain a stable position by issuing thruster commands to keep the shuttle motionless in relation to the dock. A short delay was programmed into the sequence for one final systems check before leaving the relative safety of the station.

Brett waited for the indications of satisfactory self-test, alert to any erratic movement of the shuttle. This particular autopilot had a history of malfunctioning lateral thrusters, and he did not want to be caught napping.

If there were any reasons to abort the launch, now was the time to do it. With the flick of a switch, Brett could command the autopilot to descend and re-dock with the station, or he could disconnect the autopilot and do it manually.

Autopilot commands could be issued with an array of buttons clustered on the manual controllers. Brett pressed "Launch Commit." Shuttle movement was immediate, but very slow as the rear thrusters fired a short burst to give the ship a gentle nudge toward the open door. The shuttle remained laterally centered in the dock as it crept forward gracefully past the threshold of the dock entrance and slid into space. Brett had performed this maneuver countless times, but it never ceased to impress him, in the same way that sunsets from a fighter cockpit did at 35,000 feet above the surface of the Earth. There was just something about it, the fact that *he* was the one doing this. Never mind that other pilots did it too.

The shuttle remained on a path directly out from the dock until safe separation from the station was attained. When well clear, the thrusters fired to adjust the ship's attitude and position on Oasis.

One of the digital-clock readouts on the instrument panel in front of Brett counted down to the moment of main engine burn for acceleration out of moon orbit, a maneuver known as trans-Earth injection, or TEI. The burn would last about three minutes, accelerating the shuttle to escape velocity and effectively hurling it clear of lunar gravity for the voyage to Earth.

"We're clear and effectively on our own," said Brett into the intercom. "That clock is counting down to departure burn. I have the coordinates you gave me programmed into the navigation computer. From this point on, we wait and watch."

"Tell me about the arrival."

"Main engine burn slows the shuttle so Earth gravity captures us for entry into Earth parking orbit. Once established, the navigation computer calculates when to decelerate again for reentry. When we descend to an altitude at which the Earth's atmosphere is thick enough to support aerodynamic flight, we reconfigure and proceed to destination."

"And we depart lunar orbit when that clock reaches zero?"

"Correct."

The hijacker nodded and leaned back in the seat.

Must be taking a nap. The guy acts like he does this once a day.

Brett must have dozed off as well, because when the main engines fired two things happened. Brett woke up suddenly with the old thrill of riding a barely tamed beast, and the hijacker bolted awake, his hands gripping the armrest.

With noise, vibration, and building g-forces, the shuttle departed moon orbit like an Earth-sick space traveler headed for the barn. Brett monitored the systems, scanning the instrument panel for signs of trouble, but enjoyed glancing sideways at the man strapped into the copilot's seat. He couldn't see the hijacker's face through the helmet visor from this angle, but his posture said it all. He was scared shitless.

Good. Maybe Brett could use the fear against him, end this thing without losing the shuttle, and survive it to boot.

Mother Earth, here we come.

∾

TOBY WOKE UP, CONFUSED AND WONDERING WHAT WAS happening. Trapped in this pitch-black shipping container and depressed about the collapse of his plan to rescue Brett, Toby had snuggled up next to Snooper and cried himself to sleep on the floor. But now he had no idea where Snooper was, and he couldn't feel anything underneath him. He reached out to touch something, *anything*, to orient himself with his surroundings. Nothing, which meant he was floating in zero g.

Then he heard a distorted hissing sound for a few seconds, and after a short delay he hit the bottom of the container, bounced off and hit the top. Anticipating a repeat of the cycle, he reached out for the straps he remembered were attached to the bottom of the container.

But he missed them. And while waiting for another opportunity, the hissing sounds returned. Shortly after, his head hit the side of the container. He bounced off, sensed a large object—Snooper?—pass by close before Toby's feet hit the opposite side of the container and his brain finally adjusted to the weirdness of it all and connected the dots: *The shuttle is launching.*

Toby stretched out his arms and legs to latch onto Snooper at the next opportunity. He'd read enough about the g forces developed during orbital transfers to know that floating around in a container with a robodog when the shuttles main engine fired was a very bad idea. He also knew that unless he could grab one of the straps to stabilize himself in the container before he got a grip on Snooper, he would soon find out just how bad an idea it could be.

How was he going to?—*wait a minute.* "Snooper, come."

And he heard it instantly, scraping and thumping sounds from Snooper's flailing legs and nails hitting the inside of the container as the ever-faithful robodog tried to obey his handler's command.

It took a while, but Toby finally got one hand on a strap and the other on Snooper's harness, then secured the two of them together to the bottom of the container. Snooper licked Toby's face.

He said, "You're welcome," and laughed.

When the main engine fired, the noise and vibration were unlike anything Toby had ever experienced. It felt as if something very powerful was trying to shove him toward one end of the container. Toby tucked his head against Snooper's chest and held on.

He had almost gotten used to the sensations and noise when everything changed again. Sudden quiet, smoothness, and the force shoving him toward one end of the container disappeared. As the pressure on the straps decreased, Toby and Snooper began to float, so he tightened the straps because he liked the feeling of security provided by contact with the floor. Then he remembered the backpack. He'd lost track of it in the container, but it had to be floating around inside.

He reached at far as he could above his head. Nope. To both sides. Still nothing. Spreading he legs, he moved them side to side and up, where one foot bumped against something that moved, and would keep moving until it bounced off the top of the container. He loosened the straps, pushed against the floor with one hand, and reached up with the other, where he felt nothing for a moment, until a zipper pull drifted downward against his fingers and he grabbed it.

It took a while in the dark, but Toby managed to rig the backpack to fit Snooper. The barrel of the shotgun was sticking out of the top of the main compartment with the zipper tightened against it. He thought about that for a moment, thought, *No*, and reversed the weapon. In the unlikely event that he might have the opportunity, he wanted to pull it out fast and ready to use.

But how? When the man came back he would do whatever he wanted, and there was nothing Toby could do to prevent it. He must have been crazy, thinking he could succeed against a man like this. He'd managed to keep from being caught, playing hide and seek with a maniac, but what did he have to show for it? He was stuck in a box, faithful doggie in tow, carrying some clothes and a riot shotgun. Typical runaway kid, Huckleberry Finn in space. What a joke.

Toby played a series of mind videos of his final confrontation with the hijacker to shove aside the constant fear nagging at him.

THE TEI WENT OFF WITHOUT A HITCH. BRETT WAS ABLE TO SIT back and monitor their progress without having to manually override the system, and he kept an eye on the hijacker.

The man's initial fear seemed to fade much too quickly, and at the moment he appeared to be enjoying the ride. He was humming softly to himself, tapping his hand on the armrest to the beat of the song. This did not exactly fit the profile of your average hijacker frightened of flying.

But there was more to come. Reentry into the Earth's atmosphere would provide a much more effective test of the man's ability to remain calm. In addition, Brett was hoping to simulate a contrived problem with the shuttle that would undermine the hijacker's control and provide an opportunity for Brett to terminate it.

"Want some coffee?" over the intercom interrupted Brett's thoughts.

"Sure. Want me to get it?"

"Very funny, Captain." The man removed his pressure suit helmet, unhooked from the console unit, released the seat harness, and began to float free of the seat. Brett expected him to flail around helplessly in the zero gravity, but he deftly maneuvered himself up, then back toward the ladder and down into the galley. No way he could have done that so effortlessly without training. But well trained or not, the hijacker *might* make a mistake, and Brett was going to be ready.

The interior of the shuttle was usually fully pressurized. But on some cargo missions, the cockpit, galley, and crew quarters were sealed off from the cargo bay, which was left unpressurized and unheated. Brett had planned on that configuration for this mission, but the hijacker wanted access to the bay while in transit, and that bit of infor-mation had given Brett an idea.

The environmental control panel in the cockpit worked in conjunction with a similar one beside the loadmaster's station in the cargo bay. Brett could control the environment for both the bay and the cockpit, while the panel in the bay controlled temperature and pressure only in the bay. Brett knew that if he suddenly depressurized the cargo area while the man was back there, and that certain condi-tions could be met, it would all be over in a matter of seconds.

Pressure suits were designed to be fully self-sufficient when connected to an external backpack unit. A man could survive in space for hours as long as the integrity of the suit wasn't compromised. During shorter space flights, the cockpit crew usually remained at their positions with the suits hooked to smaller, removable units built into the console between the seats. If an environmental control problem occurred, they would be protected for sufficient time to troubleshoot and correct it, or in the case of a major malfunction, don the larger backpack units.

At this moment, the hijacker was floating around in the galley in a dapper but totally worthless white outfit. Brett was still connected, and a complete decompression of the shuttle would kill the man and do nothing more than pop Brett's ears as the unit took over.

But what then? He was locked into the seat, with no way to get to the larger backpack units stored on the wall behind him. He couldn't remember how long the smaller units could support life. But that wouldn't matter if he could find a way to close the door between the forward crew section and the bay behind him with the hijacker in the bay. Brett's environment would then remain pressurized while the pressure in the bay decreased and vaporized the bastard into a fine mist.

The plan wasn't foolproof, because there were additional packs and suits in the cargo bay. The guy might be able to don a helmet and backpack if the decompression occurred slowly. The solution to this problem was to cause an "explosive," or rapid decompression. Brett would have to open a *big* hole in the structure aft of the cargo bay/crew section bulkhead.

The emergency cargo jettison system provided the only way to make that happen. Under normal circumstances, cargo was loaded on and off using the huge bay door on the left side of the shuttle. But this military ship, built to carry large, heavy items, had two additional doors in the rear.

When the shuttles were launched from Earth, the combined power of the massive boosters and main engines was more than sufficient to lift even the largest payloads. Should a problem develop after launch, however, aborting the mission and returning to Earth with a full cargo load could not be accomplished. The extra weight exceeded the shuttle's ability to sustain powered flight in Earth's atmosphere.

The solution provided a method for the rapid jettisoning of cargo from the rear doors. Brett had seen the test videos. Following a bright flash under the shuttle's tail, the two rear doors separated and fell away. They had barely cleared the ship when a huge palletized stack of cargo emerged from the rear opening, looking almost graceful as it fell away, a small parachute popped open and stabilized the jettisoned load. After a delay, three immense parachutes opened, and the cargo drifted slowly to Earth. The impact wasn't gentle, but the containers stayed in one piece.

The system was designed to work from soon after launch until passing approximately 5,000 feet above the ground during recovery. Jettisoning cargo in space while in orbit wouldn't deploy the parachutes because they weren't needed. The load would remain in orbit until recovered later.

Brett glanced over at the jettison panel. To help prevent inadvertent jettisoning, it was marked with the typical caution and warning signs common to military aircraft, including a gaudy yellow-and-black-striped paint scheme and safety-wired red cover guards over the switches.

Get the SOB in the cargo bay, hopefully with the bulkhead door closed, then blow the doors and jettison the load. If in space, the second step probably wouldn't be necessary. Without full suit and backpack, the hijacker would die instantly.

Decompression during powered flight in Earth's atmosphere would be easier to survive, especially if the hijacker thought to tether himself to the structure. This was a common safety practice for load crews, and he just might be able to hang on and live. But in both cases, if the hijacker was still alive and Brett released the cargo in sequence after the doors blew off, the guy would have much more to think about than just hanging on.

That satisfying thought was interrupted by the appearance of the hijacker floating up from the galley, holding two sealed thermos bottles of coffee. He maneuvered over to the copilot's seat and handed the coffee to Brett while he strapped in. The bottles had spouts and valves that kept the liquid inside until you sucked on it. The coffee was strong, and tasted very good.

"Any changes up here?" asked the man.

"Everything's fine."

"Not quite. I didn't notice this until now, but what's the deal with the transponder?"

Brett stiffened. *Does he know what it does?* Time to shoot from the hip.

"That's standard procedure. Helps keep us separated from everyone else. Midair collisions are a real hazard in today's aviation." *Will he buy this? Activate his fear, maybe?*

The hijacker looked over at Brett with a slight smile. After a moment, he methodically reconnected his suit leads, cinched down the harness, and set the helmet on his lap. "Yeah, I'm sure it does. But if you don't turn it off in the next few seconds, I'm going to shove this up your ass."

Brett didn't even know the hijacker had the knife beside him in the seat, but when it appeared in the man's left hand, gleaming in the reflected light of the cockpit, Brett turned the transponder to standby.

The hijacker leaned over to look at the panel and lowered the knife until it was very close to Brett's crotch. After a moment he retreated, taking the knife with him, and Brett breathed out sharply in relief.

"I'm still going to have to watch you carefully, Captain. I thought we might be able to get this done with a minimum of bullshit, but you're still playing me for the fool."

"Not true. I just figured your plan took transponders into account. They can't clear our flight path without knowing where we are, and we're going so much faster than most other aircraft. The danger of running over somebody is real."

The hijacker shook his head. "Cut the crap. Keep us stealthy and forget about the sneaky shit. Next time, I hurt you. "

Brett turned away to hide a smile.

The hijacker *didn't* know about the other modes. They were probably being tracked right now and would be for the duration of the flight.

Here we are, guys. Come and get us!

SAMAEL EXPECTED THE PILOT'S TRICKERY AND HAD NOTICED THE transponder was on before they left the station. It was like a contest being played out on more than one level. They each had private objectives, and an agenda dictated by past experience over which they had exercised only marginal control.

Being a military man, patriotic and dedicated to the preservation of his country's way of life, the pilot probably obeyed rules and complied with signs that told him to do this, or not to do that. He'd be the one without so much as a parking ticket.

To Samael, rules and regulations meant absolutely nothing. He recognized no authority other than his own.

In the physical part of this contest, Samael held all the cards. The pilot would never be able to threaten him because he'd never get the chance. The outcome of the mental tug-of-war was equally certain and simply another matter of control. Keep him thinking he had a way out, and concentrating hard on it.

But what about the kid? Getting rid of him would feel good after all the trouble the little runt had caused, but every time Samael considered that option, something warned him against it.

With another careful look around the cockpit, Samael satisfied himself he could leave for a while. According to the navigation displays, which his instructors had taught him to read, they were right on profile.

"I'm going back into the cargo bay."

The captain looked up, stared at him for a minute, and then nodded.

As Samael disconnected from the seat, he thought about the telltale interest of the pilot in Samael's statement about the cargo bay. Eyes were the great betrayer. A person could perfect the ability to lie, to weave a story that would fool his closest acquaintance. But it took a special skill to hide the windows, pull the shades down, and not reveal what was going on behind them.

Floating effortlessly was an incredible sensation. Until training for this mission, the closest thing he'd ever felt to it was scuba diving, hanging there, suspended by unseen forces, a marvelous sensation of freedom.

His employers appreciated the reality that human spatial orientation was based on gravity. In the same way a seed "knows" which way to send the root for water and nutrients and which way to push the shoot that will become the plant, the human body is designed to operate with gravity. Remove it, and a period of disorientation usually results. Unwilling to accept anything less than the hijacker's instantaneous zero-gravity acclimation the moment he exited the container, they had sent Samael into low Earth orbit and made sure he could operate at 100% of his lethal capability from the git-go.

Descending head first, Samael maneuvered down to the galley and through the crew sleeping area to the door into the cargo bay. Through a small window, it was an eerie sight. The overhead lights dimly lighted the cavernous area, and he could just make out the outline of the fighter and the cargo stack behind it.

To his right on the wall by the door was a panel with two digital readouts. Labeled "Cargo Bay Atmospheric Status," one indicated the temperature in degrees Fahrenheit and Celsius, and the other displayed atmospheric pressure expressed as a percentage of that normally found on Earth. Just to the right of the readouts, a green light labeled "Entry Permitted" was illuminated. The red light just below it, ominously labeled "Entry Forbidden," an understatement to say the least, was unlit. As he had been cautioned to do, Samael pressed it to test the bulb and effortlessly drifted away from the bulkhead, feeling like a fool. The next time he tried it, gripping a handhold mounted beside the door with his other hand, he confirmed the bulb was good.

Fifty-eight degrees Fahrenheit and normal Earth atmosphere seemed safe enough. Samael braced himself to stabilize his body and rotated the door latch. Exiting the corridor into the cargo bay, Samael floated out above the landing. Stairs descended below him to the floor. Designed to minimize the distance they extended into the cargo area, they reversed direction twice at landings similar to this one.

But there was no need to use the ladder. By launching himself off the landing, Samael could float down to the top of the stacks where the kid was trapped in the container. He was about to push off when he thought about the door behind him. He'd allowed it to close without considering the consequences. *Big mistake.*

His instructors had cautioned him about the shuttle's two-zone pressurization system. The door separating the crew and cargo areas opened inward toward the crew compartment, was spring-loaded closed and served as a "plug." Higher atmospheric pressure in front of the door and lower pressure behind it would effectively hold the seal tight even if the door wasn't completely locked.

In the case of decompression in the bay, air escaping into space would create lower pressure there, which would in turn try to draw air from the crew areas into the bay. This would clamp the door even tighter against the seal. Result? A fully pressurized atmosphere forward of the door and rapidly decreasing pressure aft. Life versus death.

Answer? *Don't ever get separated from the pilot with the door closed.*

Samael locked it in the open position, held by a latch mechanism in the wall near the bottom of the door. Then he closed his eyes and thought back to two important items in the briefings, and the modifications he had performed.

Security of the shuttle while in the docking position prior to departure had been assured by disabling the external cargo door controls to prevent entry from the outside. Disabling the pilot's controls for releasing the bulkhead door latch from the cockpit protected his personal security within the cargo bay while en route to Earth. But as he thought about it now, he remembered that the shuttle's pressurization system was designed to react to pressure loss by automatically releasing the latch to close the door and isolate the problem. He couldn't remember whether the manual and automatic systems used the same control circuitry. His modification probably rendered both inoperative, but now he realized that wasn't good enough.

Samael returned to the shuttle's tool storage locker. A piece of safety wire and pliers did the trick as he secured the door open by wiring the latch shut.

Satisfied with the fix, he moved over to the railing around the landing. Looking down into the bay, he scanned the interior for the spare backpack units. He located at least four of them. They were attached to the walls and positioned so you could approach, connect your suit and helmet while facing the pack, then turn and put your arms through the shoulder straps. Once fastened, you reached behind and released the pack from the wall.

Samael positioned himself above the railing around the landing with his head slightly lower than his feet. He held on to the railing with both hands, and using his arms with a sort of "pull up" motion, launched himself off into the bay. Even though he knew he wouldn't fall, his stomach tightened as he left the security of the landing and looked down at the floor far below him.

As the feeling passed, he returned his gaze to the top of the stack and saw that his motion was slightly off-target. No amount of movement on his part could adjust his path now. As he floated slowly toward the stack, he saw that he would probably miss his target slightly to the left.

As Samael approached the cargo, he extended his right arm and gripped the cargo netting. His body swung past slowly as he held on and stopped his movement, then pulled himself into a kneeling position on top of the stack.

Now to take care of some *really* important business. He used a short piece of strap to secure his legs to the cargo stack. As he started to untie the first knot in the rope ladder restraint, he still hadn't made up his mind about what he was going to do, just that he wasn't going to kill the kid. Two things were holding him back.

An extra hostage could always come in handy, especially when it was a kid. Most people tend to back off at the thought of children in harm's way, and he might be able to use that to his advantage.

The second factor was much less clear, harder to put his finger on, but some little voice inside him told him that he would later regret killing the kid now.

He'd thought about it a lot. All he could come up with was his begrudging admiration that the kid had been able to evade him so well. Then after almost being caught, shot at, and probably scared shitless, the little prick had come after him again.

Who would've ever believed it?

With confidence that nothing the kid could do now would jeopardize the mission, Samael finished untying the first rope securing the top of the container and tossed it aside.

TOBY HAD NO IDEA HOW MUCH TIME HAD PASSED, BUT WAITING for the inevitable was getting to him. he loosened the straps, rolled over on his back, pulled his legs into his chest, put his feet against the top of the container and pushed with all his strength. The top moved a little bit, but—suddenly that too-familiar terror gripped him. The man was close. and the voice sent Toby's pulse rate through the roof.

"Hey, kid! I'm back. Can you hear me?"

It had been different in the chutes where he had a chance of getting away, but this was the worst feeling in the world.

"Hey, KID!" accompanied by something hitting the side of the container with a cracking sound that made Toby jump. Snooper began to growl softly. Toby put his hand over the dog's muzzle.

"I hear you." His voice wasn't working too well, and he felt himself begin to shake. "What do you want?"

"What do *I* want?" The man began laughing. "I want you, runt, and here's how it will happen.

"There's one line holding the top down. When I release it, you will push it all the way open, then let yourself out while you hang on to the box. If you let go and I have to come retrieve you off the ceiling, I'll hurt you."

He really sounded mad. "Okay, hold on a minute. I've got the straps around me and I have to get them loose."

"You have thirty seconds to open that lid and show yourself. I'm counting."

On impulse, Toby leaned over to Snooper, lifted the dog's ear, and said as quietly as he could, "Snooper, stay. When I leave, find a place to hide and don't show yourself until I call you." He had no idea if Snooper understood, but he knew that after a period of voice imprinting, robodogs were capable of doing exactly what they were told to do in plain English without special commands.

"Time's up, runt. Out. Now!"

Toby patted Snooper's head, held up his hand, palm close to Snooper's face, and whispered "Stay." He released the strap around his own waist, and pushed on the top. There was an initial resistance, then it began to open and the light streaming in blinded him. He didn't remember it being this bright in the bay, but after all that time in the dark it didn't take much.

The container lid was hinged along the back edge and opened completely with no effort. Toby immediately began to float. With his left hand on the edge of the box and the right holding onto a strap, he tried to keep himself steady.

Touchy business, not being secured in zero gravity. Small movements could do a lot, and as he slowly opened his eyes to get used to the light, Toby heard the voice from behind him.

"Move toward the end of the container toward the sound of my voice, feet first. Don't look behind you, and do it slowly."

Toby began doing that. As the fingers of his right hand found the end of the strap, he let go and reached behind him for the end of the container. Unable to touch it with his fingers, Toby nudged himself backward with his left hand gripping the front edge, intending to establish control with his right hand finding the end as his left released the front. It didn't work exactly as planned, however, and he developed too much upward momentum.

Losing his grip on anything stationary, Toby floated out and up. He knew better, but that didn't prevent his efforts to change his direction with frantic arm and leg movements.

Next stop, the ceiling, if the man hadn't pushed off from his perch on the side of the cargo stack and grabbed Toby's legs. Tethered to the stack by a line, the two of them came to a stop about ten feet from the edge and above the container.

Toby glanced down and was relieved to see that when the man pushed off the container, he had almost completely closed the lid, hiding Snooper from view.

"You stupid little shit," said the man. "I told you to go slowly."

The man's face was right beside Toby's, masked and sinister, and the voice was just as ominous as he remembered it. Lifeless eyes, cold and barren, stared right through him.

Holding Toby around the waist, the man used his other arm to pull them both down the line to where it was attached to the cargo stack.

Controlling Toby with one hand, the man pushed off the stack toward the side of the shuttle and then pulled them both along using a railing attached to the wall. It was at about waist height and seemed to be there for just that purpose.

When they reached the ladder up to the crew quarters, the man stopped at a phone mounted on the bulkhead. With one arm wrapped around a vertical steel pole supporting the ladder and landings, he picked up the handset and punched a button on the face of the unit.

Then the man handed Toby the handset. "Say hello to the captain, kid. But don't be surprised if he's less than delighted to hear from you."

∿

BRETT SAT ALONE IN THE COCKPIT WONDERING WHAT THE hijacker was up to. He loosened his straps, but he couldn't see more than a few feet of the floor in the galley.

He knew the door was open. Status lights on the tele-light panel told him that. And the hijacker left his helmet in the copilot's seat. Did he not know that Brett could unlatch the door manually? This was exactly the opportunity Brett was looking for. Time to do it.

Brett triggered the manual bulkhead door release to close off the bay from the forward part of the shuttle. Staring at the tele-light panel, he waited for indications that the bulkhead door was unlatched and in transit toward closed. It took him a minute or so to realize that it wasn't happening. He frantically actuated the switch a few more times, but the door remained open.

Now was the time for hard choices. Jettisoning the rear doors would subject the entire shuttle interior to the deadly environment of space. Brett knew his own immediate survival was assured, because the smaller console environmental units were designed to disconnect from the ship's environmental system upon sensing a drop in atmospheric pressure within the shuttle. But would they last the entire voyage?

Brett had no idea how long the hijacker would stay in the bay, or if he would come and go more than once. But he knew one thing for sure. If he blew off the rear doors now, the guy would turn to mist and spend the rest of eternity on a journey to nowhere. It would be safer to wait until he was sure his own unit would support him long enough, but he couldn't take the chance.

He donned his helmet, checked the connections carefully, cinched his harness down tight, and reviewed the procedure. As he reached for the cover guard over the enable switch, he tried to swallow and couldn't. Memories of combat, the fear, and looking death in the face had removed all the moisture in his mouth and throat. But everything was ready, an almost perfect opportunity. Brett put his gloved hand on the jettison control panel and the enable switch.

The cover guard was safety wired. He pushed up on the guard. The wire snapped easily. He flipped the exposed switch, which enabled the jettison circuits by allowing electrical power to the panel, and then lifted the cover on the rear door jettison switch. With a last thought as to what this would feel like, he placed his thumb against the switch. Although he knew it made no difference, wasn't necessary, and he was being foolish, he held his breath.

"Hello Brett? Are you there?"

Brett jerked his finger away from the switch as his earphones came to life with a voice. It sounded like Toby, but that couldn't be. Stunned, unable to believe what he had just heard, he tried to make sense of it.

Then it came to him that it had to be the secret comm link they had installed in his helmet. They had discovered the malfunctioning tape recorder and fixed it. Maybe this was a real-time message—but they wouldn't involve Toby, and he should have long since been evacuated to the moon colony.

"Brett, the man's got me back here. Can you hear me?"

Brett was struck speechless. All his planning, worthless. He was wondering how it could have happened when the man's voice interrupted the thought.

"Captain, your friend is disappointed. He thinks I've been lying to him and you aren't really here."

"You miserable son of a bitch. You harm that kid and I swear I'll feed your body parts to the pigs."

"Tough talk from a glorified bus driver chained to his seat. You need to calm down before I come back up there. I wouldn't want you to hurt me."

The laughter filling the headset infuriated Brett, and he had never in his life felt so completely helpless. His only chance to stop this bastard had been taken from him. Without the freedom to act, he, Toby, and very likely Oasis, were doomed.

The intercom stayed hot for a few seconds, then went dead. Brett heard the door to the bay slam behind him and remembered the jettison panel. He quickly put the cover guards down and positioned the safety wire so that it looked intact. He turned and saw Toby at the top of the ladder between the galley and the cockpit. He had a broad grin on his face, obviously unhurt, and even more obviously very glad to see him.

"Howdy there, buddy."

"Hi, Brett. I'm really sor—"

"Cut the small talk, kid," said the hijacker as he appeared behind Toby and moved him out of the way. "And as for you, tough guy, what was it you said about my body and some pigs?"

Brett had no idea how unstable the hijacker might really be. *Time to cool things down.*

"Why don't you and I discuss our business in private? There's no reason to involve a youngster, and—"

"Shut the hell up. In case you haven't noticed, this little piece of shit is involved, and by his own doing. How the hell do you think he got on the shuttle? He's here because he chose to be. He couldn't keep his nose out of things that didn't concern him. And now he's going to pay the price of not staying at home and playing with his toys."

Not trusting himself to speak without showing his mounting fear and weakness, Brett simply nodded. The hijacker maneuvered over beside Brett's seat and studied the navigation panel for a moment.

Apparently satisfied with what he saw, he pushed off and returned to the ladder. Brett watched over his shoulder as the man positioned

Toby slightly head low pointed toward the galley, and using the rail as a handhold slowly disappeared down the narrow passageway.

Brett had spent more than his share of time in zero gravity and knew he couldn't have done it better. Economy of movement was necessary to be precise in positioning within the confines of the shuttle, and this guy had it down to the fine details.

The hijacker returned after a few minutes and maneuvered himself into the copilot's seat. After fastening the harness, he laid his helmet in his lap. "Okay, Captain, time for the next step. You can fly this thing manually anytime you want to, right?"

"Manual override is *always* an option in case the autopilot malfunctions."

"The autopilot will keep us on flight plan, then make any corrections required to enter orbit and initiate reentry deceleration at the proper moment. Correct?"

Brett nodded.

The man reached down into a duffle bag, brought out a small handheld electronic device and pressed a button. The screen lit up on what appeared be a standard hand-held GPS navigation computer until the display changed and caused a lump to form in Brett's throat when he realized it was the same as the shuttle's navigation display. *Including* steering commands. *Is there anything this guy didn't plan for?*

At this point in the journey, the shuttle was tied to an invisible flight path by the navigation computer and autopilot. They were on profile, with the command steering bars centered, traveling at speeds up to 25,000 mph and shooting for arrival to within one-half degree of accuracy. Brett watched with growing concern as the man went through a series of inputs to his navigation device, and it became clear to Brett what was happening.

The shuttle was programmed to enter Earth orbit, initiate reentry, reconfigure for powered flight in the Earth's atmosphere, and fly to the destination currently in the navigation computer. And counter to what Brett had told the man, NASA knew exactly where that was, where they were now, and their arrival time at destination. All of which appeared to be old news.

The hijacker was programming a device to provide onboard reentry steering commands to a new destination. Brett had already told him he could manually fly the shuttle through the maneuver. He couldn't help but stare at the screen on the hijacker's nav device as the words "SELF TEST COMPLETE" flashed across it.

"Figured it out yet?"

"I think so. Buy that at your local pilot supply store?"

The hijacker smiled. "Made a few software modifications, however. And although I imagine you know the drill, let me clarify what you'll do.

"Our current progress will suffice until this instrument indicates we're approaching the reentry position for our actual destination. On my command, you will disengage the autopilot and assume manual control. The onboard navigation computer will be disabled, and you will follow these steering commands. I've heard all about your exceptional skill at doing this, so don't even think about coming up with some bullshit reason why it won't work. After reconfiguring for powered flight, you will descend to and utilize a minimum-altitude profile. Questions?"

Brett shook his head and felt despair settling into his bones. Faced with the absence of alternatives, the worst possible place for a pilot to be, smothered by helplessness and mounting bad news, did he have any options for changing the outcome?

The hijacker had apparently not noticed that the military transponder modes were still operating. The shuttle could *probably* be tracked no matter where it went, and the fact that friends were watching provided Brett with a small measure of optimism. The military had teams specially trained for stuff like this. And while he hoped for intervention, he also feared it. They probably didn't know that Toby was on the shuttle.

Toby should be safe on the moon colony with his parents. Brett was certain the hijacker would never have jeopardized his objectives by taking a young hostage. If he thought the bomb was still a factor, he didn't need one. And with Brett along, the problem of flying the shuttle to destination was solved. If that were his only objective, there would be nothing to gain by taking Toby.

Brett could see no other choice but to do the job fate had assigned him. And what a legacy it would be. Brett Larsen, Captain, United States Space Command, loses the first military spacecraft to a hijacker in the history of the program.

But if he dwelled on that they were both doomed. With one final thought that his first objective was to protect Toby, Brett prepared himself mentally to face an uncertain future.

14

DAY EIGHT EARLY EVENING

The man had taken Toby to the restroom, then returned him to his room, strapped him down in a seat, and told him to stay there. He knew the voyage from Oasis to Earth took about four days. By counting meals, he figured they would be landing on Earth sometime soon.

He knew Brett was disappointed with him, unable to pursue his own plans because of a kid who was supposed to be his pal, getting in the way and fouling up the works. He desperately wanted to apologize, but never got the opportunity.

Toby had decided that one of his own objectives might be achieved just because he was here, captive or not. He disobeyed his parents and ignored the evacuation order to help Brett prevent the taking of the shuttle. So much for the first goal, although Toby didn't care about the shuttle. The hijacker was going to get it anyway, no matter what anyone did.

But with Toby onboard, Brett couldn't go through with any plan that endangered himself without putting Toby at risk, and he was more than willing to accept Brett's anger in trade for saving his life, no matter how he achieved it. That's what friends do for each other.

Toby also figured that the hijacker didn't have reason to hurt them.

They had never seen his face, and he could just drop them off anywhere, thank you. We'll thumb a ride to the nearest phone.

Spirits on the mend, Toby's excitement begin to build. He was going to Earth! Not quite first class service, and the steward was a real jerk, but Toby would finally see for himself what it was like.

As Toby put his head back against the seat and closed his eyes, he became curious if his powers had been affected by leaving Oasis. Relaxing, he allowed it to happen. Audio search was initiated immediately, and he extended it into the cockpit, where he heard movement, breathing, and familiar voices.

"That horizontal bar on my nav is on the move. Shouldn't you correct left to center the vertical one now?"

"I can, but not with the autopilot engaged. It will keep the vertical bar on the shuttle's nav display centered as long as it is accepting steering information from the computer. All it knows now is the destination we've got dialed in. When the horizontal bar begins to drop, the autopilot will maintain the capture and initiate the retro-fire to slow and enter orbit, then again later to follow it as it drops down for the reentry."

"How long do we have until that happens?"

"The computer shows . . . about . . . one hour and thirty-two minutes."

"Okay. Disconnect the autopilot before my vertical bar reaches full scale, then correct left to center it. Continue to follow the shuttle's horizontal bar until my nav shows it's time, then transition to it for the remainder of the flight."

As the voices became silent, Toby wondered what all that meant, but knew enough to realize Brett and the man were discussing the maneuver that would take them out of space and down to Earth. He began to get even more excited.

But not so excited that he couldn't sleep. He began to doze off, chin falling to his chest and back up with a snap. Finally he lost the battle and entered the special fantasy world of dreams.

He was in a fighter plane, master of the skies, vanquishing foes with the skill of an eagle. The aircraft was an extension of his will, following every command as if no control movements were required. Swift and deadly, he pursued the enemy, knowing in his heart the hijacker was his current adversary and was about to die. Closing for the kill, Toby smiled.

Suddenly all dreams of adventure and revenge vanished as the most horrendous noise and vibration Toby had ever felt shook him awake and filled him with fear.

All alone, he was terrified that the shuttle was coming apart. He screamed for Brett, crying at the top of his lungs for his friend to save him, and buried his face in his hands as his entire body was shoved into the seat, with so much pressure he thought it would suffocate him.

Is this what it's like to die?

THE INITIAL REENTRY HAD GONE WELL. BRETT WAS AMAZED AT the performance of the small nav device. The steering bar display was easy to follow, and the error update rate seemed identical to that of the shuttle's system. Even without the autopilot, he nailed the approach. He was curious how the man had acquired software to program a reentry maneuver, but he wasn't surprised.

They descended into darkness. With all the instrumentation to assist with flight path control, the task wasn't much different than daylight in terms of the piloting required. The next portion of the journey, however, would be extremely demanding, and Brett felt the tension begin to build as the shuttle slowed for reconfiguration, a capability that had transformed the shuttle program into what it was today.

A first-generation shuttle launched into orbit riding a massive fuel tank feeding the main engines, assisted by two solid-propellant rocket boosters. It was maneuvered in space with thrusters, and decelerated for reentry with the main engine's thrust acting in opposition to its forward velocity. As it slowed, the Earth's gravitational pull overcame the ability of the shuttle to maintain orbit, and the spacecraft began a descent into the Earth's atmosphere. With air flowing over its lifting surfaces, the shuttle became an unpowered glider using conventional flight controls for roll, pitch, and yaw, allowing limited control over descent rate for a gliding approach to a predetermined landing site and mission termination.

The inability to extend the shuttle's flight path beyond the narrow limits of unpowered flight created significant operational limitations that proved unacceptable for the expanded shuttle mission. Weather conditions for recovery had to meet minimum standards far more limiting than those used by the rest of commercial and military aviation. Diversion to an alternate landing site or holding for the weather to improve were options unavailable to the shuttle pilot.

The solution to this problem was to combine current shuttle capability with a second proven technology borrowed from tactical aviation.

Fighter aircraft design in the mid-1900s had been forced to compromise between two competing objectives. The first was speed, and airfoils had to be capable of withstanding supersonic flow while producing minimum drag. The swept-back leading edge wing design was an essential element in pursuit of this goal.

The price to be paid, however, was an increase in stall speed. This resulted in higher takeoff and landing speeds, and made the job of getting airborne and bringing the airplane to a stop after landing potentially more hazardous.

One solution to this problem was development of "swing-wing" technology. With wings in the forward position for takeoff and landing, the fighter's stall speed was lowered significantly. Once airborne with the wings swept back, the fighter became capable of high-speed flight without paying an excessive drag penalty. It was, in effect, the best of both worlds.

Designs of later-generation shuttles eliminated the reliance upon unpowered, gliding flight after return to the Earth's atmosphere. Wing and empennage extensions were hydraulically positioned to provide conventional control surfaces. Power for aerodynamic flight was supplied by two turbojet engines nestled into the fuselage/wing root junction and closed off by ramps. Once the shuttle slowed down, the ramps retracted and the engines were air-started. When stabilized, the engines were advanced from idle to cruise power and the pilot was now at the controls of a twin-engine supersonic jet transport.

Brett's first task was to get the shuttle slowed down, carefully following the altitude/speed profile to avoid problems with being either too fast or two slow for existing conditions.

Airfoil extension was the next priority. The shuttle was capable of gliding in the space configuration with aerodynamic controls stowed, but the ratio of distance covered along the ground to altitude lost was much more favorable when configured for Earth flight. In the event of a problem with one or both engines, the additional glide distance obtained could mean the difference between reaching a suitable airport and a disastrous off-airport landing.

Brett manipulated the airfoil controls and extended the wings and empennage to their high-speed, highly-swept aerodynamic positions. The shuttle's airfoil status display graphically presented the status of each wing and vertical and horizontal tail surface. He had flown swing-wing fighters in which the pilot could see out of the cockpit well enough to visually confirm this movement, but with the shuttle he was totally dependent upon the indicators.

As the surfaces unlocked, amber lights in the airfoil status portion of the tele-light panel illuminated, which also caused both amber "master caution" lights to come on. These lights were on the glare shield immediately in front of the pilots, and were designed to direct attention to the source light somewhere on the tele-light panel.

Brett pushed his master caution light to extinguish both, and glanced at the tele-light panel to confirm that the left and right wing, left and right horizontal tail, and vertical tail surfaces were unlocked. At this point, with the flight controls in transit, lots of things could go wrong. It was important to maintain the correct attitude and airspeed to avoid complications. Asymmetric extension was rare, but had occurred during testing when the shuttle was intentionally flown outside the established limits during reconfiguration. Excessive air loads were the culprit, and Brett flew the shuttle very precisely to avoid such complications.

In addition to the lights, Brett could feel changes in airfoil status: the solid clunk in the airframe as the wings locked into the extended position, followed almost immediately by the less pronounced feel of the tail section as it reached the travel limits. After checking the lights for an extended indication, Brett gently moved the flight controls to confirm the expected increase in maneuverability. At these higher speeds the controls were extremely sensitive and the shuttle flew much like a fighter.

Continuing on the profile, Brett began to spend more time looking outside the cockpit. Darkness notwithstanding, he strained to see something to give him a clue about where they were going. With no moonlight it was an exercise in futility, but the view was spectacular nonetheless. Blackness all around, stars above, no lights below.

Brett figured they were either over the ocean or a solid cloud cover, or both. He turned toward the hijacker. "We may have a cloud cover below us, and I need information about our destination to plan an instrument approach if required."

"Don't worry about that. Just follow the nav steering, which, by the way, is now using standard Earth GPS positioning. It's programmed with the vertical information required to keep us clear of terrain. Once we get within TFR limits, use that for vertical guidance and nav for directional steering."

The TFR, or terrain following radar, helped pilots maintain safe separation above the ground under a wide variety of conditions. A desired altitude was selected, and when coupled to the autopilot, the TFR was capable of flying the aircraft right down on the deck.

Brett began sweating. Descending to minimum altitudes at night over unfamiliar terrain with no personal advance planning violated every pilot instinct imaginable. He questioned the hijacker again, but was told to fly the commands and shut up. With no other choice, Brett prepared to start the engines.

Unlike the shuttle's main engines or the solid rocket boosters, the turbojet engines needed air, fed into the compressor through intakes molded into the aircraft's structure. Moveable ramps, controllable from the cockpit, covered the intakes and formed a smooth, low drag surface. The task now was to put the shuttle within the airspeed and altitude limits for an air start and begin the process.

A glance at the airspeed indicator confirmed what he felt, a slight shudder as the ship decelerated through Mach 1 and became subsonic. Brett noted that the wings automatically extended on schedule from their supersonic position. So far so good. Although the shuttle was capable of achieving and maintaining supersonic cruise during aerodynamic flight, the air start envelope for the engines mandated speeds below Mach 1 before opening the intake ramps.

Triggering the ramp control, Brett selected the open position and monitored the indicators as they began to move. He couldn't see the ramps from the cockpit, but knew they were opening because he felt the change.

Much of flying was like that, and it didn't matter whether the aircraft was a biplane or a shuttle. The term "seat of the pants" usually referred to smaller, lighter airplanes without hydraulically actuated flight controls and dampers which reduced the pilot's ability to feel what was going on. But all airplanes telegraphed the results of pilot actions. It was the ability to "hear" these messages that often made the difference between a good pilot and a mediocre one.

As the ramps opened, the turbojet engines were completely static. With no air flowing through them, the motionless compressor and turbine blades formed an aerodynamic wall that initially created a substantial increase in drag and rapidly decelerated the shuttle before the sudden buildup of air at the compressor face could be relieved.

The deceleration aggressively pressed Brett forward in the harness, so that the ramp position indicators and engine instruments were nothing more than confirmation of what he already knew. And as the engines began to turn, the rate of deceleration decreased because ram air was no longer restricted and could flow smoothly past the rotating blades. RPM gauges recorded this change, and as Brett increased back-stick pressure slightly to stay on profile, he reached over to the engine start panel and selected ignition on, then pressed the lock button on the fuel control for the left engine and moved it forward to introduce fuel into the combustion chamber to mix it with air exiting from the compressor section. Eyes switching back and forth between the various engine instruments, he monitored progress of the start.

RPM, oil pressure, hydraulics, fuel flow, exhaust gas temperature . . . light off, EGT rising, RPM and oil pressure increasing, EGT within limits, engine stabilizing at idle.

Procedures called for allowing the engines to warm up before increasing power above inflight idle, so Brett repeated the process for the right engine, deselected ignition, and completed the after-start checklist. With frequent glances at the nav display, he adjusted the flight controls to maintain the command steering bars centered and waited for the obligatory warm-up time to expire.

Passing 35,000 feet above mean sea level (MSL), Brett eased the throttles up slowly. Procedures called for checking the engines at a medium power setting while at altitude. Adjusting pitch to correct for the extra power, he stayed on profile and accepted the momentary airspeed increase while he confirmed the engines were within normal limits.

Looking good. He liked space flight, but there was something about the feeling of a powerful turbojet that brought him home to his aviation roost. Brett had been a fighter pilot most of his career until he got the chance to enter the Space Command. It would have been a hard decision if the new job had been strictly flying shuttles, but when dual qualification in fighters was offered, the deal was sealed.

And he'd been pleasantly surprised with the shuttle, which in spite of its size and the fact that it was purely a transport aircraft, had relatively light controls and sufficient power to be exhilarating during normal turbojet-powered takeoff, climb, and acceleration. This military version was also capable of supersonic cruise, which meant that long, boring flights were rare, and the challenges of air refueling, low altitude navigation, and formation flying were always there to make it interesting.

Approaching 10,000 feet MSL, Brett decided to clarify exactly what it was the man wanted him to do. The shuttle's reentry profile was designed to place them in a position from which transition to an instrument approach could be made. If the hijacker's GPS device program was doing the same thing, they must be approaching their destination.

"Question?"

"Go ahead."

"You said you wanted me to continue following the nav heading bar to our destination, but use the TFR. If this weather continues much lower, we're going to need an instrument approach to landing, and the TFR can't do that. Do you have an approach in there?" Pointing to the portable nav device lying on the console, Brett looked at the man as he waited for an answer.

The man shook his head. "You're assuming that this profile is taking us to our destination. I simply picked an ending point for the reentry. You still have some flying to do." The man glanced toward the instrument panel, then said, "Passing five thousand feet, ignore the GPS for a moment, hold your heading, and set the TFR for one thousand feet AGL. Descend to and maintain that while I get this set up."

So that was it. The bastard used a bogus set of coordinates as a destination just to program the nav for reentry, fully intending to continue beyond that point. As Brett set the TFR altitude, he wondered if the shuttle was being tracked by anyone, and if so whether they would be able to maintain contact at lower altitude.

He also began preliminary fuel calculations. The hijacker indicated that this profile had been planned out, but no pilot with any brains would accept that as the final word. Low-altitude, high-speed flight guzzled fuel. Even when you knew where you were, with a map of the area and full tanks, you never allowed complacency to affect preparation for the unknown.

In this case he was being kept in the dark in both a figurative and literal sense. Below him, he saw nothing but clouds and a black void. Ahead, an unknown destination and very questionable future. Before too long he would need distance-to-go, ground speed, and fuel burn rates as a minimum to decide whether they could make it.

The man put the GPS on the center console. Brett was just leveling out at 1000 feet AGL with the engines powered up to maintain a comfortable 450 knots. Although not the most fuel-conserving speed under these conditions, he wanted sufficient energy for maneuverability until he was certain of the terrain below him. Speed is life, as the saying goes, and it applied here.

The GPS was in a navigation mode. The display provided desired course, current ground track, ground speed, steering bar, distance- and time-to-go. As he checked fuel burn, the TFR light illuminated with the warning that he had descended below his selected altitude, a mistake that could turn fatal in short order.

Adding a little back pressure to climb, Brett decided to use the autopilot. Without the support of a copilot and with the uncertainties developing, it would help reduce his workload. Although the hijacker's GPS couldn't be coupled with the autopilot for navigation, the TFR could, which would allow him to spend less time monitoring altitude and more on navigation, fuel burn calculations, and preparing for the approach.

Leveling out at 1000 feet AGL, Brett engaged the autopilot in the altitude hold mode, then coupled the TFR and autopilot together. In this configuration, the autopilot would maintain the selected altitude above ground level rather than above sea level. As the altitude of the terrain below the aircraft changed, the TFR/autopilot combo adjusted accordingly.

With his hands resting near the controls, Brett confirmed with the hijacker that he was to follow GPS steering. Using the autopilot's heading control knob, he manually corrected the shuttle's heading to center the GPS steering bar.

The TFR appeared to be working properly, and the lack of autopilot pitch adjustments and steady altitude indicated to Brett they were probably over water. The TFR's job was an easy one when the surface below the shuttle was flat and level, and the ride under those conditions was generally smooth. TFR's worked on the principle all radars used to determine range from the source to any radar-reflective object. A constant series of radar pulses, transmitted directly below the shuttle, struck the surface and bounced back to be received by the TFR. Using the speed of radar energy and the time delay between transmittal and receipt, the TFR calculated the distance traveled by the pulse and displayed it in the cockpit as altitude above ground level.

Uneven terrain complicated the problem. When coupled to the autopilot, the radar altitude signals sent to the pitch controller had to be dampened or the system would attempt to correct for every bump in the terrain. This dampening worked by adding trend logic to the computer, which analyzed a series of pulses before sending pitch commands to the autopilot. If the terrain began to rise, for example, the TFR would sense a decrease in altitude but delay telling the autopilot to adjust until a series of pulses confirmed the trend.

The primary benefit of dampening was to smooth out the autopilot, but there was a price to pay in return. The early TFR systems only sampled altitude directly below the aircraft. A shuttle in level flight was in no danger of striking the ground underneath it, but might be in serious peril approaching a steeply rising terrain ahead. A dampened TFR system reacted less quickly by design. When at very low altitudes of 500 feet and below, there might well be combinations of altitude, speed, and terrain exceeding the shuttle's capability to pull up and out of danger before impact with an obstacle.

All pilots liked the dampening. Without it, the autopilot was simply too jerky, constantly pumping the controls, enough to make even the strongest stomachs queasy and the most steely-eyed fighter pilot nervous. And even without dampening, there was always the question of whether the system would pull soon enough and with sufficient g to miss the terrain.

The solution was to factor in two more altitude-sampling circuits in addition to the one directly below the shuttle. Pointing ahead at a 30- and 45-degree angle to the vertical, the extra circuits provided more accurate trend information and the system was capable of reacting well in advance of approaching high terrain. Under the current conditions of darkness and cloud cover, that was more than nice to know.

Brett continued to make small adjustments with the heading control knob to keep the GPS steering bars centered while he monitored the autopilot's altitude-hold function and fuel status. He was concentrating so hard that the hijacker's movements caught him by surprise.

Without a word, the man removed his helmet, disconnected his suit leads, released the harness and stood up. Then he left the cockpit, and when Brett confirmed by looking behind him that the hijacker had disappeared into the galley, he decided on a little spur-of-the-moment trickery.

Brett selected the emergency function on the transponder control panel keypad and shifted in the seat so he could see the passageway down into the galley. It gave him a strange combination of excitement and hope, knowing that he was essentially shouting, "Here we are!" and that someone might be responding at this very moment.

After about five minutes, Brett heard something behind him and immediately returned the transponder to its previous status. Appearing busy with his tasks, Brett ignored the hijacker as he entered the cockpit until he began to open the jump seat, situated between and just aft of the two pilot seats.

Looking back to see what was going on, Brett was astonished to see Toby standing at the top of the ladder. He looked like he'd been through hell, but he managed a broad smile when their eyes met. As the boy started to say something, Brett mouthed a silent warning and shook his head. Toby's face clouded over, but he said nothing.

The man directed Toby to the jump seat and helped him strap in. Then he returned to the copilot's seat and fastened his harness. "Take the ship down to two hundred feet and keep it there."

This was a dangerous place to be, low and fast over unfamiliar terrain, in the clouds and at night. Brett started to object, but decided it wasn't worth the effort. After selecting the new altitude into the TFR controller, he adjusted the vertical velocity to initiate a gentle pushover to about 1000 feet per minute descent. Leveling out smoothly at 200 feet, the system's corrections remained relatively infrequent, indicating they were still over water or very flat terrain. He had almost begun to relax when the first indication of trouble brought him back to reality.

Ever since the development of air-to-air and surface-to-air missiles, the problem of evading them had become an increasingly serious business. All radars emit energy, and the shuttle was equipped with a Radar Warning Receiver (RWR) capable of detecting radar pulses striking it. These signals were sent to the analyzer, where they were categorized according to various characteristics. Computers then compared the data to all known radar systems in use by both civilian and military agencies, and presented to the pilot the results of that analysis as a function of threat level.

Whenever the RWR gear was activated it provided both audio and visual warnings. The audio served two purposes, alerting the pilot that a signal had been received, and providing a unique warning sound based on the type of radar system detected and the mode of operation.

Long-range radars, typically used only for search, were indicated by a kind of laid-back sound more informative than demanding, and not requiring immediate action. Important, certainly, but not a threat.

Short-range radars normally associated with air-to-air and surface-to-air weapons systems generated a different sound that varied as the system changed modes. A search indication meant something entirely different when it was a fighter doing the looking, especially when the radar signal switched modes and the RWR system detected the difference. Each of the audio indications was distinctive, and at the maximum-warning end of the scale, triggered when the system detected a short-range radar with all the characteristics associated with a missile launch, the warning could put Brett's heart in his throat and his adrenaline on overload flow.

The RWR system's visual warnings were primarily to provide estimated range and bearing to the source of the received signal, and included a digital readout of the system's analysis.

When Brett heard the audio, he immediately glanced at the scope and knew the signal was from a fighter's airborne radar, weak power, relatively long range, search mode only, in his right one o'clock position and probably friendly.

Well I'll be damned! Maybe our friends are trying to find us.

Brett did his best to remain impassive about it, wondering if the hijacker would understand the significance of the warning.

"What was that?"

Careful, now. "Uh, radar signal of some sort, not sure what. It's long range and probably nothing."

The man chuckled at this. "Yeah, right. Nothing is 'nothing' in my business, Captain."

Another warning sounded, and Brett knew immediately it was closer, slightly stronger, and was holding at the same bearing or maybe slightly more toward twelve o'clock. He thought about the implications of what he was seeing on the radar screen.

If he were in that fighter picking up a possible contact at long range, low altitude, and knew nothing except that the bogey was capable of high speed, he'd attempt to convert the attack geometry as close to head-on as possible. He would probably get only one chance, and if he ended up cold on the roll out and outside missile range, he'd never be able to run the target down.

Unless, of course, he'd been authorized to engage head-on and without obtaining a visual identification. Then it would be a look-down, shoot-down situation and he'd be planning the reattack as a stern conversion just in case he missed on the first shot. *I wonder if the bogey*—Brett's thoughts came to a screeching halt when he realized the scenario he was creating. If this was a friendly fighter looking for them, he might not be all that friendly. The bomb had been disabled, the station was safe, and they might have decided they weren't going to let the man get away with a shuttle after all. Brett had indicated to Parker a willingness to take chances, and was accused of being a rogue warrior with a private agenda that might include sacrificing himself. *What if they're taking me up on it?*

But they didn't know about Toby. Brett got a sickening feeling in his stomach at the thought of being shot down with his young friend sitting behind him, and decided he had to evade the fighters.

He was being forced into becoming an active accomplice of the bastard in the right seat.

15

DAY EIGHT LATE EVENING

First Lieutenant Susan Strickland was wide awake, although she had every reason not to be. It had all started with the recall a day or so ago, she couldn't remember exactly when, initiated by a middle-of-the-night phone call ordering her to report to the squadron ASAP and bring her deployment kit.

Then the hurried briefings, suit up, blast off into the night sky and rejoin with the tankers for the flight to destination. She hadn't been on the ground for more than an hour when they began reconfiguring the fighters for five-minute alert status, loaded with the real stuff.

Now go get some rest, said her commander. Sure. Tell that to her heart, still racing from the coffee to stay awake and the excitement of her first real-world deployment. And where did they find these beds? You'd have to be used to sleeping on concrete to be comfortable and, let's face it, Susan liked her waterbed.

Initially they hadn't told the pilots anything. That was pretty typical, based on the traditional security concept of "need to know." And even though she didn't care for the mystery, it made sense. For the purposes of flying airplanes from one point to another, the pilots had no reason other than curiosity to know what the mission would be once they arrived. That came later.

And, of course, it happened in the form of another sudden phone call interrupting the first sound sleep Susan had been able to get. She was barely awake entering the briefing room, but that changed in a hurry.

With no preliminaries and right to the point, the major told the assembled pilots about the shuttle. Susan returned to the world of reality instantly as she listened to the situation portion of the briefing. The major provided a chronology of events beginning with an incident aboard the Space Station Oasis. Her career goal was to become a Space Command pilot, along with every other pilot she knew, and she had frequent dreams about what it would be like to fly a shuttle. Now she might just get close to one, even if not in the way she had hoped.

Takeoff had been just after midnight as number two on the wing of Captain Jorgensen. She liked him, although there had been the inevitable come-on's, accompanied by the typically juvenile attempts to determine if she would be interested in a little after-hours close formation. But once she made it clear their relationship was and would remain strictly professional, he behaved appropriately and Susan respected his competence as a fighter pilot and flight leader.

Tanker rendezvous was accomplished in the clear after a climb through dense clouds with tops about 10,000 feet. She was a little nervous while in the observation position on the right wing of the tanker, but that disappeared quickly as she got to the business of settling the fighter into the contact position for her first hook-up to the boom and received her scheduled offload.

The ops order called for the flight to remain with the tanker, topping off periodically until further orders. That might mean nothing more than hours of hanging around in formation, followed by an uneventful return to base. Susan's flight had already cycled through to refuel twice, and she was currently established on the tanker's right wing in preparation for another drink.

The mission objective was to find the shuttle. The major had been a little defensive on this point, especially when questioned by one of the pilots as to how we could lose one and have to find it. Everyone assumed NASA controlled shuttle movements to the last detail, and with today's technology and satellite coverage, communications were supposedly infallible.

But from the briefing Susan knew they had been trying to track the shuttle with varying degrees of success since it departed the station. At this point they did not know the shuttle's exact location. NASA was using speculation and flight path prediction while coordinating with the military for assistance in establishing radar contact with the shuttle and following it to destination.

Certainly this must be a first. A shuttle on the loose and no one knew where it was going, or much of the time where it was. And she was part of the effort, waiting for the word to go, while only vaguely aware of how the mission would progress once they left the tanker.

An unusual situation, to say the least. For all of her military flying career Susan had been taught that you never did anything that hadn't been thoroughly briefed. She was, however, experienced enough to know that in the unpredictable nature of tactical aviation, there were times when a fighter pilot had to react on the basis of what was happening at the moment rather than what had been talked about in the comfort of the briefing room.

Initiative. It was something you were supposed to have, use when the situation called for it, but be ready for criticism after the fact. If it worked, they called you a hero. If it didn't, that's why your wings were attached to your flight suit with Velcro. They'd rip them off in a heartbeat.

So this felt really strange. Here she was, all the briefings over with, but with so few details nailed down. And although it was in some ways a fighter pilot's dream, this absence of restrictions and the freedom to get the job done in the best way you saw fit, a significant downside could easily turn onto a nightmare.

Susan had felt it from the very beginning. Military aviation, and particularly fighter aviation, was still dominated by men, and a woman had to perform way better than average to have any chance of being accepted into the fraternity. Making the grade was good enough for Joe, but not for Joanne, and the ever-present question always seemed to be whether women had what it took to succeed in combat. Training is one thing, being shot at and having to kill the enemy is quite another.

For Susan, the answer up until now had been easy. If she held herself to a higher standard than the system did, criticism seemed to vanish. In some cases it was even replaced by a grudging respect, hastily offered and then dropped, as if they were embarrassed at having felt it. But that had been during training and routine operational flying. And while this mission couldn't be classified as combat, and the Rules of Engagement (ROE) presented in the briefing were strictly peacetime, Susan's fighter was loaded with a full complement of air-to-air missiles and that definitely wasn't routine.

And tonight, the same old question nagged at her. Could she hack it? Although she would never admit it to anyone, Susan secretly wanted the opportunity to prove it, once and for all, and get it over with, even though she felt the same way most military people did about war. Give her peace any day. It was much less hazardous to health.

The tanker boom operator's voice interrupted Susan's thoughts. "Hondo Flight, Exxon Boom, time for another drink."

Captain Jorgensen answered, "Roger that, Exxon, is Hondo One cleared into pre-contact?"

"You're cleared, Hondo One."

Susan watched as her leader eased down and back from the tanker's right wing, banked left, and slid into trail behind the tanker. She adjusted by moving her fighter into the space just vacated by him.

Since they had joined up with the tanker, three other flights of two had arrived, each taking pre-assigned positions in formation. Cycling eight fighters on and off the boom required precise control of sequence, and standardized procedures were essential to safety. All this airborne metal in close proximity created a prime situation for an accident.

"Receiver's ready."

"Exxon's ready, you're cleared into contact, One."

Jorgensen was a good pilot, and Susan admired his perfect control of closure rate as he moved the fighter slowly forward and brought it to a stop in the position required for the boom operator to extend the tanker's telescoping boom into the refueling receptacle and begin the transfer of fuel.

Susan divided her attention between flying formation on the tanker and watching Jorgensen. As he stabilized in the contact position, the boom extended to a flawless hook up. That's the way it was supposed to be done.

"Tanker contact."

"Receiver contact." This verbal confirmation of hookup meant both the fighter and tanker systems were working properly and Jorgensen was taking on fuel.

After a few moments the boomer's voice said, "You have your top off, Hondo One."

"Hondo One, disconnect . . . now."

"Tanker disconnect."

The boom pulled up and out of the fighter's refueling receptacle, streaming a small amount of jet fuel. The receptacle door began to close even before Jorgensen blanked slightly to the left, slowly moving aft and down and to assume position on the tanker's left wing. Susan would join him there when her refueling was complete.

"Is Hondo Two cleared to pre-contact?" You never changed position within the formation without clearance from the tanker.

"You're cleared, Hondo Two."

Susan throttled back slightly and began moving her fighter aft and down. When well clear of the tanker's right wing, she slid to her left until approaching the large aircraft's centerline, then banked right quickly to kill the drift and added power to stabilize in the pre-contact position. No closure, two ship lengths back, slightly low, locked there.

Boom operators were understandably touchy about this. Procedures dictated that the receiver must be stabilized in pre-contact before the boom operator would issue clearance into the contact position. Air refueling was a dangerous maneuver, and pilots could easily tense up with anticipation as they approached the boom.

"Receiver's ready."

"Tanker's ready, Hondo Two, you're cleared into contact."

This part of it was so unreal. Settling back in the reclined seat, Susan imagined it as being in an easy chair in her office, concentrating on the massive shape of the tanker looming in front of her windscreen. The night sky was pitch black, and special lights illuminated the underside of the tanker to give the receiver pilot a reference. Up, down, left, right, all meant nothing except in relation to this big aircraft.

Placing the fighter into the contact position was a matter of making it look exactly like it did the last time she did it perfectly. For each pilot it was different.

With slow, controlled closure, Susan brought the fighter forward to a stop in the contact position and held it there. The boom swung smoothly from her left until it was directly centered over the fighter, then the smaller section extended over her head and out of sight. Initially she had difficulty in training with this part of refueling because she couldn't ignore the boom. Tilting her head back and trying to watch it was a hard habit to break, but the consequences provided ample motivation. Head back, control back, immediate climb toward the tanker and the excitement would begin.

But not tonight. The end of the boom made contact with a satisfying clunk, and directly in front of her canopy the illuminated end of the large section of boom was centered on the green.

"Tanker contact."

"Receiver contact." Lights in the cockpit confirmed the hook-up, and Susan glanced down at her fuel quantity indicators to check that she was taking fuel. Now it was a matter of flying formation, staying relaxed, keeping the boom in the green.

"Hondo One, Exxon."

"Exxon, Hondo One, go."

"We just received a call from Hunter control. They want you to contact them button twelve."

"Roger that. I'll be off freq for a bit, monitor guard."

"Exxon copies."

This exchange told Susan that Jorgensen had left the primary refueling frequency to talk with Hunter control but was monitoring the standard emergency channel in the event Exxon needed to contact him in a hurry. Preoccupied with the possible significance of the call, Susan was beginning to bobble just a bit on the boom. *Easy, now, easy does it.*

Relax, it's probably nothing, just some typical stupid question. Controllers were always asking stupid questions.

"Hondo One's back up, Exxon. How're we doing with Two's fuel?"

"Just complete now, Hondo One, break, Hondo Two, you have your fuel."

"Hondo Two, disconnect now." Susan pressed the disconnect button on the control stick and hesitated momentarily before changing power until she saw the boom positively release from the receptacle and pull up and away. She reduced power slightly and without taking her eyes off the tanker reached over to the refueling panel with her left hand and closed the receptacle. Failure to do this would result in the tanks remaining unpressurized, trapping fuel in the internal and external wing tanks.

Dividing her attention between the tanker and her leader on the tanker's left wing, Susan continued to drop back until she was approaching nose-tail clearance with her leader's aircraft. Simultaneously adding power and left aileron to bank toward him, she rolled wings level as the heading difference provided closure on her new position on Jorgensen's left wing. Once safe separation was assured, she was free to concentrate on the rejoin.

Susan's fighter was so sensitive that small adjustments in pitch, power, bank, and rudder brought her smoothly but expeditiously behind Jorgensen and slightly low. Passing her leader's tailpipe, she banked right, added power, and maneuvered forward and up to a route formation position. Route formation was defined as one- to two-ship widths out, providing a more comfortable position for situations when close formation wasn't required, but tactical formation wasn't practical. She could relax, only if a little bit, and check inside the cockpit, monitor systems, and navigate without having to concentrate so much on flying formation.

"Exxon, Hondo One, we'll be leaving you now. Thanks for the gas."

"Roger that, Hondo. Come on back if you need more, we'll be on station until 0400, and your credit is always good with us."

"Wish my banker felt that way. Bye now."

You could have all the standard terminology spelled out in detail, but sometimes it boiled down to people talking to other people just like people normally do.

Susan maintained position as her leader backed down and out of formation with the tanker along the departure line. Looking past Jorgensen's fighter, she could see the lights of the big aircraft shining on the underside of its fuselage and wings, and the formation lights of the next two fighters moving up the approach line to the tanker's right wing. It was a beautiful sight no matter how many times she had seen it.

They remained on the refueling frequency as they descended below the tanker's altitude. These procedures were designed to keep everything under control until the flight was well clear. Once at the bottom of the block, with 2000 feet of altitude separation with the tanker, they could leave frequency.

"Hondo's departing the block, Exxon, switching tactical."

"Roger, Hondo. Be careful."

Susan heard two clicks of a microphone button as Jorgensen acknowledged the tanker's transmission, then, "Hondo Flight, button seven, go."

"Two." Without looking inside the cockpit, Susan removed her left hand from the throttle, punched in the channel change on the up front control (UFC), and then replaced her hand on the throttle. Glancing at the head-up display (HUD), she confirmed the correct channel and waited to check in on the new frequency.

The HUD was a transparent screen located above the glare shield. The display projected on the screen from below put whatever information the pilot wanted conveniently within view without the necessity of going head down. The ability to customize the display was essential, allowing the pilot the option of personal preference for the conditions at the time.

Susan had set up a minimum display en route to the tanker, and turned the brightness down to eliminate distracting glare as she flew formation. The dim "07" on the HUD helped because she had been able to perform the important function of changing radio channels without ever taking her eyes off her leader. Tonight, in clear air and in route formation, it wasn't that big a deal. But try it in close formation a few feet off Jorgensen's wing tip in clouds as thick as milk, and the difference was substantial.

"Hondo check."

"Two."

"We'll go to Hunter's freq in a minute, but first I want to remind you of a few things.

"Our briefings have been necessarily vague, unlike the majority of your experience so far, because of the uncertainties involved with this mission. As the situation develops you may have to react in a more autonomous fashion than you have been taught. Keep in mind the overall objective, the principles of two-ship tactical support you have learned, and let your instincts guide you. We may have to come up with a new course of action we haven't talked about. Let's stay calm and be flexible. Understood?"

"Roger that, sir."

"Okay. Go trail while we sort things out with Hunter."

"Two." Susan banked away from Jorgensen and throttled back to facilitate the transition from route to trail formation.

"Hondo, button twelve go."

Susan acknowledged the command, made the change, and waited for the check in.

"Hunter Control, Hondo's up button twelve, check."

"Two." This was a common technique to reduce radio chatter. Her leader made the initial call to the airborne controller before checking her in on the new channel, knowing she would respond before Hunter could answer.

"Hondo, Hunter, proceed to point Alpha and standby for mission info."

"Hondo copies."

Hunter Control was the call sign of the Airborne Warning and Control Station (AWACS) that would coordinate the mission, provide directions to Susan's flight, and serve as the command authority for all the actions they and any other U.S. aircraft took while searching for the shuttle.

Mission briefings had included a series of navigation points programmed into both AWACS and fighter computers. When directed to point Alpha, Jorgensen simply selected that destination and received immediate steering information, which could be displayed on the HUD and coupled to the autopilot. If the point was within range of the fighter's radar, he could also bring up a symbol on his scope showing the location of the point in either air-to-air or ground mapping modes.

Tonight's mission was a good case in support of AWACS capability. As Susan divided her attention between maneuvering into radar trail formation and selecting point Alpha in her own nav computer, the flight was already en route. AWACS was at the tail end of the chain of authority that undoubtedly began at the White House and extended directly into the hands of two fighter pilots in the dark night sky many thousands of miles away. Their specific orders were probably still being discussed, and essentially could be handed to them within a few minutes of being finalized.

As her leader banked away and rolled out on a westerly heading, Susan delayed her turn to follow. This move would help achieve the desired separation between her and Jorgensen. She wanted a 10 nautical mile (nm) radar trail, using 50 degrees offset during turns. As the range to her leader reached 1 nm, she glanced at the HUD to crosscheck her nav information with his. A good wingman always planned ahead.

The steering looked good, and they had a ways to go. Jorgensen was about 3 nm ahead, 15 degrees right on the scope. Crosschecking between the bearing to point Alpha and distance and bearing to her leader, Susan maintained a diverging heading until Jorgensen was about 45 degrees right and 9 nm range. A turn to center the radar return put him on the nose at about 10 nm with point Alpha dead ahead.

Perfect. Where do they find such women?

Susan then settled back to the relatively undemanding task of maintaining radar trail, and refreshed her memory on the major points covered in the briefing.

A shuttle had been hijacked. NASA and the Space Command were jointly involved with the current effort. The briefer pointed out the shuttle was one of the military versions, flown by a Space Command pilot. At first that seemed to be an insignificant bit of information, but the briefer didn't think so. The reason soon became clear.

The objective was to find the shuttle and follow it to destination. NASA had been tracking the shuttle well enough during the journey from the moon to Earth and approaching the reentry maneuver to predict where the shuttle would transition to powered flight. From that point it was a simple matter to draw a circle with a radius of the shuttle's maximum range. In the absence of air refueling, the shuttle would land somewhere within that area.

Simple to draw, not so simple to search. The target area encompassed thousands of square miles, but hopefully they were not faced with a needle in a haystack situation. The pilot was a factor for two reasons.

First, he was military trained, an experienced fighter pilot, and he knew what Susan, her leader, and the other pilots were up against. If he were an enemy, that would be a problem because he could anticipate their moves and take timely evasive action to counter their tactics. But, of course, he wasn't an enemy.

And second, he had flown the shuttles on military missions. Unlike the civilian shuttle pilots, he had hours of experience at low altitude, where the problem of tracking an aircraft was so much more difficult. But assuming he wanted to be found, the pilot might be able to help by doing things that would make it easier. The colonel stressed that point repeatedly. Expect assistance, but it will occur unexpectedly, with a narrow window of opportunity, and you will have to respond immediately.

One of the pilots asked why it made any difference that the shuttle was a military version. Because, explained the briefer, it is equipped with chaff, flares, and a full array of RWR gear. They didn't know if chaff and flares had been loaded, but assuming the pilot has the RWR gear on, he'll know you're coming. The ship also has a military transponder, with the capability to be interrogated on Mode 1. This feature could be used to detect and track the target.

Another pilot asked about the shuttle crew, and the colonel was quick to point out that as far as anyone knew there were only two people on the shuttle, the pilot and the hijacker. Someone then suggested this might be a factor in the shuttle's ability to evade, reasoning that one pilot in an airplane designed to be flown by two might easily be task saturated. The briefer shook his head at this idea, and pointed out that this particular pilot more than likely flew better that way. Summing it up, the briefer stressed that the pilot was capable of flying the shuttle very aggressively, but would probably try to help them find him.

Susan and Jorgensen were now cruising toward point Alpha at 35,000 feet and in no particular hurry. Hunter Control hadn't commanded a speed, which meant Hondo flight was en route to take up station and hold. Hurry up and wait was a common situation in the military, but fighter pilots hated to do that at any time, especially when airborne. With a fighter's relatively limited fuel capacity and high fuel flow, it was essential to economize whenever possible, and Susan knew her leader had selected a maximum range cruise speed en route to the nav point.

Other flights could be heard checking in on Hunter Control's common frequency. During periods of little activity it was normal practice for a number of aircraft to monitor the same channel, and then individually be called over to a discrete frequency when the AWACS controller had an assignment. Susan was able to form a picture in her mind of what was happening as other flights were each assigned a navigation point.

They were forming a line known as a "Barrier CAP." The term "combat air patrol" referred to a tactical mission in which fighters were assigned the task of maintaining air superiority over a given area. There were various ways of accomplishing that objective based on any number of considerations. In this situation, their job was to set up a line at roughly right angles to the projected flight path of the shuttle. Although there was no intention of engaging the shuttle, or preventing it from crossing the line, it would serve the purpose of locating the aircraft by placing the fighters in position for the best chance of obtaining radar contact.

When the navigation points were briefed and she took down the data, Susan had wondered how they decided where to put the line. Once the shuttle transitioned to powered flight it could turn and go in any direction. As soon as she looked at a map, however, the answer was clear.

Shuttles were marvelous machines, but they couldn't land on water. The projected point for transition to powered flight was over open ocean, and the line had been placed between that position and the nearest land. Not too hard to figure that one out, nor that the hijacker had no intention of landing anywhere under control of the United States.

Overall mission control was the job of the AWACS aircraft, positioned well back from the action but equipped with such a vast array of radar and communications gear that the controllers might as well be flying in formation with the fighters. Susan's radar was designed to be a weapons delivery system, sacrificing detection range for the ability to track airborne targets during heavy maneuvering and feed accurate range and azimuth data to the missiles. She could detect targets outside missile range, and use that capability to control fight geometry, but was effectively blind at longer ranges against fighter-sized targets, especially when the enemy didn't want to be seen.

Which, of course, was most of the time. But AWACS could look way out there and provide essential information. Susan expected that she and Jorgensen would be switched to a tactical discrete frequency as soon as AWACS had information about the shuttle's location, altitude, and heading. In addition, the controller might issue a vector to the fighters, along with an altitude and speed.

This preliminary positioning might well be accomplished long before Susan could obtain a contact on her radar scope, and was one of the distinct advantages of the AWACS-to-fighter coordination. Hondo flight could be established in the CAP in advance of the shuttle's arrival, which maximized their chances of being in the right place at the right time. Left on their own, the fighters would be forced to maintain constant radar surveillance of the shuttle's expected approach path. Although there were established formation flight patterns to accomplish this, it was costly in terms of fuel, increased pilot workload, and relied on radars ill-suited for long-range contacts.

"Hondo, Hunter Control here."

"Hunter, Hondo, go ahead."

"Proceed to a point three-hundred-twenty degrees for one hundred miles from point Alpha. Descend to angels two eight, and push it up a little."

"Hondo copies. Got any bogey dope?"

"Negative, Hondo. I'll be back to you as soon as I know any more."

"Roger that. Hondo coming right."

AWACS had just changed their destination further to the northwest, sent them to a lower altitude, and wanted to get them there sooner. The lack of a specific speed indicated that the controller had no intercept solution, but needed Hondo flight where he wanted them in plenty of time.

Susan programmed the new destination as an offset from the nav point already in the computer, and obtained her own steering as a backup. Once again, she delayed her turn until Jorgensen's fighter drifted to about 50 degrees right on the scope, then matched his turn to maintain the desired 10 nm spacing. With 40 nm range selected, and her leader about one-fourth of the way up the scope, Susan could easily monitor Jorgensen's position and still maintain an effective long-range search in both azimuth and elevation. Rolling out with the bearing to the new nav point and her leader on her nose, she checked her range and adjusted heading to cancel a slight drift to the left. With everything stabilized, she returned her attention to the task ahead.

Hunter Control's immediate objective was to position Hondo flight in relation to the big picture and as a part of a coordinated effort. Susan and Jorgensen would then establish their CAP and wait. If the shuttle tried to breach the line in Hondo's sector, Hunter would provide directive commands to adjust the CAP accordingly, then commit them on the intercept and assist them in obtaining a radar contact sufficient for taking control.

The task was complicated, however, because the shuttle was designed to be hard to find on radar. Stealth technology utilized a combination of aircraft shape and special coatings to reduce radar reflectivity. Nose-on or tail-on aspects were especially difficult, and the chances of detection were best on the beam where the radar signature of the aircraft was the largest. Head-on to the shuttle, which was by necessity where they would have to be during the initial portion of the intercept, Susan knew that she might be able to get momentary radar contacts, or "hits," on the target, but could not rely on radar alone. Fortunately, she wouldn't have to.

Susan's fighter could "interrogate" radar returns. Symbology on the scope then indicated one of two levels of interrogation, whether the contact was squawking Mode 1, and whether the code was that specified for the current period. Hopefully the shuttle pilot would have Mode 1 turned on, although it was highly unlikely that the code displayed would conform to any published plans. For Hondo's ultimate goal, it wouldn't matter. They needed help finding the shuttle on radar, not identifying it as the one contact they wanted among multiple targets. Once that was accomplished, they could go in close and take a look to confirm it was in fact the shuttle.

In addition to radar and IFF/SIF, another method of detection was the Infrared Search and Track System, or IRSTS. Jet engines emit heat in a narrow range of IR energy. Heat-seeking missiles detect this energy and send guidance signals to the flight controls so the missile can track and hit the heat source. Stealth didn't count for much to a missile that went after engines.

The IRSTS used the same principle to find a target, and although the information received was less accurate then that derived by radar, it was certainly better than nothing when you were trying to find a stealth aircraft. When a heat source was detected, the IRSTS displayed it on the scope. Azimuth was the most accurate parameter, followed by elevation, and then range. Susan's radar could be slaved to the IRSTS, which helped obtain a radar contact, so stealth aircraft were also designed to defeat this system with shielding to reduce the IR signature as much as possible. In frontal aspects the target aircraft blanked out most of its own IR energy. But from directly astern there wasn't much that could be done to prevent the IRSTS from obtaining a fairly solid IR signal.

Susan's mind was filled with the specifics of Jorgensen's briefing and she tried to review them carefully. He had instructed her to use any and all means to find the shuttle, which meant she would have to be very precise in coordinating her use of radar, IFF/SIF, and IRSTS so that the disadvantages of one system would be offset by the advantages of another.

"But don't forget," he had said. "The goal of using all this magic technology is to reach the point of not having to use it at all. One tally-ho is worth a thousand sweeps."

And that was the final objective. Put your eyeball on the target and don't lose sight. Susan's vision was in the eagle-eye category. She had never failed to read the bottom line on the eye charts, along with the tiny stock number and date printed in the bottom right hand corner. But tonight she would need all the help she could get. It was pitch black out there. The shuttle certainly wouldn't have any exterior lights on, a dark shape against a background of nothingness. And the pilot would probably be forced to stay in the clouds, which also decreased the capability of the IRSTS.

Clear of clouds, however, Susan had one other method for finding the shuttle. Night Vision Goggles, or NVG's, used the same infrared principle to create an image based on heat differential. Adapting the system to fighters had been a long process, but was finally accomplished by utilizing the same principle as Susan's helmet-mounted sight.

The infrared sensing hardware was mounted in the airplane, and aimed with the pilot's head movements. With the flick of a switch, Susan could activate the NVG system. Wherever she looked, the NVG's sensors followed and routed the image to her visor. The advantages of this approach were never clearer to Susan than tonight. Until the latter stages of the intercept, she would be using a combination of radar, IFF/SIF, and IRSTS to position her fighter for the end-game objective of obtaining visual contact with the shuttle. With all the cues pointing to that small piece of darkness where the elusive target had to be, Susan had only to engage the NVG and confirm the visual identification (VID). *Piece of cake. Yeah, right.*

Susan was dividing her attention between maintaining radar trail formation on her leader, checking navigation to the CAP point, and scanning her engine instruments when she felt a momentary surge of pride. She was part of all this, strapped in the cockpit of this marvelous machine, slicing through the night sky at 450 knots and

28,000 feet above the water en route to a possible rendezvous with another craft that had last been at rest on a space station orbiting the Moon. Absolutely incredible!

Lord, don't let me screw this up. The universal fighter pilot's prayer.

"Hondo, Hunter, turn immediately heading one four zero, direct Point India, descend angels one five, buster."

The radio had been routinely busy for the past ten minutes or so, and Susan had mentally tuned out all the chatter that didn't apply to Hondo. This transmission changed all that because the controller's voice was unmistakably insistent.

Turn southeast to a new cap point, descend, and go as fast as you can go in military power. Something was definitely happening, and Susan's heart rate spiked as she returned her concentration to maintaining the assigned trail position during Jorgensen's turn. Is this it?

Do your job, Susie, and let's go find this stealthy bastard!

Following the call from Hunter Control to descend and push it up, things began to happen quickly. There was a lot of radio chatter, but because the AWACS controller was working at least one other frequency in addition to Hunter common, Susan learned in bits and pieces that the shuttle pilot had managed to select emergency on his transponder. With this enhanced radar signal, the AWACS radars were able to establish a few minutes of solid ground track and determine the most probable intercept point.

Hondo flight was the first to leave the tanker for their CAP point. The overall plan presented in the situation briefing called for each of the two-ship flights to be in place well in advance of the shuttle's earliest possible transition to powered flight, but something must have gone wrong. Still on the tanker and out of the picture for the moment, the other fighters were not available to help when the transponder signal appeared on the scopes. In addition, the projected flight path of the shuttle was farther away than anticipated, and Hondo flight was closest to the action.

As the only two in position to do anything, Susan and Jorgensen were now in full afterburner trying to reach the new CAP point in time to get set up. Susan was in trail formation, but was not trying to maintain visual on her leader. They had entered the clouds passing

15,000 feet, and with her radar she was able to keep track of his position and still search the area in front of the two-ship.

"Hondo, Hunter."

"Go for Hondo, Hunter." Jorgensen's voice was as calm as ever.

"I show you fifty miles from point India. When you get there establish the CAP and start looking for this guy. What's your fuel state?"

"We'll have no more than thirty minutes remaining at point India if all we do is orbit. You have relief on the way?"

"That's affirmative. Bison just departed the tanker, and we're moving the refueling track closer to India now."

"Hondo copies."

Since no one knew exactly when it might start or how long this operation would last, the ops order called for sufficient fighter assets to maintain continuous coverage in the CAP. But the sudden appearance of the emergency squawk had compressed the time factor and now it was simply a matter of trying to get Hondo in position quickly, then relieve them sooner than originally planned. Afterburners were marvelous devices, but the cost in fuel was a significant factor.

Susan's nav computer showed point India at 13 nm ahead when the AWACS controller said, "Hondo One, I show you four miles from India, suggest you turn up track for the first look and have number two take spacing behind you."

That was about right. Susan was 9 nm in trail with Jorgensen, and he was 4 nm from India. He would make a left turn toward the shuttle's projected approach path and begin searching, while she turned right and proceeded to the other end of the orbit. The objective was for one fighter to be rolling out at the far end with radar coverage as the other fighter turned away to reposition.

Jorgensen had briefed relatively long legs for the CAP orbit. In combat situations, that would be risky because the two fighters would be too far apart at times to maintain mutual support. But in the absence of threats, with AWACS in support to help clear the area, and the objective being to find a stealth aircraft, he wanted more time for each leg with the radars looking for the shuttle. Two minutes was the standard unless he changed it in the air.

"Hondo One, point India."

As she watched Jorgensen's fighter turn left and drift off the scope, Susan hacked the clock and began to plan her pattern. The nav computer told her everything she needed to know, because with point India as the reference, the racetrack orbit was anchored on the point. As she turned down track the time and distance-to-go were displayed on the HUD. The first pattern would be flown with her leader searching for only one minute. All she had to do was time her turn so as to be rolling out up track just as he began his turn to reposition. Beginning with Susan's first pass, all subsequent legs would take the full two minutes.

Watching the time-to-go readout on the HUD, Susan began her easy turn with about 45 seconds displayed. As she rolled out up track on the hot leg, one minute to go and Jorgensen's call occurred almost simultaneously.

"Hondo One off cold."

"Hondo Two in hot."

Airspeed at a comfortable, fuel-saving 350 knots, Susan engaged the autopilot and concentrated on the radar. At 15,000 feet above the water with the search pattern depressed slightly and maximum range selected, she was covering a large area but sacrificing contact range, especially against a stealth target. At this point she had no choice, because without knowing more about the shuttle's location, it would be self-defeating to narrow down the search. But if given some indication of where to direct her attention, the radar could be concentrated into smaller sectors to enhance the chance of contact.

AWACS, IRSTS, and IFF were also available, and she would need them all.

16

DAY NINE MIDNIGHT

All the previous considerations about trying to stop the hijacker were so much old news. With no way to determine the intent of the fighters hunting him, Brett had to assume the worst.

Impact with the ground was also a real threat, especially without the benefit of advance planning. Screaming along at low altitude was dangerous enough when you could see ahead and knew your exact position. But in pitch-black nothingness, with only a vague idea of where in the hell they were, Brett was anxious to pick out something on the horizon for a reference.

When he leveled off at 200 feet above the water, the visibility was difficult to determine. The cloud layer seemed to be dissipating, but he couldn't see any stars, and nothing on the horizon indicated anything but more water. This was like being in a dark room traveling at 450 knots, staring at a wall. What's on the other side?

But the autopilot and TFR were operating well, so he left them coupled while he assessed the potential threat indicated on the RWR. If the fighters were looking for them, their task would be much more difficult with the complications of night and weather. The RWR gear steadily became more active. Every time the audio sounded the hijacker seemed to tense up a little more, but he stopped asking questions when Brett told him to shut up. The building tension in the cockpit apparently was sufficient explanation, and the faster events began to happen, the more it must have become evident that Brett had his hands full.

He continued to follow the GPS steering with manual inputs to the autopilot heading controller while he analyzed the RWR indications. When trying to evade an airborne threat at low altitude it was common practice to avoid a long, straight run. Periodic course alterations, or "head fakes," made it more difficult for the fighters to determine your destination and complicated the task of interception.

Brett was considering a modified head fake. It was entirely possible these fighters were here strictly by coincidence, on a mission having nothing to do with the shuttle. If that were true, and he turned away from the destination on the GPS, he should notice a divergence in which the RWR indications would drift off toward one side of the nose as the fighters failed to respond to his course change.

But if they were hunting him, and the fighters were able to obtain contact, they would immediately turn to stay as close to the shuttle's twelve o'clock position as possible in an attempt to maintain cutoff.

Decision time. Brett needed to know the answer before he got any closer to the fighters, and on the spur of the moment came up with a plan.

"What the hell are you doing?"

The man didn't like what he saw. Telling him to shut up wasn't going to hack it." I'm turning away from the destination. I—"

"I can see that, damn it. What for?"

Brett struggled to remain calm, concentrating on flying the shuttle, but he had to explain the objective so the man would remain quiet and let him analyze what was happening.

"Those indications we've been getting are U.S. fighters, and they may be hunting us. I want——"

"They aren't hunting us. Take my word for it. They can't interfere because I've got the hammer and they know it. Now reverse this turn and get back on course."

Brett lost the internal battle. "ARE YOU SURE?" he shouted. "Are you absolutely sure the bomb hasn't been found and disarmed?" The hijacker's expression was the first time Brett had seen anything like a loss of composure.

Arguing with the guy wasn't working. Brett eased off the bank to shallow the turn as he explained his reasoning. "It's the kid I'm thinking about. They don't know he's on board. If they don't interfere, we're still going to get there. But if you're wrong, and I don't do this my way, I can guarandamntee you those fighters have what it takes to find and kill us."

Brett had said all he could. He rolled out with the shuttle's course reversed 180 degrees. This might tell him more than a lesser turn would have anyway. The man said nothing, and didn't appear ready to interfere, so Brett pulled the power back to slow up and monitored the RWR.

AFTER 17 MINUTES, SUSAN HAD COMPLETED 4 SEARCH LEGS. THE only contacts had been with ships on the surface and commercial aircraft cruising by. AWACS had access to civilian air traffic control agencies and had confirmed all the airborne contacts were scheduled air-carrier operations. Everyone expected the shuttle to be at low altitude, but they couldn't rule out the possibility of the pilot trying to sneak by as an airliner. She was just turning up track for her fifth leg when AWACS called.

"Hondo, Hunter Control, we have a possible contact bearing zero seven five, one hundred forty miles, very low."

Hondo One off cold. That's yours, Honda Two."

"Hondo Two, roger, in hot." Susan rolled out fifteen degrees left of the up-track heading of 090 degrees to put the contact on the nose. She used the cursor control on the throttle to bump the radar cursors against the side of the scope to select narrow scan. This concentrated the radar search pattern in a smaller area and allowed her to slew a 60-degree scan wherever she wanted on the scope.

Then the IRSTS blipped. Susan immediately slaved the radar to it and hit the IFF interrogate button on the chance that the shuttle's Mode 1 might be operational.

Bingo. "Hondo Two, I have a very weak IR contact on the nose with Mode One interrogation!"

"Easy, Two, take your time." It was Jorgensen, who undoubtedly recognized the excitement in Susan's voice. She barely heard him as she focused her attention on the possibility that this might be their elusive target.

Susan almost forgot about converting to 180-degree aspect, and luckily there was still time. Turning left, she displaced the intermittent hits to the right on the scope, but not too far. She needed to obtain cutoff, but if the target turned left suddenly, she could get caught with an unexpected drift off the right of the scope and lose contact.

Playing the drift by turning right in small increments to maintain the contacts between 15 and 30 degrees right on the scope, Susan confirmed with the AWACs controller that the target's heading appeared to be 270 degrees. When her heading was about 060 degrees and the target was 30 degrees right, she turned hard right to a heading of 090 degrees to convert her intercept to a head-on pass. She couldn't get any more cutoff than that.

Susan had extended her hot leg as briefed rather than turn away. Jorgensen had continued down track until the situation proved to be more than a false alarm and was now in trail with her. Although unusual for the less experienced of the pilots to be in the lead, there were provisions for the wingman to assume tactical lead of the formation when the situation warranted. Susan had pushed up the power and was accelerating as she descended toward the water. Although still in the clouds and capable of running the intercept on radar, her chances of success would be better for lots of reasons if she could get in clear air. The shuttle might stay in the clouds, but it was better to look up at a target than down. In the off chance that he was flying below the weather, she wanted to do the same.

As she closed on the target, Susan ran the cursor to the bottom of the scope and changed the display to the next shorter range. This concentrated the radar energy and improved her chances of a solid contact and lock on. With the help of intermittent IRSTS contacts and IFF interrogations, she was beginning to pick up what she thought was the shuttle. Her conversion to head on had worked well, and now it was a matter of obtaining offset at the correct range and timing the turn to achieve the desired shadow position.

"Hondo Two, this is One, how do you read?"

The radio seemed to intrude suddenly on her world, and Susan felt a spasm of fear that she hadn't heard previous transmissions from her leader. "Loud and clear, One. How me?"

"Listen up, Two. Do you have a level two Mode One confirmation?"

Shit. He must have asked me that more than once. And I haven't even figured that out for myself.

Susan triggered another interrogation, and glanced at the scope display for the result. A level one IFF hit would tell her the target was squawking Mode 1, but not the specific code for the current period. If this contact was the elusive shuttle, and the system had been programmed correctly, it should respond with a level two display.

Uh-oh. No such luck. Mode one is turned on, but isn't squawking the right code.

"That's a negative, Hondo One. Level one only."

"Roger. Continue, and stay cool, I had to call you three times."

Not good. She had been concentrating so hard on the intercept that she never heard Jorgensen's calls. The absence of a level two confirmation meant that they would have to complete the VID without knowing for sure whether they were on the right target. The chance there could be another U.S. military aircraft out here that nobody knew about was remote, but the ROE were clear on this point. With renewed determination to do this right, Susan interrogated the contact again and stared at the scope where the shuttle had to be.

Faint, but there it was. Susan attempted a lock on, and after three tries she had it, dead ahead, 31 miles, about 3 degrees low. Symbology on the HUD and the scope provided valuable information for the intercept: closure-900 knots; aspect-180 degrees; target heading-272 degrees. Susan was directly in front of the target, on a collision course. And as she passed 10,000 feet in the descent, the target was about 9,000 feet below her. The shuttle was right down on the deck. No way she could get below him.

Reviewing her checkpoints for the stern conversion, Susan had just keyed the mike button to confirm with Jorgensen which side he was on when something changed.

The target began to drift right slightly. Up until now the track had been steady down the nose, so this must be a heading change. Scope symbology confirmed Susan's suspicion just as the radar broke lock. All those nice cues went away and it was right back to interpreting the situation through raw data.

No matter, I can do this.

The drift just picked the direction of turn. She would offset him to the right and use his turn to help convert. That'll cool it off somewhat, but it's too late to do anything else.

Susan got another lock, and was comparing drift rate, target azimuth, and range when she noticed the closure readouts on the radar scope and HUD. Confused, she concentrated on the readout, entering a mode often referred to as "tunnel vision." Ignoring other information, Susan began to lose situational awareness.

He must have turned left. Small heading change, though, or with his speed he would have drifted further to the right side of the scope. Closure should still be high, about—what the hell?

Closure 350 knots.

Why so low?

BRETT HAD PUT THE FIGHTERS IN A TAIL CHASE, THE WORST position for them versus a high-speed target at low altitude. If they had been setting up a barrier CAP on the shuttle's projected course, this just threw a load of shit in the fan. Depending on how well they had been able to monitor the shuttle's position since the descent to low altitude, they had probably planned to intercept him in a general area, using a number of two-ships to cover the most logical courses.

Brett didn't know exactly where they were, but the fighters certainly knew where they were. The thought occurred to him that being over water might make his head fake ineffective. If the nearest land was behind the fighters, they knew the shuttle had to make a run for it and pass through the barrier CAP. Turning away from the CAP toward open ocean shouldn't elicit any reaction. Why chase a target that has to come to you? Brett was about to give up on the attempt to determine the fighter's intentions when it happened.

RWR audio and strobe, six o'clock, closer in range than before. If this was a random hit, it shouldn't repeat, because the fighters would be orbiting a nav point and wouldn't try to maintain contact. Brett decided to try something, find out for sure if he was the target. He disengaged the autopilot, snapped the throttles to idle, and extended the speed brakes, rapidly slowing the shuttle to less than 250 knots while allowing the automatic system to extend the wings forward.

"What the hell are you doing now?" The man was squirming at this sudden change in configuration. Good. Brett ignored the question. Extending the slats, he waited for the speed to decrease further. He wanted the shuttle in a slow flight configuration, and lowered flaps according to the speed schedule until just above the stall.

At the first burble, indicating that airflow over the wing tips was just beginning to separate, the shuttle's lateral stability decreased slightly as the ailerons became sloppy. Leaving the left throttle at idle, he advanced power on the right engine, adding right rudder to prevent yaw and keep the nose straight. As the throttle reached military power, he banked right slightly to further help control the aircraft's tendency to yaw and roll left. The next move would require precise control.

Brett moved the right throttle outboard, then forward until the first stage of the afterburner lit. The sudden increase in thrust required more rudder and aileron, but he was able to control it and even increase power into the second stage before he began to feel approaching disaster. If he lost control now, the shuttle would snap roll left, and end up nose low, upside down, at less than 200 feet above the water.

This was certainly not a normal maneuver, but Brett was confident he could pull it off. There was even time to notice the man was petrified, unable to move, hands gripping the armrests hard enough to crease the cushions.

Welcome to the world of real aviation, you bastard.

The flying was automatic, even with this unusual combination of control inputs. Brett allowed his senses to coordinate with his hands and feet as he detached a part of his attention and assigned it to the RWR indications. With an idea of what he expected to see, he waited patiently.

And there it was. *Good guess, Larsen, suspicion confirmed.*

The fighters were definitely looking for them. He still didn't know why, but with the bomb disabled and Toby's presence on the shuttle unknown to anyone else, Brett had no choice but to assume they would shoot if given the chance.

He could picture the fighter pilots' reactions. If they had seen the emergency IFF squawk, they probably had been able to confirm a position and course at sufficient range to move the CAP directly in line with the shuttle's path. They were undoubtedly working with AWACS, taking directions from a controller and getting intermittent radar contacts. It was like trying to solve a mystery with minimal clues, feeling in the dark most of the time. Expecting the target to maintain course, they would be coordinating with AWACS and each other so one of them would be in position to search the approach corridor at any given time.

Then suddenly things changed for them. What had been a series of momentary radar hits, maybe with occasional IRSTS blips and IFF interrogations, indicating closing range with overtake, had turned into a solid IR signature. The closest pilot would have immediately slaved his radar to the IRSTS, obtained a radar lock-on, and noticed lower overtake than expected on a target going away.

Reaction? Chase. Don't let them get away. And the fighter's radar would do what it knows best, switch from a search mode into a ranging mode to help launch and guide a missile. At speeds of Mach 2 plus, missiles need accurate information as to target range and angular movement. The faster the radar pulses are sent out and received, the better the information, and RWR gear was designed to detect the change and alter the audio indications accordingly.

And as the tone became constant and higher pitched, and the strobe confirmed the fighter to be in the shuttle's six o'clock position, Brett knew for certain they were waiting for him. One of the pilots had detected the afterburner plume on the IRSTS and responded as predicted, which also set the stage for the next move.

Assuming the worst, that the fighters had been given the authority to shoot the shuttle down, Brett had to penetrate the barrier CAP and separate beyond missile range. There may be more than two fighters out there, but probably not close enough to be a threat at the moment. Glancing at the GPS, he knew the hijacker's destination was just over 250 nm away. If he could throw a wrench in the fighters' intercept plan just long enough to punch through the CAP and run for it, they might have a chance.

The shuttle was capable of supersonic speeds at low altitude. Fuel burn was a severe limitation, but it was for the fighters also. Depending on how long it had been since refueling, and how much burner they had used so far, once in a tail chase they might be forced to break off the intercept. If another two-ship was positioned further away and between the shuttle and its destination, Brett might be faced with the same problem again. But he couldn't think about that now. These two fighters were the immediate threat, and he knew the shuttle would be hard to find regardless of the numbers.

It was time for the rest of the head fake. Brett slowly advanced the left engine to reduce the asymmetric thrust condition and terminated afterburner on the right, adjusting the flight controls and throttles to maintain his heading in level flight and the airspeed right at stall. His objective now was to reverse course in the face of the pursuing fighter before the pilot could detect the change. Brett guessed the pilot would leave the radar slaved to the IRSTS, which was perfectly capable of tracking a non-afterburning engine tailpipe, and the fighter's radar would probably maintain lock-on. He wanted to use that to gain a little time, a small advantage, by throwing in some confusion.

The pilot flying the fighter was probably the less experienced of the two. If your objective is to set up a barrier CAP, you don't leave it and chase after a target that isn't obviously trying to get through. One of the common head fakes against a barrier CAP was to send in a decoy to make a run at the barrier and then turn off when one or more of the CAP fighters leave it in pursuit.

Brett's plan was a modification of the decoy, and timing was critical. With at least one of the fighters in pursuit, his objective was to trick both the pilot and his radar for a few seconds. The shuttle was slowed down to very near stall speed, and the fighter's radar would indicate positive overtake when the pilot would be expecting low or even negative overtake in a stern chase on a supersonic-capable aircraft. The pilot undoubtedly had a preconception about what he would see, and Brett hoped to use that to create doubt and hesitation.

The fighter's radar might also be used to Brett's advantage. Small doors on the shuttle's tail, opened on command from the cockpit, dispensed chaff as an anti-radar defense. Radars like things that reflect energy, and the thin strips of foil packaged in chaff bundles came apart when ejected into the slipstream. Blossoming into a nice radar-reflective cloud, the chaff was designed to break a radar lock on the shuttle by giving the pursuit radar's tracking circuits something else to see.

Brett knew that all U.S. fighter radar systems were equipped with features that reduced the effectiveness of head fakes and included countermeasures to the problem of chaff. Numerous clues clearly visible to the pilot on the HUD could be used to decipher the current situation. But if Brett's assumption was correct, and the closest fighter to him was piloted by the less experienced wingman, there was always the possibility of taking advantage of the inevitable confusion inherent to combat situations.

The purpose of anti-chaff logic was to prevent transfer of lock-on to chaff by programming the tracking circuits to ignore target shifts with very sudden changes in overtake. The shuttle was currently slowed to 160 knots and the fighter was probably doing 500 plus, maybe more if the pilot was still in pursuit. With a difference of about 340 knots, when the fighter's radar attempted to shift lock to the larger chaff target, the logic would reject the shift because the chaff instantly slows when it is dispensed and becomes stationary. This immediate change in overtake to the fighter's current airspeed was the key to the radar's ability to ignore the chaff maintain lock on the shuttle.

But there was a way to fool the radar. Dispensing chaff when the pursuing fighter was off the beam provided the best situation. At this point in the target-to-fighter flight path geometry, the relative speed difference was very close to the fighter's own airspeed. As the radar started to shift lock to the chaff, only a small change in overtake would occur. The anti-chaff logic circuits therefore had much more difficulty detecting the presence of chaff, and often the radar would transfer lock almost with no indication to the pilot. The word "almost" was important, and Brett's plan was designed to take advantage of it.

Even if he could successfully defeat the fighter's anti-chaff logic and the radar shifted lock from the shuttle to the chaff, other clues were available to alert the pilot of the fighter. An "aim dot" on the HUD, a "collision course cue" on the scope, and a sudden shift in the target's azimuth all pointed to the change. But depending on the geometry of the attack, these clues might be dramatic or barely perceptible, especially to a relatively inexperienced pilot full of adrenaline, breathing hard, struggling to do everything right and probably scared shitless. Brett was planning on the latter.

All three of the additional cues relied on the sudden change in azimuth to be effective. If Brett was flying faster and turned into the attack, the pursuing pilot would have e better chance of noticing the target drift from dead ahead to one side or the other and pull to the inside of the turn for cutoff. But with the shuttle slowed down, Brett knew that he could turn back toward the pursuing fighter and keep the radius of the turn very small. This would reduce the angular movement of the shuttle's radar return on the fighter's scope, and the pilot probably would remain nose on to the shuttle. Distance from the fighter to the shuttle was a factor, and although Brett didn't know how far back his pursuer was, he sensed there was sufficient range between them to pull this off.

And if Brett popped the chaff when he was about half way through the turn with the fighter off the beam, the attacker's radar would smoothly transfer lock to the chaff. The anti-chaff logic would ignore the small change in overtake, and the pilot might not notice the slight shift in the target's azimuth and small changes in the aim dot and collision course cue.

It was called "free" maneuvering. In air combat, every offensive move had a corresponding defensive counter, and tactics for defeating an enemy were designed to provide you with an opportunity to do something without your opponent knowing about it. Brett wanted to reverse course on the fighter closest to him and be accelerating in his face before the pilot recognized what was going on. If the ruse worked, the shuttle would be past the closest pursuer and in a good position to evade the second fighter before they could regroup.

Come on, hands, don't fail me now.

Brett pushed the throttles to military power, and with left rudder and aileron rolled the shuttle into a steep left bank. Afterburner would have been better, but he was concerned the fighter pilot would note the sudden heat increase detected by the IRSTS. With the maximum back stick available and the shuttle shuddering around the turn, Brett brought the nose through 180 degrees in about ten seconds, dispensing the chaff halfway through. As he eased back stick and rolled out, he selected afterburner and felt the satisfying punch in the ass as the spray nozzles in the burner cans added vaporized fuel to the exhaust and the igniters fired.

Talk about a head rush. Turbojet engine exhaust always contained unburned fuel as a by-product of incomplete combustion. Afterburners were very basic. Dump in more fuel in a vaporized state and strike a match. The rapidly expanding gases accelerated out the tailpipe and shoved the shuttle forward so quickly that the g-forces pinned Brett back into the seat. Even in the midst of the current serious situation Brett's reaction was the same as always.

God, how I love this.

But there was no time for grinning. Brett selected flaps up and retracted the slats and speed brakes in one motion. The wings swept back automatically on schedule with no action on his part, and in a move that brought a gasp of terror from the hijacker, Brett pushed forward on the stick until the shuttle was about 30 degrees nose low. The radar altimeter and the terrain avoidance system sounded the warnings of impending disaster.

Alarm bells, and, "ALTITUDE! ALTITUDE! PULL UP! PULL UP!" filled the cockpit as Brett yanked back on the stick and leveled the accelerating shuttle at less than 50 feet above the black water. In full afterburner, the ship surged ahead through the Mach and Brett let her run. He had flown shuttle prototypes at over two times the speed of sound at low altitude during testing of the TFR, but knew they were capable of quite a bit more than that.

~

SUSAN'S AIRSPEED WAS APPROACHING 500 KNOTS. THE TARGET had to be doing about 450 knots, and she was expecting the closure to remain high until she passed his wingtip and was well into the conversion. Staring at the HUD, she tried to decipher what was happening.

Of course! He's turned much further than I thought.

With her brain spring-loaded to Jorgensen's emphasis that the shuttle was capable of rapid acceleration and supersonic speeds, Susan concluded that the target had turned away and put her in a stern chase. As she keyed the mike button again to tell her leader, something else didn't seem quite right.

Closure 350 knots. Why so high if he's going away? It should be about 100 knots or so.

Susan read it as negative overtake, rather than positive. In a panic that the target was getting away, she slammed the throttle into afterburner and accelerated in an attempt to stay close. The next series of events happened so fast the result was guaranteed from the outset.

Closure should be decreasing or at least holding. His max speed should be about . . . wait a minute. Why is it increasing? What the hell? Slight drift to the left. Turn to keep him on the nose. Closure now 550 and still increasing. Drift just stopped. Shit, now he's drifting right. Roll the hell out and look at this for a second. Airspeed 600, overtake 600. Did the son of a bitch just stop?

Susan had been so intent on trying to decipher the problem she failed to hear Jorgensen's first warning, which now, repeated for the second time, burst in on her consciousness like a commandment from on high.

"HONDO TWO, DON'T FOLLOW HIM! BREAK IT OFF! HE'S TURNED AWAY AS A DECOY MOVE. SUSAN! THAT'S CHAFF! HE POPPED CHAFF! DO YOU READ?"

~

AT THIS POINT BRETT NEEDED ABOUT NINETY-NINE PERCENT OF his attention devoted to staying alive, but the other one percent concentrated on the RWR. The audio indication of radar lock on had ceased before he rolled out, and he noticed a momentary strobe from twelve o'clock as he leveled out just above the water. Apparently the chaff had worked, and now the immediate question was whether the pilot had detected the turn soon enough to reposition and was close enough to be a threat.

Glancing at the GPS, Brett altered heading to the right slightly to center the vertical steering bar and return to course. Shortly afterward, the RWR gear lit up with the same friendly fighter indication, this time at six o'clock and in search mode. When the audio failed to shift to a higher threat mode, Brett concluded that his pursuer was caught in a tail chase, stagnated outside missile range.

Good. Satisfied that at one fighter was out of the picture, Brett returned all one hundred percent of his attention to flying, but only for a moment.

RWR hits, friendly, on the nose, search mode, then drifting right, one o'clock, two o'clock, closing. The proper move for Brett now in most situations would be to turn right into the threat and keep the fighter at high aspect. But that would allow the trailing fighter to close range by using cutoff to the inside. He was also concerned about getting too far off course at this low an altitude. The man had planned for being able to clear obstacles at 200 feet in this general area, but that might not apply at 50 feet, and the profile may call for a climb sometime soon. A glance at the hijacker told Brett he wouldn't be getting much direction from him for a while. The bastard was white as a sheet.

Suddenly the RWR gear sounded off again, indicating a shift to a higher threat mode and a radar lock on. A quick glance at the scope showed that the fighter ahead was drifting to right four o'clock and closing. The shuttle's stealth capability was most limited on the beam, where the radar signature was more a function of size than anything else. A larger profile reflected more energy, and it was obvious to Brett that this second pilot was flying a perfect stern conversion.

Without even thinking about it, Brett popped some chaff, and immediately heard its effect as the audio ceased and the fighter's radar broke lock. *Take that, fella.*

Okay, but only for a moment. Brett got two quick RWR hits at five o'clock, then a solid lock on warning at six. This guy was good. Brett's thoughts were jerked back into reality when the seriousness of what was happening terminated his admiration for a fellow fighter pilot.

If he shoots, we're in big trouble. Brett put all his concentration into flying as fast and as low to the water as he could. It was the only remaining defense other than the chaff and flares, but if he used either of these at the wrong time it would only serve to highlight his position.

WHEN SUSAN FIRST REALIZED SHE HAD BEEN DUPED, SHE WAS too stunned to react. But at 600 plus knots, passing 1000 feet above the water in a 10 degree dive, she had little time for remorse and her immediate survival instincts took over.

Yanking back on the throttle, Susan pulled on the stick and leveled her fighter at about 500 feet, then snap rolled left and pulled hard in a max-g turn to reverse course. With her G-suit clamping hard on her legs, abdomen, chest, and neck, grunting in a classic L-1 maneuver to keep from graying out, she noticed what appeared to be breaks in the clouds just below her. Glancing to her left as she passed 90 degrees of turn, by pure chance she saw a huge black shape streak by underneath, followed by the unmistakable bluish-white plumes of twin afterburners.

"HONDO TWO'S GOT A TALLY HO ON THE TARGET!" Her transmission came out muffled by her oxygen mask and distorted by the high g-load, but Jorgensen had years of experience interpreting this sort of excited verbiage and probably understood.

Susan's call wasn't strictly accurate at the moment, because she didn't have the shuttle in sight as she rolled out of her turn. Frantic to remedy the situation, she pushed the nose over to descend below the clouds and triggered both the IRSTS and IFF to obtain a quick contact.

The IR blip was immediate, the shuttle's afterburners leaving more than enough heat source at this close range to be discernible through the clouds. With an IFF hit in the same location, Susan knew just where to look for the radar contact. A stealth aircraft wasn't much easier to find on radar from the stern than head-on, but if she could just stay close enough, she might be able to regain the tally and keep it. If the shuttle pilot stayed in afterburner, and he would have to in order to outrun her, once below the clouds that would be relatively easy.

Susan triggered an automatic lock-on sequence with the radar slaved to the IR contact. As she descended into the clear at about 200 feet, she could discern just enough of a horizon to maintain orientation. The water appeared black, but it had texture, probably from sea swell, and what appeared to be land ahead was backlit by a faint glow. The sky above was just a dark ceiling, lit up in her vicinity by—

Holy shit, my lights. Should they be on?

Jorgensen never said anything about turning them off. They always would in combat, but this isn't combat.

Or is it?

Everything seemed to become instantly clear. She saw the twin bright lights ahead against the dark of the land, nestled precisely in the center of the TD, or "Target Designator" box, which provided a visual cue to the position of the target on the scope. It had to be the shuttle's afterburners, and she had to tell Jorgensen. But just to make sure, she engaged an NVG search and was immediately rewarded with a ghostly five-second IR image of the shuttle with two intensely bright holes of heat defining the exhaust nozzles.

"HONDO TWO, TALLY HO THE TARGET DEAD AHEAD, RANGE ABOUT SEVEN MILES!" That ought to get him excited. She found the bastard.

"Hondo Two, One copies, I'm in your left eleven o'clock about four miles with a tally. Do you have a visual?"

Susan was struck speechless for a moment. She had heard some radio chatter going on, but in her excitement most of it didn't register. Her situational awareness was instantly updated with that one call, typically calm, cool, from Jorgensen the ice cube, all business.

Standard terminology differentiated between visual contacts by referring to the target as a "tally" and your leader or wingman as a "visual." Swallowing hard, Susan acknowledged the call.

She had fallen for a beautifully executed head fake, rolled out 7 nm in trail, and her leader had performed the classic stern conversion. A little far back at 3 nm, but who was she to nit-pick him? And how could she have missed the contact? She broke lock on the shuttle, and Jorgensen's fighter was right there, big as a damned house. Susan started to lock on to make it easier to follow him, but paused to consider the consequences of that. Better to let the radar sweep ahead and clear the area for strangers, although they didn't expect foreign military reaction to their following the shuttle. The situation briefing had emphasized that diplomatic efforts were in progress to set up clearances to go wherever the shuttle did.

Susan began looking for Jorgensen's lights. And there they were, slightly left of the nose and high. High? The cloud cover must be lifting. She initiated a slight climb away from the water. There was never any good reason to stay at a lower altitude than called for by the situation, especially now.

The next few minutes were filled with radio chatter between Jorgensen and Hunter control. Susan realized there might have been lots of that before as they entered the CAP and ran the intercept, but she couldn't remember much more than what happened in her own cockpit. Now she heard it all.

They were in a tail chase, holding their distance back from the shuttle, and fuel states were fast becoming a factor. Hunter had more fighters on the way, but they were far behind and struggling to catch up. Although at higher altitude and able to fly faster on less fuel, they would be too late to take over from Hondo. The tanker was racing after them, so when Susan and Jorgensen broke off they would have less distance to fly for a drink, but it wasn't looking good.

The shuttle stayed low, but climbed to about 500 feet above the terrain as it made landfall. After crossing some low cliffs at the coast, the lights of a city flashed by underneath and the three aircraft were now over what appeared to be a flat plain. Susan figured it was mostly rural, because there were few lights to be seen, although the clouds had dissipated and there were stars overhead. This had turned into a night low level three-ship in-trail chase. Kind of pretty, actually.

Hunter had just mentioned the possibility of coordinating foreign landing clearance at a divert field when things suddenly changed.

"Hondo, Hunter, we've just picked up multiple targets approaching your position from the west. Contact is intermittent, appear to be at very low altitude, bearing two eight zero."

"Roger, Hunter."

Susan glanced at her fuel quantity to figure what her absolute minimum acceptable fuel state should be. Hunter and Jorgensen had discussed when to break it off based on the tanker's position, but you never left these decisions entirely in the hands of anyone but yourself. As pilot-in-command, it was ultimately Susan's responsibility, and running out of fuel was an unforgivable mistake. She'd be selling shoes at Foot Locker in a heartbeat.

The shuttle appeared to be descending, and Susan returned her full attention to flying. Jorgensen followed him down, and it would be much harder for her to maintain the tally and visual. She pushed over gently and kept the two aircraft just above the dim horizon. This was time to be very careful. A rock could appear suddenly between her and the other two aircraft. She glanced at the TFR to verify it was working and available to warn her. Then all hell broke loose.

"HONDO, POP-UP TARGETS YOUR LEFT TEN O'CLOCK TEN MILES CLOSING FAST!

~

BRETT SAW THE FAINT OUTLINE OF LANDFALL AHEAD IN THE darkness and climbed slightly. Without the benefit of preflight map study, he had no idea what the approaching terrain was like. At these speeds, death was only a split second away.

The climb would also reduce his ability to terrain-mask the shuttle. The RWR gear indicated two fighters in pursuit. The first one might have been able to close in range in spite of Brett's speed. *If this guy shoots, you better be ready, Larsen.* Then sudden audio made his heart jump.

Another RWR signal, twelve o'clock, holy shit! More fighters, but —*what's going on here?*

The RWR gear was really active now. Brett had to concentrate very hard to pull his attention away from the six o'clock signal and ignore that audio in favor of the new one.

Fighters, more than two, search mode, bearing from left eleven to right one o'clock. *Oh shit.*

These guys aren't friendly!

~

WHAT THE HELL IS THIS?

Susan glanced inside and her heart skipped a couple of beats as she saw what appeared to be four targets tracking down both sides of the scope on collision courses. Before she could react, the RWR gear audio sounded with that awful high-pitched tone indicating lock-on by short-range fighter radar. She hesitated, dividing her attention between the sudden threat and the two aircraft ahead, when the decision was made for her.

Audio, red launch light, brilliant white lights at her left eleven o'clock, and her own voice screaming over the radio, "HONDO BREAK LEFT MISSILES IN THE AIR OH JESUS!"

The last part wasn't standard, but neither was this. All thoughts of the shuttle, Jorgensen, and the mission vanished as Susan reacted to an immediate deadly threat.

With the dark night as a background, the missiles were easy to see as they leapt out to do their grisly work. The first two appeared to be on Jorgensen, so she ignored them. But the second set, spaced about two seconds apart, were definitely on her.

Susan instinctively rolled into a left bank and pulled hard into the missiles. Known as a "break" turn, this was the correct defensive move when fired upon at close range because it increased the closure rate between her fighter and the threat. Her objective was to rapidly close within minimum range of the missiles before they had a chance to arm and detonate. Eyes locked on to the twin deadly streaks of light, Susan suddenly realized this was the wrong thing to do.

At longer ranges and with time to arm, missile tracking circuits loved the increase in overtake generated by a break turn and were more accurate in front-quarter or head-on situations. These two missiles had plenty of range. Susan's next actions were reversions to training, pure and simple.

She rolled out of the left turn and banked right, but not so much to lose sight. Turning away from the missiles, she put them on the beam, snap rolled to wings level, and pushed hard on the stick to bunt the aircraft in a steep descent toward the ground.

Even with indications that the missiles were radar guided, you never really knew. The rule was to always assume you were being attacked by both radar and heat-seeking missiles. Susan popped chaff and flares simultaneously to break the enemy fighter's radar lock on and decoy the heat-seekers.

Both missiles were following her descent. Still accelerating in the boost phase, the bright exhaust plumes were easy to see, and she knew she was in real trouble. Now it was only timing, luck, and maybe some skill between her and death.

Susan's fighter was almost through the Mach, so energy wasn't a problem. But the ground certainly was, and timing the pull up. Too soon, and the missiles had enough range to correct. Too late, and she impacted the ground, or the missiles tore through the skin of the fighter and detonated. As fuel and hydraulic lines severed, the ship would explode in a ball of fire or rapidly become uncontrollable. With only a few seconds to go, the image of her own death became far too real, and she popped more chaff and flares out of desperation as much as anything else.

The first missile was pulling lots of lead, and appeared to be pointed well in front of her. Radar-guided missiles were designed to do this, especially on the beam where the angular rate of movement of the target in relation to the missile's flight path could result in a "square corner" during the terminal phase of flight. To avoid a miss as the warhead's destructive power passed to the rear of the target, radar missiles flew a lead-collision course almost from the moment of launch. Accurate ranging and proximity fusing worked together so that even without a direct hit, detonation of the warhead was timed to fill the sky with a cloud of deadly fragments and let the target fly through it.

Susan knew an object on a collision course with her fighter visually appeared to remain in the same position on the canopy, and one with lead moved forward at a rate based on the relative speeds and flight path geometry. The first missile was turning hard to get in front when it seemed to quit trying and began to drift aft. Susan almost laughed with joy as she saw it and heard the confirmation as the RWR audio quit abruptly.

The attacking fighter's radar had broken lock, probably to her chaff, and the missile lost guidance. Susan said a very short, silent prayer, and did one of the hardest things any fighter pilot can do. She ignored the first missile and concentrated on the second.

With the realization that it was still tracking, but in the absence of RWR audio, and holding a pursuit course rather than pulling lead, Susan knew it had to be a heat-seeker. Even in the midst of her fear, she felt a strange admiration for the fighter pilot who had done this to her. Surprise, low altitude intercept, two missiles a few seconds apart, one of each to complicate the problem of evading the threat. *What a guy. Or gal.*

Susan saw the ground just in time, a rushing darkness below her. Looking to her left to face the airborne threat, she saw the first missile pass above and behind, grunted hard in anticipation of the g-forces, pulled with all her strength, and yanked the throttle to idle.

The fighter responded like the thoroughbred she was, reversing the descent just prior to contact with a water-covered rice field, and passing close aboard to the right of a small hill rising sharply from the flat terrain.

Three factors in combination saved Susan's life. The missile was tracking her down and had to turn the corner to follow her back up. The beautiful, hot heat plume from her fighter's afterburner suddenly disappeared, and although there was still plenty of residual heat in the tailpipe to track, it went away suddenly as the hill came between the missile's seeker head and the source. Losing the target, the missile's flight control and detonation circuits did what they were designed to do.

The missile's canards went full deflection to pull lead on the last known target position and the warhead detonated. Most of the fragments struck the hill, smashing harmlessly against the dirt-covered rock, but a few passed over the top and struck the tail of Susan's fighter with a series of quick thunks in the airframe and the sound of tearing aluminum.

Holy Mother of God, I'm hit.

Warning lights in the cockpit. *Hydraulic pressure low, engine overheat, but she still responds. Watch out now, it isn't over yet.*

Susan climbed at a 60 degree angle, which on top of everything else was extremely disorienting. The horizon she had been using for reference was gone, with clouds or haze in the way, and the attitude indicator was showing mostly blue. Better than mostly black, but both require corrective action.

Susan gently pushed the fighter's nose down to what she thought would be close to level flight. Ignoring the warning lights for the moment because the fighter was still responding to control inputs, she tried to recover her situational awareness. Where was Jorgensen and was she still under attack?

The RWR gear was silent, no bright lights streaking her way, no sign of the fighters that had engaged her. Susan checked her heading, then rolled right to look below her in the direction she thought Jorgensen would be.

Nothing but blackness, then a bright flash that could only be a missile warhead detonation. The radio was strangely silent at a time when she would have expected it to be very busy.

"Hondo One, this is Two, say your position."

Silence, then, "Hondo Two, Hunter Control, do you read?"

"Roger that, Hunter, have you heard from One?"

"Negative, Hondo Two, not since he answered your break call."

"Be advised, Hunter, I just saw what I think was a missile detonation below me...uh...southwest of my position. I haven't seen—"

The sound interrupting Susan's transmission was one of the most dreaded in all of aviation. Personal Locator Beacons sent out a distress signal to assist rescue personnel in locating a downed aircrew member or a crash site. High-pitched, piercing, and aggravating as hell, the

PLB smothered Susan's transmission until she turned off guard channel.

"Hunter, do you read Hondo Two?"

"Roger, Hondo Two, do you have that PLB?"

"Affirmative, Hunter. Do you have a bearing?"

"It's southwest of your position. We will continue to monitor. What is your fuel state?"

A good question, but with a bad answer. "Bingo minus a thousand. And I'm hit, not sure how bad yet. The jet responds okay, but things don't look good."

"Hondo Two, recommend you steer zero five five and climb. We have a tanker on its way."

"Wilco, Hunter, but I want to take another look in the direction of that—"

Susan cut her transmission short when she saw it. Another explosion in the same general area, but much larger. Jet fuel burns with a characteristic yellow flame, and although she couldn't see the accompanying black smoke as confirmation, the flickering nature of the fire was unmistakable even at this distance.

"Uh, Hunter, Hondo Two here. I have a visual on a crash site. I'm going to go check it out."

"NEGATIVE, HONDO TWO, NEGATIVE! You don't have—"

The controller's transmission abruptly stopped, and Susan thought for a moment that her radio had quit. Then a different voice said, "Hondo Two, this is the senior director here. Listen carefully please. Your only chance to bring that ship back safely is to turn toward the tanker now. All indications are Hondo One took a hit and went down. We have other assets on the way to conduct the SAR. Do you copy?"

Susan couldn't answer, the suddenness of the events overwhelming her emotions. A few hours ago she had been sitting at a table with Jorgensen, talking about how they were going to come out here and find the shuttle. Different than the normal day-to-day mission, certainly, but who would have ever thought this?

"HONDO TWO! Do you read me, over?"

"Hondo Two copies. Say again the vector to the tanker."

"Heading zero six zero. Recommend climb to your max endurance altitude. The tanker will be in your twelve o'clock position for two hundred miles."

"Roger." There wasn't much else to say at this point. Susan selected guard channel to determine if the PLB was still there and it was.

She tried to picture Jorgensen hanging in his chute, or maybe he was on the ground by now, and said a silent prayer for his safety.

BRETT HAD BEEN IN COMBAT ENOUGH TO KNOW THAT NO MATTER how well you plan out what you want to happen, there are times when you have no idea what is going on with the big picture. And when that occurs, you end up reacting to a very small portion of the available information, instinctively doing what seems appropriate at the moment.

His situational awareness had been right in step with events as he planned and executed the head fake against the first fighter. And he was confident the second pilot, as good as he apparently was, would probably not be able to stay with him for long. The nagging question remained, however, as to what their mission was, and would they shoot?

With all his attention concentrated on flying the shuttle within 100 feet of the water, Brett had to analyze the RWR gear to answer that question by carefully following the principle of task prioritization. Audio was easy to assess, and he could do that almost without thinking about it. But before he diverted his attention from the flying, he had to determine if he had a few seconds to do that safely. His current altitude, attitude, approaching terrain, and trends all had to be considered and automatically coupled with his hands and feet.

But when the RWR audio changed so drastically, his attention had been immediately riveted to the scope. Bearings in front of him were out of synch with his current assessment of the situation. He was certain there were only two fighters in the vicinity and that both were behind him. The computer analysis had been like a spear in the heart as the RWR gear received the signal, compared it to known characteristics of all the world's weapons radar systems, and flashed the warning on the screen.

Brett's next reaction was probably more luck than anything else. He looked up to search for the threat without even considering whether he had a chance in hell of seeing anything, and just happened to notice a change in the horizon.

Solid black, just like it had been since they reached low altitude, but only to about half way up the windscreen. Now there was a jagged line, backlit by a dim glow, and it had almost taken him too long to recognize the danger.

The TFR warning was louder than RWR audio and sufficiently different to break through any mental fog. The voice screamed, "TER-RAIN! TERRAIN!" and Brett responded instantly.

He hauled back on the stick so hard and fast that he had no time to prepare, and he grayed out as the sudden onset of g-force pulled the blood from his brain. The shuttle responded well enough to miss the ridge line, and was still climbing when Brett regained sight.

With vision blurred and spots floating in front of his eyes, he pushed forward gently and lowered the nose to level flight. The RWR gear was silent, indicating the absence of immediate threats. As he rolled to look back to the east he realized why.

It was hazy, but he could make out the ground below him, a city just to the west of the ridge line creating the glow that helped save him. He saw two bright dots streaking through the blackness, and watched them in fascination as they detonated about a second apart.

Rolling in the other direction to look where the missiles had come from, Brett saw two or three other moving lights, larger than the first, but not as bright and definitely not as fast. They appeared to be swirling, and then he realized they were probably afterburner plumes. This was an air-to-air engagement, sure as the night was dark.

Positive confirmation came in the form of two more small bright lights, appearing near one of the afterburner plumes and accelerating into the inky blackness. Someone just launched missiles, and they both seemed to be tracking the same point.

And at least one hit the target. As the missiles detonated there was a third flash, which blossomed into a sustained fire, entered a spiral

path, and ended in a very large explosion. Brett had seen enough
airplanes hit the ground to know what it was, and he hoped the pilot
got out, a universal feeling within the fraternity that transcended any
friendly/enemy distinction.

This, however, was a friendly loss. The PLB blared over guard
channel, and Brett knew one of his own was in trouble. He considered
what he might do to help but the voice of the hijacker brought him
back to his own problem.

"What the hell happened?"

"We almost hit a ridge line."

"Where are the fighters?"

"Gone, from what I can tell. One of them may have been shot
down. Those other guys friends of yours?"

"Apparently so. But there may be more of everything still to come,
so let's get back down on the deck."

Brett was relieved at being able to return to basic piloting. This
whole thing was getting more and more bizarre. The sudden appearance of the other fighters was one more indication that the forces
behind this operation were indeed playing a strong hand.

Brett leveled the shuttle out at 500 feet AGL and coupled the
autopilot to the TFR. In the relative calm of the moment he concentrated on fuel calculations, using the distance-to-go and ground speed
on the GPS, crosschecking against time-to-go and current fuel burn.

The man busied himself with the duffle bag beside him, taking out
two more objects about the size of the GPS. Brett glanced over and
saw a portable radio and what appeared to be a second GPS navigation
computer. After a few minutes working with the radio, the man
removed his headset, put a small earpiece in his right ear, then replaced
his headset and lifted the radio to his mouth and made a call. As a
conversation took place, Brett's curiosity mounted by the second.

The hijacker reached out toward the center console and set the
second GPS beside the first. With two key strokes, he selected a direct
course to a navigation point and said, "Take us there."

~

As Susan turned toward the tanker, she had to force her brain to leave Jorgensen's fate behind and devote full attention to her own problems. The senior director was right. The search and rescue had been initiated, and she would be no more than a liability to that effort.

Carefully advancing power, Susan initiated a climb and divided her attention between the engine instruments, warning lights, and navigation computer. Selecting the economy mode on the UFC, the HUD went blank for a few seconds and then lit up with the climb and cruise display. Turbojet engines were most efficient at higher altitudes. The best profile was to climb at military power, the highest throttle setting without using afterburner, and then descend at idle to destination. Depending on the distance-to-go, that might include a period of cruise at an optimum altitude, but the tanker was headed in her direction. All she knew was that it had been 200 nm away a moment or so ago.

Susan selected a maximum endurance profile and entered 100 nm as distance to destination, figuring that the tanker would probably fly that distance in the time it took her to do the same. With the jet responding well enough to control inputs, her primary concern was to keep the engine running. The red overheat warning light was so bright that it blinded her every time she looked at it, so she decided to quit looking at it.

There were two separate engine temperature warning systems. The overheat light was the less serious of the two, indicating excessive temperature in the rear portion of the engine in the afterburner section. An engine fire light, however, was evidence of trouble in the primary combustion section, and Susan was concerned she might not be able to obtain full climb power and remain within the engine exhaust gas temperature limits.

The EGT gauge showed just below red line as the throttle reached the military stop, and Susan breathed a sigh of relief. Maybe it would hold together long enough to get her out of this. As the airspeed approached best climb speed, she adjusted pitch to maintain it and glanced at her fuel.

Whoa! She didn't want to look at that either. Susan had never seen the gauge read that low, and seriously began to doubt whether she could make it.

"Hunter, Hondo Two here, I'll need a tanker turn, and from the look of things I'll get only one shot at it."

"Roger that, Hondo, do you want to call it?"

"Yeah, but let me know if you see something you don't like."

"Roger. Come left five degrees. The tanker will be twelve o'clock for one-hundred-fifty miles."

"Hondo two copies."

Usually a tanker rendezvous was set up with a head-on situation because it was the fastest way to close distance between the fighter and the tanker. Once the fighter had the tanker in radar contact, control of the intercept was passed to the fighter, which continued on a straight course while the tanker turned in front. The geometry was designed for a tanker roll out ahead of the fighter at a mile or slightly less with controllable overtake.

Successful intercept geometry depended upon many things, not the least of which was mutual agreement among the players as to airspeeds to be flown, procedures to ensure altitude separation, and who was in control. Under normal circumstances Susan wanted the tanker to be offset about 26 degrees to one side or the other of the nose at about 21 nm and with 2000 feet of altitude separation, at which time she would call the turn.

Entering the clouds again as she climbed, Susan asked whether the tanker was in the clear. When told it was, she instructed Hunter to have the tanker descend no lower than a thousand feet or so above the tops. No need to make this thing any more difficult than it already was. Just as she was about to ask for a frequency change, Hunter called.

"Hondo Two, push button one seven."

"Hondo." Susan selected the channel and waited.

"Hondo Two, Hunter Control here, Exxon's up this freq and twelve o'clock for one twenty-seven."

"Hondo copies." Susan didn't bother to search for the tanker yet at this range, but wanted to clarify her plan. "Exxon, Hondo Two, how do you read?"

"Five by, Hondo, how me?"

"Five square also. I'm going to be sucking fumes by the time we get together. The best plan is for you to start the turn in closer than normal, and I'll need a harder turn." If she rolled out closer than desired, it would take less fuel for Susan to drop back than to chase the tanker down.

"Sounds good, Hondo, we'll turn on your command."

"Roger that. And I'm going to keep climbing rather than level off below your altitude. You'll be easier to see looking down, and it'll take less fuel for me to drop down to your altitude."

"Exxon copies."

Susan broke out of the clouds at 24,000 feet and kept climbing. "Hunter, Hondo Two, bogey dope."

"Tanker is slightly left, ninety-five miles, level."

Susan adjusted her scope and caught a very faint hit there, and with an IFF interrogation confirmed it was friendly. "Hondo Two contact. Any other friendlies in that location?"

"Negative." That meant the other fighters must be either on their way back to base or past her toward Jorgensen's last known position.

"Exxon, Hondo Two, what's your altitude?"

"Exxon's at angels two eight."

"Roger. Descend to angels two six. That should put the tops about two thousand feet below you. Let me know if they look higher in your area."

"Exxon copies."

Susan leveled off at 30,000 feet. Adjusting the tilt of her radar slightly low, she tuned the scope and got a slightly better contact on the tanker at 5 degrees left for about 85 nm. Tankers were big targets, and soon she would be able to lock him up. Normally she would run the intercept no lock on, because it was good practice for combat when there were plenty of good reasons not to lock on, but here she needed all the help she could get.

The master caution illuminated suddenly and drew Susan's eyes to the tele-light panel. There were many other amber caution lights lit up and she had a hard time determining what the new one was. Then she saw it, backup hydraulic system pressure low. She still had the primary and the utility, at least for now.

Returning her attention to the scope, Susan tuned the display for a better contact and interrogated again just to make sure. The tanker was drifting slowly to the left, and it looked like she might not have to do much else to set things up. She wanted the tanker about 10 degrees left at 40 nm, which would be correct if their headings were close to reciprocal.

"Hunter, Hondo Two, how's it look to you?"

"Good, Hondo, maybe just a little too much offset for this range."

"Concur. Break. Exxon, come five left please."

"Exxon, five left, roger."

That should reduce the drift, keep him closer to the nose. Susan watched the target close inside 40 nm, switched scopes and locked him up. Now the tracking circuits kept the antenna pointed directly at the tanker, and the HUD provided a continuous readout of critical information. The TD box appeared just to the left, kind of wobbly at this range, but if all went well she could use it to get an early visual and complete the intercept with the old eyeball.

With the instrument panel darkened to maximize outside visibility, the flickering master warning light got Susan's immediate attention. Looking down, she saw a faint glow in the engine fire light. When she glanced at the EGT gauge, she knew why.

It was pegged off the scale at the top. Susan retarded the throttle and managed to get the EGT below redline with the engine at about eighty percent RPM. Not enough to maintain altitude, but it was about time to descend anyway.

Tanker 12 left, 35 nm, slightly low, but not descending. He must be at 26,000 feet. Susan eased back on the stick to slow her rate of descent and her airspeed. With the reduced power setting and a sick engine, she wanted to avoid being too low. With any number of ways to increase her rate of descent, it would be easy to correct for being too high.

Tanker holding 12 left, 30 nm, Susan passing 28,000 feet, which meant his heading must be slightly to the left of reciprocal if the offset stayed the same for the last 5 nm. "Hunter, Hondo, I'm shooting for something closer and tighter than the standard 26 left at 21 miles, but the tanker's heading looks a little too tight. Do you concur?"

"Affirmative, Hondo. Suggest two degrees right for Exxon."

"Exxon, roger, two right."

Okay. Looking good, tanker tracking slightly left, 15 degrees left now at 25 miles. I'm passing 27,500, tanker is 1500 feet low, ease back a little, slow this rate of descent.

Tanker 20 left, 20 nm. TD box empty. Why the hell can't I see him? "Exxon, you got your lights on?" Long pause. Then a bright red rotating beacon, strobes, and a mass of exterior lights that looked like downtown Cincinnati.

"Sorry about that, Hondo, we went into a self-protective mode when we heard about the shooting. You got us now?"

Tanker 25 left, 15 nm, 1000 feet low. "I have the visual. Start your turn, and haul it around." The tanker was at Susan's left 11 o'clock position, slightly low, rolling into the turn, and she instinctively pulled off some power because it looked so much closer than usual. Which, of course, it was, but as the tanker began to drift toward the nose, Susan could tell it was going to work out pretty well after all. She couldn't see the change in aspect except by the lights, but it was no problem knowing when the tanker's nose passed through her position. All the landing lights damn near blinded her.

"Hondo Two, Exxon boom here, radio check."

Susan recognized the voice as the same boom operator from earlier this evening. "Hondo Two has you loud and clear, boomer, how me?"

"You're beautiful, Hondo, come and get it."

Which was exactly what she intended to do. This was one of those times when formalities of radio procedure took a back seat to an understanding between professionals. The boom operator had seen Susan's work on the boom just a few hours ago, and undoubtedly knew she wouldn't suddenly run into him because of abbreviated, non-standard terminology.

It looked like she still might be hotter than desired on the roll out. Susan turned right slightly and pulled the power off a little, easing the stick over to descend to the tanker's altitude. Glancing inside at her fuel, she felt her heart jump when she saw less than five hundred pounds indicated on the gauge.

Don't look at the fuel now. It is what it is, and it'll be less in a hurry if you don't get hooked up right away.

Eyes back on the tanker looming below her, Susan popped a little speed brake to slow her overtake and toggled open the air refueling door. When her closure rate slowed to what she wanted, she retracted the brake and added power.

Talk about sudden bright lights. Amber master caution and red master warning lights seemed to fill the cockpit with an eerie glow and Susan knew she was in trouble.

Utility hydraulic pressure low, engine overheat. *Goddammit to hell.*

"Uh, Hondo, boomer here, your door isn't open."

"Exxon, Hondo, I may need a toboggan."

"Toboggan" referred to a maneuver in which the tanker pulled off power and began a descent so that the receiver could maintain airspeed by trading away altitude. In this situation, if she could just get some fuel she might be able to nurse the engine back to safety.

The tanker pilot must have heard only the word "toboggan," because he responded by reducing power and starting down. The move caught Susan off guard. As the tanker began to accelerate away she frantically tried to stop him.

"HOLD ON, EXXON! I have some power, I just need you to start a slow descent so I can keep it back."

"Exxon, roger, what rate of descent do you need?"

"Try five hundred feet per minute."

"Roger."

Susan maneuvered to make up the distance she had lost and tried to concentrate on the door problem. The door was electrically controlled and hydraulically actuated by the utility hydraulic system. She realized she should have tried to open the door sooner. Maybe there had been a slow leak.

Or maybe the system was holding pressure only until a system demand was made. Or it might be the simultaneous use of the speed brakes and the door was too much for a damaged line. *The speed brakes are off the utility, aren't they? Considered as a secondary flight control?*

Susan was closing in on the boom, trying to answer her question, when she realized that it didn't matter. There was no alternate way to get the door open. It either did, or it didn't. Holding her breath, Susan recycled the air-refueling switch to the open position. Almost afraid to look at the warning lights, she adjusted power and slid forward into the contact position. Concentrating on her references, she was vaguely aware of the boom sliding out to the side like it always did, and then moving back to the centerline and extending behind her head.

The clunk was solid, satisfying, and almost sexual in the pure pleasure of it. Susan felt a tremendous relief and then remembered to breathe. With a quick movement, she took her left hand off throttle and gave a thumbs up to the face of the boom operator in the window as he grinned at her from behind his headset microphone.

Susan had heard quiet before, like in the mountains, but nothing like this. When the engine quit it was as if all sound in the universe just stopped. The sudden loss of thrust resulted in a rapid descent back and down, and although she instinctively shoved the throttle up it didn't help a bit.

"EXXON, TOBOGGAN! THIS IS FOR REAL, I NEED A TOBOGGAN!"

"—push it up you're at the outer limit!"

Susan never had time to repeat her transmission, which had been covered up by the boomer's call. He should have been disconnecting rather than talking, but it was too late now. The boom was yanked out of the receptacle with a wrenching sound of tearing metal, and the master caution light illuminated for lots of reasons. Susan still had flight controls, the wind-milling engine would give her that as long as she had primary hydraulics and maintained sufficient glide speed, but as for powered flight it was all over.

"Hunter, this is Hondo Two. Mayday, mayday, mayday. I've flamed out, going down, squawking emergency."

"Hondo Two, Exxon pilot, we're in a toboggan, can you make it to us for another hook up?"

"Negative, Exxon. My receptacle's damaged, and I'll be in the clouds shortly. Can you follow me down, try to pinpoint my position for the SAR?"

"Affirmative, Hondo Two. Break. Hunter, Exxon here, if you can keep us close to Hondo we'll try to pick her up visually below the clouds."

"Exxon, Hunter Control, steer zero niner zero and level angels two five. I want altitude separation before we turn you back."

"Exxon copies."

Susan was calmer than she had ever been in an airplane. With the inevitable staring her in the face, she carefully went through a mental checklist for the ejection, trying to remember all the things the technicians had told her about the proper position, the ejection sequence, actions to perform once hanging in the chute, her survival equipment, and water landings.

Exxon and Hunter were busy coordinating, and although she wasn't paying much attention to them, she knew that Hunter would also be on other frequencies setting up the search and rescue. If she did her part right, there was no reason she couldn't survive this.

Passing 10,000 feet, Susan keyed the microphone and said, "See you guys, soon I hope. Hondo Two's out of here."

Feet out against the rudder pedals, butt pushed back in the seat, elbows in, chin tucked in, Susan reached between her legs, gripped the ejection ring, and pulled up sharply.

What a ride. Canopy thrusters fire, the clear dome over her head disappears, sudden cold and wind like nothing she had ever felt, then the seat accelerating up the rails and a feeling of being compressed from the head down and arcing over on her back. A series of sounds, stuff happening behind her head, and the seat just starting to tumble when the stabilizer chute popped and settled everything down.

The seat reached the top of its trajectory and was just starting to descend when Susan heard a pop behind her head and felt the smooth sound of nylon sliding, a kind of swishing, then a whump as the drogue chute opened and began to pull the main chute out of the bag, accompanied by a feeling that something had pushed her in the back and butt.

Oh, shit! The seat's gone. Then, *Of course it is, dummy.*

Now a big swishing and a real solid whump as the main chute

opened and Susan felt her harness dig into her crotch and inside of her legs, jerking her almost to a stop.

Thank you, Lord.

Talk about quiet. Faint sound of what might be a jet. Exxon? Then a splash. Heard it all the way up here. Susan looked down to see if she could see the fireball, then realized there wouldn't be one. No fuel.

Goodbye, lovely steed. Rest in peace. Sorry it will be so cold and dark.

Procedures. Check the canopy. Looking over her head, Susan could just make out the mushroom cap shape of the parachute and see that it was fully open. *That's reassuring, to say the least. Wonder who packed it?*

Release the mask. Susan disconnected the bayonet fitting on the right side of her oxygen mask and let it hang from the left side, then remembered the suggestion to get rid of it. She released the left side bayonet and the communications cord, then pulled the hose free of the attachment point on her harness and dropped the mask toward the dark water below.

Flotation device. Susan had to fumble for a minute to find them, but when she pulled the cords to the "horse collar," the CO_2 canisters popped and filled the two bladders with a satisfying hiss. The thing was designed to keep her head upright in the water even if she lost consciousness, and was automatically activated by contact with salt water. She couldn't imagine waiting until then to find out if it was going to work.

Survival kit. Hoping it was where it should be, Susan reached down by her left hip and confirmed that the attachment fitting was intact. The kit contents were contained in a hard shell with a cushion on top that served as the pilot's seat. With few exceptions, procedures called for the kit to be in an automatic mode, so that it would deploy as the seat separated from the pilot during the post ejection sequence. Leaning to her left, Susan looked down and was relieved to see the kit hanging just below, and beneath that the reassuring sight of the life raft, self-inflated and suspended from a line.

How about that? It all worked as advertised, and now all she had to do was survive the possibility of drowning, dying of exposure, or being attacked by "Jaws."

Susan pondered for a moment whether there were sharks out

here, and then remembered a nature special that said sharks were known to inhabit every ocean in the world. *Time to think of something else.*

Ah yes. Parachute landing fall. Her training had included practicing PLF's on land and water. Pilots were not required to take actual jump training, which was fine with her. Most pilots were inherently opposed to jumping out of perfectly good airplanes.

And although water wasn't as hard as land, the potential for trouble was every bit as serious. Susan's next task was to determine wind direction. The worst condition was with the wind at her back, because it resulted in the maximum velocity relative to the landing surface, pitched her over on her face as she hit, and increased the risk of injury. For a water landing, it also created one of the most dangerous situations, of being dragged through the water face down if she didn't get the chute collapsed. Susan had been taught techniques to handle this situation, but it was best to avoid it altogether.

Having the wind in your face was better because it actually resulted in the slowest lateral velocity at impact, but compromised the PLF by pitching you onto your back. The recommended technique was to turn in the chute by pulling down on the risers until the wind was off your right or left side at a 30- to 45-degree angle.

All of this depended on determining wind direction, and the life-support instructors had covered a number of different ways to do that. But she had to see the surface, which proved to be impossible from her present height. She couldn't tell how high she was, and had no clue as to the sea state awaiting her. In these conditions, the best tactic was to be prepared for landing at any time, and look level. Looking down was the wrong thing to do, and at the same time almost impossible to resist.

Susan had heard a pilot say his plan was to watch the raft. It was suspended about 30 feet below her, and she decided to try that. If she saw the surface in time to determine her drift, she might have time to adjust for the wind. If not, she would at least have a warning just prior to landing in the water as the raft touched down.

Water landings were especially dangerous. With her flotation device inflated she couldn't sink, and with the raft attached to her she'd be able to get out of the water quickly, but the period just after touchdown would be the most critical.

In calm winds, the canopy would most likely land on top of her. Talk about panic. Her training had included this scenario, and it had taken a strong will to remain calm, remember there was plenty of air under there to breathe, and practice the procedures. Roll over on your back, find a seam in the nylon, reach behind your head and pull yourself along hand over hand until you come to the edge of the canopy.

With strong winds, the danger of drowning was especially high. The canopy would likely remain full of air even after touchdown, and the procedure was to prepare for collapsing the chute immediately. The canopy risers were attached to Susan's personal harness at two points, one above each shoulder. The fittings were designed for easy release, but required two actions as a precaution against accidental activation. Susan had been taught to follow the harness from her shoulders up to the fittings with her hands, place her fingers just below the safety covers, and push up to expose the release mechanisms. Then with fingers resting there, look level and wait.

Susan decided it was time to do that, and with no small amount of concern pushed up on the safety covers. And although Susan's harness had a strap above her head connecting the two shoulder straps, and she knew that release of one side would not collapse the chute, it was still a gut check. Just the thought of falling suddenly was enough to cause her bowels to flutter.

But she did it, and leaned sideways to watch the raft. It was plenty dark, but the raft was a bright international orange and it seemed to gather what little illumination there was.

Okay, now, if I can see the surface soon enough I'll try to determine my drift. If the sea has any swell, or whitecaps, I can watch my feet or the raft in relation to that and then let these covers back down and pull down on the shoulder strap in the direction I want to turn my body. Need to be careful, though. I don't want to try any turns below a thousand feet, and if I misjudge it and don't have my hands on the release fittings I could hit before I'm ready.

Looking at the raft, Susan tried to remember if she had ever been told any guidelines about how to judge height above the water. She knew depth perception over smooth water was inaccurate at best. She thought there was a guideline that if you can see individual whitecaps or swells you are below a certain altitude, but she wasn't sure. Then she saw something.

It looked like white ripples. Without hesitation Susan released the fittings and reached as high up on the shoulder straps as she could. Looking at the surface between her boots, she tried to assess her drift direction and rate.

How long am I going to wait? This is the worst way to touchdown, and leads to misjudging altitude and being surprised when you hit. I better just forget it and go back to plan B.

Susan leaned her head back and looked at the shoulder harness fittings. She was thankful for the training she had received, especially for the small things that could become important.

Sitting in the airplane, the parachute fittings were draped over each shoulder and connected to her personal harness. On a day-to-day basis she would connect and disconnect them by reaching just forward of the top of her shoulders. But the life support technicians always pointed out during refresher training each year that when you are actually hanging below the parachute, these fittings are much higher than that. Easy to reach, but not in the same place. Following an ejection when your heart is pounding and you're in shock, a small thing like that can create hesitation, confusion, and lead to big trouble.

Susan felt better looking at the fittings as she reached over her head, and carefully slid her gloved fingers under the right side safety cover and gently pushed up. She repeated the process on the left side, and looked down to her left to find the raft.

Stunned for a second or two, Susan wondered if the raft had come loose. It wasn't where she expected it, and during this period of doubt events accelerated out of control. She realized too late that she was within seconds of landing in a trough, and the swells must be at least 10 feet or more.

With the wind at her back, the raft was trailing behind her and out of sight as it touched the water. When her boots hit the surface, Susan was so surprised that she failed to release the fittings. The chute, still filled with 30 knots of wind, pulled her face first into a rising swell and buried her beneath the cold, salty sea.

Susan's hands were ripped off the fittings as she was dragged up the slope of the swell, and in a split second she knew if she didn't do this right it was all over. She arched her back, trying to get a breath of air, and found out immediately why this was not the way to do it. She was being pulled through the water so fast that her head was almost completely submerged. With mounting pain in her lungs and her mouth filled with water, the panic almost took over.

Reach over your head as far as you can and grab the shoulder straps. Leading with your shoulders and arms, push with one side and pull with the other to rotate your body so that you are lying on your back. Then bend forward at the waist like a sit up. This will create a bow wave around your back, neck, and head and leave a pocket of clear air in front of your face. You can get all the air you need in this position.

Susan fought down the fear and with all her strength forced her hands up against the rushing water and found the straps. Straining hard, she managed to rotate about half way when she seemed to leave the water and become airborne. Gasping for breath, she opened her eyes just in time to see the backside of the swell as the wind-filled chute pulled her momentarily clear of the crest and slammed her face first into the next massive trough.

Eyes stinging, flooded with the cold salt water, Susan got mad. Bellowing like a weight lifter going for a personal best, she repeated the maneuver and made it over on her back. Needing air badly, wanting to take a huge breath, she bent forward at the waist and felt the water begin to pile up against the back of her head and neck.

Her first breath was mostly water. *Where's the goddamn air they talked about?*

Susan summoned the last of her strength and bent her chest forward toward her knees and held it there.

Immediately she became aware that her head was almost clear. Her next breath was mostly air, a truly glorious feeling, filling her lungs and renewing her with the will to survive.

Holding the position and breathing in big gulps of cold air, Susan reached up on the straps with both hands until she found the release fittings. With the memory of many practice sessions during water survival training, she pushed up and under followed by in and down.

Two sharp tugs spaced a split second apart signaled the release of the chute as it was pulled away by the wind. Susan settled into the sea, supported by the horse collar. Bobbing like a cork in the stormy ocean, her emotions took over and she began to cry.

But not for long. Susan knew she was going into shock, and she had never been as thirsty in her life as at this moment. She was also shivering, and the next few minutes would be critical for her survival.

Reaching into the sea at her left hip, Susan found the survival kit floating beside her, and attached to it the line leading to the raft. Hand over hand, she pulled the raft to her and let the training take over.

Turn the raft upright if need be. Don't worry if it appears swamped, it will float even when full of water. Find the small end of the raft and with the handles on the side, position it in front of you. Pulling toward you and down, slide your body up and over the small end of the raft as far as you can. Let go of the first two handles and reach up for the handles at the large end of the raft, pulling your body the remaining way into the raft so that you are face down.

Now roll to your right until on your back. That will put the survival kit either in your lap or off to your left side. If you roll in the other direction the kit will impede the movement and you may be tempted to release it. Do not release the survival kit from your harness until it is positively secured to the raft.

Susan sat up in the raft, which was half filled with water. Her next priority was to protect herself from the elements. The cold water had already lowered her body temperature to a dangerous level, and hypothermia would kill her very quickly without preventative action. She heard a jet overhead, and wanted to hear a friendly voice in the worst way, but knew they could pinpoint her position without her contacting them immediately. The PLB in her survival kit had been activated during the ejection sequence and would send out a continuous emergency signal until she turned it off.

Working quickly, Susan removed her helmet. Using it as a bailing bucket, she furiously tackled the task of getting the water out of the raft. It helped warm her up, but she also found that looking down as the raft pitched and rolled in the swells was doing no good for her stomach.

She decided to put out the sea anchor, designed to stabilize the raft. After trying unsuccessfully to remember the instructions, she elected to let out enough line so that the anchor was in a trough when the raft was at a crest. Typical fighter-pilot solution, shoot from the hip, also known as the "John Wayne" approach. But it seemed like the thing to do, and did reduce the raft's reaction to the swell.

Susan put up the storm cover, which was a tent built into the raft to protect her against the wind, rain, and sea spray. Once she had it all zipped up, her body heat helped create a reasonably warm environment. It also brought back the nausea. Using her flashlight for illumination, Susan quickly opened the survival kit and found the seasickness pills, washing them down with a full can of water. She needed to inventory the kit, but that could wait.

The radio in the kit was secured to one half of the hard shell. Susan released the clips and turned off the PLB, selecting the voice function.

"Mayday, mayday, mayday, this is Hondo Two on guard. Over."

"Hondo Two, this is Exxon, what is your status? Over."

What a wonderful sound. "Good to hear you Exxon, thanks for staying around. I'm in the raft, no injuries, should be fine for a while. Any word from Hondo One?"

"Uh, negative, Hondo Two, nothing as yet. Be advised we have launched the SAR effort and will stay on station as long as we can. There are several merchant vessels in the area responding, and may be able to get to you before the choppers do. How copy?"

"That's a roger, Exxon, Hondo copies. It's a rough sea out here. Depending on how far out they are, I would think they'll want to wait for daylight anyway."

"No problem with that, the nearest vessel estimates your position mid-morning. How many radios do you have?"

"Two, with spare batteries for each."

"Roger that. Recommend you shut them down for now. We can vector the ships in close enough with hourly updates. How about we come up every hour on the hour? We'll get a voice check, then have you transmit the PLB for ten minutes, then come back on voice. That work for you?"

Susan considered getting some sleep, then realized she might not be able to relax enough to do that for a month or two. "Yeah, that's fine. Anything else?"

"Nothing, except we're all cheering for you up here."

Susan was in no mood for cheering at the moment, but the thought was nice. "Thanks. Talk to you on the hour. Hondo Two out."

"Exxon out."

Susan turned off the radio and decided to inventory the survival kit. The raft was still doing a fair amount of pitching and rolling, but the pills seemed to have done the trick for now and she was suddenly very hungry. Tearing the wrapper off an energy bar, she bit into it with less than her usual manners and tried to remember the last time she had eaten.

Ah. Back at the mess hall, with Jorgensen. Sitting across from him, eating bacon and eggs, briefings out of the way, getting ready to launch out on a real adventure. The memory of it didn't sit well, and Susan almost lost the first half of the energy bar.

What a bucket of shit. Sent to find a shuttle, end up with two fighters down, one pilot missing, one on an unscheduled cruise. So many questions.

Was this my fault? What if I had run the intercept better, not fallen for the head fake? It would have been me out there in front. Who the hell were those fighters and what does all this mean?

Susan was wrong about the sleep. Or at least her body thought so, and whether it was a matter of relaxation or fatigue, she drifted off, head slumped on her chest, mouth open, snoring.

17

DAYS NINE THRU SIXTEEN

Toby woke up slowly, not at all like his usual up-and-at-them start to the day. Maybe it was because he had no idea what time of day it was, or he was so tired when he went to sleep, or because he was weighted down by something.

That must be it. The feeling was so unfamiliar. It was like wearing a second skin. Then he remembered Brett's comment about gravity. There's no getting away from it, even for a second.

You can say that again. He felt like it was just too much trouble to move. Good excuse to stay right where he was, and a good time to take stock of the situation.

Toby wanted to be excited about being on Earth, but found it impossible. The circumstances were nothing like he had envisioned. It was almost as if the long-awaited anticipation had been taken from him by his own actions, and going "home" for the first time hadn't actually happened and would never come again.

What had he seen so far? The journey to Earth seemed like a nightmare, and he had no idea what went on toward the end of the flight, with all that activity and being jerked around in the middle of a pitch-black nothingness. The landing was spectacular, and he had a thousand questions for Brett about what happened.

And then when he was taken off the shuttle, excitement building in anticipation of what it was going to be like, the man brought out the blindfolds. The only way Toby was able to control his panic was to concentrate on the fact that Brett was just in front of him, and he managed to activate his space search and follow his friend without mishap.

And when he got to the room and the blindfold was removed, it was just a room. It didn't look anything like his room on the station, except that it had four walls. So far his introduction to Earth had been a real disappointment.

But he liked the food. The man returned after a short delay with a tray full of stuff. Some of it looked like what his mom made, but the flavors were very different. Toby ate so much he thought he was going to be sick. The only thing that saved him was falling asleep. He didn't even remember getting into bed.

And he wouldn't have gotten out of bed now if he didn't have to pee. Toby decided to get it over with. As he pulled back the covers and got up, the thought occurred to him that if he ever had to do anything quickly in this full gravity he'd be in real trouble. It was like trying to move through molasses.

Walking into the small bathroom, Toby thought that at least one thing was the same as on the station. This floor was just as cold, and he longed for his warm, fuzzy slippers. Standing there at the toilet, toes curled under to reduce the contact between the bottom of his feet and the frigid floor, Toby looked down as he began to pee and was horrified to see the stream drop much faster than on the station and completely miss the bowl.

Cutting off the process in mid-stream, he found himself in a predicament. Holding it back was particularly hard now, and there was no way to step forward without stepping in his mess.

And then he remembered something and had to stifle a chuckle. It wouldn't do to laugh right at the moment, but he couldn't get the picture out of his mind. It was a sign on the wall of the bathroom in Brett's fighter squadron, just above the urinals.

NOTICE

PILOTS WITH LOW MANIFOLD PRESSURE,
SHORT PITOT TUBES, OR POOR EYESIGHT
ARE REQUESTED TO TAXI IN CLOSE.
THE NEXT PILOT MIGHT NOT BE FLOAT RATED.

IT WAS ALMOST TOO MUCH, BUT TOBY HELD IT IN AS HE FOUND some towels. After wiping the floor he finished the business at hand. Here on Earth he would have to remember to step closer to the urinal. It wouldn't do to have anyone question his manifold pressure or pitot tube length, whatever they were.

Returning to the larger room, Toby noticed a bundle on a small table beside the door and opened it to find some clothes. They smelled good, appeared to be freshly laundered, and he decided to clean up. There was a small shower, some soap, and a towel. He stepped under the hot water, and sighed in ecstasy as the steamy liquid seemed to wash away his immediate concerns. This really felt good.

The clothes were okay, too. They fit as well as anything he had brought with him. He bundled up the dirty clothes and wondered if he could get them cleaned. The only change of clothing he brought was in the bag strapped to Snooper's back, and who knew what had happened to them? Lost and gone forever, probably, along with his faithful companion and the shotgun.

Wish I had that gun now. I'd surprise the heck out of whoever came in that door the next time and make him take me to Brett. Then we'd get out of here and I'd be able to see what Earth really looks like.

Combing his hair, Toby heard the door to the outer room open and turned to see an arm reach in and put a tray of food down on the small table. He smelled some more good stuff, and hungrily sat down on the bed with the tray in his lap.

Toby was just finishing when he heard the door open again. Looking up, he saw the man in black walk in and close the door behind him. He was still masked, but after seeing him that way for so long it looked normal.

It was no less frightening, however. Toby crawled up on the bed. The man stood in the center of the room for a moment, then went over to a small desk, pulled out a chair, and sat down. He leaned, back, crossed his arms, and stared at Toby, eyes giving away nothing. Toby was getting nervous, wondering what was going on, when the man spoke.

"I trust the food and accommodations have been adequate?"

Toby didn't know what to do. Brett had said to steer clear of people, and to speak only if spoken to. The man was speaking to him. Maybe a nod will suffice. So he nodded, meeting the man's stare, determined not to look away.

"Good. I see you found the clothes. Are those your dirty ones over there?"

Another nod.

"I'll see to it they're laundered and get them back to you. Did you bring any other personal belongings with you?"

Toby almost nodded before he caught himself. It wouldn't do to tell him about the backpack. *May I have my shotgun, please?*

"I . . . uh . . . don't have anything else. Left it all on the station."

"All right. The toilet articles in the bathroom are for you. I'll get you some extra clothes." The man pointed to the tray on the bed beside Toby. "Had enough to eat?"

"Yes, sir."

The man motioned for Toby to hand him the tray, which he took and replaced on the table. "You and I have some negative history built up. It occurred to me last night maybe we should try to clear the air a bit."

Toby was unsure how to respond. He never expected to sit down for a friendly chat with the man, and wasn't particularly interested in doing so now. He remained silent.

"Well, Toby, that's your name, isn't it?"

Toby nodded.

"I don't expect you to understand all of what I'm going to say, but it's important to talk about a few things. You don't appear eager to say much, and that's okay, but I hope you'll listen and answer a few simple questions. Fair enough?"

Toby nodded, just wanting to get through this as quickly as possible.

"When did you arrive on the station?"

"I was born there."

"Really. I had always thought they didn't allow births on Oasis, population control and all that. You might be the first, huh?"

"Yes, sir."

"Do you have any family on Earth?"

Should I be talking about that with this man?

"No."

"Okay, well, you live with your mom and dad on Oasis, I guess. Do they ever talk about living on Earth, what it was like? You know, family stories, when they were kids?"

"Uh . . . sure . . . I guess so."

"Ever hear your parents say it used to be better? Comments about things getting worse for raising kids, no discipline, crime out of control, stuff like that?"

"Sometimes. My Dad talks about my grandfather, what he used to say about it. He was killed during a robbery."

The man looked saddened by that "I'm sorry about your grandfather. Mine had a great influence on my life, taught me a lot. And I can remember hearing him talk about how things had changed from the time he was growing up and when he raised my father."

Toby found himself becoming interested in the conversation. This stuff couldn't hurt anything. "My dad says one of the reasons he and Mom volunteered for Oasis was to leave all that behind. He called it a fresh start."

The man grinned and laughed softly. "I understand that. Well, let me share something with you. I'm on a mission with the objective of reversing the trend your dad talked about. I can't go into the details, but the shuttle will play a big role in our plans, and we need it to succeed. I'm sorry about the trouble this has caused for the station, and the tragic loss of life, but we never intended to hurt anyone.

"And I'll bet if you were in my position, and were a dad with a family to protect, you'd want to do the same thing. You might not pick the same means, but the time has passed for gentle measures. Action is required, and now."

Toby wasn't sure what action the man meant, but he had heard his father talk about how bad it was getting on Earth and knew his parents had run away from it. Was this man telling the truth? And could he do anything to make it better?

The man broke the silence by asking, "I assume this is your first trip to Earth. Have you wanted to see what it was like?"

"Oh, yeah, all the time. Ever since I can remember."

"What do you want to see the most?"

"I can't pick any one thing. I've heard so much about it, seen pictures, it all seems so strange. But the real reason is that I want to be a pilot."

The man smiled broadly at this. "A pilot? Really? I suppose lots of kids do at one time or another. I—"

"No," interrupted Toby, "it's not like that with me. I'm going to be one."

The man stared at Toby with a questioning look, then seemed to accept it just to get on to something else.

Toby hated it when adults didn't take him seriously, and most especially about being a pilot. "I can't train to be a pilot up on the station. The only way to do that is on Earth, and I'm going to live here so I can start my training early and get my student certificate on my sixteenth birthday and my license on my seventeenth."

The man nodded. "Well, now, I just believe you might. You seem determined enough. You friends with the pilot?"

"Oh yeah, Brett and—"

Stop this! What are you doing talking with this man about Brett?

"Hey, hold on a minute. I can see you still don't trust me. But let me share something with you. That pilot was ready and willing to do something really stupid to stop me. If I hadn't gotten tough with him, convinced him to do what I told him, he might have been real trouble. I've got nothing against him personally. If he does his job, that's all I care about."

"But he has. He flew you down to Earth. You have the shuttle and you can let him go now."

The man shook his head. "It might seem that way, but as I said before, I can't go into all the details right now. I still need him, and maybe even you."

Me? What does that mean?

"Why are you looking at me like that? You should be eager to help. You just said you wanted to live on Earth, but you seem to forget your mom and dad left because it was getting so bad. Helping would be an investment in your own future. You could have a hand in it."

"There isn't anything I could do."

"I'm not so sure about that. Let me ask you a question, Toby. You don't have to answer if you don't want to, but I'm really curious. How did you get away from me in the chutes?"

Be careful here. What's this all about? "I know my way around. I just ran away."

The man scoffed. "I agree, but there's more to it. You didn't *just* escape. You stayed around, then escaped, with more than a little luck at the last second. There were a number of times you could have taken off, but you didn't. You seemed to be playing with me, and you pulled it off. How did you do that?"

This was definitely getting out of hand. Toby had allowed the man to maneuver the conversation around to a subject he had no intention of discussing. "I didn't do anything special. It's just that you made me mad."

"Why?"

"Because you were in my space, and I wanted to pay you back. Up there on Oasis it's hard to be alone. Everything is so closed in. There's no privacy anywhere. The chutes are a place I can go to get away from other kids and be by myself."

The man seemed very interested, and Toby was glad to have directed the conversation away from the subject of escape.

"Why wouldn't you want to take your friends with you?"

"Most of the other kids don't like it in there. I've got one friend I take with me sometimes, but he won't go by himself."

"Why don't they like it the way you do?"

"I don't know. Maybe it's the darkness, feeling squeezed in by the chutes, and being afraid of getting lost."

"And you don't feel any of that?"

"No, sir. I did at first, but decided I wanted to explore around and just made myself do it."

The man leaned forward in his chair, looking straight at Toby. "Are you a loner?"

"A what?"

"Do you like to be alone?"

That was strange question. "Yeah, I guess so. I don't know if I like it so much as I don't mind it. It doesn't bother me."

The man leaned back in his chair, put his hands together behind his head, and straightened out his legs so that the chair rose up on the two back legs. You couldn't do that on Oasis. All the furniture was bolted down.

The man said, "So when I invaded your space you felt like paying me back. You tricked me, didn't you?"

Toby had done more than trick him, and he knew it. He was kind of proud of it, actually. "It was fun."

The man laughed. "I bet it was. How did you do it?"

"I just ran you around some."

"Weren't you afraid?"

"No, not really. Maybe toward the end there a little, but not for long."

"Why weren't you afraid?"

Toby was getting into this, the man seemed really interested in him as a person. Maybe he wasn't all that bad a guy. "I knew where you were."

Silence. The man's eyes widened slightly, but returned to the look of casual interest so quickly that Toby made nothing of it.

"That place is a maze. Noisy, dark, chutes going every which way, but you were able to anticipate my moves. How'd you do that?"

"Lots of practice. My friend Rooster and I play a game like hide and seek, and I always win."

The man stared at Toby, then looked down at the floor and shook his head. "Practice, huh?" With his gaze back on Toby, he said, "Not good enough. And let me tell you how I know that.

"You did something to me no one has ever done before. Do you understand that? I've played serious versions of hide-and-seek with some dangerous people, and they don't hold a candle to you."

Toby had long suspected what the man said was true. In so many instances with adults he had been able to manipulate them at will, and in more than a physical sense. This man seemed to understand.

The man let the chair fall forward, leaned over with his elbows resting on his knees, and clasped his hands together. He looked at Toby with soft, inquisitive eyes, the first time they'd ever looked like that, and asked, "You ever tell anyone about it?"

Without even thinking about it, Toby shook his head.

"Embarrassed?"

"Yes."

"Think it makes you so different from other kids that you'll never be accepted by them?"

Toby nodded.

"Well, let me tell you something. I've felt like an outsider all my life, and never more than when I was a kid. Nobody seemed to understand me. They were always suspicious, jealous of the things I could do they couldn't, and they ganged up on me constantly. Sound familiar?"

Another nod.

"Tell you what. Why don't we go for a walk? I'm sorry we don't have the run of the place, but we can get you out of this room. You're probably ready to see something besides four walls. Right?"

"Yes, sir!"

SAMAEL WAS IN A VERY GOOD MOOD. HE HAD GONE INTO THE kid's room with no clear picture of what he wanted to accomplish. But there was something still nagging at him, some unfinished business.

And boy, was there. He was still shaking with the discovery of it, the implications of what it might mean to him. The kid was a hard nut to crack, which told him a lot even before he found out any particulars.

The friendship and kindred-spirit approach proved to be the key. The kid was starving for someone to understand him. He had been holding the secret in for so long that when it started flowing you couldn't have stopped it by choking him to death. He would have been like a snake, thrashing around long after death, still telling all about his powers.

And what powers! There hadn't been the time or opportunity to observe them all, but the one demonstration was proof enough. Samael had taken the kid to a spot where no one was likely to walk up on them, and asked him to find out what was going on behind a wall.

It was a command center, completely soundproofed. The kid heard discussions between a man Samael knew to be in the room and his counterpart over a mile away in the shuttle hangar. Not only could the kid hear through the wall, it was almost as if he had crawled into the radio and heard the transmissions as they were received.

And even without additional confirmation, Samael was certain the kid was telling the truth. He had no reason to lie, and every reason to share his pent-up frustrations. Up to now Samael's plan had been forming slowly. But now with this sudden revelation he was committed to going ahead.

The seeds of the idea had been planted for years, and most recently nurtured by the success of this assignment. It was to be the culmination of everything and allow him to leave the business at the top, a world champion, undefeated. There was the money, of course, but the real satisfaction was that there had never been anyone better.

And still it wasn't enough. Where would he go? What good was all the money without a place to spend it in the fashion you intended? The allure of the wealth had become tarnished by the harsh reality of conditions on Earth. He could probably find a place and fortify it well enough, but then what? He'd be a prisoner in paradise, with freedom of movement slowly being eroded by the mounting pressures of a world gone mad.

During the voyage back from the space station, Samael concluded there was another, far more rewarding possibility. Throughout his career, he had never worked for anyone as smart as he was. And although every one of his employers had more money, at some point wealth became an inadequate measure of who's on top. A far more telling criterion was available, which became the catalyst for the cancellation of his retirement plans.

Power. Money could buy it, but the best kind was derived from the use of situational control to exert your will over others. And this was the opportunity of a lifetime, just waiting for someone bold enough to reach out and grasp it. Samael was about to embark on a journey that was more than a culmination of years of work, more than a reward for services rendered, and far more than he had ever dared dream.

And then there was the irony of it all. Success or failure involved a shuttle, a pilot, and a thirteen-year-old boy.

BRETT WAS DOING PUSHUPS WITH HIS FEET ON THE BED AND HIS hands supported by two chairs when someone knocked on the door. Wondering why anyone who held another person prisoner would bother being polite, he yelled, "Come in!"

Pausing at the top of a pushup, Brett looked up to see the hijacker enter the room with a tray of food. Ignoring him for the moment, he slowly ground out three more repetitions and then stood up, breathing heavily.

"Hungry?" the man asked.

"Yeah. I could eat something. But what I really need is less gravity."

The man set the tray on a table. "May I sit down?"

Brett was wiping his face with a towel, chuckling softly. "You're really something. Why don't you cut the crap and just say what you came for?"

The man didn't respond for a moment, then nodded his head. "Okay, if that's the way you want it. Your services are still required. That may be bad news in your view, but you might also want to consider the good news. As a man with usefulness to my mission, you live. The moment you become excess baggage that may change. I'm sure you get the picture.

"We're in the process of preparing the shuttle for launch. We don't need your help getting it ready, but as a pilot you have every reason to be involved. And before you think of this as an opportunity to try anything sneaky, let me introduce you to someone. Lin!"

Brett glanced at the door as it opened and watched a man enter.

He was obviously Asian, and dressed in black like the hijacker, but without the mask. The word "PILOT" was printed in white on the front of his shirt. He looked vaguely familiar.

"Captain Larsen, I'd like you to meet Lin. You and he will be spending quite a lot of time together, and you might as well consider him as being your shadow, as it were."

Brett couldn't concentrate on what the man was saying. Along with the obvious question of what the hell was going on, he couldn't shake the feeling he knew Lin, but from where?

His captor continued. "We're going to return the shuttle to Oasis, and you will pilot us there. Lin will serve as copilot, not only to assist you, but to learn as well. You will share your knowledge with him freely. Consider yourself his instructor, and teach him all you can about the shuttle. And before you choke on your tongue, let me assure you he has previous space experience, is an extremely fast learner, and much of your instruction will be like a refresher course."

Brett was stunned. Of course. That's where he had seen him.

The man stood, offered the chair to Lin, and turned to Brett. "I suggest you two spend a while getting acquainted, or maybe reacquainted, as the case may be. Come see me when you're through here, Lin."

Lin bowed very slightly as the hijacker turned and left the room. Brett was almost too shocked to speak, and stared at his new copilot with unabashed curiosity. "What about Toby?"

"Who?"

"Toby. The kid who came with us from Oasis. What will become of him?"

"I know nothing of these things." Lin's voice was as smooth as silk, with the slightest trace of an accent. "I am here to assist you and learn as much as I am able with regard to shuttle operation. I—"

"I heard what the man said. Where do I know you from?"

Lin smiled, ignoring the rebuke and obviously pleased. "I thought you did not remember, Captain Larsen. I am honored that you recognize me, even if only slightly. I was a foreign pilot member of a shuttle crew, and you helped train me."

There had been so many students over the years. Then Brett

remembered an intense young man who seemed to bore into you with his eyes as he took in every word. He almost never spoke, asked no questions, but performed every task with flawless precision. Brett recalled thinking he must have been a robot with a computer for a brain.

"If I may suggest, Captain, we should get started as quickly as possible. There really isn't much time."

OVER THE COURSE OF THE NEXT FEW DAYS, TOBY FOUND LIFE ON Earth could be interesting in spite of the unusual circumstances that had brought him here. He exercised, ate like a king, slept like a baby, and gradually began spending more and more time with the man.

Toby discovered one of the disadvantages of living on a space station was absence of bicycles. The man had come to his room on the second morning and taken him outside. At first Toby was mesmerized as he stood in the sunlight soaking up the view. The man seemed to understand, then suggested Toby concentrate on learning about one thing at a time, rather than trying to embrace everything at once.

They had just started off on a walk when a man on a bicycle came peddling around the corner of the building, startling Toby so much he jumped back against the wall. The man in black laughed, then asked if Toby had ever ridden a bike. When Toby said he'd seen them only in movies, the man picked that as the morning's lesson.

Toby spent the rest of the morning getting the hang of it. Each day thereafter they went for a ride. Toby learned quickly, and focused his curiosity on the surrounding countryside as they took a different route along the miles of roads surrounding the complex.

Today they stopped on a small hill overlooking a lake. Without realizing it, Toby had begun to think of the man as a friend. The subject of his powers hadn't come up since the first day they talked, and Toby was curious about the results of the test they conducted.

It hadn't been like a challenge, just a question about how it worked. Toby mentioned his ability to hear outside the apartment on Oasis, but the man didn't appear to believe him. Toby suggested a demonstration, then afterwards became concerned about what he had done.

But not for long. For the first time since discovering he had special abilities, Toby felt as if a massive weight had been lifted from his shoulders. The man listened as the words just seemed to pour out, carried away by the wind, and Toby's long-held fear of being considered a freak had vanished along with them.

Toby sipped from a bottle of apple juice. "When you asked me to listen past the wall?"

"Hmm?"

"I heard the one man, you know, talking to someone, but there was a lot of other noise in the background."

"I'm sure there was."

"Well, it seemed like you didn't believe me at first. I was wondering if . . . uh . . . you think I'm weird or anything."

The man laughed. "Don't get me wrong. I'm not laughing at you. It's just that you have no idea how unique you are. I think you've probably felt like a freak, knowing you were so different than the other kids, afraid to tell anyone for fear of being laughed at. But I'm jealous, and wish I had half the ability you do. You have no reason to feel anything but pride."

Toby was silent for a few minutes, looking out at the lake, thinking hard about what the man had said. He'd never considered himself special, gifted, or anything like that. When he discovered his powers, he never associated them with any other part of his life.

"You know what destiny means?" the man asked.

"You mean like fate?"

"Yes. Something that's inevitable, you can't do anything about it. As far as I'm concerned, destiny brought us together. You remember when I told you I was committed to doing whatever I could to reverse the course our civilization seemed to be on?"

Toby nodded.

"And this whole thing with the shuttle and the pilot had to do with that mission?"

"Yes."

"Well, I don't need to point out that you're involved because of what you did, not anything I or anyone else did."

"Excuse me, sir, but that's not true."

The man looked surprised at the contradiction, and then with a slight smile asked, "Why isn't it?"

"Because I would never have done what I did if Brett hadn't been in the middle of it." Toby then related the incident in which he overheard the phone conversation between Brett and the general. "I felt I couldn't let Brett go through with it, at least not without help."

"And you decided to jump right into the middle of this, knowing all the while that you'd be challenging a man who shot at you?"

Toby didn't answer for a moment, lost in thought. "I didn't plan on that. I just figured I could outsmart you like I did in the chutes. And I wasn't thinking about being alone, but that I'd be working with Brett. He'd want to send me back, but after the shuttle departed he couldn't and he'd have to let me stay."

"I agree you had external reasons to do what you did, but that's missing my point. You don't see this in the same way I do, for two reasons.

"First, you're young, and don't look at what kids do as anything unusual. But you did something I can't even imagine a kid doing. You voluntarily walked into a situation you had to know would be dangerous.

"Second, you've lived with your abilities long enough to accept them as part of who you are. And while you seem to be concerned about them making you weird, as you put it, you can't help but respond to things that happen to you in light of those abilities. Like this situation, for instance. You probably wouldn't have considered doing this without the previous experience evading me. You were able to accomplish that only because of the very power you've been so afraid to acknowledge."

"What does that have to do with destiny?"

The man chuckled softly. "If you believe in destiny, even a little bit, you also have to accept that one of the reasons we find it hard to embrace is the mystery which shrouds it. Do we understand it? No, and we never will. But in this instance your presence here makes all the difference in the world. You and I are sitting on this hill, and like it or not, our immediate futures are inseparable."

Toby understood the idea, but was still confused. "How can I make a difference?"

The man stood up and motioned for Toby to follow him. "Let's take a stroll."

They walked down the side of the hill and over to the edge of the lake. In the past few days Toby had seen many things that were incredibly new and fascinating, but the sight of water lying out there on the ground was almost spooky.

The man suggested they walk around the lake, and after about ten minutes of silence, he said, "I've been beating around the bush, but I have something I want to talk with you about."

"Sure."

"You may not have thought much about what was going to happen after we arrived here on Earth. I hadn't considered what to do with you before because I didn't plan on having a passenger."

"What will happen to Brett?"

The man stopped suddenly, and gripped Toby by the shoulder. "The captain will play an important role, and that was in the plan from the very beginning. I don't like having to take him, the shuttle, or anything else by force. But as I've tried to explain over the past few days, there's been a crisis building on Earth for years. We don't have the luxury of gentle measures, or the time to recruit volunteers. It will all become clear to you soon enough, but for now I want you to consider what I have to say. Will you do that?"

Toby didn't really have a choice, but he was more than a little curious. "Yes, sir."

As they continued walking, the man said, "It's a harsh world out there, with ruthless men who will do anything to see this mission fail. It all has to do with money, power, control of food, water, minerals, and much more. I have people committed to help me, but the methods of accomplishing the task and its potential outcome are by no means decided. I need your help. This may seem ridiculous, that I would be asking a boy your age to get involved, but as I said before the time for waiting is over."

"But if this is as serious as you say, how can I do anything?"

The man walked to the edge of the trail and sat on a boulder with a flat top. "Have a seat over here for a minute."

As Toby sat down the man said, "I'm a key player in this effort. My enemies know if they can eliminate me their chances of winning are vastly improved. I expect them to try very hard to achieve their goal. I've spent most of my adult life involved in activities with this danger, and here I am, proof of some abilities in that regard.

"But this is different. On Earth there's room to maneuver. But not in space. To you, this," said the man, extending both his arms and indicating their surroundings, "is foreign because there's so much of it. The station is your home. But to me Oasis is a tomb, and it cramps my style."

Toby found all this to be very interesting, with the guy talking around the subject without ever saying what he did. But he seemed sincere enough, and Toby's curiosity was in overdrive.

"I need someone to watch my back," said the man.

Toby was dumfounded. "I don't know anything about that kind of stuff."

"You don't have to. But you told me you have the ability to sense beyond your immediate surroundings. I cannot overemphasize how valuable that could be."

"But you don't really know that. I don't understand it completely, and there was a period on the shuttle when I was convinced it was all gone. Most of it may be now, I just don't know."

The man waited a few seconds and seemed to be thinking about what to say next. "For as long as I can remember, one of the secrets to success for me has been to follow my instincts. They've never failed me, and something tells me you're a key to this. It has to involve your powers.

"What else *could* it be? You're not part of the original plan. And even after you dropped in unannounced, it wasn't necessary for us to relay that to anyone and try to use you for leverage. The only advantage you give me is so significant that I can't ignore it."

"I'm sorry, but I just don't understand how I can help."

"If you were to stick to me like a shadow, with your abilities tuned up and working, no one could sneak up on me. You'd be able to warn me, because any threat to me is a threat to you."

"Would it be dangerous?"

"Could be, but the time for easy solutions has past. And we could work on it. There are people here I trust, and I think we could figure out a way for you to warn me and then get out of the way. Is this thing you told me about directional?"

"Sir?"

"Can you tell where the threat is coming from?"

"I knew in the chutes whether to go left or right to stay clear of you, and a few times when you were stalking me I sensed danger from a certain direction."

"Excellent. And here's something else for you to think about."

"What?"

"If I succeed in this, and I think you could be a key factor in improving my chances, you will have done the best thing you could to protect the pilot and your family and friends on the station."

"But they're mostly gone. Evacuated to the moon colony."

"That makes what I said all the more true. The sooner we get those people back on the station, the better it will be for everyone. If I succeed, things can return to normal, and you might get something out of it you haven't even considered yet."

"Something for me?"

"You bet. What would you say if once this thing is done, and your family would have to agree, of course, we might arrange for you to come on back to Earth, live with someone here, continue your education and take flying lessons?"

Toby was stunned. It took him a moment to speak.

"Oh, mister, do you really mean it?"

OVER THE NEXT WEEK BRETT CONCENTRATED ON THE TASK AT hand and tried not to think of anything else. He hadn't seen the hijacker since the first day, and although he attempted to ask Lin about Toby, the copilot insisted he had no idea who Toby was.

Lin was ravenous for information. In a way that helped, because Brett was constantly answering questions. They spent long days working, most of it in or around the shuttle. At first Brett had a difficult time concentrating on his instructional duties, preoccupied with what he was witnessing. If asked last week whether he thought it would be possible to duplicate a shuttle preparation and launch facility outside the United States and in the absence of NASA cooperation, he would have scoffed at the idea. But not now.

Walking through the vast complex, Brett was tempted to conclude he was viewing the results of the most extensive copycat effort in history. They had a shuttle and the facility to launch it. The small space fighter had disappeared, swallowed up within the cavernous maw of the massive structure. The most logical inference was that it had been taken to study, its metallurgy, avionics, computer hardware and software, and propulsion systems dissected like a laboratory frog. Somebody wanted a dehydrated manned space program, add water and there it was.

But this scenario didn't track with returning to Oasis. If the objective was to steal the technology, why wouldn't they keep the shuttle in addition to the fighter? The only logical answer was the objective had to be Oasis itself.

With that nagging conclusion as a constant companion, Brett maintained the image of a man resigned to the inevitable, with no other choice but to do as he was told. And as the launch day approached, he struggled once more with his personal commitment to stop this thing no matter what the cost.

Unless part of the price included Toby. If Brett launched for the return journey knowing that Toby had been left behind, he was determined to take action. Oasis *must* be protected.

～

SAMAEL ALMOST COULDN'T CONTAIN HIS EXCITEMENT. Manipulation of the boy had gone better than he ever expected. Toby seemed eager to test his skills. Using a member of the assault team, Samael set up a series of situations during the morning while he and

Toby were out on the trails, and in the afternoon at one of the combat training facilities.

Toby appeared apprehensive at first, until Samael introduced him to the man who would be the "attacker." He had a kid or two of his own, and they seemed to like each other immediately.

The attacker showed Toby his sidearm, explained how it worked, and assured him that the gun would remain unloaded for the tests. Then he brought out the training knife and let Toby see that it wouldn't hurt anyone.

Toby had said there were three manifestations of his powers, and the tests were designed to demonstrate each of them. In the morning session the attacker planted simulated explosive devices along the trails, testing Toby's ability to detect spatial anomalies, objects that didn't fit into the background and were out of place.

The first one was covered with sand, and although Toby sensed it, Samael was concerned about how close they got. Later on there was one beside the road hidden among some grass, and the detection occurred much sooner. Toby explained he had felt the heat difference. The device was an empty land mine casing, and in the bright sunlight the dark color had absorbed more heat in relation to the surrounding sand and grass.

The attacker also lay hidden for a sudden surprise assault, and Toby discovered him every time. Part of it was heat, and part spatial, but Samael was impressed with how well it worked.

Then came the simulated attacks themselves, and the kid's reaction was absolutely uncanny. It didn't matter how fast, how quiet, or how sudden the attack was, he was able to pick up the threat outside lethal range of most hand-held weapons.

During the afternoon sessions they used a mock-up city block where combat training was conducted. After repeating some of the morning objectives, Samael took Toby into a centrally located building, and had the attacker take up random positions within the facility and turn on a small portable radio. Using a diagram of the training facility, the boy was able to pinpoint the source of the sound even with the radio volume turned low. By late afternoon, Samael was convinced that with the boy at his side, he would have a significant advantage, and it was time to put things in motion.

As the afternoon sun settled to the horizon, Samael, Toby, and the attacker stood in the street of the training facility. It was a debriefing session, and they talked about the various situations during the day.

Samael congratulated Toby on the good work, and sent him back to his room for dinner. As Toby rode off on the bike, the attacker said, "Quite a kid. Is he from Oasis? And how the hell does he do that stuff?"

Samael didn't answer and went over to his bike. Opening a pouch of the saddlebags behind the seat, he unzipped a soft-sided cooler and took out two beers. Handing one to the attacker, he waited while the man twisted off the cap and tilted his head back for a long pull.

Then he drew his pistol and shot the man in the chest. The impact of the bullet almost knocked the man's feet off the ground, and the body landed hard on the compacted Earth with a muffled thump.

As Samael de-cocked and holstered the weapon, he walked over to a large trash container, opened the lid, and took out a body bag. He laid it beside the body, and rolled the man on top. Bringing the sides of the bag together, he closed it and dragged the body off the street and over to the dumpster. In one motion he lifted the body's upper torso and laid it over the edge of the dumpster with the feet dangling outside, then reached down and gripped the bottom of the bag and tossed it over and in with the rest of the trash.

After closing the lid, the Samael trotted over to a storage shed and found a small trenching shovel. Returning to the pool of blood on the ground, he carefully scooped up some stained dirt and took it behind the nearest building. Heaving it as far as he could into a grassy area, he saw the dirt break up into small clumps and fall out of sight onto the ground. He repeated the process, then took unstained dirt from different areas in between the clumps of grass and scattered it over the area where the body had lain, tamping it down with the flat back side of the shovel.

Stepping back to admire his work, he felt satisfied this was good enough. He returned the tool to the shed, recovered the two beer bottles, tops, spent cartridge case, and left the compound.

Now he was really excited.

~

RACING ALONG THE TRAILS, TOBY WAS HAVING THE TIME OF HIS
life. The feeling of freedom was absolutely wonderful, with all that sky
above him, being able to see so far in any direction he looked, and
with no one to tell him where to go or what to do.

The man had said to go straight back, but to heck with that.
Toby found a dip in the trail and used it as a ramp to practice
jumping the bike, and found he could either go for distance or
height depending on how he timed the maneuver. It occurred to him
that if he had a bike on Oasis he'd be able to go much higher and
farther, and decided to ask the man if he could take one back
with him.

Breathing heavily from the exertion, Toby stopped at the top of a
small rise to catch his breath. He was able to see the lake from there,
and took out the pair of binoculars the man had given him to watch
birds and some of the small animals they had seen. Scanning the valley
below, he paused to survey his temporary home on Earth.

It looked like a bowl with a piece cut out of the side. A stream
came out of the mountains at the far end, winding through the flat
bottom of the bowl and exiting through the opening to Toby's right.
To his left were some buildings, nestled up against the steeply rising
terrain, and he could just make out the straight lines that appeared to
be painted on the side of the mountains. When he had asked the man
what they were, he was told they were hangars, and until then Toby
hadn't even noticed the runway.

Toby knew what camouflage was, and he was looking at an elaborate example of the concept. The predominant ground feature was
some form of low vegetation, growing in clumps with patches of dirt
and grass in between. The pattern had been painted right over the
runway surface, so that the straight edges of the hard pavement were
hardly visible. The first time he saw it from this location, he thought
the stream cut right through it, but now with the binoculars he could
make out the details. They had diverted the water under the runway

through a culvert, and painted the concrete so that it looked as if the stream continued in an unbroken flow right across it.

Scanning to his left with the binoculars, Toby took a closer look at the buildings. Although painted the same way and not easy to see, they weren't particularly interesting and offered nothing to hold his attention. He was about to put the binoculars away when he saw two men standing beside the trail. Focusing the binoculars to get a clear view, Toby almost fell off the bike.

It was Brett, leaning up against the side of a building and talking with someone. This was wonderful. He had asked the man about Brett, and was told not to worry about him, but of course he did. And now there he was, looking okay, and the urge to see him was almost too hard to resist.

He started off down the trail but suddenly thought better of it and skidded to a stop. The man had told him to go straight back and avoid people. Brett had cautioned him about talking with anyone. Without knowing who was down there with Brett, he could be doing the wrong thing on both counts. Toby raised the binoculars again and watched as the two men continued talking, then saw Brett give the other man a slight wave with his hand and turn away.

Toby followed Brett with the binoculars as he trotted over to what looked like an outdoor exercise area. There were a number of small structures arranged in a group, and Brett stopped at the first one and began doing sit-ups. Toby scanned the area around the exercise stations and found a route down a dry creek bed that provided reasonable concealment. He wanted to talk with Brett, but didn't like the idea of rushing down there in plain view on his bike.

It was a rough ride off the trail, but once in the creek bed the ground was mostly gravel and the going became easier. After a few minutes, Toby was surprised at how deep the ravine became. He was getting concerned about being able to climb up the increasingly steep sides.

A strange feeling came over him. He stopped to think about it for a moment, and realized that for the first time in his life he was lost. Unable to see very far in the ravine, Toby decided it was time to get reoriented. He left the bike and scrambled up the side.

Toby was about three-fourths of the way to the top when he came to a ledge. He couldn't see the top, but with one foot wedged into a crack in the wall he was able to reach up and with both hands gripping the edge pull himself up.

Or try to. This wasn't nearly as easy on Earth as it was on Oasis. And although he had become stronger with all the recent exercise, he ended up hanging off the ledge by his fingertips. He tried to support himself by wedging his foot back in the crack, but he couldn't find it.

Okay, time to pull yourself up in one motion. Ready . . . one . . . two . . . THREE!

Toby made it, at least part way, with his upper body lying on top of the ledge and his legs hanging off. He wasn't in danger of falling, but needed another handhold to pull himself the rest of the way up. Without looking, he reached out, feeling for something to grab, and put his right hand on something smooth, round, and moving.

Toby's immediate reaction was to tilt his head back and look in front of him on the ledge. What he saw was so terrifying that for a second or two he was unable to react.

But the snake changed all that as it seemed to come alive and reared back, head high, upper body curved to strike.

Toby's only thought was to get away, so he let go and fell off the ledge.

BRETT HATED EXERCISE JUST FOR THE SAKE OF IT, BUT FELT THE benefits were worth the effort. Flight physicals helped provide the motivation. Once a year he was required to assume various embarrassing positions while a doctor probed and prodded, listened and examined, with the ever-present possibility of finding something which could end his flying career.

That was especially true of EKG's, which Brett hated far worse than exercise. Wired up with a computer delving into the workings of his heart, Brett would swear that he could feel things going wrong, including extra beats, not enough beats, or beats of the wrong kind.

He was determined to help himself avoid heart trouble by regularly putting the old pump through its paces.

The hijacker had no objection to Brett getting the exercise, but wanted Lin with him. It wasn't for fear of an escape. The surrounding terrain was too rugged, and Brett wasn't even close to being in shape for substantial physical exertion in Earth's gravity. But today Lin had decided to take some time off, and Brett was on his own for an hour or two.

His usual routine involved circuit training, or proceeding from one exercise to another with very little rest. He also preferred exercises in which he lifted his own body weight, and this group of stations allowed him to put together a nice sequence. Before long he was sweating profusely, breathing hard, and about to begin his third circuit.

The scream cut through the air suddenly and stopped Brett's pushups. Kneeling in the dirt, he listened while trying to soften his breathing. For a moment he considered finishing the set, but it sounded close, and he decided to check it out. Brett looked down toward the runway and the valley below, searching for any signs of human activity. Finding nothing, he trotted in the other direction between the stations and up the sloped side of a long rise that curved down past the exercise area.

Reaching the top, Brett looked down into the ravine and saw the upper torso of a figure lying at the base of a ledge. Scrambling down the steep slope, he reached the flat top of the ledge and recognized the motionless form of Toby sprawled in the dirt below.

Abandoning caution, Brett hurried down to a relatively flat ledge at the bottom, then traversed over to where Toby lay motionless. With a pounding heart, Brett knelt down beside his friend.

Toby was breathing, with no blood evident, but Brett didn't dare move him for fear there might be neck or spinal damage. Placing his hand under Toby's jaw, he felt for a pulse and then yanked it back when Toby's eyes popped open suddenly and his body jerked slightly.

"Jesus!" Brett exclaimed, partly in surprise, and mostly with relief.

Toby's eyes seemed to be unfocused for a moment, then settled down and stared right at Brett. With a slight smile, he tried to get up.

"Toby, don't move. You may have injuries that would be worsened."

In spite of Brett's objections, Toby insisted upon sitting up and resting with his back against the ledge. He asked about the snake, which was long gone, and or the next fifteen minutes talked non-stop about his activities for the past week. Brett listened without interrupting, becoming increasingly concerned about the relationship between Toby and the hijacker, and about the growing suspicion Toby was holding something back.

When Toby seemed to have run out of steam for a minute, Brett asked, "So, would you say you and the man have become friends?"

Toby appeared startled by the question. "Uh, no, not like you and me. But I was getting real bored just sitting in the room, and it didn't seem like it would do any harm to learn how to ride a bike."

"And that's all you've been doing, just riding bikes?"

"We usually take some food, a lunch or something. And there's the binoculars, and skipping the stones on the lake."

Brett shook his head. "I'm not talking about that, Toby. It seems to me you've forgotten what this man did to get us here in the first place. It's one thing to enjoy your first trip to Earth, and I'm not saying you shouldn't be excited about it. But I'm hearing something deeper, kind of like you two are partners or something."

Toby stared at Brett as if he had just been caught eating the last piece of cake. "What do you mean?"

Brett could see the fear in Toby's eyes, and decided not to question his young friend further. It probably was nothing more than trying to stay busy, and now wasn't the time to dig any deeper. "Nothing. But let me tell you something. This whole thing is becoming worse by the minute. The man wants me to fly the shuttle back to Oasis.

"I have no idea what he plans to do with you. I don't think you're in any danger, but I'm going to ask him to send you to the States. I have to know you're safe before I leave."

"But Brett, he's already told me he wants me to go with you and—"

"What the hell are you two doing?"

Brett looked over his shoulder down the ravine and saw the man in the mask walking toward them, his weapon in his right hand hanging by his side. Brett stood, and walked out from the ledge a little to make sure the man could see that he wasn't armed. "I was exercising up there," he said, pointing behind him to the top of the ravine, "when I heard a scream. I found Toby lying here unconscious. He fell while trying to climb up this ledge."

The man continued to walk toward them, and Brett heard a rock falling from above him and bouncing down the slope to his left. He turned and was shocked to see a group of men, all carrying short-barreled assault rifles and dressed in black combat clothing, spread out in a fan shape and advancing down from the top of the ravine. He noticed each man was wearing a baseball cap with a number printed in white on the front, and the same number was repeated in other places on their clothing.

The man in the mask came up the side of the ravine to where Brett and Toby were, then stood in front of them while he slipped the sidearm inside his waistband in the middle of his back. He looked right past Brett and in a loud voice said, "Twenty?"

"Yes, sir," a voice answered from behind Brett.

"Make certain twenty-seven learns how to walk without dislodging rocks and announcing our presence. I expect silence no matter what the terrain."

"Yes, sir."

The man then looked at Brett. "Is the boy okay?"

Brett tried not to show his relief at how calm the situation had remained as he answered. "I think so. I was worried he might have a spinal injury, but he appears to be fine. If you have the medical facilities, I'd recommend he be kept there for observation overnight. He did get a nasty bump on the back of his head."

The man nodded as he leaned down and examined Toby's injury. Then he stood up and rapidly barked orders at the men. One led Toby down the ravine while another retrieved the bike. The rest started back up the side of the ravine as the man motioned for Brett to do the same.

Approaching the top, Brett saw a man standing just back from the edge. He recognized Lin and started to say something but stopped when he saw the pilot was very nervous, looking past Brett at the man who followed. Lin had a bad cut on his cheek and a bruise that extended up to the hairline.

"Lin will take you to your room, Captain."

Brett turned to face the man and said, "Look, I've been wanting to talk with you about Toby. He's of no use—"

"Lin will take you to your room."

The hijacker turned, walking past Lin without a word. Lin motioned for Brett to follow him and began climbing the slope. As Brett fell in trail, he knew he'd have to find out why Toby was returning to Oasis.

And somehow change it. With Toby on board it would tie Brett's hands as effectively as it had on the journey down, and there was the other thing bothering him, too.

It was the look on Toby's face, and that light in his eyes when he had said the man wanted him to return to Oasis.

What on Earth is going on?

18

Things were going well, but you could never be too careful. Samael shouldn't have let the kid go back by himself. And although he couldn't have anticipated Lin would violate orders and leave the pilot alone, it still rankled him that the two mistakes allowed this to happen.

Although confident of maintaining control, he didn't want to deal with having to struggle against the pilot's influence any more than necessary. Lin would be on the pilot like glue, that lesson had been reinforced well enough, and Samael would see to it that the kid remained under his own supervision at all times.

Which shouldn't be too difficult given the circumstances. Samael would soon need Toby's services on a continuous basis anyway, and what better way to supervise him than that?

After taking Toby his food, Samael checked with the operations supervisor to ensure the shuttle preparations were on schedule. Then he went to the assault team's quarters to make certain the men were occupied. At this time of the evening the squads would be released to do as they wished, but if the squad leaders were doing their jobs, the men would be busy enough to keep them occupied for at least another hour or two.

As he strolled through the barracks, Samael found groups being briefed by their leaders, and saw no strays wandering about. He needed privacy and no surprises. Once convinced, he left the barracks and set his own plan in motion.

His employers had hired him to bring a shuttle, a space fighter, and a pilot back to Earth. And although Samael had been involved with the selection and training of the men, his services were not required from this point forward. He'd been cleared to depart the complex, but he remained under the guise of wanting to observe the shuttle launch. The money was waiting, payment in full, and that was supposed to be the end of it. For them, maybe, but not for him.

Samael left the barracks and went through his usual routine of walking around the complex, which he had done every night about the same time since he arrived. Toward the end of his tour, he approached a building set off from the rest, light visible from a window and at the bottom of the door. Glancing about, he checked for signs of activity on the grounds. Finding none, he dropped into a low crouch and quickly scurried up to the building. He pressed an ear to the wall and heard a conversation.

Damn. Have to wait. He went around to the other side of the building, then darted across a space between it and a storage shed to hide in the shadows. After about ten minutes he heard the door handle turn before he saw it. The door opened slightly, probably with the visitor standing just inside and preparing to leave. Muffled voices drifted to him in the slight breeze, and he silently urged whoever it was to hurry the hell up and go on about his business.

After a another minute or so the visitor exited the building and walked off in the darkness. Samael caught a glimpse of him as the interior light from the room illuminated the doorway, a man dressed in standard black combat clothing with the number 40 printed on the front and back of both the shirt and baseball-style cap. The Squad Four leader, probably there to discuss some detail of the approaching mission.

Samael decided to wait. He knew the interior layout of the building, and the light streaming through the windows was from a desk lamp where the occupant always sat to work. And although Samael was certain the man inside was alone, he also knew the chance of more visitors would be much reduced once the man began preparations for bed.

After an hour or so, the light from the desk lamp went out. Samael hacked his internal clock and waited fifteen minutes. Then he took a careful look around, walked up to the front door, and knocked.

From inside a voice: "Yes?"

"Sorry to bother you, Number One."

After a short pause the door opened and Samael entered. He knew the routine and walked to the center of the room without looking about, standing still until he received an indication it was okay to proceed.

The voice from behind him. "Are you armed?"

"No."

"Have a seat."

Samael sat down in a chair facing the man's desk and waited. From behind and to his left he heard a distinctive shuffling sound as the man came around from behind and took his seat at the desk. With his one eye staring directly into Samael's, the man turned his head slightly to the left and nodded.

Samael spoke slowly and distinctly in deference to the man's compromised hearing. "I have a minor incident to report. Probably of no consequence, but that should be for you to decide."

"Of course."

"Early this evening I found the boy and the pilot by themselves. I do not know how long they were alone, and I've made no attempt to ascertain what they may have discussed. They are adequately separated now, and will remain so permanently."

"Need I ask how this occurred?"

"Temporary lack of judgment. I have disciplined the parties involved and there will be no recurrence."

"I should hope not. On another subject. I thought you would be gone by now."

Samael internally welcomed the shift in topic. He had gotten in the room on a thin reason to begin with, and could now remain longer providing an explanation. "I had so planned. But the project was far

more interesting than I had imagined. I have decided to wait around
to observe the launch. I trust you have no objection."

Number One turned his head to one side, covered his mouth, and
began to cough. Samael had seen the ploy often enough to know its
purpose and the reason for it. The man was annoyed at this unexpected development, and he would undoubtedly object.

After a moment, Number One appeared to recover. "Not as such,
although I'm sure you're aware that we have consistently avoided
exposing the mission to the dangers of extraneous personnel. Your
contribution, valuable though it may have been, is old news. I would
prefer that you depart the premises."

Samael had expected this reaction as well. "I understand your position. I'll do so in the morning."

The man nodded, then stood up behind the desk. Samael got up
and walked toward the door, then stopped and turned. "Oh, I almost
forgot. I left a small package with Number Two for safekeeping. He
said he would put it in the wall safe. May I have it now?"

Number One frowned slightly. "He didn't say anything to me."

"There would have been no reason to. It was nothing more than a
personal favor to me. I'll wait and see him about it." Samael turned
toward the door and heard another predictable response.

"Number Two is away from the complex and will not return until
just prior to launch. I'll have him mail it."

Samael paused at the door, knob in hand. That was bullshit. Two
had been at dinner earlier that evening. Number One obviously
wanted Samael out of the picture as soon as possible.

Samael looked over his shoulder. "Come now, Number One. You
don't really think I'll be strolling down to a post office in the next few
months. You may have the barrier of space travel between you and
retribution, but my situation requires different tactics. I'll leave here as
soon as I retrieve the package."

Samael turned and opened the door. As he stepped out on the
landing, the man set the stage to end this charade for both of them.

"Hold on a minute."

Glancing back, Samael watched Number One turn from the desk
and shuffle toward the wall behind the desk.

Quickly now, go!

Samael pulled the door almost closed, hurried to close the distance between him and Number One, approached from his left side, and struck him on the temple with a shot-filled leather sap as he was dialing in the combination to the safe. Samael caught him under the arms as his knees buckled and lowered him silently to the floor.

Then he closed the door all the way, dragged the body into the small sleeping room, and laid it on the bed. Although a weak and erratic pulse indicated the blow was very likely fatal, he covered the man's face with a pillow for a few minutes.

Samael turned out the lights, left the building and entered the crawl space underneath the floor through a small access door. All the structures in the complex were of pier and beam design, with enough space to crawl to the center of the building. After activating the timer of an explosive charge placed there well in advance, he retraced his path and snuck off into the night.

TOBY HATED HOSPITALS. THEY SMELLED STRANGE, AND EVERY time he got near one the thought of all the uncomfortable things that went on inside made him exceedingly nervous.

No one spoke to him, and he didn't try to start any conversations. The guy who brought him to the hospital just walked off, and the doctor, or whatever he was, examined him for about thirty minutes before calling in the nurse.

Some nurse. Toby had found that in spite of how much he disliked hospitals, he actually liked most of the nurses. Crisp, white uniforms, pleasant smells, and bodies underneath the starch that he could only guess at. He enjoyed guessing though, and was looking forward to trying when a man entered the examination room in response to the doctor's call.

After handing him two pills and a glass of water, the man led him to a room and left him there. Another man brought in some food a few minutes later, and Toby found that he was once again hungry enough to eat everything on the tray.

Stomach full, aches and pains slacking off some, Toby lay down on the bed and fell asleep almost immediately. He was dreaming about pretty nurses he had known when a persistent voice and gentle shaking tore him away from the pleasant image of smooth curves under white blouses.

Struggling awake, he sat up on the edge of the bed as the man's voice hammered through to his consciousness. ". . . and I'm sorry to wake you up, Toby, but I need to talk with you about something."

"Whatimisish?"

"Here, drink this."

Toby accepted the glass with both hands, feeling the cold, wet promise of what turned out to be orange juice. Suddenly very thirsty, he finished most of it in one long drink.

"More?"

"Uh huh. S'good."

"I'm sure it is. Those pain pills will do that to you."

Toby drank another full glass before the man spoke again.

"Feeling better?"

"Yes. Thanks. What time is it?"

"Late. I won't keep you long, but it's important that we have a talk now, get a few things settled before tomorrow."

Toby nodded, handed the glass to the man and stretched. He was stiff, and sore in a few spots, but he'd had worse injuries. "What about?"

"We should be leaving for Oasis tomorrow night. I want you to stay here, get a good night's rest, and I'll come get you about ten o'clock tomorrow morning. You'll have breakfast at the hospital, we'll have lunch and dinner together tomorrow, and when I'm not involved with other duties I want to work with you about how we'll handle your duties."

Toby nodded, still sleepy from the nap, and tried to assimilate what the man was saying. "My duties?"

"We'll go into detail in the morning, but from tomorrow night on you'll be with me most of the time until my mission is completed. We'll have plenty of time to talk about your future during the voyage."

The mention of his future got Toby's attention, and cut through the fog of sleep with no problem. "How long do you think it'll take?"

The man shrugged. "Too many uncertainties to predict. But the best thing you can do to hurry it along is to do your job well. Everything else will fall in place in due time." The man stood, walked to the door, and while appearing to test the lock with a key said, "You should be able to fall asleep quickly. Those pills last quite a while, and I'll tell the orderlies to wait for your call to bring breakfast. Goodnight."

Toby watched as the man closed the door and heard the lock snap shut.

Is that to keep me in, or someone else out?

THE MORNING AFTER THE INCIDENT WITH TOBY, BRETT LEFT HIS room with Lin for the vehicle assembly building and noticed a faint smell of burned wood. As they walked toward the massive doors into the side of the mountain, he glanced to his left down an alleyway between two buildings and saw what appeared to be the remains of a structure, leveled and still smoldering.

Lin was uncharacteristically tight-lipped, and had been so ever since yesterday evening. Brett asked him about the injury to his face, but he let the matter drop when Lin offered no explanation. Probably because it was a *wound,* and Brett was hoping they'd all kill one another off anyway.

Turn-around time had been completed in slightly better than the average time at NASA. Walking through on a last inspection, Brett couldn't help but contrast the current procedure with the original concept.

NASA had wanted a simple, reusable, and low-cost vehicle for use in supporting a space station. The only part they got right was the reusable. With almost every step of the development process there had been changes in what they wanted the shuttle to do, so that the result was a hodgepodge of capabilities.

Over the years since, the most significant changes had occurred with the decision to aggressively build and supply Oasis and the lunar colony. This fourth-generation shuttle benefited not only from the lessons learned and technical advances made by the earlier programs, but also from dedication to a single-purpose design.

Reducing turnaround time was absolutely critical to the effort. The process evolved from a slow, tedious, labor-intensive, step-by-step procedure to a relatively rapid, automated sequence that could be repeated with great efficiency. Brett had never been involved this closely with launch preparations before, but these people knew what they were doing.

Once in the cockpit, Brett monitored Lin performing various systems preflight tests. Usually this would be a crew task, but Lin wanted to do it by himself under supervision. As he watched the copilot work, Brett considered the reason for the request, and decided that it may well be in preparation for a time when Lin might be doing it alone. Interesting thought.

As was the comment Toby made last evening about the man wanting him to return to Oasis. There were so many questions, and so few answers. Brett felt completely isolated from reality. He had no clue as to the situation on Oasis, how he might be able to prevent the shuttle's return, whether he could ensure Toby's safety, and what the man's ultimate plan for him might be. He was pondering these uncertainties when Lin's voice interrupted him.

"Is this correct, Captain?"

～

SAMAEL APPROACHED THE SECURITY GUARD. "HOW THE HELL DID this happen?"

"Don't know. We got a call around five about an explosion. Might have been the heater. By the time the truck arrived it was fully involved."

"Anybody inside?"

"Not sure. Been too hot to get in close, but if you ask me there's a crispy critter over in that corner."

Samael nodded at the guard and stepped over some hoses, dodging a firefighter as he struggled to disconnect a fitting. Walking around to the corner where the bedroom had been, he didn't need to get particularly close to know there was a charred body visible in the remains of a bed.

Good. Looks like an accident, and there is no time for anyone to investigate. This should get things moving in my direction.

Appearing to inspect the fire-gutted building, Samael stayed at the scene for a while, then left and walked to the assault team assembly area. It was a large open warehouse structure with a smaller room at the rear. The sight of so many men busy preparing for combat stirred his blood, and he stopped to observe the activity.

No need to count them. Samael knew the plan called for one hundred men, divided into ten-member squads. There were nine groupings of men gathered loosely together, some cleaning weapons, others busy packing gear into duffle bags or reorganizing the equipment harnesses they wore. He had done that countless times also. Take everything out, try a new way, end up putting it back together the way someone had first taught you. Lessons born of experience usually have sound reasoning for what they teach.

All gear was black, and each man was assigned a number printed in white on his clothing. Squad leaders used numbers ten, twenty, and so on, with the numbers one through nine reserved for the leadership cadre.

None of these men had names, at least as far as any of the other men were concerned. They were recruited as mercenaries, and the number system provided a simple yet effective method of maintaining anonymity while allowing for ease of communication.

The man now reduced to charcoal in the burned-out building had been their leader. His untimely departure left a small but very important vacancy in the ranks, which probably was the topic of discussion at this moment in the room at the rear of the hangar. Samael could see a man with the numeral "3" on his clothing gesturing with his hands, agitated, obviously angry about something. There were eight other men in the room, and that's where Samael was headed.

Without hurrying, of course. He just dropped by to see how things were going, to say so long and good luck. Samael had trained many of the men, and they knew he had been the point man for the entire operation. They also knew what being "on point" meant, which gave Samael an advantage.

Stopping to talk with a man in the group nearest the room, Samael paid little attention to his own conversation as he waited for the right moment. He had positioned himself so he could see into the room without really looking at it. When Number Seven began speaking to Number Three, Samael excused himself abruptly and walked up to the room.

"Am I interrupting?" he asked as he opened the door. The conversation ceased, and all eyes were on him. "Something the matter?"

"Yeah, you could say that," said Number Two. "One died in a fire last night, and Three seems to have an objection to the rules of succession we established."

"You're damned right!" shouted Three. "He put the whole thing together, and it isn't a standard operation."

"Nobody ever said it was. But you had every opportunity to object before, or walk away if you didn't like the arrangements. You expect us just to drop it because one man bites the bullet?"

"He's not one man. He was the *main* man in case you hadn't noticed."

"Not quite true, gentlemen." It was Seven, and Samael closed the door and watched as the man came to the front of the group, and folded his arms over his chest. "From what I can gather, there's more to this than thinking One was indispensable. Five and Eight over there seem to have more of a problem with Two taking over than with One's absence."

This started a chorus of comments, everyone talking at the same time, evidence of a group without effective leadership.

"Hold On!" shouted Seven. As the room quieted down he continued. "We agreed command would transfer straight down the line. I don't remember hearing any alternatives offered. It's as if none of you ever considered that One would buy it, and now that it's happened you seem to question our earlier decision.

"Consider this. One wasn't the main man in the first place. Just to set the record straight, that man right there," said Seven, pointing at Samael, "planned this operation. He's already been there and back. I don't see any major pieces of his anatomy missing, which tells me he must have done something right."

Samael was smiling inside, but unreadable on the surface. *Keep it up, Seven.*

"I say put him in command. Anybody got a better idea?" Seven looked around the room, inviting input. Three took him up on it.

"His part in this is over. One said that from the beginning, and he's supposed to be gone by now."

"Lucky for this group he's not," said Five. "What a bunch of pussies. The reason for the succession rules among our group was to provide backup leadership. It's obvious to me the rest of you were erroneously assigned."

Samael was leaning against a wall, letting this play out. But with that comment he uncrossed his legs and got ready to move. This was a room full of dynamite, men who had been on both sides of the leader-follower equation, and who were volatile in more ways than one. The room filled with a tense quiet. Three looked ready to challenge Five about that insult when Seven prevented a serious situation from becoming a disaster.

"No need to fight among ourselves. I'd like to remind you all that we've contracted to do this. A failure to honor that commitment before we even get started would be more than hazardous to our combined health. Long arms reaching as far as you can run and the memory of an elephant make for an unforgiving employer. Wouldn't you agree?"

The question hung in the charged atmosphere like a fog, enveloping every man in the room. Samael held his breath as the implications of a self-generated failure seemed to sink in. He could sense the easing tension.

"So," said Seven, "are we unanimous?"

No one objected, although Samael knew not everyone agreed. He mentally noted the men who seemed to accept it, those who were uncertain, and especially those who opposed.

That bodyguard may come in handy. I'm going to be trapped on a space station with at least two, maybe three men who would just as soon see me dead.

Two looked at Samael. "No one bothered to ask you."

Success was so sweet. "I noticed. I also am in no way offended by the assumption I would accept, or by those of you who appear to be . . . how shall we say . . . reluctant. I have never considered leadership to be a mantle of privilege. I believe we must earn the right to lead. The moment I prove myself unworthy of your support, I'll relinquish command to the next in line and the rest of you can do as you will. Fair enough?"

There were nods, a few looks of satisfaction around the room, and the rest appeared uncommitted. It was time to take command and let them know who was really in charge.

"And now, for my first official act as commander, I pronounce sentence on a traitor."

Samael did this as well as any man alive, and a lot better than countless dead ones. He began the move while he was still talking. His hands were on his hips, and with his left hand coming up as if to punctuate the point he was about to make, his right hand reached behind his back. Instinctively he assessed the individual reactions among the men and made split-second decisions about which one or more might be a threat.

But he got them all looking at his left hand. If there really had been a traitor other than himself, that man would have been the most dangerous. But not this time, and he had the pistol out of his belt and past his right hip before he noticed any reactions to his move.

That changed immediately when he extended his arm and pulled the trigger, the bullet entering Three's skull just above the left eye and exiting in a shower of gore. As Three crumpled to the floor the other men reeled back in surprise and shock, most of them reaching for weapons in habit patterns developed through years of experience in a dangerous profession. Samael expected nothing less, and was ready with a calculated response.

He dropped the pistol on the floor. "Hold!" he shouted, "I'm unarmed," and held his hands held out and visible to the other men. The next few seconds would make the difference between success and failure.

In the ringing aftermath of the gunshot within the confined space of the room, Samael stood perfectly still as he waited to see what would happen. Some of the men outside in the assembly area had grabbed for weapons and were cautiously approaching the door. Seven held his hand out in a "stop" gesture, then motioned for the men to back away. It was time for Samael to speak.

"I'm at the mercy of the group, but hear this before you act. Three opposed Two's becoming commander and the suggestion that I take over because he was planning to do that himself. You can check it out for yourselves. He planted a device under One's quarters and murdered him early this morning."

"How in the hell do you know that?" It was Two, pointing his pistol directly at Samael's chest.

"I have been investigating that possibility since I got back from the station. One had suspicions, and asked me to stick around and see what I could find out."

"Some investigator you are. Why didn't you prevent it if you knew so much?" Five walked between Two's weapon and Samael, and stood close to him, looking into his eyes.

He thinks he can catch me in a lie, that I'm not good enough to hide it when my life is on the line.

"I didn't know about the bomb until this morning. I had evidence pointing to Three from other sources, but all indications were that the move would be made after departure. I should have considered the possibility of an earlier attempt and discovered the bomb before the fact."

Five's expression remained unchanged for what seemed like an eternity, then softened somewhat. Samael instantly knew he had bought the explanation. Turning away to face the group, Five said, "Okay. I'd like to have more time to check this out, but under the circumstances we have to decide now, gentlemen. You either believe him or not. Which is it?"

Samael watched carefully as one by one the men appeared to decide in his favor. He also noted that Two was the last to do so, and filed that detail away for future reference.

"You sure made a mess in here . . . One? Is that what we call you?"

Samael turned to Five. "I would recommend we do that. Eight, have two men come in here and remove the body. Somebody call the custodians and tell them to clean this place up. I'm going to my quarters for my gear, and I want to meet with you men in one hour. Where can we do that?"

"There's a conference room off the command post," said Two.

"I'll see you there at ten thirty hours." He then knelt down, picked up his pistol, replaced it behind his back and walked out of the room.

The assault team members were standing in groups, watching everything. Samael walked in a straight line toward the large hanger type door at the far end of the assembly area, intentionally causing some of the men to move out of his way. It wouldn't take five minutes for every one of them to hear the details, and his reputation would be firmly established as a commander worthy of respect, loyalty, and a healthy dose of fear.

WHEN BRETT ARRIVED AT THE HANGAR AFTER A PRE-LAUNCH nap, the shuttle was in the vertical position but still in the pre-launch building. It would not be towed out until just prior to launch, a precaution necessary for keeping all the activity hidden from the prying eyes of reconnaissance satellites. Surprise was the key to avoiding interference.

Procedures for Earth launch usually called for completion of cargo loading before raising the vehicle into a vertical position. The size and weight of the larger components made it impractical to load them in any other way. Fueling, however, was always performed with the shuttle vertical, and after the cargo was on board. The only exception to this sequence was for passenger flights, to avoid the unnecessary risk of refueling with a cargo bay full of people.

The passenger-boarding gantry consisted of a ladder and a platform positioned adjacent to a side door in the shuttle. Ladders were also temporarily installed within the interior. Passengers climbed the external ladder, entered through the door, then climbed or descended to their assigned rows. A horizontal set of stepping pads provided access into the rows and the individual seats.

Lin was being his usual busy-beaver self, and Brett allocated a small portion of his attention to monitoring him while the rest considered his situation and what he could do about it.

Short of being killed trying to escape or taking his own life, he had no way to avoid returning to Oasis. The fighter was offloaded, obviously for the purpose of reverse engineering. He hadn't seen Toby or the hijacker in more than two days, but apparently the three of them were in this together one more time. The last word he had received indicated the bomb had been disabled, and the hijacker didn't know that.

Brett tried to come up with a reason why the hijacker would bring Toby. It was obvious he never planned to take him to Earth, which meant hostages weren't part of the plan. Why would the man need one with the bomb as leverage?

But Toby had inserted himself into the equation. Maybe the hijacker figured Toby's presence on the return trip would provide extra insurance against Brett trying something. He might have notified the authorities he had Toby, but it probably wouldn't make any difference.

Looking at the problem from the perspective of the decision-makers, Brett believed the situation would change decisively the moment they realized losing the shuttle and the fighter wasn't the end of it. Within a very short time after launch, they would have to consider the new threat to the station. Their options would include destruction of the shuttle, or at the very least a decision to prevent it from docking with Oasis. The threat of death against a pilot, especially one who volunteered, or even a teenager, would never tip the scales enough in favor of the hijacker.

In spite of the uncertainty before him, Brett began to doze off. The combination of a large pre-launch meal, the reclined seat, and fitful sleep over the past few nights caught up with him. He was dreaming Toby had escaped and they launched without him when the sound of voices awoke him with a start.

Looking behind him, he saw the masked figure climbing into the cockpit, and heard the familiar voice of his young friend acknowledge an order to strap into a crew seat.

I guess that answers that.

WITHOUT THE BENEFIT OF EXTENSIVE TRAINING IT COULD HAVE turned into a disaster. Samael had insisted from the beginning on strict discipline and unhesitating obedience to orders. Each of the men picked for the assault team was interviewed with that in mind, and he rejected a number of otherwise outstanding applicants because they might have had problems integrating into a cohesive unit.

Loading went very smoothly. Usually he would have liked to dry run something as complicated as this, but there wasn't time. There was no horseplay, and not much talking. Halfway through the process he left the gantry and made his way into the cargo bay. He was impressed with the efficiency of movement as the men snaked up and down the ladders and into the rows of seats. Even these grown men could have become unruly from the excitement of it. The fact that space travel was routine didn't mean it was common, and the vast majority of people had never been near a shuttle, much less traveled on one.

The shuttle was transferred from the hangar out to the launch position so smoothly he wasn't aware of movement until they were just clearing the hangar doors. The pilot seemed impressed with the speed this was accomplished, and said NASA's tractors were much slower. He also mentioned the shuttles were normally moved to the launch pads and sat there while final preparations were made. Of course NASA had no reason to hide launch preparations, and wasn't in the business of surprise shuttle flights.

From the beginning of the operation, planning sessions had emphasized the requirement for secrecy. And although the possibility of interference was minimal, they took every precaution to stay out of sight. Once the hangar doors were opened, there wasn't much time to contemplate things before the shuttle was clear of the structure and final countdown began.

Samael's first launch was nothing like his second. Riding the jump seat was infinitely better than being stuffed in a box, and this time he was awake to experience all the sensations.

He would never forget the feeling. Main engine ignition was accompanied by awesome sound and vibration, along with a light so bright it seemed as if the sun were rising behind the shuttle. The two solid rocket boosters ignited and the massive ship seemed to suddenly free itself and with astounding grace lift off the pad and accelerate into the night sky.

He had been briefed on the basics of the launch sequence, but the words simply couldn't prepare him for it. Samael almost passed out about twenty seconds into the launch when the shuttle rolled 180 degrees onto its back and he was looking out the windscreen at the inverted horizon. He knew that the boosters were supposed to separate about two minutes after liftoff, but without the mission clock on the instrument panel he wouldn't have known it happened. Another worrisome moment occurred at about eight minutes when the shuttle's main engines seemed to throttle back, and Samael looked over at the pilot to observe his reaction. The captain appeared to be sleeping. A short time later the engines throttled back again, then quit abruptly. Even in the midst of his sudden concern, Samael was amazed at how smooth and silent the ride was. About ten seconds later, he felt something and asked the pilot what it was.

"External tank separation."

I knew that. He concluded it was all over for the time being and tried to remember what came next when the orbital maneuvering system fired to boost the shuttle into a higher orbit and circularize it.

And then it became boring. The pilot worked with Lin doing whatever pilots do en route to the moon. After a while Samael realized the Earth wasn't getting any smaller. He didn't know a lot about it, but was sure you had to leave the Earth behind to get to the moon.

"What happens next?"

The pilot looked at him with an expression of barely veiled disgust. "Just like leaving the moon, we have to use Earth's gravity to slingshot us out of parking orbit to achieve escape velocity. And we have to do that at the correct time so that we intercept the moon about four days from now. It wouldn't be a good idea to miss it."

"You mean we could miss it?" Samael couldn't remember anything about missing something as big as the moon.

The pilot smiled a little. "Well, we don't want to hit it exactly, but pass close enough and at the correct speed so that lunar gravity grabs us into orbit. It's a small window, with some real bad shit waiting if we screw up."

Not really wanting to hear about bad shit at the moment, Samael let the matter drop and waited patiently for something to happen.

After a few orbits, he found it hard to tell how many, the main engines fired and he was on his way to a new destiny of his own making.

∼

SAMAEL WAS VERY CAREFUL TO ENSURE HIS CAPTIVE REMAINED restrained. But with a trained copilot available, he decided to alternate their time on the flight deck and allowed the pilot to sleep in one of the crew rooms.

A side benefit of that arrangement enabled him to meet with his officers and squad leaders in the galley area and talk freely without being heard. Samael set up daily meetings to discuss en route training and activities for the men. Their problem was unique. No one had any experience with how to maintain the physical and mental edge of men trained to perfection in assault tactics during a period of relative inactivity in zero gravity.

Keeping busy was the key, and the squads rotated through a series of activities. They practiced moving about in weightlessness. Multi-station exercise machines using internal resistance were bolted to the floor in one corner of the bay, and the men took turns on the circuit.

Samael had designated another area for briefings. Squad leaders set up easels and used diagrams of the space station to review assault tactics and areas of responsibility. The men would form a semi-circle, seated and strapped to the floor, while the squad leader stood by the easel with his boots fitted into clamps.

He would have preferred to give the men access to their personal gear, but decided to leave it stored on the pallets. Soldiers have an irresistible impulse to unpack, check, and repack their combat gear. He had watched men all over the world do it. But in the zero gravity environment of the shuttle, there was too much potential for loose items. He didn't want any arguments over who belonged to which knife.

Such disagreements often ended in fights. The squad leaders assured him they had personally checked every man's pack, and that would have to do.

His relationship with Toby was turning out well. Samael spent a few hours each day strengthening it by eating meals with him and going over the details of what he would be doing in his capacity as a bodyguard. But when he noticed a casual attitude creeping into the boy's actions, he decided to crank down the screws a bit.

He took Toby into the galley for the daily meeting with his staff and squad leaders. Their initial collective response had been nothing more than curiosity as to what the boy was doing there. But when it became apparent Toby would remain through the meeting, things changed. Before it was over, Samael had identified no less than five of the group who displayed open hostility. His purpose was twofold, and the move appeared to have worked on both counts.

Positive that sooner or later there would be an attempt on his life, he wanted his attackers off balance, and he needed Toby's powers up and running, with the boy scared enough to be alert.

One look in Toby's eyes after the meeting confirmed the result. Samael added a comment or two about how dangerous these men were, and the us-versus-them situation became well established. From then on he took Toby with him wherever he went and firmly settled the issue for all concerned. The staff and squad leaders had to get used to the fact that the boy was always there, and Toby always appeared nervous and tense in their presence.

With the situation on the shuttle handled, Samael was in full control of his immediate future. And although he had no direct way to affect what the other major players were doing, he felt confident they would not be able to interfere.

His employer was effectively out of the loop. By taking control of the assault team, Samael had put himself in the position of holding all the cards. They either played the game his way, or they lost it all.

The United States government had probably been rendered help-less. Whatever their objective had been, the encounter with the fighters had been settled in his favor. At this point the possibility of Earth-based interference had been eliminated.

Oasis authorities were undoubtedly operating under the direction of POTUS through NASA. But Samael was certain that when it came down to taking specific action, the Oasis commander would be given broad discretionary powers in selecting a plan and determining the appropriate response to conditions as they changed. In the absence of direct orders to the contrary, he also knew the general would act in the interest of saving lives. If they hadn't believed in the bomb, they would have never let him leave Oasis with the shuttle. For the same reason, they would be unable to prevent him from returning.

Unless, of course, they had managed to disable the bomb. Unlikely, but he had to consider it. What would he do in their place?

Simple. Lock the place up tight and don't let them dock. If that turned out to be the situation, Samael would be unable to do much about it, except return to Earth with a reasonable chance to escape.

Barring that possibility, he also had no doubt the assault teams could take control, and probably without firing a shot. The original plan called for nothing more than brute force to overwhelm the relatively small police contingent on the station. Learning the station police were issued weapons with special ammunition could have been a serious problem. But disaster was averted by his capture of the cop and the sidearm. Samael's allies had analyzed the bullet material and manufactured it in quantity. His assault teams were now equipped with the same ammunition. Although he didn't expect armed resistance, they would be ready in case he was wrong.

With nothing left to do for the moment, the waiting became like an intermission prior to the final act. Samael would consider every contingency more than once before they arrived at the station, but he was confident no major flaws existed.

Oasis, here I come.

19

DAYS EIGHTEEN THROUGH TWENTY

General DeSilva was being subjected once again to an inevitable reality of life. He had been convinced it couldn't get any worse as he watched the shuttle depart, knowing his career was down the toilet, his legacy established as the commander who lost hundreds of millions of dollars' worth of spacecraft to one man. But he was wrong.

The next few days were like a dream, sitting in the War Room monitoring the attempts to find and disarm the bomb. The two cops provided valuable information, but the evidence supported only one logical conclusion. The man wasn't bluffing.

The corporal had been able to examine the bomb and its associated arming system in great detail. When technicians analyzed his debriefing and combined it with the video, they concluded it would be suicide to attempt a breach of the reactor room's outer perimeter.

So his only choice was to watch and wait. The reports of the attempted intercept and loss of two fighters were of only passing interest, and DeSilva was privately relieved when the shuttle disappeared. His only remaining objectives before suffering the shame of a forced retirement were to eliminate the bomb threat, bring his people back from the moon colony, and turn over a relatively undamaged space station to his successor.

And then the duty officer charged into his office and brought the news. The shuttle was on its way back. At that moment, General DeSilva became absolutely convinced that he must have done something to deserve eternal existence in perpetual agony. This current nightmare simply would not end.

NASA seemed incapable of making a decision. A debate raged about whether the hijackers really would allow the bomb to detonate if Oasis were the final objective. They considered destroying the shuttle when it arrived, or locking Oasis down to prevent the shuttle from docking, or allowing it to dock and then defending the interior of Oasis.

As far as General DeSilva was concerned, the analysts were spending far too much time hypothesizing what could be done under the assumption the bomb was a bluff. But bombs had detonated on Oasis, and that's all the proof DeSilva needed.

Hours of contemplation had produced very little progress until he allowed himself the luxury of devising his own plan. He asked himself a hypothetical question about what would be the perfect solution to the current problem. And the answer was, recover the shuttle, deny the bad guys use of the station, and eliminate the bomb and anyone associated with it as a threat.

Then he tried to figure out a way to do that and ran up against the same stone wall until he got past his own self-imposed fear about letting the shuttle dock. What if the hens weren't in the hen house, the foxes were allowed inside, and he locked the door behind them?

General DeSilva drafted a message to NASA explaining his idea, but didn't send it. His decision was prompted by a combination of two cardinal rules in the military. First, don't ask the question if you can't stand the answer, and second, it's always better to ask for forgiveness than permission.

The general felt the uncertainty of the past few weeks lift from his shoulders. And although he trusted his staff, he purposely conducted his preparations quietly just to make certain the Oasis rumor mill didn't jeopardize his ability to act swiftly when the time came. He needed the element of surprise on his side, not only for its effect on the bad guys, but also for its ability to spur his own people into action.

Welcome back, mister. Come on in, the door's open.

Lying in the hospital bed, Andras gritted his teeth against the pain of his wounds and the frustration of failure. The collapse of his plan to find and kill the bastard was bad enough, but mild in comparison to having a second chance and no way to take advantage of it.

His wounds were serious, but the new ammo had probably saved his life. The first shot hit him in the leg. He was on his way down when he was hit two more times. The vest stopped one, and the third was a glancing blow to the side of the face. The spreading of the special bullet combined with the angle caused substantial tissue damage without penetrating very deeply. He was disfigured, but he would survive.

Andras avoided being evacuated to the moon colony by convincing the doctor he was too sick to travel. Rumors were flying around about the shuttle coming back, and he couldn't check it out lying in a hospital bed. He'd been trying to come up with a solution to the problem all morning when he heard a familiar voice outside his room.

It was Dan, talking with someone at the nursing station. Andras thought he'd been evacuated to the moon colony. *What's he doing back on Oasis, and what does he know about my dealings with the hijacker?* Only one way to find out.

"Hey, Dan! It's Andras! I'm in room seventeen!" Andras waited for a few seconds before the door to his room eased open. Dan peered in, and seemed to pull up short at the sight of Andras's condition.

"Hello, Sergeant. How you doing?"

"I'll live. I thought you'd been evacuated."

"I was. I objected, but they ordered me to get out. Said they didn't need me and I'd just be in the way."

"What changed?"

"I healed up fast, for one thing. I wasn't hurt that bad. With these new developments it was easy to talk them into letting me come back."

Andras sat up in bed, wincing with the pain but doing his best to ignore it. This was his way out. "Tell me all about it. I don't hear jack shit in here."

Dan walked over to the corner of the room and sat in a chair. "The shuttle's on its way back. Took everyone by surprise. They flew it to somewhere in Asia, at least that's what the rumors say, and we lost a couple of fighters trying to intercept it."

"Lost fighters to a shuttle?"

"Somebody else got involved. Details are sketchy, but apparently it was the result of a fighter-to-fighter engagement. Anyway, the shuttle disappeared for a week or so, then launched from there with no warning. Everyone thought we'd just lost one, kiss its ass goodbye, and now we know exactly where it is and can't do a damned thing about it. The press are calling it 'Shuttlegate.'"

To hell with the press. "The brass have any ideas why they're coming back? And do we know Oasis is the destination rather than the moon colony?"

Dan shook his head. "Not at this level, anyway. If they know something, they aren't saying."

"What do you think?"

Dan looked at Andras as if he'd asked him to explain the theory of relativity. Andras knew why, of course. This was probably the first time he'd ever asked Dan his opinion about anything.

"Uh . . . well . . . I think everybody figured they only wanted the two spacecraft. But now it appears the shuttle was just a means to an end. Unless they brought a lunar shuttle with them, they can't make it to the colony without taking Oasis first."

If a corporal can come up with it, surely the idiots in the War Room can. "I bet you're right. That's why you're back, isn't it? Have every cop here to help stop it?"

Dan laughed softly. "Not hardly. I had to beg them to let me come back. Told them I'd be useful in the event of a complete evacuation, help get everybody off. They bought it, and it's in the emergency plan anyway. Cops are the last ones to leave."

"So there's no plans to fight for the station?"

"Not from what I can see."

Andras's mind began working overtime. Here was an opportunity to get out of this if he played his hand right, but he'd need Dan's help. He was also worried Dan might suspect his complicity in all of this, or at least be aware of his shoot-to-kill authorization when Dan was being held captive.

Andras had to know if he could trust Dan, and he made the snap decision to ignore the first problem for the moment and concentrate on the second.

"I need to talk to you about our decision to go in when you were held captive in the core."

Dan looked at him with a completely neutral expression and said, "What is there to discuss?"

Something hidden may be going on here. Dan had to know about it. *Why isn't he mad? I sure as hell would be.*

"I want you to understand the reasons why the Battle Staff decided to try and stop the guy. It was—"

"Excuse me, Sergeant Cadogan, but there's no reason to explain. I know the decision was made in the best interests of the station. I would never have expected it to be altered for me or anyone else. In situations like that you do what you have to do."

"Okay, but when you're the one left out there hanging it's not so easy to see it that way. Did you know we had shoot-to-kill authorization?"

Dan nodded. He didn't respond for a few seconds, then added, "The other guys seemed embarrassed, or maybe guilty about it, almost as if it was their fault. I told them the same thing I'll tell you.

"I knew it might come to that, and it wouldn't matter who was in there. We all take the same risks in this job. It was my turn in the barrel, and . . . well . . . here I am. Must have been my lucky day."

"What happened to you in there?"

"Long story. I'm sure you also have a tale to tell, but I've got to get back to work. Bring you anything?"

Andras shook his head and motioned for Dan to come closer to the bed. "Do you agree with letting that bastard take over the station? Assuming that's what this is all about."

"What does my agreeing with it or not have to do with anything? If they tell me to leave I guess that's what I'll do."

"What if I told you I plan to stop this guy, or die trying? Would you help me?"

Dan grinned. "With what? The trying or the dying?"

Andras grinned back, at least the best he could. He'd refused to look at himself in a mirror, and asked the nurses to remove the door to the medicine cabinet in the bathroom. Dan didn't seem particularly grossed out by what he saw, however, and that was good.

"I'm definitely not planning on the dying part. But you and I both have good reason to disobey orders, if it comes to that. It's real personal with me, and I bet it is with you too."

"You're right. But you may be jumping the gun. They could decide to fight. I just got back today, and I don't know what the situation is. What if they've found a way to defuse that bomb?"

"That's what I mean. I can't find out anything. These damned hospital toads won't tell me what's going on. I'm sure they know. It's impossible to keep a secret around here."

Dan was shaking his head. "So what? Why are we talking about this? There's no way you can do anything, all bandaged up like that."

Without a word, Andras pulled back the sheets on the bed and swung his legs over the side. Then he stood up, and managed to keep a straight face in spite of the pain. Dan reached out, but Andras shrugged off the assistance.

"I'm not hurt as bad as it looks. I got the doc, he owes me a few favors, to declare me too sick to be moved so they wouldn't send me to the colony. I'll be ready to go when the time comes. How far out is the shuttle?"

"Not sure. I would guess a couple days."

"Good. I'm getting up at night when the nurses are out there doing their nails, or whatever it is they do rather than check up on me. I can accomplish my own rehab right here. Look at this stuff."

Andras walked unsteadily over to a closet and opened it. There was a pile of physical training equipment on the floor. "I've got these weights. I can put them on my ankles or wrists, and these rubber-band things work great. I asked the doc to send over a trainer, and he showed me a program that's designed to get my strength back."

Dan sat back in the chair. "That's fine, Sergeant, but I still don't see what this has to do with us."

That's my cue.

"I was waiting for you to say that. Let me get some water and I'll be more than happy to tell you."

Dan was on his way from the hospital back to Police Central when he decided to extend his break and visit one of the quick-stop refreshment stands scattered about the station. Although many of them were shut down because of the evacuation, he knew there was one close by when he smelled the aroma of brewing coffee. After a short search following his nose, he took a seat in the corner of the small eating area and sipped the hot liquid as he thought about his conversation with Andras.

He'd never liked the sergeant. Andras's style had always been dictatorial, with no indication he ever wanted, much less needed, your opinion. But there was a marked difference in the way Andras treated him in the hospital room. It was almost as if the man cared what he thought. During the last hour Dan felt accepted as a real partner and not a flunky.

Confused as to what he should do next, Dan poured a second cup of coffee and returned to his seat. He had to make up his mind how he felt about three separate, and yet connected, issues.

Something didn't feel right about Andras and the hijacker. There was the sports bag stuffed in the man's duffle. And what about the radios? The hijacker appeared glad to have obtained Dan's, like it was a great stroke of luck. Then seemingly out of nowhere the man had two, and possibly a third. If he'd brought them with him, why was he so interested in taking one from a cop?

But the real source of Dan's unease was from the incident in the reactor room. Because while the police attempt to capture the hijacker and the shoot-to-kill authorization were logical, Andras's individual actions were hard to understand.

Andras Cadogan may not be a shining example of an effective supervisor, but when it came down to procedure, particularly in tactical situations, he did it by the book. Dan could not understand why Andras got himself in that situation without backup. He could only conclude the sergeant had acted out of some personal agenda, like trying to take the hijacker by himself.

Was any of this sufficient evidence not to trust him? For whatever reason, and it might well be nothing more than revenge, the sergeant wanted to plan for armed intervention even if it meant ignoring orders to abandon the station or allowing an uncontested takeover. He was ready to continue alone if he had to.

Dan's thoughts kept coming back to the realization he felt the same way. His own motivation stemmed from the day of the initial incident when he elected to enter the shuttle's cargo bay by himself and helped the hijacker accomplish his objectives. In a thoughtless attempt to further his own career, he'd handed the man three things that might have ensured his success, If given the chance to correct that grievous error, he knew in his heart he couldn't turn it down.

Partners again. Who would have ever thought it?

THE TRIP BACK TO OASIS PASSED QUICKLY FOR TOBY. ALTHOUGH he wished the visit to Earth could have lasted longer, it did help satisfy some of his curiosity. He wouldn't have to take any more insults from the other kids, and he was going to make sure they knew the man had promised he could go back to Earth, finish his education, and learn to fly.

And he was on an important mission, as part of the solution to real problems. They would settle the current crisis, get the people back from the moon colony, and life would return to normal. He missed his parents, and looked forward to hanging out with Rooster.

Twice a day the man took Toby to the exercise area in the cargo bay. They spent an hour or so using the machines, and Toby discovered he enjoyed the feeling of a good workout. He decided to become more active in sports, and knew his dad would like that.

During his second visit to the bay, Toby remembered Snooper. The stacked cargo had been removed, and along with it the container where he left the dog. He wondered what had happened to him, and felt a sense of sadness at the loss of a faithful companion. Toby hoped Snooper had gotten away, was free on Earth, and enjoying the wide-open spaces. It didn't matter that Snooper was a robot. He deserved some fun too.

One evening the man came to his room and told him they'd be docking late tomorrow.

"What'll happen when we get there?"

"I don't expect any trouble with the docking. They have nothing to gain. Once we leave the shuttle, your purpose is to remain alert and warn me of any threats.

"Remember that we cannot let anyone stand in the way. It doesn't matter if they're acting directly against us or simply trying to defend the station. Do you remember what that means to you?"

"I'm not to relax my guard when around people I know, friends or not. I'm to consider everyone an enemy, and be ready to warn you."

The man smiled. "Very good, Toby. And you know that my men are no less suspect. We can expect someone among them to betray me. It will come in the form of a sudden attack. It's you and me against all the rest of them, right?"

"Yes, sir. But you also said there'll come a time when—"

"Yes, but for now you must forget all about the future. No daydreaming. It's second-by-second, minute-by-minute, you know the drill. Okay?"

"Okay," answered Toby.

But was it?

～

BRETT WOKE UP WITH A START, CONFUSED AS TO WHAT DAY IT was. Then he remembered they would dock with Oasis later this afternoon.

A knock on his door signaled the arrival of breakfast. Brett unzipped his sleeping bag as Lin entered, set the food tray down and snapped the hooks that kept it from floating around. Brett finished breakfast, completed his normal morning routine, and waited for Lin to return.

He had decided to be ready for the unexpected by reducing his workload as much as possible during the docking. Lin wanted to manually dock the shuttle, he was more than qualified, and Brett agreed to let him. Hopefully he'd never be able to make use of the training again.

Lin returned to escort Brett to the cockpit. As he exited his room behind Lin, Brett glanced down the corridor toward the door onto the landing high above the cargo bay floor. It was open for the first time during the trip, and he could see into the bay. The view sent a shiver of cold fear through him. The bay was crawling with men, dressed in the same black uniforms and armed to the teeth. He'd acknowledged to himself the probability that the takeover would succeed no matter what anyone did trying to prevent it, but this sudden, ominous confirmation of the hijacker's preparation and intent removed the last measure of Brett's hope.

Lin waited while Brett strapped in to the left seat and then secured the waist restraint. As the copilot took his position, Brett performed a quick check of the cockpit and found everything to be in order. He had to admit that Lin was exceedingly meticulous in the performance of his duties. In other circumstances, they might have made a good team, and very possibly been friends.

Space travel was totally automated. No pilot worth the name liked to admit it, but the crew could have gone into hibernation for the journey and it would make no difference. Departure from Earth-parking orbit had occurred with Brett and Lin doing nothing more than staring at the flight displays when the main engines fired to accelerate the shuttle to about 25,000 mph for the free coast to the moon.

Until the shuttle outran Earth's gravitational pull on the third day, speed steadily decreased to about 3000 mph. Once crossing the "speed bump," lunar gravity took hold and the shuttle began accelerating toward rendezvous with the Moon and lunar orbital insertion using the Moon's gravitational field to "capture" the shuttle.

But because en route speeds were too high to accomplish that maneuver, and failure to decelerate properly risked the dreaded "skip" past the Moon and subsequent never-ending journey to nowhere, the thrust of the main engines in a controlled burn had established the shuttle in an elliptical orbit, subsequently circularized to await final rendezvous with Oasis.

The shuttle was currently established in an approach orbit higher than the space station, at a slower speed, with Oasis closing from behind. Final rendezvous and docking could also be accomplished hands-off, but the tolerance for error was so critical that pilots always maintained an especially close watch and were prepared to take manual control.

In this case Lin would hand-fly the shuttle through the docking with Brett acting as a safety observer. The rules were precise and well understood. Lin was in complete control of the shuttle and would perform the maneuver without instruction from Brett.

As they completed final preparations, Brett considered taking control during the latter stages even if Lin had the maneuver wired. It would shake the copilot's confidence. It might also affect the hijacker's trust in Lin, which could in turn alter his plans. Brett had another concern, that whenever the hijacker considered Lin capable of operating the shuttle solo, his own usefulness would cease. Why keep an extra pilot around you have to guard all the time?

Brett and Lin had nothing more to do than monitor the autopilot as it established initial approach orbit. At this point, the shuttle was traveling backwards in a higher orbit and slower speed than Oasis, which was catching up for final rendezvous and docking. Brett had been so involved with the cockpit that when he looked out the windscreen the sight almost took his breath away. No matter how many times he'd seen it, the effect was the same. There sat Oasis, bright against the black of deep space, the stark lunar surface bathed in sunlight, and it filled Brett with the wonderment of having traveled 240,000 miles in less than 80 hours from liftoff.

Brett sensed movement behind him as the hijacker entered the cockpit, Toby following like a puppy. As the hijacker sat in the jump seat, he told Toby to strap in to one of the auxiliary crew chairs against the rear bulkhead, and then spoke into a hand-held radio. Brett caught the word "minutes," glanced at the time-to-go readout, and guessed he was providing a countdown to docking.

The crew normally wore full suits during docking, but the hijacker had ordered them not to. Lin had beads of perspiration glistening on his forehead, and when the hijacker ordered him to turn on the ship's radios, Brett noticed a slight tremor in the copilot's left hand and arm as he reached for radio panel and flipped on the master switch. Nervous pilots make mistakes, and Brett repositioned his seat forward to be ready at the controls just in case. It also occurred to him he might not have to make up an excuse to take control.

Brett returned his attention to the spectacular view out the windscreen when from behind him the hijacker reached out to the center console and flipped the switch to make the jump seat microphone hot. In spite of knowing what was coming, the words still made Brett jump.

"To the Commander, Space Station Oasis, do you read me?"

A DISTRESSINGLY FAMILIAR VOICE FILLED THE ROOM FROM THE overhead speakers, breaking the expectant silence as the men in Command Central peered out the window at the approaching shuttle. General DeSilva had been watching the small, bright dot of light, and as usual got the impression that the shuttle was much too far away to be able to rendezvous on this pass. It was hard to comprehend the closure rates involved at this point.

He sighed and snatched up the handset off the console. "This is General DeSilva of the Space Station Oasis. Go ahead."

"Good afternoon. I presume you've had advanced notification of our return visit, and you're prepared for us to rendezvous and dock."

"We're expecting you at loading dock seven."

"Seven? No . . . I don't like that number. How about five? That's it. Five will do just fine."

What a prick. It takes hours to set up a dock. "You'll either have to use seven or wait."

"I think not. We'll use five and not wait. Get it done, General."

DeSilva waited to answer, giving the illusion of a hurried decision process. In reality they could use any of the docks with minimal preparation. When it got busy around here they cycled shuttles in and out like a drive-through quick-lube.

"We'll try, but you may have to make another pass. I can't open the doors to five until the area is ready." DeSilva wanted the man thinking something was afoot, that some intricate plan was being thwarted by the change in loading docks. The hijacker would be suspicious, and aggressive in his approach to disembarking the shuttle.

DeSilva ordered the move, which took no more than ten minutes. Now all they had to do was watch the shuttle rendezvous and dock. Everything was in place, the station's personnel primed and ready for action.

In the absence of direct orders to the contrary, General DeSilva had made his move, unwilling to sit back and do nothing. They may judge him harshly, but they would never be able to accuse him of indecision in a time of crisis.

Speaking over the station's public address system, he gave the order.

"Open the doors to the hen house."

DAN DIDN'T LIKE DISOBEYING ORDERS. AND IF THERE HADN'T been so much going on he probably wouldn't have been able to get away with it. Everybody he passed in the halls was in a hurry, rushing around to take care of last-minute items, and Dan made sure he appeared the same way. When the general's order to open the doors came over the PA, Dan hurried to the nearest chute entrance and climbed inside. He did *not* like it in here. It was way too confining. *Don't think about it and hurry up.*

He made his way through the chutes to the exit closest to his apartment, dropped down to the floor and entered his apartment.

Over the past few days he'd managed to stockpile what he needed, and it took him only a few minutes to dress for combat.

Checking his watch, Dan confirmed the docking would occur in about an hour. It never ceased to amaze him, but from the moment a shuttle launched from Earth they knew within a very narrow time frame when it would dock. All those miles with so much precision. The last time he'd flown on a commercial jet, the airline hadn't been able to takeoff within an hour of schedule, much less land on time.

Dan checked his radio. Andras had provided him with one set to a discrete frequency, unmonitored by any other radios on Oasis. The ability to communicate would be essential, and they'd agreed on a radio check thirty minutes prior to the shuttle's scheduled arrival. Almost time.

He went to the bathroom, then rummaged through his gear for a food bar and ate it as he rechecked his weapons. The bar made him thirsty, so he went to the kitchen and filled a water bottle. He might be hiding for a while, and he knew from experience the tension would make his mouth dry. He was taking a long drink when the radio came alive.

"Delta Bravo, you up?"

Dan spilled water all over his chest as he reached for the radio, sending the water bottle crashing into the sink. Silently cursing his clumsiness, he keyed the mike button and answered, "Roger that."

"How's activity over your way?"

"Quiet. Most of the remaining lifeship pods are concentrated near essential work areas. The living quarters are deserted."

"Don't count on that. Proceed with caution when you leave for the core. Use the chutes. If you run into any brass it could mean trouble explaining what you're doing. I don't want to have to use force against our own."

Dan could just see himself taking down another officer. Just how dedicated *was* he to this plan? "Copy that. You leaving now?"

"Already gone. I'll be in position before the shuttle arrives and get a look at things. Let's talk again on the hour."

Twenty-five minutes from now. "Okay. Delta Bravo out."

"Alpha Charlie out."

Dan refilled the water bottle, put it in his pack, and paused to look around the tiny apartment he had called home since arriving on Oasis years ago. He wouldn't really miss it, but for some reason it saddened him. He cared nothing about anything *in* the apartment because he didn't bring anything of personal value with him from Earth, and Oasis was far from a shopper's paradise.

No, the pause wasn't about things, but the sense of duty and commitment to other cops, even Andras, and especially to those who would come after Dan. He left the apartment and hurried toward the most important thing he would probably ever do for the rest of his life, however long that might be.

Dan wasn't particularly religious, but if he survived this, he just might renew his relationship with a higher power.

ANDRAS WAS A BIG MAN, AND INJURED TO BOOT, SO THE CHUTES were out. But he'd studied diagrams of the station and plotted a route to the central core that avoided the areas most likely to be active. He saw a few people, but they'd walked past without looking at him. Maybe the sight of a disfigured cop in full combat gear was something they had no desire to acknowledge.

His wounds were still painful, which made for slow going, and one of the bandages felt wet. But he needed to be in position in the central core prior to the shuttle docking, and if he couldn't take the man down, the condition of his wounds didn't matter.

Andras had done a lot of thinking while confined to the hospital. The end result of those contemplative hours was a profound sense of shame. He finally admitted to himself that in his previously distorted view of the world, the blame was always shifted to other people. None of the disappointments in his life was ever his fault. His motivation to get back at "them" was the driving factor behind his decision to help those bastards take the shuttle. Now that he'd seen the results of his actions, it was as if he'd suddenly awakened to the truth.

And a harsh truth it was. He allowed his own failures to cloud his judgment to the point that he considered it acceptable to betray his country, his fellow crew members, and himself. With that conclusion at center stage, Andras reviewed the scenes of his life like a bad play and decided to change the final act.

Although he would have preferred using the Alpha Team, having Dan to help him was a stroke of luck. With the general's orders to avoid confrontation, Andras couldn't very well have eight to ten cops doing exactly the opposite.

But two of them might just pull it off. Dan was mobile, and could track the target. Andras couldn't move about very well, but he wouldn't have to. Pursuing the man wasn't necessary if you knew where he'd show up.

Approaching the central core, Andras stepped into a restroom. He spread out the Oasis diagrams on the counter and reviewed what he'd learned from one of the cops who'd seen the robodog tapes.

All doors into the reactor room were armed to activate a count-down timer attached to the bomb. Only one door could be entered normally. All the others had been secured from the inside. Although the hijacker probably planned it so that any assault had to come through that one door, it also forced him to enter there.

The reactor room was circular, surrounded by a hallway formed on one side by the wall of the room and on the other by the innermost bank of machinery in the central core. Empty spaces in the machinery banks provided room for expansion. These spaces were accessible by removing vertical panels forming the walls of the hallway. Andras's destination was a space directly opposite the door the man would use.

Glancing at his watch, Andras was surprised to see how little time remained before the shuttle was scheduled to dock. He expected the man to take care of the bomb soon after arrival, and he hurried to set up his little surprise.

LIN SAT IN THE LEFT SEAT AND HAD CONTROL OF THE SHUTTLE. Samael felt a bit uneasy about that, but the captain didn't seem concerned. Dockings were dangerous, and if he was willing to sit through it as an observer, so be it.

As he watched from the jump seat, Samael was amazed that anyone could do it. He knew the shuttle's instrumentation provided precise information to guide the pilots, but they still had to maneuver the shuttle through the rendezvous and docking.

He confirmed time remaining with Lin and left the cockpit to check on the men. What a sight. From the top of the ladder down to the floor of the cargo bay, Samael stared at his men, positioned in front of the side cargo door, grouped into teams based on the order in which they were to disembark and their individual objectives for the initial assault. They had been briefed to expect little or no armed resistance, but unlike combat operations on Earth, mission planning could not take advantage of current intel and surveillance. Hopefully their training and discipline would handle any surprises.

Samael rechecked to ensure the bulkhead door between the crew compartment and the cargo bay had been secured open. The pilot appeared to be compliant, but counting on that would be a serious mistake. An opportunity not given is an opportunity that cannot be taken.

When confident everything was in order, he returned to the cockpit and paused behind the jump seat to stare at Oasis, a massive structure, hanging there with no visible means of support. Glancing at the time-to-go readout, Samael had to clamp down on his emotions. They were getting very close.

Lin was manually adjusting his maneuver and propulsion thrusters to precisely follow the steering commands displayed on his instruments. The captain could have been asleep for all the activity he displayed, but Samael noticed that his hands were all but touching his controls.

By the time Lin established the shuttle on the approach path, the doors to the landing dock had just opened completely. In spite of knowing they'd departed Oasis from an identical space, Samael found it hard to believe they could fit this huge machine inside.

But here they were, damn near close enough to reach out and touch the station. As the nose of the shuttle passed the threshold, Samael watched with reluctant admiration as Lin precisely maneuvered the huge craft into the bay and stabilized it above the floor.

At this point Samael couldn't detect any relative movement between the shuttle and the docking bay. During mission planning, he had read about orbital mechanics and watched a few videos, but no amount of pre-study could have prepared him for the stark reality of this moment.

Two objects traveling thousands of miles per hour had been established in identical lunar orbits and then merged into within a few feet of each other. Nothing but the physical laws of motion connected them, invisible and mysterious to the point of being incomprehensible.

The next maneuver would lower the shuttle to a touchdown, where it would be locked in place. Samael was bent over in the jump seat looking out the windscreen and up at the windows of the docking bay control room when it happened.

BRETT HAD BEEN WATCHING A PICTURE-PERFECT APPROACH TO docking. It kind of rankled himthat a pilot with far less hands-on flying time in shuttles could perform this maneuver so well. That thought notwithstanding, if his depth of experience had taught him anything, it was the critical importance of never, ever, taking anything for granted and always being prepared for the totally unexpected, *especially* when watching another pilot at the controls who isn't ultimately responsible for *any*thing and *every*thing that might go wrong.

The shuttle's thruster control system was designed so that if a nozzle failed, the opposing nozzle automatically shut down to counteract the asymmetrical force and prevent going out of control, defined as any situation in which the flying machine does something the pilot didn't tell it to.

In this instance, when Lin eased downward on the flight controls, all of the nozzles affecting downward vertical acceleration should have fired simultaneously. When one located on the upper outboard portion of the left wing didn't, and its opposite on the right did, the result was an immediate displacement of the shuttle from the desired state of equilibrium. The bay was much larger than the shuttle, and although there was room for some excursion, proximity to the floor made the situation heart-stoppingly critical.

Brett thought he was alert and ready for anything, when in reality the instantaneous thought for any pilot almost always is something like, *Is this really happening?*

By the time he recognized that Lin had lost control of the shuttle, Brett's peripheral vision had already picked up a view he never expected to see, of the loading dock floor though his side window. He grabbed the flight controls and shouted, "I'VE GOT IT!"

In the next few seconds, the fate of the station, the shuttle, and everyone involved hung in the balance.

The shuttle was rolling to the right rather than settling down onto the floor of the dock. Brett tried to counteract it, but Lin had failed to relinquish control. With separate, uncoordinated inputs, the shuttle began to oscillate in both pitch and roll.

In less than a few seconds the spacecraft dipped suddenly to the left and nose low, the windscreen filling with a close-up view of the docking bay floor, followed in the next few seconds by a reversal of the movement in the opposite direction and an opportunity for a close visual inspection of the ceiling.

Similar excursion cycles followed in rapid succession as Brett struggled to gain control and screamed, "LET THE GODDAMN HELL GO!"

Lin finally yanked his hands off the controls and held them up.

The sudden loss of control inputs from Lin's seat resulted in immediate response to commands from Brett's, and the shuttle made one last spectacular maneuver in all three axes just before it slammed down on the docking bay floor.

But it stayed put. In the relative calm and silent few seconds that followed, Brett noted three green lights illuminated on the instrument panel and confirmed, "Docking complete."

NUMBER TWO'S VOICE CAME OVER THE RADIO ASKING WHAT THE hell was going on. After a quick command to standby, Samael leaned toward the captain. "Is the shuttle damaged?"

The captain turned to him, his face uncharacteristically white and with a sheen of sweat. "Oh yeah. Don't know how bad. I'll have to look at it."

Samael followed the pilot's gaze up at the control booth and noticed an expression of concern. "What's the matter?"

"The booth appears deserted. Normally a controller closes the docking bay doors and initiates pressurization and rotation procedures. It can be done automatically, but—"

The sound of klaxons and flashing red lights signaled start of pressurization and re-rotation. Samael was expecting some sort of trickery and had a back-up plan if the authorities tried to leave the dock open. "Is that good or bad news?" he asked.

"Depends on your point of view. I imagine you'll like it. When all that racket stops, we'll have gravity and atmosphere in the bay."

Waiting in silence, Samael sensed the changes over the next ten minutes or so. When the lights and klaxons ceased, he turned to Lin, who was slumped over in his seat, head down. "Stay here with the captain and monitor the pressurization. Do not leave the shuttle for any reason."

Lin nodded, eyes closed and without looking up.

Samael unstrapped from the jump seat and turned to Toby.

"Let's go."

AS THE SHUTTLE APPEARED IN VIEW AND LINED UP ON THE FINAL approach path, General DeSilva had reviewed his preparations for flaws. He was in the control room overlooking docking bay five, currently manned by a minimum crew. Normally there'd be frequent radio chatter between the pilots and the senior controller, but today no crews would be entering the bay to service and unload the shuttle. The lack of activity in the booth was soothing. The general settled back to enjoy the beautiful sight of the shuttle docking when the voice of the senior controller interrupted the moment.

"Excuse me, General DeSilva?"

"What is it now, Major?"

"There's someone to see you at the door, sir. A technician who says you wanted him to report here."

"Send him in, please." DeSilva turned as Chip entered the room with a robodog at his side. Every person in the room seemed intently interested in the dog, and the thought occurred to DeSilva that it was a good thing there wasn't much to do. "Hello, Chip. And who might this be?"

"Good afternoon, sir. This is a new dog, right out of the box. I thought it appropriate to call him 'Surprise.'"

The general chuckled. "I trust he'll live up to the name. Did you make the program change?"

"Yes, sir. But I can't say for certain the time delay you wanted will work. A robodog's reactions are designed to be immediate, and speed has always been an essential element of their behavior."

"I understand that. We'll just have to accept the uncertainty. How long will it take you to insert him?"

"No more than thirty minutes, sir. The procedures we used with Noser have been copied with Surp."

Surp? Does everything have to have a nickname? I wonder what they call me.

"Good work. Get it done, and don't be late for your evacuation deadline."

"Roger that, sir. Good luck."

As Chip left the control room General DeSilva returned his attention to the shuttle. Using binoculars to inspect what he could see of the cockpit through the windscreen, he confirmed that both pilot seats and the jump seat were occupied. He thought he might have seen the legs of another person in one of the additional crew seats, but couldn't be sure.

As the shuttle closed the remaining distance to the bay, General DeSilva wondered if the hijackers had brought another trained shuttle pilot with them. It wouldn't surprise him, nor would it make a bit of difference if they had.

Watching the massive spacecraft come to a stop above the bay floor, DeSilva marveled at the sight. He'd seen hundreds of dockings, but it never ceased to amaze him that they could do this.

And with a perfect safety record, too. Never so much as a scratch during his tenure as commander. The credit for this went to many people, but the general was convinced his insistence on flawless performance had something to do with it.

He didn't know of any pilot flying the shuttles or person manning the control consoles who couldn't make a mistake, or be distracted, or fall asleep at the wheel. But he was equally sure that visible command presence and leadership went a long way toward eliminating dangerous combinations of these factors.

The crew of the control room seemed eager to get on with it, and DeSilva couldn't blame them. As soon as the shuttle settled down to the floor and was confirmed locked in position, the bay doors would be closed, pressurization begun, and the plan was a go.

Then without warning, the right wing of the shuttle dropped and the ship began to oscillate in the hover position above the floor. Following a collective gasp from every occupant in the room, General DeSilva heard the duty controller say, "Oh my God, hang onto your hats, boys."

It was over almost before it started, but not without visible impact between the shuttle, the floor, and one wall of the bay. So much for a perfect safety record.

The control room was silent, with no action on the part of the crew. DeSilva recovered from his shock and said, "I believe the next move is yours, Major."

"Uh . . . sorry, sir." To the control room crew, "Close outer doors. Commence pressurization."

General DeSilva used his radio to report the docking to the War Room and then went to the window for a better view. He noticed damage in two places, and the possibility occurred to him that the shuttle might not be safe to fly. With the binoculars, he focused on the cockpit, saw the pilots completing the docking checklist, and caught a glimpse of other two people. One appeared to be rather short in comparison with the other man. Maybe they brought a small person for all the tight places on a space station a criminal might want access to.

Once the doors were closed and pressurization began, DeSilva turned to the controller. "Tell me again about the way this works and how we'll leave it."

"Yes, sir." The major turned in his swivel chair to face the general. "The process is almost fully automated. Normally, all we do is respond to what we call 'consent stops.' The automated sequence is designed to pause for confirmation of systems status before continuing. The technicians are here primarily to handle malfunctions, and they can assume manual control of the process at any stage.

"When we leave the booth today, the launch controls will be locked. In that condition, the shuttle is trapped in the bay until the proper code is entered in the keypad. Once that's done, the launch sequence can be initiated. Assuming no malfunctions occur, one person could do it, even without knowing the system well, by simply pressing the consent switches in order at the proper time."

The general nodded. "How much would a person have to know?"

"The code, of course, and it changes on a regular basis. I get the current code for the bay I'm working from command central on my way to the booth." The major turned to face the console in front of him and pointed to a group of buttons. "You really don't even have to read the designations. As the automated sequence pauses, the next button flashes until you press it. Then it goes steady as the launch proceeds through the next step. It's a real no-brainer."

DeSilva said, "I'm in the wrong job. This is right down my alley." Both men smiled and turned to look into the bay as DeSilva asked, "So what keeps one of these guys from reversing the process?"

"The code sequence. Any security system can be bypassed, but this one is designed to be especially difficult. And they probably won't have the specialized equipment to decode this lock."

"How much longer?" the general asked.

The controller turned to look at a bank of instruments on the wall. "About five minutes. You agree, Johnny?"

"Yes, sir," replied a technician behind them. "And can I say something, General DeSilva?"

"What is it, son?"

"I was . . . uh . . . talking with the guys, and well . . . we don't mean to be disrespectful, but it's just not right to run away without a fight. Why don't we stop this thing here and now? We're not afraid of these scumbags."

"I know you aren't, and we've all thought of doing just that. But for now, trust me that what we're doing is not really running away."

An alert tone sounded and the major glanced at the panel. "Pressure equalized, sir."

"Very well. Are we through here?"

"If there's no unloading, yes sir."

"Look! The cargo door is moving!" said one of the technicians.

DeSilva stood transfixed as a steady stream of men dressed in black combat gear began pouring out of the shuttle and fanned out into the bay. He'd told himself to expect the unexpected, but never this. After a pause with everyone in the room starring at him, he said, "Shut this place down, gentlemen, and let's get out of here."

"Yes, SIR!" chorused in reply.

CONCEALED IN THE DARKNESS OF A CHUTE ENTRANCE AND looking past a slightly opened hatch cover, Dan watched men pour out of the shuttle, none of them masked. He and Andras had discussed the possibility that the original hijacker might not return, and Andras insisted it was a sure thing. When he said, "I *know* this schmuck, and he ain't gonna be showing his mug to nobody," Dan got the impression that his partner's bad imitation of a mafia button man's movie dialogue might by another indication that he's not telling all he knows.

Their plan considered that Dan might not see the hijacker leave the shuttle, or another person might approach the bomb. But with Andras in position, whoever showed up was in for a surprise. Dan waited a few minutes after the last of the men had left shuttle, and was about to radio Andras when he noticed movement at the threshold of the shuttle's cargo door. Raising his binoculars, he scooted a little further out of the chute.

A Space Command pilot appeared at the cargo bay opening, then stepped out onto the loading ramp. Another man not quite in full view appeared to be close-controlling the pilot's movements. When Dan saw the mask, he fumbled with the radio and almost dropped it before calling Andras. "I have the target. I say again, I have—"

It was as if a hand grabbed his throat. Immediately behind the target, the Williams kid stepped out and followed the man down to the floor of the bay. Dan was stunned. How the hell did the kid get here?

"Delta Bravo, Alpha Charlie here, confirm you have the target."

"Hold on a minute. We got trouble."

"What the hell you talking about?"

"Wait a minute, damn it!"

Dan watched them circle the shuttle, stopping to look at what appeared to be damage to the spacecraft.

Arriving back at the ramp, the man said something to the boy, then took the pilot back into the shuttle. Toby leaned against the ramp, crossed his legs, and appeared to be waiting for the man to return.

A few minutes later the target came out of the shuttle alone and walked across the floor of the loading bay to the exit with Toby attached to him like a shadow.

Dan picked up the radio. "Delta Bravo for Alpha Charlie."

"What's going on? Why didn't you answer me?"

"Shut up and listen. The target has that Williams kid with him. Copy?"

Silence.

"Alpha Charlie, do you copy? Over."

More silence.

Dan cursed under his breath, slammed the hatch cover closed, and backed out of the chute, his mind swirling with questions and not a single answer.

"WHAT WAS THAT?" TOBY WHISPERED.

The man looked down at him. "You tell me. That's what I pay you for, isn't it?" He pushed through the door.

Toby hurried to catch up as they advanced into the deserted space station. The man moved as if he knew exactly where he was going, then abruptly turned around and went back the way they had just come. Was he lost?

The man stopped at an intersection. "Give me one of those patented searches."

Toby had practiced during the voyage back, refining his ability to call up the audio and space search modes at will. After about thirty seconds he said, "Nothing so far."

The man stared at him. "On a space station with a population of hundreds even under minimum manning you can't find anything?"

"Maybe they're all together in one place." Toby motioned to a clock on the wall. "It's the middle of the early shift. They'll be at work-stations."

The man shook his head. "Okay, let's go. Stay alert."

For the next ten minutes they continued in the same random movement pattern. Toby still couldn't tell where they were going, except that they were getting closer to the central core. The man stopped at an intersection, glanced at the corridor designations on the walls and referred to a station diagram.

Toby closed his eyes, yawned, and it hit him: man-sized object nearby, warm, no sound, not at floor level. Toby opened his eyes when he heard the rustling of paper as the man folded the diagram.

"What?" the man asked.

Should I warn him? "Nothing. I'm just a little tired."

"Tired won't hack it. Stay alert."

The man turned and walked down the corridor. Toby was lagging behind as the man reached the next intersection. An internal threat warning almost took his breath away.

"DUCK!" Toby shouted, not understanding why.

The man had just stepped into the intersection when from behind the corner to his left Toby saw movement. He was vaguely aware of something happening at the right edge of his vision, but his attention was fixed on the barrel of a shotgun as he saw a flash of flame, heard the punishing retort of the gunshot, and felt the concussion. The barrel jerked back out of view, simultaneously with the first of three quick shots accompanied by flashes of light from behind the corner to Toby's right. Then silence.

Toby froze in place, ears ringing. Staring at the empty intersection, he didn't know whether to move forward to see what had happened or turn around and run for his life. He decided to let his senses help and closed his eyes.

Silent audio. Toby wondered if loud noises could shut it down. Then he spatially detected objects on both sides of the intersection, followed by movement to the right. Toby opened his eyes and stared at that edge of the wall blocking his view. Holding his breath, he expelled it in a rush as the man stepped into the intersection, moving slowly, his face contorted in pain, blood on his upper body, and holding his right arm with his left.

He stopped in the middle of the intersection, staring ahead and above him at something in the crossing corridor. Then he grimaced, closed his eyes, sighed heavily, looked directly at Toby and smiled. "How did you know what to say?"

Toby couldn't hear him very well, and he had to speak loud just to hear himself. "It just came to me all of a sudden."

"And none too soon, either. Come here. I want to show you something."

Toby couldn't move his legs very well. They seemed to have rooted on the spot, and he wasn't sure he wanted to look around the corner.

"Come on," ordered the man. "You need to see this."

Toby obeyed. When he turned his head and looked, it took him a moment to absorb the details.

Bloodstains, a combination of splatter, drips, and a slowly advancing puddle, appeared stark against the white wall and floor. The source of the blood was above Toby's eye level.

A man, slumped over at the waist, bent in half and very still, was hanging from a strap around his waist and looped through the rungs of a ladder leading up to one of the chute entrances. He was dressed in black, and a baseball cap with the number "2" imprinted on the front lay upside down in the pool of blood. One of those short black shot-guns hung from the man's limp right hand, secured to his wrist. Blood dripped from various places on the body, and as the impact of what he saw took hold, Toby turned to his left, leaned over, and vomited his breakfast onto his shoes and the floor.

AFTER INSPECTING THE DAMAGE, BRETT SECURED THE SHUTTLE with Lin, who had been grim-faced since the docking incident. Obvi-ously embarrassed, he avoided eye contact, and for the first time since Brett had known him, Lin was in a hurry. Within a minute of completing the checklist, he left the cockpit with nothing more than a command to stay put mumbled over his shoulder. As if Brett could do anything but, since Lin had changed the passcode and enabled the shuttle's security system.

With nothing more to do, Brett was sitting in the copilot's seat waiting, when fleeting movement at the edge of a docking bay window caught his attention. He leaned forward to get a better view through the shuttle's windscreen and stared in disbelief as a figure in a full pres-sure suit drifted across the window and disappeared behind a section of wall separating the windows, followed by a second figure. Then he noticed the lights on the airlock panel.

Spaced at regular intervals in the outer walls of Oasis, airlocks served as exit points for extra-vehicular activity (EVA), necessary on a regular basis for inspection and maintenance. These small rooms could be closed off from the station's normal atmosphere and depressurized quickly to the absolute vacuum of space. Maintenance personnel could then open an outer door, exit the room and go about their business. Inherently dangerous, EVAs were treated with the utmost respect, because a malfunction in the airlock could jeopardize many more people than those directly involved with the work being performed.

Under normal conditions, since the airlock would most likely be used by a person entering from the station in preparation for an EVA, it would be fully pressurized with the inner and outer doors secured closed to provide a double seal against the possibility of a major air leak. The airlock control panel immediately adjacent to the inner door allowed someone inside the station to manipulate the atmospheric conditions within the lock. The status lights on the panel were used to confirm the airlock's condition.

Each airlock was also equipped with another control panel mounted in the outer skin of the station so a person could safely enter the lock without help from the inside. Brett watched the status lights change from green to red, indicating that the airlock was being depressurized from the outside.

It took no more than a few minutes for the outer door-open light to illuminate, followed by a closed indication, then re-pressurization.

Who the hell are these guys? Is this a rescue attempt?

Brett's heart rate began to increase as he saw the green light come on and then the indication that the inner door had been unlocked. He stared at the door, expecting to see the symbolic knight in white armor charge into the bay. But when nothing happened, he tried to figure out what they were waiting for. And then it dawned on him.

The shuttle is a fortress, you idiot.

Agitation building, Brett considered the possibility they were waiting for him to do something. He looked up at the loading bay's control room window and barely visible in the darkness, saw a black-mask-covered head. Brett's initial fear that it might be the hijacker disappeared when the man's hand appeared above the windowsill and pointed to his ear.

Cursing himself for not having thought of it earlier, Brett grabbed his helmet and put it on. Peering out the windscreen, he looked up at the head and immediately heard a voice.

"Captain Larsen?"

"YES!" Brett shouted, and instantly regretted it. This was a receive-only comm setup, and if Lin had heard that, Brett might have blown the whole deal. He gave a vigorous thumbs-up out the window, and looked back down the companionway.

What if Lin comes up here? Are you going to kill him?

"We're going to get you out of there. Do you know if and how many hostiles are on board?"

Brett shook his head and gave a thumbs down.

"Can you find out without alerting them?"

Brett considered this for a few seconds, then decided he had to go for it. Holding up one index finger, he looked for acknowledgment that his message had been received, got it, pulled off his helmet and stepped into the companionway. He tiptoed through the galley, past the tables, and entered the corridor separating the individual crew quarters. The door to Lin's room was still closed. Brett continued to the end of the corridor, where the bulkhead door was latched open. He lay down on the floor, inched himself out over the threshold and onto the landing. At the edge, he peeked down into the bay and got a solid adrenaline hit as he saw a group of five men lounging around the closed cargo door. There may be more out of view from his position on the landing, but he didn't want to risk another look.

Brett scooted backwards into the corridor, then rose into a crouch and walked back past Lin's room into the galley. When he got to the cockpit he pulled on the helmet and held up five fingers.

"Five? Is that correct?"

Brett extended his hand up to the window, held it horizontal, and waggled it back and forth.

"Approximately five?"

Thumbs up.

"Are there any hostiles in the galley?"

Brett shook his head and pointed toward the rear of the shuttle.

"In the cargo bay?"

Vigorous nods.

"Listen carefully. Make certain the port in the belly of the shuttle, the one that leads into the chutes from under the center table, isn't secured from the inside. Return to the cockpit and prepare to open the cargo door on my command. Make sure the cockpit is closed off from the companionway and sit tight."

Brett nodded and gave a thumbs-up signal. Leaving the cockpit again, he pondered two important details as he descended the companionway.

The men in the bay must know how to operate the door and had closed it from the inside after the others left. A signal from the cockpit to open the cargo door probably took precedence over any conflicting inputs from the door control panel in the bay, but he couldn't remember for sure.

But if the cops were planning to use the chutes to enter through the escape port in the belly, they were in for a surprise. The shuttle's gyrating docking maneuver hadn't accurately aligned the chute hatch and the port. If the hatch was open, however, they could still enter the shuttle, but they wouldn't be able to get there without the risk of being seen. Hopefully they knew all that and had planned accordingly.

Brett entered the galley and went to the center table. Looking toward the crew quarters for any sign Lin had alerted on Brett's activity, he lifted the table to expose the hatch cover. With excitement building over the possibility of getting out in one piece, Brett reached down and gave the handle a hefty pull.

The effort almost pulled him on his face to the floor. The hatch didn't budge. Brett looked down to determine why. Safety wire held the handle in the closed position. The hijacker didn't miss much.

Brett removed the safety wire with a pair of wire snips he found in the top tray of a toolbox stored in the utility equipment locker. He tried the handle again and rotated it to the open position. To make sure the hatch wasn't stuck, he tried to open it. No luck. *Is the hatch sabotaged? How do I—?*

A noise from the direction of the crew quarters. *Lin?*

Brett lowered the table, moved to the wall at the entrance to the corridor and waited. After a minute of silence, he checked around the corner. Nothing. He returned to the table, raised it and tried the hatch again. Still no luck. And then it occurred to him what the problem might be.

In the cockpit, he found that the shuttle's air conditioning system was operating, which was normal, but the outflow valves usually opened on the ground were closed. With the cargo bay door also closed, the influx of outside air from the docking bay had created a differential pressure effectively locking the hatch. They had either missed the switch during the docking termination checklist or someone had changed it later.

Brett turned off the flow of conditioned air. In this configuration, the shuttle would remain pressurized until a door or the outflow valves were opened. But if the cops planned to enter through the hatch, they'd be unable to force it open without explosives, which he was certain they were not planning to do.

Unable to clarify the situation with the man in the booth, Brett decided to take a chance. He returned to the cockpit and put the helmet on as he prepared to manually depressurize the shuttle. The man's voice was waiting for him.

"Ready?"

Brett held up another "Wait a minute" sign with his finger, then carefully manipulated the manual pressure-release valve. It was held closed by positive pressure, and he felt the resistance in the mechanism. Trying to avoid a sudden release, he slowly increased the force and hoped for the best . . . when his ears popped as the valves opened. Lin and the men in the bay would have felt it. *Will they understand the significance?* Brett took off the helmet and went to the top of the companionway. The man in the booth was probably wondering why he didn't just do as he was told, but he had to handle this.

When the sound of boots on steel announced that someone was climbing the stairs from the floor of the cargo bay up to the landing, Brett remembered the open equipment locker. He rushed down the companionway, entered the galley, and knelt down in front of the locker over the open toolbox.

I'm just looking for a tool to fix something in the cockpit. That's logical, isn't it?

As footsteps approached from behind him, Brett lifted the top tray out of the box. Reaching in to appear busy hunting for a tool, his hand came to rest on the handle of an awl. He slipped it under his sleeve just as the soldier entered the galley from the corridor.

"What the hell you doing?"

Brett looked over his shoulder. The soldier held an assault rifle, muzzle pointed in Brett's general direction. He appeared alert and very suspicious. Brett smiled. "Just some routine maintenance. Usually the ground crews—"

"Get your ass up from there and move away from that hatch."

Brett realized much too late that he'd left the table up and the hatch exposed. Did this guy know the handle had been secured? Would he notice that the wire had been removed?

The soldier stepped into the galley. "Where's the other pilot?"

"In his room. He didn't get much sleep in the last day or two."

The soldier moved carefully around the galley, then turned his back on Brett and ascended the companionway into the cockpit.

He can't be too worried about me. Get ready.

After about thirty seconds the soldier came back down into the galley. The assault rifle was hanging from his right shoulder on a short sling, and his hand was resting lightly on the handgrip. The weapon was still readily available, but it was as if he didn't expect to use it.

"I've never been up here," he said. "Quite a set up. What's with the hatch?"

Brett jumped at the opportunity for conversation to divert the soldier's attention. "Our through-flight procedures call for checking all the emergency systems on the shuttle. The hatch handle is supposed to move easily, but it seems to be stuck. I was just looking for something to tap it with. I can't budge it by hand."

The soldier appeared to accept the problem as a personal challenge to show the wimpy flyboy how a real man could muscle the handle open. "Let me try it," he said. "Pull it to the right?"

"Correct. But be careful. It's an awkward angle, and if the handle gives suddenly you can bash your knuckles on the side there."

The man grunted something unintelligible, and his manner indicated he wasn't in the least bit worried about hurting his hands. He knelt down over the hatch, and with his right hand moved the assault rifle behind his back so it wouldn't swing in front and in the way.

Brett stood behind him, feet rooted into the floor, frantically wondering what to do next. The handle was already rotated fully open, and couldn't have been moved any further to the right with the strength of ten men.

Reaching down with his right hand, the man gripped the handle and pulled. Brett saw his body shift forward and to the left as the force against the stationary handle acted against his weight and heard the man expel a breath of air.

"Goddamn. Sonofabitch's stuck big time. It'll take some real muscle here, and I'm just the guy for the job."

Brett was astonished to see this idiot shove up the sleeves on his shirt, lean down low over the hatch, and take a few deep breaths as he gripped the handle.

It just seemed like the right thing to do. As the man took a final deep breath, Brett slid the awl out of his sleeve. Hearing the grunt of effort as the man pulled hard on the handle, Brett stepped forward, raised the awl high over his head, and drove it down full force into the base of the man's skull.

The awl punched through a combination of soft and hard stuff with equal ease, and Brett was both shocked and horrified as blood spurted and the man instantly lost all control over muscular functions. The body collapsed to the floor in a heap, shuddered spasmodically for a few seconds, and lay still.

Brett stood motionless, frozen in place by this turning point from which there would be no retreat. Lin or the other men in the bay could come in here at any time, and his days of being a pilot for this group were over. He began to move the body when it occurred to him that he had to get word to the man in the booth.

The masked head was still there, and the voice was clearly pissed. "Where have you been? You want out of that tomb or not?"

Brett almost answered again before he caught himself. He gave the thumbs-up signal continuously until he heard the voice respond.

"Be ready to open the cargo door on my command."

Brett gave another thumbs-up, and saw movement to his right. The door to the airlock opened, and two men sprinted out into the bay. They were dressed in pressure suits, helmets and gloves removed, but heavily armed. The image of knights in white armor flashed through Brett's mind for the second time. The men quickly disappeared out of view underneath the shuttle, and Brett jumped in surprise as the voice screamed in his ears.

"NOW! NOW! NOW!"

Brett selected the open position on the cargo door control, and felt another slight pressure release as the "in-transit" light on the door panel illuminated. He sat there watching like a spectator when it dawned on him that the body was still lying on the hatch. The man in the booth had told him to stay in the cockpit, but he couldn't do that now.

Scrambling down the companionway into the galley, Brett almost vomited when he came upon the results of his work with the awl. The passage of time, no matter how slight, allowed him to look at the scene with a little more clarity and he didn't like what he saw.

A few deep breaths helped, and with his jaw set in determination to do what he had to do, Brett hauled the body by the feet off the hatch and over to the equipment locker. There was no time to do anything about the blood.

Then, as if the volume control on his ears had been suddenly turned on, Brett heard the sound of gunshots accompanied by yelling. Some of the shots were close, from down in the bay, and some were muffled. He moved forward toward the corridor into the crew quarters, and was startled breathless when the escape hatch burst open without warning and a man's upper body appeared in the opening.

Brett froze. The cop's weapon was trained on his chest, and the thought suddenly occurred to him he might be mistaken for a bad guy. He was about to say something when the cop's eyes moved off and seemed to take in the scene, staring at the body of the soldier. When his gaze returned to Brett, he nodded. "Good work."

But only for a moment. The cop pulled himself into the galley, did a quick check for threats, then gave his partner a hand up through the hatch. The first cop then proceeded down the corridor and looked into the bay while the second moved beside Brett. The sounds of the firefight had died down, but the diversion was doing its job of keeping the other men preoccupied in the bay. The first cop motioned back toward his partner, who then touched Brett's arm and motioned toward the hatch. Brett had just started to move in that direction when a crew sleeping room door opened.

For a moment it was like slow motion. Lin stepped into the corridor and stood facing the wall opposite his door. He was looking to his right toward Brett and the second cop, and Brett felt a stab of fear when he saw the weapon in Lin's right hand, held muzzle down by his leg.

Lin then looked away from them and to his left down the corridor toward the other cop. Brett heard a whispered, "Gun, behind you," spoken into his radio by the cop standing beside him, and his partner immediately turned from the bay and faced Lin.

"Lin," said Brett, "drop the gun and come with us. You aren't a part of this like the others. Pilot to pilot, now, come on. Give it up."

Lin turned and looked at Brett. His face was red, eyes puffy, almost like he'd been crying. The expression was one of a tormented soul underneath trying to escape.

Then it changed, starting in the eyes, and Lin's face transformed itself into a picture of inner peace and contentment. "Goodbye, Captain Larsen." As Lin raised the pistol toward the cop standing by Brett, three rapid shots from the other cop sent Lin to the floor.

The rest was a blur. Brett was literally picked up and thrown down the hatch. The two cops pushed him ahead of them as they ran to the airlock. Once inside, they commanded him to don the extra suit they'd brought, spurring him on with additional incentive to hurry by locking the inner door and punching the pressurization controls before Brett had even put a leg in.

Brett had enjoyed every EVA he'd ever done, but this one was nothing more than going through the motions. The cops hustled him through every step, and once back inside the shuttle turned him over to an EMS technician. Brett refused treatment, insisting he was fine, and demanded to see the general.

"You're too late for an audience with him, Captain," said the tech. "He's busy evacuating this station, and you need to haul ass to this location." He handed Brett a piece of paper with the numerical designation of a lifeship pod.

"But I need to see the general. There's a boy—"

"Don't know nothing about it. Don't want to. I'm getting off here now, and I suggest you do the same. The folks on that pod," he said, pointing to the paper, "are holding it. How long do you think you'd wait for a stranger to show up?" With that the man closed his medical bag and hurried down the hall.

Brett stood alone, struggling with the decision. If he tried to find DeSilva, what would that do for him? As the commander, the general would probably be on the last pod to leave. But if all the other cops were gone how would Brett get help? Would DeSilva stop the evacuation to find Toby? He'd have to, wouldn't he? But what if he can't?

Too many uncertainties. Brett decided he had to find Toby. In all the confusion, the chances that people had become separated were too great, and who would expect a boy to have made a quick voyage to Earth and back? They probably were hunting for him on the moon colony right now.

Toby had to be with the hijacker. *But where?* They'd left the shuttle together after the other men fanned out into the bay and disappeared into the station, so he might not be with a group.

What would the hijacker do first?

The bomb. Of course. The first message Brett received via the comm link said it had been disabled, but the hijacker probably didn't know that. The station let the shuttle dock, which seemed a little strange to Brett if the bomb really was out of the picture. But with the plan to evacuate, it might not matter because the hijacker would end up being trapped. Not a bad idea at all, except for Toby.

Brett struggled to remember War Room discussions about where the bomb would most likely be placed to cause sufficient damage to render Oasis uninhabitable. The central core, something about the reactor room, and disabling the power or atmospheric systems seemed to be the key.

So be it. Brett had never been near the reactor room, and didn't particularly like the idea of going now, but how hard could it be to find? He knew what "central" meant, and where it was in relation to his current location.

Toby, I hope you're okay.

~

IT BROUGHT BACK MEMORIES OF COMBAT OPERATIONS IN AN urban setting, except this time Dan was the one avoiding contact rather than seeking it. He didn't know the chutes well enough to feel comfortable navigating them, and in any case he figured it would take far too much time to crawl the distance he had to go. But he knew his way around the station and had been able to move in the open quickly without encountering anyone. He estimated that about a hundred of the hijacker's men had left the shuttle, and it was as if the station had swallowed them up. When he almost ran into one patrol, his police electronic master key provided access to an apartment, where he hid until the danger had passed. Since then he remained cautious, moving from cover to cover, but still hadn't found the target.

The original plan was for him to find the hijacker and stay close enough to monitor his position while coordinating with Andras. He was to remain undetected as long as possible, then herd the target toward the reactor room. They wanted him to approach his objective with attention focused behind him and give Andras the element of surprise.

The presence of the boy changed all that. Dan was afraid Andras wouldn't see the kid before he ambushed the hijacker. Dan had tried unsuccessfully to contact Andras every few minutes, and finally decided his primary objective now should be to set up an ambush of his own.

Using a station diagram, he determined the most direct route from the shuttle to the reactor room. If the hijacker did that also, Dan would probably never catch up. But maybe the guy had other things to do on the way, which hopefully didn't include joining up with other members of his team.

Dan was trotting down a corridor approaching an intersection when caught a whiff of a foul odor. He stopped. *What the hell is that?* Two more steps, and he peeked around the corner. Someone had vomited on the floor. Moving to his right to avoid the mess, Dan stepped into the intersection and was assaulted further by the stench of recent death from the body of a soldier hanging from the rungs of a ladder, blood everywhere, including bloody shoe prints leading off down the corridor, complete enough to see two different heel prints. Checking the bottom of his own sole, he confirmed that one person was wearing police-issue combat boots, and the other looked like standard Oasis footgear. In a smaller size . . . *like a kid would wear.*

Dan drew his sidearm and forgot all about his hurting lungs as he sprinted down the hall.

～

THEY STOPPED AT A REFRESHMENT CENTER. THE MAN ORDERED Toby to clean up. After doing the best he could, he came out of the restroom and smelled the food. He almost vomited again.

"What's the matter?" asked the man. "Lost your appetite?"

Toby nodded and took a seat at the food bar.

"Ever seen anything like that before?"

Toby started to share his experience in the chutes when he discovered the cop, but decided not to. "No."

"First time's always the worst. I wanted you to see it. Without your warning, that's what could've happened to me."

"Will there be more?"

"Probably. But I can tell you this. When the word gets out about this, it may give them pause. Particularly when they see us together, and realize you're always with me, and that you must have been with me when the attack occurred. I'm limping, but you're okay, except for a little barf on your shoes. Come on."

Toby followed, and as they walked, the man removed the pistol from behind his back and replaced the magazine with a fresh one from a holder on his belt. "Where are we going?"

"You'll see. Just stay close and keep those antennae out there. It isn't over until it's over."

When they came to an entrance into the central core the man said, "Do your stuff."

Toby searched for about two or three minutes, changing the angle and distance of his pattern until he was convinced no threats existed in the vicinity of the door. "It's fine."

"Step back."

Toby watched the man open the door and check both directions, then motion for him to follow. For the next five minutes or so they continued deeper into the core, pausing periodically for Toby to search ahead and behind. When they came up to an intersection Toby felt was probably near the center, the man stopped. "Take your time."

Toby stepped up and closed his eyes. For the first minute or so there was nothing, until he detected a shape that seemed to be at the limit of his range. It was warmer than the background, man-sized.

"Something?" asked the man.

"Uh, yeah, I think—"

A now familiar sensation hit Toby, an intrusion warning of impending threat that took precedence over any other search in progress. He turned to look behind them back down the hallway. The man reacted by moving out into the intersection to face in that direction.

"What is it?"

"I think . . . there might be someone behind us."

Before Toby could say anything about the shape he'd detected in front of them the man grabbed his shoulder and pulled him back into the intersection. They hadn't moved more than a few feet when footfalls approached. Fast ones. The man stepped to the side. With most of his body protected by the wall, he drew his weapon, placed his left forearm against the wall with his clenched fist extending past the edge, where he rested his right hand gripping the pistol. Toby watched with fascination, not realizing that he was still standing exposed in full view.

"You enjoy being a target?"

Before Toby could move, a full-blown warning hit him as a cop rounded the corner in a full sprint.

The muzzle blast from the man's weapon hit Toby hard. The man stepped out into the corridor and walked down the hall, his pistol trained on the body of a cop crumpled against the wall.

Toby closed his eyes, took a few deep breaths, and immediately felt it.

Another warning, a combination of spatial warmth and movement, approaching from the same direction as the cop.

"Uh . . . mister?"

"What?"

"We got another one coming."

The man looked back at Toby. "Where?"

Toby pointed. "That way." The man hurried forward a few steps, and seemed to be dividing his attention between the cop and whoever might be coming their way. The warning signs increased, and Toby became frightened.

"It's getting really close now."

The man backed up quickly. As he got to Toby he motioned in the direction they had been traveling. "Move. Keep a good search going."

Toby remembered the original sensation he had received before the cop ran up. "There may also be someone up ahead of us."

"I wouldn't doubt it."

Toby walked up to the next corner and stopped to search out in front. He was aware of the man as he moved up close behind him, and within a few seconds located the shape he'd found before.

"It's probably a person, and I don't detect any movement."

"Sound?"

This took longer, with more concentration. It was really quiet, maybe shallow breathing, a faint rustling that might be clothing, then the muffled cough.

"It's a person with a cough."

The man nodded, moved in front of Toby and peered around the corner. "I anticipated there'd be a move or two by someone in my group. Probably a surprise thing like before, someone waiting in hiding. But the cop's actions don't fit. He was moving much too fast, and I can't figure out why. It was very stupid."

"Is he dead?"

"I don't think so, but he might as well be. Okay, listen up. I want you to be in front, and follow my directions. I'll point which way I want you to go. There'll be no talking, and you have to move as quietly as you can. I—"

"But I didn't think this was about fighting cops. You said the people who'd try—"

"Shut up. I didn't tell you everything. It's too complicated for you to understand. It's like taking the shuttle. I would have preferred to do that without violence, but there are too many narrow-minded people out there who can't understand the stakes.

"Like these cops. They're nothing more than robots in their own fashion, brainwashed to think what they do is right and anything is justified as long as it's in the name of law and order. I can't sit down with each one and explain why they should back off and let me proceed. Even if I could they'd never understand."

Toby listened to the man's words, but had the distinct impression that his own confusion had nothing to do with it being complicated.

The man motioned with his head. "Let's go."

Toby turned the corner, moving deeper into the core. At each intersection he stopped and searched forward, then behind them. After indicating it was safe, he followed the direction indicated by the hijacker, and it didn't take long to realize that the man's erratic movements assumed he was being followed.

Toby continued to receive only intermittent hits behind them, and the original stationary shape remained in the same location. As they got closer to the reactor room, Toby heard a faint squeak. He hadn't been audio searching, so the sound was close.

The man heard it too, and he walked slowly back the way they had come. "You hear that?"

"Yeah."

The man motioned for Toby to continue. He proceeded to the next corner, where he stopped and closed his eyes.

There it was, much clearer now. Definitely a person, somewhere close in or near the corridor ahead. Toby turned and motioned to the man, indicating with sign language as best he could that the threat was very close. The man nodded, then mouthed, "Stay here," before turning and disappearing back down the way they had come. Toby returned his attention to the corridor, and worked on refining his sense of the shape.

One of the things he'd discovered during his recent practice was that the more he concentrated on a specific location or sound, the less he picked up from the surrounding area. It was a tradeoff between accuracy and coverage.

Accuracy was the hardest to obtain because it took very close control. Toby's powers were so directional that when he moved the center of his search pattern he knew exactly when he drifted off the person hidden ahead because the sensation of heat dropped off. He was practicing with it now, and never sensed the other person.

MOVING AS FAST AS HE DARED THROUGH THE DESERTED corridors, Brett had stopped to peer around a blind intersection when the sound of gunshots echoed down the hallway. He hurried to the next intersection and checked in both directions. To his right, a dark shape lay barely visible about twenty yards away.

Heart pounding, he advanced and found a cop lying face down on the floor with a small amount of blood near his head. Brett knelt down, saw no evidence of a spinal injury, and rolled the limp body face up. The name tag pinned above the right breast pocket identified the man as Corporal Bishop. He was breathing and had a strong pulse. Brett couldn't remember the details about how to put an unconscious person in the recovery position, and he didn't know whether trying to wake Bishop up might not be the right thing to do, but he had to try something.

But before he could, the cop groaned, became restless and slightly agitated.

Brett gently restrained him. "Corporal Bishop, can you hear me? My name is Brett Larsen and I'm trying to find Toby Williams. He's—"

"Toby?"

"I'll try to get EMS for you, but I've got to find the boy. Do you—?"

The cop shook his head, grimacing with the effort, and pointed to his radio in a belt holder. "Ra . . . radio. Call for assist . . . assistance."

Removing the radio from the holder, Brett glanced up at the wall and saw damage from the bullets. "Bishop, have you been shot?"

"Fell. Hit the damned wall."

He seemed really pissed. Brett knew the feeling. Keying the microphone, he called the police. "Corporal Bishop to Police Central, officer down, needs assistance. I say again, officer down, needs assistance, location fox seven delta one zero." Brett repeated the coordinates stenciled on the wall. Squeezing Bishop's hand, he said, "Good luck. I've got to find Toby."

The cop grabbed Brett's arm. "Take my gun."

Brett had never pointed a handgun at a human being, much less one hiding behind a kid. But the time had come to change that if circumstances required. He reached over Bishop's body, unsnapped the thumb break, and removed the pistol. "Thanks," he said, patting the cop's shoulder.

As he tried to stand, Bishop grabbed his arm. "Don't rack the slide. It's ready to rock. Good luck."

Brett thanked him and stood up. Although he felt more confident with the firearm, he knew he was way out of his element. The thought of confronting the hijacker and the building tension made Brett's mouth so dry that he stopped at a water fountain. As he leaned down for a drink he heard the voices, faint, but definitely the deeper tone of an adult and the distinctive voice of a youth.

But where were the voices coming from? Brett rushed to the next intersection and eased his head around the corner. The result reminded him of a favorite saying among pilots, "I'd rather be lucky than good." The voices were distinctly clearer. He crept forward. Approaching the next intersection, he heard the man say something about cops.

A quick peek around the next corner produced a glimpse of a man, dressed in black, and masked.

Brett's heart pounded with adrenaline. He would never be able to sneak up in the corridor without being discovered. And if they moved off when he wasn't looking he might lose them. His only choice was to get ahead of them. The bomb was in the core, that's where they were headed, and so was he.

Moving laterally to a parallel route, Brett hurried two intersections down and scrambled up a ladder to a chute hatch. Dropping inside, he crawled back in the direction of their anticipated route, and carefully popped a hatch open. From this higher vantage point and relatively hidden position, he hoped to catch sight of them on the move, verify the direction, then move ahead again.

After about five minutes of no contact, Brett was afraid he'd lost them. He opened the hatch further, and moved forward so his upper body was sticking well out of the chute for a better view of the corridor to his left. Then he realized someone was approaching from the right. Without moving his head, Brett looked as far as he could to the right and almost swallowed his throat.

Toby, walking slowly in the middle of the corridor with the hijacker about ten feet behind him.

Brett had put the pistol inside his waistband in the small of his back. If he could get it out he'd have a relatively clear shot without putting Toby in the line of fire. But he was holding the hatch open with one hand while bracing his upper body with the other. When he tried to relax the pressure on either, it upset this delicate balance and he almost fell forward out of the chute. The hatch cover squeaked, only a little bit, but enough to alert the man.

Brett held his breath, arms trembling with the strain of holding his body absolutely still. The man walked back down the hall, then turned and came back to where Toby was standing. They talked about hearing a noise before finally walking down the corridor.

Once back inside the chute, Brett lay there for a moment waiting for his pulse to slow, then struck out for one final dash in the chutes. By his calculations he could exit at or very near the reactor room by moving through three or four more sections.

Crawling into the dimness of the chute, Brett hoped the next hatch cover he tried was well lubricated.

No more squeaks.

TOBY WAS CONVINCED THE SHAPE HE SENSED WAS A PERSON sitting or kneeling down. He'd been refining the image for a few minutes when he remembered that narrow search patterns increased his vulnerability to surprise. Relaxing his concentration, he scanned a larger area and got an immediate hit as a second shape seemed to appear out of nowhere.

It was another person, standing, and moving. Toby drew the search in and found the first person, then alternated between them and determined the mover was closing the distance toward the stationary person. Suddenly a voice startled him.

"Hey."

Who was that? It didn't sound like the man, and why would he give away his position by saying anything?

"Can you hear me?"

Toby didn't need enhanced audio to hear this voice. His search evaporated as he realized it sounded like Brett.

"Give it up, mister. Lin's dead, the shuttle's non-flyable, and they're evacuating the station. Let the boy go, he's of no use to you now."

Toby heard footsteps. He stepped out into the intersection and stared down the hallway surrounding the reactor room. The man appeared from around the corner of the next intersecting corridor, back-stepping and with his attention directed up toward something above him. Toby followed the man's gaze and it all became clear.

Brett's head was just visible sticking out of a radial chute. The man raised his pistol and fired. Brett's head disappeared inside the chute and the cover slammed shut. The man continued firing, the bullets impacting on the closed hatch cover.

Something snapped inside Toby. All the talk about the man's mission, saving Earth and Oasis for future generations, and Toby's commitment to help became old news. The man was shooting at Brett.

As Toby rushed forward, an overwhelming fear engulfed him from the right as a wall panel exploded outward into the hallway. Toby screamed as something hit him, knocking him into the wall of the reactor room. As he slid to the floor, a much heavier gunshot pounded his ears. A big cop was standing with his back to Toby, looking down at his shotgun. Through the inverted "V" of the cop's spread legs, Toby saw the hijacker throw his gun, charge and body-slam the cop. The shotgun fell to the floor, and the two men tumbled backward toward Toby. From his position on the floor he watched as the two men fought, grunts and curses filling the air.

The cop screamed. The hijacker stood up, a small, knife, dripping blood, protruding from between the second and third fingers of his right hand.

A cop with a horribly disfigured face was holding his bleeding stomach. The sight almost made Toby sick.

The man stood over the cop and began to laugh, his voice filled with anger and hatred.

"Look at this, you miserable son of a bitch, lying at the feet of your conqueror holding your guts in your hands. Thought you could double-cross me and get away with it."

The man leaned over to wipe the bloody knife on the cop's sleeve, stood up, and slipped the knife back in its sheath. "I should kill you now, but I want you to die slowly."

As the man turned around, Toby looked up. The man's mask had been torn off in the struggle. Toby stared, wanting to look away, but it was as if his eyes were drawn to the sight.

"The hell you looking at?"

Toby couldn't find the words to answer. All he could think about was that he had seen the man's face. He remembered a movie about a kidnapper who had to kill his victim for that very reason.

The man turned around, looking behind him where the cop was lying. The mask was on the floor, and stained red with blood. "Well," he said, turning back around, "I don't think I'll try to clean that one. No matter. The reasons for it have become unimportant. Oh, and before I forget, thanks again. Your scream gave me just enough warning."

Toby's gaze shifted to the cop, who was moaning in pain, and then at the shotgun lying on the floor. The man noticed.

"It jammed. They'll do that on occasion. He made a big mistake trying to clear it. He should've rushed me, used it as a club, gone for his weapon, something. My pistol was empty. He gave me the chance and look at the result."

The man stepped over to the shotgun, picked it up and did something with it to eject a shell, catching it on the fly. After examining it, he shook his head. "You can't trust anybody anymore. I didn't know they had shotguns up here. Good thing for me this idiot loaded it with cheap government-issue ammo." The man removed the rest of the shells, then walked over to Toby and stood over him.

"Get up. We've still got work to do. Then we'll talk about our new relationship and how it changes the terms of our agreement. Come on."

Toby got up, but stood his ground. "What do you mean, new relationship?"

The man turned so suddenly that Toby reeled back against the wall opposite the reactor room door. The man stood over him, his face red and contorted.

"Listen, you little shit. I've been more than patient with you, playing along like we were partners, but that was just to get this thing done in the easiest way possible. Do you actually think I needed to ask for your cooperation?" The man backhanded Toby across the face.

Toby lost his temper and reason at the same time. He tried to kick the man in the leg and ended up on his back from a blow to the side of the head. Scrambling backward to get away, Toby saw someone—Brett!—appear from around the corner behind the man and run toward them. The man ducked his head, pivoted around, crouched low, with his legs in a wide stance.

Running full tilt, Brett slammed into the man. They went down in a pile. The hijacker ended up on top, pounding Brett with the unloaded shotgun.

Toby got up looking for a weapon. The man's empty one was lying by the cop. A second pistol lay nearby. Toby picked it up and pointed it at the man's back. "STOP IT OR I'LL SHOOT!"

The man paused, the shotgun raised to strike Brett another blow, and turned his head. His eyes zeroed in on the gun, then glanced toward the cop and the other pistol on the floor. For a split second he seemed confused, but then he began to laugh and stood up. Facing Toby, he put one hand on his hip, holding the shotgun at his side, and shook his head. Brett lay unmoving on the floor behind him.

"I'm having a hard time believing this. After all we've been through together. But listen, before this goes much further, are you sure you know how to use that? It's cocked, isn't it? Won't do you much good if it isn't cocked. And you're sure that isn't mine? The empty one?"

Toby's hands were shaking. He'd never fired a pistol, but had seen plenty of videos and knew the basics. Did he have to cock this one? He didn't know, but the pistol was too big for his hand, and he was afraid if he tried to cock it the man might rush him.

And regardless of what he was saying, the man stayed where he was. If Toby had to cock it, why was he waiting?

Trying to keep his voice from cracking, Toby said, "You'll find out soon enough how much I know about a *loaded* gun if you don't back up."

The man stepped back with his hands held out to his sides. "Easy, kid, someone could get hurt. Put the gun down and let's talk—"

"Shut up and move back. And drop that shotgun. I'll shoot if you don't, and I mean it."

The man made a "calm down" motion with his free hand, dropped the shotgun, and moved back a few feet. "Okay, easy does it."

Toby held the gun on him and moved closer to Brett, dividing his attention between the man and his friend.

Brett was bleeding from the face and appeared to be unconscious. Toby feared that he might be dead, but he didn't know how to tell. Turning his full attention to the man, he gripped the pistol with both hands and straightened his arms while pointing it at the man's chest. "Move back more. I'm warning you. I'll shoot if you try anything."

The man nodded and stepped back a few feet. Toby wanted a little more room, but Brett groaned and Toby looked down at him, relieved that there was some sign of life. Then Brett's head rolled from one side to the other and Toby noticed the wound. As he bent down for a closer look the warning bells in his head rang at maximum volume and Toby squeezed the trigger.

The punishing sound and recoil of the gun took Toby completely by surprise. As the pistol clattered to the floor, he stumbled backward and tripped over the legs of the cop. Falling on his back, Toby looked between his feet and saw the man lying in the middle of the hallway.

Did I shoot him? Is he dead?

Toby lay there, propped up on his elbows, when he saw something out of a horror movie.

The man sat up slowly, holding his chest, head hanging down. Then he raised his head, looked at Toby, and grinned. "I guess you didn't need to cock it after all. But you know what?"

Toby couldn't have responded if he wanted to. The man reminded him of a superhuman villain in a video, coming back to threaten the hero after being torn to pieces.

"You need to hold it tighter."

The gun was lying on the floor, about halfway between him and the man. Could he get to it? Should he try? The man was fast, but he looked hurt. Toby was looking for signs of a chest wound when the man almost got to his feet before Toby realized what was happening. He rolled to his right, pushed himself up, and ran straight to the reactor room door, the closest way to put something between him and his pursuer.

Toby grabbed the handle as he hit the door with his shoulder and felt an initial resistance give way when the latch opened. He burst through the doorway into the dark interior, turned left and sprinted for his life. He couldn't outrun the man in a straight test of speed, but with his knowledge of the station and the man's wounds, all he needed was enough time to get into the chutes.

Samael had first discovered that cops on Oasis were issued protective vests when he found the corporal wearing one. They were very thin and light, made from a material he couldn't identify. He got another one off Cadogan after the first reactor room incident, and had decided to wear two just in case.

He always expected his adversaries to wear vests and aimed accordingly. Lucky for him the kid didn't. It hurt like hell, but the combination of the special ammo and the double layer of vest material prevented the bullet from penetrating even at this close range. His other injuries forgotten for the moment, he scrambled to his feet and went for the pistol.

He was sure the kid would do the same, and was surprised when he ran for the door. He also thought the door was locked, and was surprised again when it had opened and the boy disappeared into the darkness.

As Samael charged through the door and turned left, he realized the alarm was sounding. With his earplugs installed he was lucky to have heard it at all. He reversed direction and ran toward the keypad mounted just inside the door. As he approached, the countdown timer showed almost twenty seconds. Plenty of time.

Samael paused to confirm the passcode in his mind and began

entering it. Then he became aware of a soft, rhythmic sound, unusual and yet familiar, increasing in volume and approaching from his right. He tried to ignore it and concentrate on entering the code, missed a key and glanced to his right.

The robodog closed on Samael with blinding speed.

He turned to meet the threat and the dog slammed into Samael's crotch and knocked him back onto the floor with the dog tearing at the protective cup, cracked in the first robodog attack, and which gave way under the force of this dog's viselike jaws and crushed Samael's testicles like a couple of grapes.

He bit into his tongue as he fought to maintain consciousness through the excruciating pain and went for the stun gun, but the dog was tearing at him so hard that his hand kept getting pulled off the holster. He was barely conscious when the bomb detonated.

Samael heard it, felt the horrific concussion, and screamed.

TOBY KNEW BETTER THAN TO LOOK BEHIND HIM. HE RAN AS hard as he could looking for another door out into the central core when he saw the open air conditioning duct hatch, performed one of his patented leaps and grabbed the lip of the duct. He had just pulled his upper body inside when a massive WHUMP and shock wave reverberated through the reactor room. Pausing to look below him, he saw no signs of pursuit but noticed a faint, flickering glow and cloud of smoke advancing through the corridor. Then he heard the emergency klaxon and saw the red flashing warning light mounted in the ceiling.

He was tempted to go back the way he came to find Brett, but the man might still be in pursuit. Toby pulled himself the rest of the way into the duct and crawled to the point where the duct met the chute system, scrambled to the nearest exit into the central core and dropped into the corridor just outside the reactor room. He jogged down the corridor looking at the placards on doors in the outer walls until he found a utility storage room, yanked open the door and pulled out a flatbed pushcart used by maintenance guys.

Toby pushed the cart in front of him as he ran. Rounding a corner he saw Brett and the smoke pouring out of the reactor room. Toby rolled the cart up and knelt down by his friend, who moaned softly.

"Brett, listen to me. We've got to get you on this cart so I can move you away from here. There's fire. Do you understand? The station is on fire."

Brett opened his eyes, but looked as if he had trouble focusing. After a moment he seemed to shake off his confusion and looked directly at Toby. "You all right?"

"Forget about me. You're hurt. Help me get you up on the cart."

Brett nodded and mumbled something about that being a good idea. "Pilots don't like fire."

With Brett's feeble help, Toby rolled him onto the cart and pushed it to where the cop was lying. He looked dead, but Toby had to find out. As he touched the cop's arm, the sergeant turned his head and looked directly at him. Pain contorted his mangled face, but the voice was surprisingly clear, and vaguely familiar.

"What're you doing?" the cop asked.

"I'm going to get you out of here. There's a fire."

"Forget about me. Is the pilot okay?"

"He's hurt, don't know how bad. I can push you both on this cart. Help—"

"Where's the hijacker?"

"Don't know. Haven't seen him since the explosion and that's the way I want to keep it. Are you Sergeant Cadogan?"

"Hard to tell, isn't it? Take the pilot and get the hell out of here. You don't have much time."

Toby wanted to do that, but it didn't feel right. The cop seemed to read his mind.

"Look. I'm a dead man. You can't help me, and I'm not going to help you try. There's no way you can get me on that cart, and the longer you wait the less chance you and the pilot have. Do as I say right now."

Toby heard the words but didn't want to believe them.

The cop smiled. "It's okay."

Toby looked into the cop's eyes and nodded.

~

THE CART WAS LOW SLUNG ON SMALL WHEELS AND VERY maneuverable. Toby found he could get the thing up to speed, then hop on the back and by shifting his weight steer it pretty well. Brett looked up once or twice, glanced ahead, then back at Toby and closed his eyes. It was almost as if he didn't want to acknowledge how fast they were going.

Toby moved away from the center of the station, using elevators to change floors and avoid traveling in a straight line. As far as he knew, everyone had evacuated except for the men that arrived in the shuttle. He wanted to hurry, but took time every so often to search for threats. The soldiers could be anywhere, and the man might still after him.

Toby had almost blocked out the sound of the klaxons, but turned his attention to the warnings when the computerized voice began announcing the automatic lockdowns. He'd been through enough drills to know what that meant.

The most serious threat to life on Oasis was loss of environmental control, and leaks due to malfunction or damage had to be immediately isolated. The systems were designed to do that automatically, which could trap them in one of the segregated areas. A harsh reality, but a necessary one. "Cut off an arm to save the body" was the phrase used in training, even for youngsters.

Toby stopped to get his bearings, then changed direction toward where he expected to find a lifeship pod. After a few minutes of searching, he found a lifeship symbol hanging from the ceiling of the corridor. But a yellow sticker placed diagonally across the lifeship keypad controls labeled it as INOPERATIVE.

Pushing the cart up to speed, Toby raced down the corridor to the next lifeship location and skidded to a stop. The keypad was not placarded. He punched the door-open button and looked down at Brett. He wasn't moving.

I've got to get some help. What's wrong with this door?

Toby reached for the door-open button again and noticed the red warning light on the panel.

POD DEPARTED.

Toby peered through the small porthole in the door at the gaping, dark hole in the outer station wall.

Toby shook Brett gently. "Brett, wake up."

His friend slowly opened his eyes. "Where are we?"

"At a lifeship station. I've tried two so far with no luck. What—?"

"What do you want with a lifeship?"

"Brett, we've got to get off the station. There's been an explosion, remember? Sections are shutting down. How can I find a lifeship station that works?"

Brett closed his eyes, then suddenly opened them. "Holy shit. I forgot about that."

"About what?"

"The pods." Brett coughed, winced in pain, and seemed to collect himself before continuing. His voice was shaky, but better than before.

"There was some trouble with the pods. Not enough to handle the population. Forget about trying to find one."

"But we've—"

"We don't know how much of the station is being shut down, but it can't be all of it. Let's just get in a section that's okay."

Toby knew better than that. Brett wasn't thinking straight. "You've got to concentrate. The announcements are continuous. Every few minutes another section shuts down. I can't figure out where to go. For all we know the problem affects everything."

"That's impossible. This station—"

"You want to bet your life on that? And you're forgetting we're the only good guys left. Why should we stay around with a small army looking for us?"

Brett seemed to wake up. "I'm glad one of us is thinking straight. Okay, get us to the shuttle."

Toby was now certain Brett's head injury had caused some brain damage. "What are you talking about? We've got to get to a working lifeship pod, abandon the station, and wait to get picked up. It's our only chance."

Brett lowered his head back down on the cart, closed his eyes, and shook his head. "I'm kind of shaky now, but you'll have to trust me on this one. I don't think there are any working pods left. But even if there are we have no way to find them. I do know where the shuttle is, and I'll bet no one is guarding it."

"You must be crazy. After that docking, the shuttle isn't flyable. You told the man yourself when we looked at the damage. And you're in no shape to fly it anyway."

Brett, lying there with his eyes closed and in obvious pain, grinned. "What makes you think I tell the truth all the time? Just get us to the shuttle and I'll show you what I mean. Besides, you always said you wanted to learn to fly. Now's your chance."

Toby stared at his friend. "Now I know you've lost your mind."

"Stop arguing. The longer you wait the less chance we'll be able to make it there. Let's go, and don't worry about speed limits."

ANDRAS LISTENED CAREFULLY TO THE ANNOUNCEMENTS AND knew the lockdowns were occurring from the central core outward, and the net effect would be to drive any knowledgeable survivors in that direction. With no operative lifeship pods left, the bad guys would eventually be cut off with no method of escape, with one possible exception. And although the hijacker might have died in the explosion, Andras couldn't shake the hunch that the guy was a perpetual survivor.

Andras knew all about stomach wounds. He'd seen some nasty ones, enough to know they were usually fatal *and slow*, which in this case might be a blessing in disguise.

He removed his combat harness and vest and rigged a makeshift compress for his wound. Not the best of dressings, but it wouldn't have to do much more than hold him together for a while. He pulled himself over to the shotgun and gathered up the shells that were lying about on the floor. Cursing the crimped one that had jammed, he discarded it and loaded the rest.

He crawled to the nearest equipment locker, found a cart and pulled himself onto it. Using his arms, he managed to make good time along the corridor to an elevator. The shotgun made a handy extension to reach the call button, and he repeated the process to make his way from the central core to the shuttle loading dock. En route he passed one of the closed lockout doors and heard the faint cries and pounding from the other side.

Bye-bye, you sons of bitches.

Andras used his electronic access card to enter the control booth above the loading dock and wheeled himself to the window. Propping himself up on an elbow, he peered over the bottom edge and saw three men standing around the open cargo door of the shuttle. At least one of them appeared to be wounded. Two others lay unmoving on the floor of the bay by the loading ramp.

The pain that had dogged him since the fight returned with a vengeance. Andras gritted his teeth against it. After a moment the pain subsided somewhat, but the episodes were closer together and lasting longer.

Andras had a buddy who worked as a docking bay controller. Visiting on several occasions, he had watched enough dockings to know the basics of pressurization control.

Andras rolled himself over to the console, struggled against his growing weakness and managed to pull himself up into a chair. After a moment to let the dizziness subside and catch his breath, he examined the console and thought out the sequence. Normal de-pressurizations were relatively slow affairs, but the system was designed to allow for a more rapid process in the event of a malfunction. The man had showed Andras how that would work, and the lesson hadn't been wasted.

He used his electronic access card to power up the console and initiated the sequence. Once the command verification was made, a green GO button began to flash, and Andras pushed it with a silent curse and rolled in the chair over to the window, where he peered out and down to watch the fun.

Any station crew member would have known what the warnings meant, but these guys were your standard garden-variety mercenaries, told only what their employers wanted them to know. They'd probably been ordered to stay and guard the shuttle, and that's what they were doing. Even when the klaxons in the bay started up, all they could do was to run around brandishing their weapons, looking for someone to shoot. The men calmed down after a few minutes, then went back to their guard duties as the pressure in the bay began its precipitous drop.

After a short period Andras noticed one of the men yawn, then begin taking deep breaths. He said something to the man next to him, they both turned and talked to the third man, and within the next minute or so all three of them were struggling.

Andras enjoyed it immensely. The last man to pass out had finally tried to enter the shuttle, probably to search for an oxygen mask. He died at the threshold of the cargo door. Andras arrested the depressurization and after a wait of about ten minutes, reversed the sequence.

He wanted his target to enter the bay, become diverted by the bodies, and then find out what it was like to meet the same fate.

It would've been much easier just to lie there and die. But Samael *had* to survive long enough to get his hands on the person who designed these damned dogs. When that happened, the world would have to redefine the word sadistic.

Shrapnel from the bomb had ripped open the dog's side, with wires hanging out and sparks every few seconds. The dog's innards were toast. With some satisfaction, Samael realized the dog had saved his life by shielding him from some of the shrapnel. He shoved the carcass off and rolled on his side, fighting against the comforting nearness of unconscious bliss.

Do not pass out. You'll die here on this floor if you do.

Smoke billowed everywhere, alarms blared, and a computerized voice announced shutdowns. He rolled over on his stomach and struggled to his knees to wait for the dizziness to subside. The smoke was thick above him, so he stayed low and crawled out of the reactor room, closing the door behind him.

With the wall for support, Samael stood and leaned against it. It wasn't until he looked directly at the pool of blood on the floor that he realized the pilot and the cop were both gone. And what about the kid? Although tempted to believe he'd been killed in the explosion, Samael couldn't shake the feeling that their paths would cross again.

Anger had never been a prime motivator for him. But with a plentiful supply of it to fuel his revenge, Samael blocked out the pain and concentrated on the computerized voice. After a moment he formed a picture of how the bomb damage was affecting the station's atmospheric control zones, and he willed his legs forward toward the only destination that made any sense.

Once clear of the immediate danger of fire, Samael stopped and tried the radio. His transmission was immediately followed by the garbled sound of two or more simultaneous responses, which rendered them both almost unreadable. He was able to make out the panicked voice of a squad leader asking for instructions. The plan called for the squads to fan out and secure widely dispersed critical areas. This violated the principle of concentration of force, but with the chance of organized resistance being so remote, it was the fastest way to gain complete control.

It also meant the lockdowns were trapping his assault teams in death zones. Samael thought about trying to reestablish order, but decided it would be useless. He'd placed the bomb to provide a real threat to the station's survival, and it appeared the theory had been correct. Oasis was rapidly becoming a tomb.

Listening carefully to the announcements, Samael referred to his station diagram and crossed off questionable areas to find an escape route. Limping down the corridor, he hurried as best he could toward a final rendezvous.

EXITING AN ELEVATOR AT THE LOADING DOCK LEVEL, TOBY TOOK a moment to search the immediate vicinity and found nothing. He rolled the cart with Brett into the corridor and pushed it up to speed before hopping on the back. He didn't bother to slow down at the intersections ahead, abandoning caution in favor of getting to the shuttle as quickly as possible.

They passed three empty docks before reaching their destination. Toby stopped just short of the last corner and left the cart as he edge toward the entrance, pausing to search the area ahead. Arriving at the doors, he stayed below the windows and directed his search into the bay.

He had no problem telling where the shuttle was. It was the biggest single object he'd ever sensed, resting alone in the massive bay. Turning his attention to the presence of people, Toby found shapes of the right size, but without the distinctive temperature differential. They were warmer than the surroundings, but not warm enough.

Carefully rising to the bottom of the windows, Toby peered into the bay. When he saw the men he pulled his head back down. He had sensed seven man-sized shapes, five in one location and two in another. The five were lying around the entrance to the shuttle's cargo hold and they appeared to be sleeping.

Why would they be sleeping? The two separate shapes were probably in the shuttle, not visible from his vantage point outside the bay. Toby thought for a minute, searched the area again, then decided to take another look.

The men were absolutely still. He watched for about five minutes, and finally made his decision. Moving back from the doors, Toby trotted back to the cart and found Brett awake and extremely curious.

"Where have you been? I woke up, you're gone. Worried me to death."

"You look fine to me. Now quit complaining and let's get to the shuttle."

"Hold on a minute. Do you know what's going on in there?"

"No. But we don't have much choice."

Toby shoved the cart around the corner and pushed it down the corridor. He stopped at the loading dock doors and reached for the control panel.

"Stop," said Brett. "The bay isn't fully pressurized."

Toby looked at the door control panel and saw the red warning light.

"It's being pressurized. Someone is doing that either from inside the bay or up in the control booth. Have you looked—"

"There's no one alive in the bay."

"Then there has to be someone in the booth. We have to find out who it is before we try to make it to the shuttle."

Toby nodded. "I'll be back in a minute." He hurried down the hall to the elevator and rode it to the control booth level. The lights were out in the booth. Toby searched, found the familiar evidence of human presence, and then carefully looked in the rear window. The light in the loading bay illuminated the booth interior just enough for Toby to see the big cop. He was slumped in a chair by the window overlooking the bay. Toby opened the door and entered.

He was almost close enough to touch the cop when the big man suddenly spun around in the swivel chair and leveled a pistol at Toby's nose. After a moment of panic, Toby breathed a sigh of relief as the cop lowered the gun into his blood-soaked lap.

"You could get shot sneaking up on people with guns, kid." His voice was very weak. "You got the pilot with you?"

Toby nodded.

"Good. Take him into the bay and get on the shuttle. It might be your only chance, so be quick about it."

"We can't get into the bay. The red light is on."

The cop shook his head. "It won't be by the time you get back there. Now go."

Toby stared at the big cop's face. He was sweating profusely in spite of the cool atmosphere in the booth. "Why don't you come with us? I'll help you on the cart and—"

"We've already discussed that. And even if I weren't dying, there's no safe place for me anymore. Now get the pilot on the shuttle and leave the station. Hurry up."

Toby thought he saw moisture building in the sergeant's eyes, but couldn't be sure. He opened his mouth to say something, but the cop pointed to the door and motioned for him to leave.

As Toby returned to the docking bay Brett yelled at him. "What the hell's going on? Was there anyone in the booth?"

Toby ignored the question, looked at the door control panel and the green pressurization status light, and jabbed the door-open button. With an audible pop and hissing of air, the door began to move as he walked around the cart to push it into the bay.

Brett stared at him. "What's the matter? You look like you've seen a ghost."

"You're right."

Lying on the cart, Brett couldn't see the shuttle until Toby lowered him down the sloped ramp and onto the bay floor. Brett's throat constricted into a knot when he saw the men, but before he could say anything Toby said, "They're all dead."

Calm. Matter of fact. This was some kid.

Toby never even slowed. He gathered speed on the level bay floor and shoved the cart up the shuttle's cargo ramp and into the hold. Turning left, he maneuvered around the piles of equipment left by the troops and stopped at the bottom of the ladder. Toby stepped around to the front of the cart.

"Any suggestions on how we get you up to the cockpit?"

"I'd like to try climbing up."

"Lots of luck. You haven't even been able to sit up without losing it."

Toby was right. Brett looked above him and remembered the block and tackle. "There's equipment on the landing used for hauling supplies up to the crew level from the floor of the hold. If you lower it to me I can hook the strap on and we'll pull me up."

Toby took the steps by threes and in less than a minute swung the utility crane out over the edge of the landing. He climbed over the railing, grabbed the leather straps on the end of the cable, and stepped off into space. The block and tackle arrangement slowed his descent, and he touched down by the cart.

Toby rigged up a harness for Brett, then went back up to the landing and tossed the other end of the cable down. With Brett doing what he could to help pull, Toby hauled on the cable until they raised Brett above the level of the railing. After swinging the crane over the landing, they lowered him and disconnected the harness.

Toby helped Brett make his way slowly down the corridor of the crew quarters. When he saw Lin's crumpled shape lying at the entrance of the corridor into the galley, Brett stopped.

"I wish there were some other way to do this. There was a fight in here and two people died. We can't leave them on board. I can't move them by myself, and that means you have to. Can you handle it?"

Toby was staring down the dim corridor toward Lin's body. After a moment he nodded. "In the last few weeks I've seen my share of dead people. I just hope it never seems normal."

Brett stared at his young friend, wishing he could take him in his arms and make it all go back to the way it was. No one should have to grow up this fast. Squeezing Toby's shoulder, he said, "I feel the same way. Let's get this done."

Stepping around Lin's body, Brett was shocked at the sight. Being here when it happened wasn't the same at all. Swallowing hard, he decided the easiest way to do this was through the open hatch. They needed to get it closed quickly, just to make sure all access to the shuttle was blocked off.

The soldier was closest. Brett helped as best he could. The two of them maneuvered the body head first down the hatch. It knocked over the ladder the cops used to rescue Brett and hit the floor of the bay with a sickening thud. Toby was looking down at the body when he asked, "What happened to him?"

I killed him. Up close and personal, not at all like with an airplane.

"I don't want to talk about it. Now help me get Lin over here."

It took longer, but they did it. Brett told Toby how to use an onboard hose and they washed and brushed off most of the blood before closing the hatch. With Toby's help, Brett made it to the companionway and slowly climbed up to the cockpit. Once in the pilot's seat, he asked Toby to get them some food, then closed his eyes and thought about their next move.

Oasis was dying. The soldiers were more than likely cut off from returning to the shuttle. If some of them did make it back, they wouldn't be able to get inside the shuttle without using heavy weapons or power equipment, which they probably didn't have. They would also be reluctant to damage the shuttle if they realized it was their only means of escape from a dying space station.

Brett hadn't told Toby, but their own chance of escape wasn't all that good. The odds of launching the shuttle were slim. With no one to operate the bay controls, the shuttle would have to be pressurized.

One of them would have to use the airlock to exit and make his way to the booth, depressurize the bay, open the outer doors, and return. Brett was in no condition to try it. And although there were small pressure suits that would fit Toby, the chances of something going wrong were simply too great.

But they had another option that might work. The shuttle was designed for extended space travel and could provide the two of them with food and shelter for months. They were onboard, ready to lock the shuttle down, and then it was a matter of waiting. The station would become sectioned off by automatic lockdowns, trapping the soldiers where they were, and eventually allow Brett to call for rescue without fear of interference.

Brett heard the sounds of movement in the companionway and opened his eyes to find Toby standing beside him with a tray of food. "This stuff looks pretty bad, but there sure is a lot of it." It was a standard joke between them.

Brett thanked Toby and accepted one of the infamous space versions of the veritable MRE. He was taking his first mouthful when he remembered he hadn't initiated the shuttle's pressurization. Directing Toby to the control panel, he told him how to close the cargo doors, select the manual mode, and dial in positive pressure. This action sealed the shuttle, and made certain any decrease in the docking bay pressure would not affect the interior.

Toby wasn't eating. Brett motioned to the food on the tray. "We can joke about it, but it's all we have at the moment. You'd better have some and get used to it."

"I'm not very hungry right now. Don't you think we'd better get going? There'll be plenty of time to eat later."

Brett put down his fork and motioned for Toby to sit down on the jump seat. "When I suggested we come to the shuttle it wasn't because I thought we could get off the station. That's just not possible under the circumstances. But we can—"

"It's flyable, isn't it? When we looked at the damage you weren't telling the truth when the man asked you about it. You said so."

"As far as the shuttle itself is concerned, you're right. But we can't get the bay ready for launch without someone in the control booth. All we can do at this point is to lock the shuttle down and wait for rescue."

Toby was shaking his head. "That's not true. Can you fly the shuttle?"

"Toby, listen to me. In order to launch we have to—"

"No, Brett, listen to *me*. There is someone in the booth, and we can get out of here if you will just quit talking and start flying."

Brett had to concentrate hard to comprehend what Toby had just said. "Someone in the control booth?"

Toby nodded.

Brett leaned over to look up toward the booth. And there in the corner, barely visible in the shadows, were the head and shoulders of a man.

"Who the hell is that?"

"Tell you all about it later. Now get the shuttle ready to go. If you don't hurry we'll be trapped in here."

Brett had a momentary thought, about how the adult-child relationship often reversed itself when aging parents required special care. He wasn't anywhere near ready for that with Toby, but the young man knew what he wanted to do, and under these extraordinary circumstances he appeared to be right.

"Okay. But if you're waiting for me, you're behind. I need a copilot, and he's not in his seat."

Toby grinned, his face lighting up, and as he took his place in the cockpit Brett called the booth.

"Shuttle to Launch Control, do you read, over?"

THIS WAS ABSOLUTELY THE MOST FANTASTIC EXPERIENCE OF Toby's life so far. He concentrated so hard he totally forgot about the events that had put him here. Once the shuttle was in a stable position above the bay floor, Brett rotated the shuttle so the control booth was directly in view out the windscreen.

His voice a hoarse whisper in the headset, Sergeant Cadogan had coordinated with Brett to depressurize the bay, open the doors, and assist in the launch sequence. Toby could now see his shadowy figure behind the booth's window, and watched as Brett took his right hand off the controls and in slow motion raised it in salute.

Cadogan sat up straighter, returned the salute and held it for a few seconds before lifting his arm in a wave of goodbye. As Brett turned the shuttle to exit the bay, Toby watched the cop for as long as he could. The man had helped save their lives, and sacrificed his own in the process. Toby felt a surge of sadness that he'd never thanked him, and hoped his own wave conveyed the thought.

Once free of the bay, Brett stabilized the shuttle in a stationary position on Oasis. Pointing to the lifeship pods, visible as bright points of light around the station, he said, "In a moment I'm going to call the moon colony and coordinate our rescue. We'll probably have to wait awhile. They still have a lot of pods to pick up, but we're in good shape here."

Brett didn't look very good. "How're you feeling?" asked Toby.

"Not real hot. I need to close my eyes for a while and rest."

"What do you want me to do?"

"Nothing, except maybe eat some of that delicious food and relax. The shuttle will maintain this position on the station automatically. I'm really tired."

Within a few seconds Brett's face relaxed and he fell sound asleep. Toby used the seat controls to recline the back. He felt as if the weight of the world had been lifted from his shoulders. So much had happened that it all seemed like a bad dream with no end, and he was ready to wake up and resume his life.

There would be obstacles, of course. Running off on his own would be hard to justify. But when the station was back in operation, he would return with his mom and dad. It might never be the same again, but he'd adjust, regain their trust, and come up with a way to get their support for his plan to be a pilot.

Although his cooperation with the man haunted him, Toby felt that in the end he had made up for it. Brett probably would have died, and the man might have succeeded in his final goal, whatever that was. With no one else to tell the tale, Toby was determined to forget his mistakes and turn the negatives of the past into a positive future.

The tray he'd brought to Brett still had lots of food on it, but he remembered some other choices in the pantry that looked better. Testing his stability in the weightlessness, he descended through the companionway down the galley floor. Landing softly on the balls of his feet, Toby gripped a handrail to steady himself and looked out into the galley.

Something wasn't right. The pantry door was open and items were lying about. He was positive he had closed the door. Was he mistaken? Was someone else on the shuttle?

Toby moved out into the center of the galley and held onto a table for support. Then it occurred to him that a simple search would do the trick. In spite of his enhanced powers, vision was still his most natural sense, and he had to think consciously about using audio or space search. Closing his eyes, he began the process out toward the corridor and crew quarters ahead.

The warning hit him like a freight train out of the darkness, sudden, massive, and overwhelming.

～

LOOKING DOWN AT THE CRUMPLED BODY OF THE KID, SAMAEL saw a drop of his own blood drift into his peripheral vision. It must have come from the head wound and hung there, a red shiny dot. He blew at it, sending it slowly away into the galley. The bandages were becoming soaked through. He needed to tend his wounds, rest, and get the hell out of here.

Samael had known the boy wouldn't leave the pilot, and that they would return to the loading dock. He also figured by using the chutes and their connection with the shuttle's escape hatch, he could probably get there before they did.

The first complication had been the hatch. He couldn't get it open. He was about to abandon the attempt when he sensed a change in air pressure and the hatch swung open.

The next surprise was finding that the chute opening in the floor of the dock wasn't lined up with the emergency hatch in the bottom of the shuttle. He'd been considering what to do next when the boy entered the dock pushing the pilot on a cart. Peering out from under the partially opened chute cover, Samael watched them enter the shuttle and smiled.

He climbed out of the chute and closed the hatch. With the shuttle between him and the control booth, Samael moved to the open emergency hatch in the bottom of the shuttle. Someone had placed a short ladder there, and he was able to pull himself up into the galley. Ignoring the two bodies, he walked back to the aft bulkhead door and heard the boy talking with the pilot about rigging a harness. Hiding in a crew sleeping room, he waited.

A short time later they passed by his hiding place and stayed in the galley for about ten minutes, dealing with the bodies. When he felt the shuttle pressurize, Samael knew he was home free. Then after the launch it was simply a matter of making his way into the galley, using all his skill to avoid triggering the boy's alarm system, and the trap had been set.

He was in no condition to chase anyone, and knowledge of the boy's powers had helped him stage the attack. With the element of surprise as his only advantage, Samael used the open pantry door as a diversion. He expected the boy to stop, close his eyes, and start searching in front of him. Attacking from the rear was the best chance of getting close without alerting him too soon.

Stuffing himself in the small locker had been easy enough once he removed a shelf. He'd never attacked anyone in zero gravity, but it worked quite well. Coiled up in the locker, he simply shoved out with his legs and propelled himself into the galley. One blow to the kid's head sent him down like a sack of potatoes. Patience had paid off, as it usually did, and he was back in the driver's seat once again.

After tying Toby's hands and feet, Samael ascended the companionway and confirmed the source of the snoring was indeed the pilot, alive, but not all that well.

What a crew. Cuts, bruises, maybe a broken bone or two, and you couldn't make a complete body from the remaining working parts.

But he was alive. And with this shuttle he could still revert to his original plan. Retirement under the circumstances can't be all bad.

"Hey there, pilot, wake up. Time to go to work."

BRETT WAS SOUND ASLEEP WHEN SOMETHING GRABBED HIM BY the throat. He opened his eyes to find the hijacker standing over him.

"Surprised to see me again?"

Brett nodded, but even that small movement hurt. He couldn't breathe very well. Surely the man wasn't going to kill him now, but if he squeezed any harder he might.

"Sometime you'll have to tell me how you did it."

"What?" It was a barely audible croak.

"I leave you locked away in the shuttle, men with guns minding the store. Next thing I know you're yelling at me from that damned space sewer in the wall. I thought you might be trouble sooner or later, but not like this."

"Where's Toby?"

"Forget about him. He's been more of a pain in the ass than you have. The two of you together are quite a team."

"Have you hurt him?"

The hijacker turned ugly, like he flipped an internal switch. "Sure. And I'll hurt him more anytime I want, along with you and anyone else who gets in my way." The man drew back his hand and hit Brett across the face with a vicious backhand blow. "Now get this bucket ready for action."

The hijacker abruptly released Brett's throat and turned away, disappearing down the companionway into the galley. Brett stared after him, face stinging, drops of blood floating into his vision, and became frightened.

After all we've been through, it comes down to this?

TOBY'S FIRST AWARENESS WAS OF A SPLITTING HEADACHE. HE HAD to remain perfectly still to keep from getting sick to his stomach. He tried to open his eyes, but couldn't focus very well and there was a bright light in his face. All he wanted to do was go back to sleep.

"Does that hurt enough for you?"

In spite of the pain, Toby opened his eyes. The blurred face was right there, smiling, a vision from his nightmares come back to haunt him.

"You lied to me," Toby said. "You made me believe you were trying to do good things and you're nothing but a thief."

The man shook his head and laughed softly. "Bullshit. I didn't make you believe anything. Once I began to talk about flying you would have sold out your own mother to get what you wanted. I simply threw out the bait and you took a bite of it."

"That's not true. I never—"

"Shut up! I'm through talking with you. You made a deal and then turned on me like the snake you are. The only reason you're alive is that it's too much trouble to kill you. There's no place to toss your body until we get to Earth. It would stink up the place. Now get up."

"I can't. My head—"

"Damn your head to hell! If it hadn't been for your treachery I might have made it and that really pisses me off. Now get up!"

If there had been any gravity, Toby never would have made it. He used the bed frame for support as he sat up and noticed the restraints around his ankles. "What's this for? Where would I run to?"

"Nowhere, and I'm going to make sure of it. Now come on."

Toby floated unsteadily off the bed and in front of the man, who guided them both out of the room, through the galley and up the companionway into the cockpit. Brett turned to look at Toby as the man put him in the jump seat. The look in Brett's eyes scared Toby more than the rough hands strapping him in.

20

DAYS TWENTY-ONE THROUGH TWENTY-FOUR

The first time Toby had made the journey from Oasis to Earth he was so excited that the time passed by very slowly. During the return voyage to Oasis he stayed so busy that he hardly remembered the trip at all. This trip began as a nightmare and got steadily worse because Toby was so worried about the future that he could hardly eat.

His primary responsibility was to dress the wounds. The hijacker showed him what to do, then watched him intently as he ministered to him and Brett. Toby also prepared the meals, and the man never let him out of his sight.

He didn't know what kind of medicine it was, but the ship's supplies provided the man with a steady supply of some pills. For some reason the hijacker used only about half the amount that he gave to Brett, and it didn't take Toby long to notice the difference. Brett got sleepy following medication, and was usually given his dose just prior to a rest period. But the hijacker took it randomly, and never seemed to sleep.

About halfway into the trip, Toby went to the medical supplies locker to prepare for the dressing changes. The hijacker was close by, but positioned off to the side near the food preparation counter. Toby noticed there were only a few pills remaining in the container.

He compared the label with other pills in the locker. When he found some, he decided to move all the pills into the same compartment so they would be easier to find the next time he needed more. He paid close attention to the labels and noticed there were two containers of the same pills in a dosage twice that of what he had been using.

The next day the hijacker nodded off periodically after taking the medication. Toby began to wonder if there might be a way to take advantage of the medicine's side effects. His eagerness to talk with Brett encouraged him to take the chance.

The following afternoon, with the hijacker's back turned toward him, Toby opened the medicine locker and positioned it to block the man's view if he turned around. Being careful not to let any of the pills get away from him in the zero gravity, Toby transferred some of the double-dose pills into the original container.

Later during the dressing changes, Toby's pulse raced when the hijacker reached out for the pills. The double-dose ones were on top, and hopefully had stayed there.

Within the next hour the man began to yawn, nodded off a few times, and then fell sound asleep. Toby waited for a few minutes, then got Brett's attention and pointed to the man, making a head on the pillow sign with his hands and head. Brett nodded, and gave Toby a "so-what" look. Toby emphasized his point by reaching out and punching the man on the shoulder.

Brett's face registered his surprise.

Toby leaned over toward Brett and whispered, "I drugged him."

Brett looked over at the man, then back at Toby. "You did what?"

"I gave him a double dose of the medicine."

Brett seemed impressed. "Well done," he said softly. "Aren't you the devious one?"

"When I have to be. Now what're we going to do about this guy?"

~

SAMAEL WOKE UP WITH A SUDDEN FRIGHT THAT HE'D BEEN OUT for a long time. One glance at the instrument panel clock confirmed he'd slept for about six hours. He never left the boy or the pilot unre-strained, but it was a serious lapse in his security plan.

He scanned the cockpit and found nothing suspicious. The boy and the pilot were both sound asleep. Although neither of them could have moved very far, it was entirely possible they could have spoken without awakening him.

But the more intriguing question was why he'd fallen asleep. Samael's profession was generally intolerant of unplanned naps. He knew the painkillers could cause drowsiness, but he'd tuned the dose over the past week to make sure he didn't take too much.

So what happened? Six hours was like an eternity, and Samael was positive he would never sleep that long without planning to do so. The small pack used to carry the medical supplies was tied to his seat. He found the pill container, and quickly determined there were two dosages inside, and the container's label listed the smaller of the two.

The kid again. The little shit probably switched the pills, waited until he fell asleep, and made some kind of escape plan with the pilot.

Samael made a pact with himself to make absolutely certain it never happened again.

BRETT HAD ERRONEOUSLY ASSUMED THEIR DESTINATION WOULD be the same as last time. But when the hijacker refused to divulge the coordinates, Brett began to speculate on what the plan was and what to do about it thwarting it. One thing was for certain. He and Toby would never survive if they just went along for the ride.

Toby's ingenuity with the pills had presented them with the only chance they would have to talk. The man was extra cautious after waking up from the long nap, and Brett had not seen him take another pill.

But the opportunity had been well used. Brett hated the thought of putting Toby in danger, but the reality was they both were in serious trouble no matter what they did. It was going to take bold action to make any difference.

Using a combination of whispered conversation, notes, and hand signals, Brett tried to convince Toby the best thing for him was to make a run for it at the first opportunity once they arrived on Earth. The man was hurt and couldn't move all that well.

But Toby insisted he'd never be able to do that. He was in zero gravity on the shuttle, and the man had him in leg chains and tied in a seat most of the time. Toby also refused to consider leaving Brett. If Brett's injuries prevented running for it, Toby wasn't going anywhere, period.

They kept coming back to the same conclusion. There really wasn't much they could do, except be ready to seize any opportunity. Brett instructed Toby on the emergency operation of the rear cargo bay doors, and they discussed his original plan for trapping the hijacker in the bay. They agreed that if the hijacker went into the bay he would undoubtedly take Toby with him. But the plan could work if Toby managed to separate himself from the hijacker and make it back to the crew compartment.

If Brett lived through this and for a hundred more years, he would never forget Toby's response to these cautions. "You handle your end, I'll take care of mine. If we get that bastard in the bay don't worry about me."

The shuttle's automatic systems had operated flawlessly so far, more than just a convenience, because Brett wasn't certain he'd be any good at manual control. His mental processes seemed to be slowed up, a kind of fuzzy feeling, not at all conducive to exact flying. In the absence of specific directions from the hijacker, he was running through the checklists, preparing for either orbital insertion or reentry, when the hijacker entered the cockpit.

As the man strapped into the right seat, Brett said, "I need a destination."

The man nodded and reached for the GPS lying on the center console. After performing a series of keystroke actions, he placed the unit back where Brett could see it. "Go there."

Brett began the now familiar process of following the GPS steering commands, noting as he did so that the destination appeared to be somewhere close to the good old U.S. of A.

Well I'll be damned. I would have never thought he'd try that.

Brett considered whether it would be to their advantage to delay. What was going on out there? Were they being tracked? Did anybody give a shit?

The horizontal bar was just starting down. Brett had to follow it or come up with a reason not to. He—

"Do it."

IT WAS ANOTHER SPECTACULAR RIDE. THE SPACE PART WAS fascinating, but Toby found the transition to normal flight and the low altitude stuff even more interesting. He didn't know the specifics, but had read enough about the shuttles to understand what Brett had to do during the process.

In space the sensation of speed was non-existent unless you were close to another object, like in a rendezvous. But then everything was done so slowly that it was difficult to detect movement. Coming out of orbit had been accomplished well above any clouds. Approaching the reconfiguration part of the procedure they entered a wispy layer that looked like white cotton candy, visible even in the darkness. The sight of the clouds racing by the windscreen was absolutely fantastic, and the shuttle's incredible speed had been thrilling to experience.

As Brett began the process of extending the shuttle's normal flight surfaces, they broke out of the high layer into a clear area with more clouds below. Toby temporarily lost interest in the view outside while watching Brett's actions in the cockpit. When he looked back outside he was startled to see how close they were to the lower layer. These were a different type of cloud, much thicker, and puffy like cotton balls. Brett leveled the shuttle out just above the tops, and Toby instinctively knew why.

The sensation of speed was a head rush beyond belief. Brett seemed to be flying the ship as close to the tops of the clouds as possible without touching them, and often maneuvered to avoid a high mound of cloud, staying in the "valleys" and avoiding the "peaks." Toby knew there was no danger to the shuttle, but watching from the jump seat as they approached the mounded top of a cloud and flashed by it, he remembered the last time when the ground was this close. The thought made his bowels feel a little loose.

From the right seat, the man said, "Having fun?"

"Aren't you?" Brett answered.

The man responded with another question. "The RWR gear is on, right?"

"Absolutely."

"What do you make of the lack of activity?"

Brett didn't answer for a moment. "Maybe they just don't care. You're no longer a threat to the station. This shuttle can always be replaced, and what's one pilot more or less? They may not know about the boy."

Brett turned to look at the man as he said that, and from his position on the jump seat Toby could clearly see the concern on his face. The man ignored the comment, and motioned toward the navigation computer.

"About thirty minutes to go. Begin a descent. I want to check out the weather between us and the surface."

Brett used the autopilot to start down. Entering the clouds, the shuttle began to bounce around and Brett told the man he was slowing down because of the turbulence. After a few minutes they broke out between layers, and Toby could see more clouds below and through holes in the undercast what looked like water. The man loosened his straps and leaned forward to get a better look below the shuttle. Then with a finger pointed skyward, he told Brett to climb back into the clouds and stay there.

Brett was startled when the hijacker began to unstrap from the copilot's seat. You could get hurt in turbulence like this. What was the man up to? And then when the hijacker told Toby to come with him, Brett's stomach cramped up.

Turning to watch them descend the companionway, Brett saw Toby lose his balance as the shuttle bounced hard in the turbulence. He instinctively pulled the power back to slow down. Recommended turbulence penetration airspeed was a compromise between maintaining control, structural integrity, and passenger comfort, but was biased toward the high side because it assumed everyone would be strapped in. With Toby walking around, a slower speed would be better to minimize the chance of being tossed about and injured.

After a few moments Brett saw the BULKHEAD DOOR OPEN light illuminate. They'd probably entered the cargo bay. With the exception of Toby being in there with the man, this was the situation Brett had hoped to create, in the Earth's atmosphere, low enough for Brett to survive a rapid decompression, and the man unrestrained within the bay. Toby's words came back to him.

If we get the bastard in there, don't worry about me.

Brett glanced at the jettison control panel and felt a combination of excitement and fear. He wanted so badly to drop this son of a bitch into the ocean from 20,000 feet, but without being able to coordinate with Toby, he couldn't take the chance.

Brett's ideal plan under the circumstances relied on the shuttle's design as a multi-purpose transport. Over the objections of the anti-military crowd, it included systems for low altitude extractions of cargo. Essential for such operations was the ability for loadmasters to work safely in the bay and communicate with the cockpit when the rear doors were open.

Brett had done his best to instruct Toby on the personnel restraint and intercom systems in the bay. But at this point he had no way of knowing if and when his young friend would be ready for the big event. When the voice suddenly broke into his thoughts over the intercom, it was definitely the wrong one.

"Slow to your minimum maneuver speed and keep it there."

Why are we doing this?

Brett disconnected the autopilot, retarded the throttles to idle, and waited as the shuttle slowed up. The wing sweep and leading edge slat controls were set on automatic. As the speed decreased he felt the wings sweep forward and the slats extend from the front of the wing to direct airflow smoothly over the upper surface. Lights on the control panel confirmed the configuration changes. Approaching the minimum maneuver speed for this configuration, Brett advanced the throttles to maintain it and reported that to the bay.

"My speed is set. What now?"

No answer. Brett repeated the call, and was startled as the red glow from the tele-lights on the door control panel lit up the dark cockpit.
REAR AIRSTAIRS UNLOCKED.

WALKING DOWN THE CORRIDOR TOWARD THE CARGO BAY, TOBY had held onto anything he could find to steady himself in the turbulence. He'd almost fallen down the companionway. As they reached the rear bulkhead door, the man opened it and ordered him out onto the landing.

The bay was full of gear, everything neat, strapped down tight. The man had a grip on the back of his shirt, which seemed completely unnecessary given the shackles. Once on the floor of the bay, the man directed him toward the rear and around the edge of the bay to avoid the gear and the rows of seats. When they reached the back of the bay and about ten feet from the rear doors, he told Toby to sit on the floor and secured the chain between his ankle cuffs to a heavy metal support for the pallet system.

For the next few moments Toby watched the man prepare some equipment. The heavy duffle bags were connected together and the entire bundle was attached to what looked like a huge parachute.

The hijacker opened a soft-sided bag and took out an insulated jumpsuit. Pulling the lower portion over his legs, he slipped his arms in and zipped it up to the middle of the chest. Then he reached into the bag and brought out a protective helmet with goggles and a personal parachute. Toby felt an immediate stab of fear at the image of open cargo doors and falling out into the darkness. The man seemed to sense his reaction.

"You wondering about this?"

Toby didn't know what to say, so he didn't respond.

"If I were you I would be. I'd be thinking about what it'll be like, and get myself ready for it."

Toby swallowed hard. "For what?"

The man laughed. "You mean a smart kid like you hasn't figured it out yet?"

"I don't know what you're talking about."

The man moved closer and stood over Toby. "Maybe not, but you will." He turned away, then stopped and faced Toby. "And come to think of it, you might as well know now, so you don't have to sit there with nothing to do. The man leaned over, his face only inches from Toby's, his breath smelling of mint.

"You know what an oasis is?"

"You mean like in the desert?"

"Yeah. Like in the desert. The vision of a water source on the distant horizon when you've been traveling in the heat and dryness of the trackless sand is one of the most alluring sights in the world. And the space station Oasis is appropriately named, whether they realized it or not.

"Imagine the view. You're on Earth, the world is coming apart, and you look up on a clear night at the full moon and the bright spot of light circling it. An oasis in the sky, the promise of survival. The space station and the moon colony are the only places remaining that will avoid catastrophe.

"How much would a person be willing to pay for a ticket? It would have been like an auction reserved for the very rich, with their survival on the block. We could have controlled exclusive access to the only sure method of escape. Offer for sale the opportunity to sit on the fifty-yard line and wait until it's all over, then go back and rebuild whatever's left, according to the blueprint you decide to use. And we could have had it all."

The man stood erect, his face impassive, resigned, emotionless. "I had a feeling about you after our first encounter in the chutes, and later during our stay on Earth I decided to change my plans after I confirmed you possessed special gifts. Nothing could have stopped me, except *you*."

Toby wanted desperately to say something. He knew the stakes were as high as they get, and there must be words that could save his life, if only he could think of them. But in the silence that followed, all he could do was watch as the man turned away and walked over to the duffle bags, then dragged them to the rear of the bay and put the bundle at the base of the huge rear cargo doors. Toby squinted to see better in the dim light, and noticed an upside-down set of stairs built into the rear doors.

The man secured the bundle to the stairs, then walked over to the sidewall and looked at two switch panels mounted there. After donning a headset, he appeared to be speaking over the intercom. Toby watched carefully, remembering what Brett had told him about the operation of the communications panels in the bay. For all the good it would do him. The shackles restricted his movement to no more than a foot or so on either side of the pallet support rail.

The sudden change was immediately apparent. The engine noise decreased, and Toby could hear and feel the effect of the flight control extensions on the speed and attitude of the ship.

The man moved to his left a foot or so, and stared at another switch panel in the wall of the bay. Toby thought it contained the rear door controls, where the loadmasters could manipulate the doors during cargo transfer operations. Then the man reached out and pushed one of the buttons, and Toby saw a red light on the panel illuminate. He couldn't read the label, but knew enough to be concerned. In aviation, green and blue lights are generally advisory, amber lights indicate a need for caution, and red lights mean warning. What kind of warning?

Toby's eyes followed the man's movements as he stepped back away from the rear of the bay and approached the helmet and parachute lying on the floor. He picked the items up, carried them past Toby and over to the wall behind him. It was only then that Toby noticed another set of switch panels, which appeared to be identical to the ones at the rear. He remembered Brett had mentioned there were multiple communications and control panels positioned in the bay so the loadmasters were never too far from one.

Time seemed to stand still for a moment. The man took out a small device that looked like a GPS. After staring at it for a moment or two he put on a headset and spoke into the microphone, pointing to his right as if directing Brett to turn. The shuttle responded, and the man appeared to command a rollout as the shuttle returned to wings level.

He returned the device to a pocket in the jumpsuit and zipped it up. Then he donned the helmet, cinched the chinstrap down tight, and slung the parachute over one shoulder. Toby stared in anticipation of his next move when the man looked right at him, smiled ever so slightly, and mouthed, "Goodbye."

Before Toby could respond the man reached out to the door control panel and pushed the illuminated red button. Toby felt his ears pop, the air expel from his lungs, a sudden onset of cold and wind, and saw the atmosphere within the bay mist up like the fog he had seen in the early mornings during his short stay on Earth.

Toby watched in horror as the airstairs moved down to reveal the pitch-black nothingness through the gaping hole in the back of the shuttle. Aware of movement behind him, he turned just as the man was stepping past him toward the open airstairs. Without thinking about anything other than the paralyzing fear gripping his heart, Toby reached out and grabbed the man's leg.

"Mister!" he shouted over the roar of the wind noise, "Let me loose from here! With his injuries Brett may need my help to land!"

The man jerked to a stop as Toby held his leg, and looked down with an expression that transformed itself from something reasonably human into that of a savage beast. "You simple-minded little shitbird! Haven't you been listening? You . . . and . . . the . . . pilot . . . are . . . going . . . to . . . die . . . now!"

The man used his free hand to strike at Toby's head in conjunction with every word. With the blows raining down, Toby covered his head with his hands and tried to curl up into a ball. He felt himself losing consciousness, into a world without pain. Sliding into blackness, he decided to let go and quit fighting it.

It felt like a dream in which his mom was wiping his face with a warm washcloth, but something wasn't quite right. She was always very gentle, and this was a rapid, almost frantic swiping of the cloth over his face.

And then suddenly the realization hit that this wasn't his mom at all. Opening his eyes, Toby saw the blurry image of Snooper and heard the dog's characteristic soft bark of greeting. Snooper's face was visible at the top of his field of vision, head cocked to one side, ears alert and eyes staring at him.

Toby stared back at his ever-faithful attack robodog, who must have followed his instructions to the letter when Toby left him in the shipping container: *Snooper, stay. When I leave, find a place to hide and don't show yourself until I call you.*

And this loyal companion had apparently done exactly that, including one better. He didn't need to be called when the man began striking Toby.

Toby reached out. As Snooper moved closer to put his head into Toby's hand, Toby caught a glimpse of a body lying on the floor. This reunion would have to wait.

Rising up on an elbow, Toby concentrated on fighting the dizziness and commanded Snooper to stop licking him. He couldn't see anything with the dog's massive head in the way.

The hijacker was lying still. Toby forgot about the blood trickling down the side of his own face when he saw that the back of the man's neck was covered with it, oozing from an open wound. He was wondering what could have done that when he glanced at Snooper and noticed the dog's teeth.

"Good boy!" he said, scratching Snooper's ears. Then Toby saw the man's leg twitch, and realized things weren't over yet. The shackles around Toby's ankles were connected by a short length of chain the hijacker had passed through a slot in a pallet support railing. Toby considered trying to find the key, but decided it would take too much time.

Pointing to the chain, Toby told Snooper to bite it. Using his hands and repeating the command, he managed to get Snooper's jaws around the chain, but couldn't come up with the right combination of words and motions to get him to bite hard. And then he got an idea.

With his legs close together, one foot on either side of the railing, Toby lifted the chain up so that the loop was well above the floor. Coaxing Snooper into biting the chain again, and with his hands holding the chain on either side of the dog's jaws, he began to pull the chain gently to initiate a tug-of-war as he had seen videos of people doing with real dogs.

Snooper responded immediately by lowering his head, growling softly, and resisting Toby's attempt to pull the chain out of his mouth. Steadily increasing his efforts, Toby ended up pulling with all his strength as Snooper crouched down, front legs spread out, rear end high in the air, and held fast without giving an inch.

Then Toby relaxed his pull, allowing the chain to slacken a bit. Snooper used the opportunity to move back a step, then looked at Toby with an expression that seemed to say, "Are you giving up already?"

Toby waited a few seconds longer, watching Snooper's mouth where it was clamped around the chain. The instant he saw the dog's jaws begin to relax, he jerked the chain as hard as he could. Snooper reacted perfectly, clamping down hard to hold on and pulling back against what he perceived as a sneaky attempt to win.

Snooper ended up on his butt as his teeth bit cleanly through the chain with a metallic snapping sound. Toby laughed, staring at the dog sitting there with the severed length of chain in his mouth. "Come here," he said, and when Snooper stepped close Toby hugged him hard.

More movement from the man got his attention. Toby got to his feet, struggling to keep from falling down. His head hurt, and his legs were unsteady. With a whispered, "Heel" to Snooper, Toby walked with faltering steps toward the front of the bay. All he had to do was to join Brett in the cockpit. With the man isolated in the bay, they could utilize the jettison system to get rid of him. Toby was approaching the ladder up to the rear cabin bulkhead door when Snooper growled and turned.

Looking back toward the rear of the bay, Toby saw the man stand up and turn toward him. Could the man reach him before he made it up the ladder and into the crew area? How could Toby prevent him from getting into the cockpit? Then he realized Snooper would attack the man and might kill him, but certainly keep him occupied long enough. He was about to start up the ladder when it occurred to him that Snooper would end up being jettisoned along with the hijacker.

I don't care if he is a robot. He's my dog.

Then Toby noticed the backpack. It was still attached to Snooper's back with the pistol grip of the shotgun sticking out the top. As the man leaned over and coughed, Toby reached down and removed the weapon. He'd never been able to read the manual, but the image of the man ejecting the shells from the cop's shotgun after the fight gave him the right idea. Toby tentatively pulled back on the slide and felt it move to the rear and stop.

Glancing down, he saw the shell, resting just below the opening in the side of the weapon, waiting to be loaded into the chamber. With a hard pull on the slide, he racked the round home, checked that the safety was off, pointed the shotgun at the hijacker and screamed over the noise. "Stay where you are mister! I shot you once and I'll do it again!"

The man laughed, then shouted, "Goddam you and that freaking animal all to hell!"

As the man's arm raised, Toby saw the pistol and pulled the trigger. The punishing noise and recoil took him completely by surprise. As he stepped back with his left foot to regain his balance, Toby tripped over Snooper's tail and fell to the floor by the foot of the ladder as the sound of a pistol shot reverberated within the bay.

The bullet splattered against one of the steps and Toby felt a hot stinging sensation as the fragments hit him. He was crawling behind the first step when Snooper growled and left Toby's side.

Three more rapid shots followed. When no bullets struck in his vicinity, Toby peered over the step and saw Snooper hit the man on a dead run, knocking him back and down to the floor. Then he saw a bright flash and a shower of sparks fly up. Snooper seemed to rise up a few inches and landed on the floor, legs pumping and body twitching.

The man struggled to his feet, looked down at Snooper, and fired twice more into his side, screaming, "Bad dog! Bad dog!" Then he turned to look at Toby, grinned, and threw back his head and laughed again. Toby wanted to run for his life, but couldn't get his legs to move. He was still looking at Snooper's lifeless body when the laughter faded. Shifting his gaze to the hijacker, he stared directly into those dead eyes and heard the man shout, "You're next!"

With surprising agility considering his bloody appearance, the man rushed Toby with the pistol held down by his leg. Fueled with adrenaline and in spite of the pain from his own wounds, Toby took the ladder steps three at a time and knew his only chance was to get the rear cabin bulkhead door closed and locked before the man got to him. The door could be opened from either side, but locked only from within the cabin.

The ladder made two switchbacks prior to the top landing. At the second of the platforms, Toby couldn't resist the temptation to glance down and check how close his pursuer was. Toby's spirits soared with hope that he might make it. With renewed effort he reached the top landing at full speed and used the railing to help him turn quickly toward the open door.

Toby leapt through the doorway and came to a sudden stop while grabbing at the latch holding the door open. He expected it to release easily, but it refused to budge and he felt a stab of pain in his hand. One glance told the story. The man had secured the latch open and Toby had cut his hand on the sharp end of the wire.

His next move was completely unplanned. It was as if a vision came to him, and he knew that trying to escape forward was the wrong thing to do. Even if he reached the galley or cockpit well ahead of the man, there was no way to keep his pursuer out of the cockpit. His only chance was to lure him back into the cargo bay.

Toby heard the man's boots pounding on the ladder as he turned back toward the door and rushed out onto the landing. Seeing movement in his peripheral vision to his right, and knowing he had no more than a few seconds to spare, he reached out with his left hand and toggled the lever releasing the arm on the utility crane. With his right hand gripping the strap harness at the end of the line, he released the brake on the line with his left hand, took two steps forward toward the railing, and leapt over it and off the landing.

Toby felt the man's grip on his right ankle just as he cleared the railing and began to fall. Kicking with his left foot, he heard the man grunt with pain as the combination of the kick and Toby's weight pulled his right ankle free. But now he was falling headfirst. With only the drag of the block and tackle to slow him down, Toby knew the sudden stop at the end was going to be final.

And then a sudden jerk in the line, accompanied by a scream, snapped Toby hard as his grip on the line helped flip his body around. He landed feet first on the floor of the bay. Legs crumpling from the impact, Toby's right ankle broke, and he almost fainted from the pain. Dreading the sight, knowing this was the end of it all, Toby opened his eyes and looked up at the landing.

And he almost laughed. The man's hand was red with blood and jammed in one of the pulleys at the top of the crane. He must have reached out and grabbed the line to stop Toby's escape. Friction between the line and his gloved hand had instantly pulled his arm up and the hand into the block and tackle.

Maybe it's not quite over.

Toby managed to get up, and hobbling toward the rear of the bay tried to remember all Brett had told him about the personnel restraint and intercom systems. He heard an angry shout from behind him, looked over his shoulder and saw that the man had removed his hand from the pulley and was descending the ladder.

Hurry up.

Passing Snooper's body, Toby said, "Thank you, boy," and felt the tears begin to flow. But heightened determination and the delicious desire for revenge provided a calmness to his actions. The man was shouting something behind him, but it didn't matter. His pursuer didn't seem interested in shooting at him now, probably because he wanted to get up close for the final confrontation. All Toby wanted was for the bastard to keep coming.

Toby had his sights set on the aft communications panel. He'd gotten a clear view of it while chained to the floor. With a specific set of actions in mind, he hobbled up to it and turned to face the hijacker for the last time.

His pursuer seemed to be in no hurry. Toby stared as the man stopped by Snooper's body and began to shout something about how sorry he was to have hurt the nice doggie. His voice was taunting, vicious, and dripping with sarcasm. Then he bent over and began to stroke Snooper's head, and appeared to be talking to him. It was just the opportunity Toby needed.

With the man looking down, Toby reached out to the communications panel and keyed the intercom microphone. A headset hung nearby, but the man could easily see him use it. He would know immediately Toby was trying to contact the cockpit, and probably just shoot him and be done with it. Leaning to his left, so that his mouth was closer to the microphone without being too obvious about it, he said, "Brett, don't answer this. Get ready to open the rear doors and do it when I tell you." Toby repeated the transmission two more times, cutting off the third call when the man stood up and continued toward him.

What a sight. His pursuer was shuffling forward slowly, his body ravaged by wounds, grinning all the while. holding the pistol in his right hand, dripping blood. Toby tensed his body, not knowing if he would be able to fasten the restraint line quickly enough, but determined to do this no matter what. It was entirely personal now.

The man stopped. "Well, looks like it's just you and me this time. Whenever I think I have you cornered one of those goddamn dogs jumps me from behind. I don't know who I hate worse, you or them."

In spite of the situation, Toby wasn't afraid. Part of him was detached, kind of like looking in on this scene from the outside. He found it surprisingly easy to stand his ground, look the man right in the eyes, and wait. Then a movement behind the man got Toby's attention.

Avoiding the intense desire to shift his gaze, he focused on the man's face. "You know, I really would have liked to work with you and done those things."

The man seemed to love this, closing his eyes, leaning his head back and laughing heartily. Toby glanced behind the man and his heart almost jumped out of his chest.

Snooper was dragging himself toward the man with his front legs. There were holes in his body, wires exposed here and there, and his rear legs were dragging behind him. Love for a real animal couldn't be any stronger than this. As the man stopped laughing, Toby forced himself to stare right at him and maintain his expression.

But the man was suspicious. "What are you thinking about now, you little shit?" The man raised the pistol and leveled it at Toby's face. The dark hole in the end of the muzzle seemed to be much larger than he remembered.

Snooper clamped his jaws around the man's right ankle. Toby heard what could only be the sound of bones cracking as the man screamed and his body jerked backward. The pistol discharged, the bullet striking the wall above Toby's head and the muzzle blast hitting him like an invisible hammer.

Toby screamed, "Open the doors open the doors open the doors!" into the intercom and hoped Brett heard his original call and obeyed him. The next few seconds passed in a blur of action.

Toby heard muffled popping sounds. As he looked toward the doors he saw them separate from the rear of the shuttle and begin to fall away into the blackness. Glancing back toward the man, he saw him trying to pry Snooper's jaws free from his ankle. Toby realized that even if the man didn't succeed, Snooper was incapable of further attack and the man wasn't in any danger of falling out of the shuttle.

Then Toby remembered Brett's description of the maneuver and realized the shuttle was still level. Where was the steep climb angle that would cause the man to lose his footing? As Toby reached for the intercom transmit switch to call Brett, the deck of the shuttle began to tilt up to his left, and he realized he hadn't restrained himself.

Toby grabbed the harness and threw it over his arms. He barely got the chest strap fastened when he lost his footing as the shuttle entered a steep climb. With the harness fastened only around his chest, Toby felt himself sliding out of it. Glancing down between his legs, the sight of the open doors and the dark night below him brought a rush of fear. Toby locked his arms at his side, and while hanging from the wall of the shuttle reached down between his legs searching for the leg straps. He found one, got it fastened, and had just found the other when he felt secure enough to return his attention to the man.

The hijacker was frantically trying to find something on the floor to hold on to as he slid down the sloping deck with Snooper still attached to his right leg. The extra weight of the dog pulled him toward the vast opening in the rear of the shuttle. A landslide of loose items left in the bay pelted the man, and he appeared to be losing the battle. Toby watched with mounting anticipation at seeing the man fall to his death.

Then the man stopped kicking, calmly looked to his right and behind him, and released his grip on a pallet support railing. As he began to slide faster down the slanting floor, he rolled over twice to his right and grabbed the heavy straps of cargo netting securing some equipment to a pallet. With his motion arrested, he dug his feet into the netting and appeared to be securely stopped.

Toby could not believe what he was seeing. The man was still very much alive, and even had the presence of mind to look over at Toby hanging suspended by the restraint straps. He smiled and mouthed something Toby couldn't hear over the incredible wind and engine noise. Reading the man's lips, he thought the message was, "Nice try."

The angle of the bay floor stopped increasing, then began to lower toward a normal flight attitude. The hijacker would soon be able to climb off the pallet. His duffle bags and parachute had fallen to the rear of the bay and were lodged against the cargo door jam. He could still escape.

It was another of those flashing images, a bit of memory released by chance or some combination of stimuli. Using the restraint strap, Toby pulled himself closer to the comm panel and reached out for the microphone switch.

"Jettison the cargo, Brett! Jettison the cargo now!"

As the shuttle approached level flight Toby heard the engine sound increase to a punishing level. Looking toward the rear of the bay and out into the darkness, he felt the surge of acceleration and saw the twin bright glow of the afterburners as they lit off. The shuttle rotated nose up and the cargo pallets slowly began to move.

Slowly at first, then with increasing speed, the pallets rolled down the rails toward the massive opening in the rear of the shuttle. Toby's eyes were drawn to the figure clinging to the cargo netting, and his gaze settled on the face of the man. Toby smiled. Releasing one hand from his grip on the restraint strap, he waved to the hijacker as the pallet accelerated down the rails and out into the black void.

Illuminated for a few seconds by the afterburners' twin plumes, the pallet appeared to hang suspended as the forward edge dropped and it began the long fall toward Earth with the man still clutching the netting. The last thing Toby saw was the body of Snooper, flailing about but still attached to the man's ankle. As the first pallet fell out of sight, the steepness of the deck angle allowed Toby to see a chute open. He didn't know the pallets had chutes on them, and it was fascinating to watch.

Toby began to shiver uncontrollably as the cold hit him. He was still secured by the restraint straps, lying on the floor of the bay. He tried to get up, but fell back when he tried to put weight on the injured ankle. Crawling over to the wall where the intercom panel was mounted, he used the strap to help him stand and hold on to the wall for support. With one hand, he put on a headset and positioned the boom microphone against his lips.

"He's g-g-gone, Brett."

As the sound of Brett's voice filled the earpieces, Toby glanced behind him. He had almost gotten used to seeing the gaping hole, as if staring out into thousands of feet of darkness was a normal condition. Suddenly the realization hit that the man *really* was gone, and a headlong release of emotion surged over Toby.

Big racking sobs took his breath away. Brett called him a few times, but Toby was unable to answer. Recovering slowly, he told Brett he was fine, but needed to come forward and get warm. He didn't mention the ankle. There wasn't anything Brett could do about it anyway. After releasing the harness, Toby hobbled slowly forward. He had just reached middle of the bay when he felt the shuttle bounce and heard a muffled explosion. All thoughts of being cold vanished. With Brett's voice screaming over the PA for him to get up to the cockpit, Toby gritted his teeth against the pain and hurried toward the ladder.

The shuttle entered a descent. The floor of the bay slanted down, and the unseen hand of gravity shoved him forward. Reaching the ladder, he looked up at all the steps and decided to use the crane.

Stepping into the cargo strapping, Toby pulled on the other end of the line so the large open squares in the netting came up around his legs. He continued pulling and used the mechanical advantage of the block and tackle to assist his arms in hauling himself up beside the stairs.

He reached the top just as the shuttle nosed over into a steeper dive. The movement threw Toby against the railing, which helped him grab on and pull himself over onto the landing. After struggling free from the cargo strapping, he stood and hobbled into the corridor.

And then he smelled the smoke. Looking up, Toby saw the dark haze hanging against the ceiling. A quick glance behind him and up at the roof of the cargo bay confirmed there was a lot of it. Crouching down, Toby limped forward to the galley and realized he might not make it to the cockpit.

A pall of smoke covered the top half of the galley, and the flickering light off to one side confirmed an active fire. With the lessons of disaster training to guide him, Toby instinctively looked around for personal breathing equipment, or PBE, designed to provide a quick donning, self-contained breathing apparatus as protection from smoke and fumes. Peering into the galley, Toby saw one fastened to the wall. He stayed low, removed the device from its holder, and donned the mask. Entering the galley, he moved to his left to stay away from the flames and hobbled to the companionway. He used the handrails for support and hopped on his good leg from step to step up to the cockpit. The same smoky haze hung in the air, and the glow of red and amber lights was visible through the gloom.

Brett had donned his helmet and was struggling with the controls. Whenever Toby had watched him hand fly the shuttle before, it seemed almost effortless, with small movements of his hands and feet. The shuttle was in a dive. Toby knew what an altimeter was, and things didn't look very good at all.

"Brett, what—?"

"The SOB planted a bomb. Sit down and strap in."

The intensity in Brett's words energized Toby as he climbed into the copilot's seat and fastened the harness. Brett began to instruct him on proper positioning when things went completely haywire.

The shuttle seemed to swap ends, and went from a dive to a steep climb faster than Toby would have thought possible. He felt a sudden jolt, and heard a strange shrieking sound as the world began to come apart around him.

In a strange transition to slow motion, Toby glanced over at Brett and saw him take his hands off the controls and place them on the armrests. The thought occurred to Toby that this wasn't the right time to quit flying the machine. He stared in fascination as Brett pulled up on some handles and opened his hands to grip what looked like big triggers. When Brett's hands squeezed, the slow motion part of the scene ceased to exist.

In a mixture of sight, sound, and action, Toby was overwhelmed by the ejection sequence as the capsule separated from the shuttle. When he finally looked outside the windscreen, he saw nothing but darkness until from above him and to his right a large piece of the shuttle fell past, rotating slowly and trailing flames and smoke.

Shortly thereafter a flash of light from below signaled its impact with the surface. An eerie quiet settled upon them. As Toby wondered if this was what it was like to die, he felt the capsule hit, sink much too far below the surface of the sea, and bob back up to rest on the gentle swells.

Toby looked over at Brett. As the pilot removed his helmet, he seemed to sag into the seat for a moment, then take a few deep breaths. They stared at each other for a long moment, saying nothing until Brett finally grinned and asked, "So, you still want to be a pilot?"

Toby smiled back through the faceplate of the PBE, and after slowly releasing the straps and pulling the device over his head, he nodded. "But if it's all the same to you, could we leave off the emergency procedures part for a while? I haven't been on a normal flight yet."

They were still laughing about it when the choppers arrived overhead.

21

DAY THIRTY-TWO LATE AFTERNOON

It was one of those evenings he'd heard his dad talk about, sitting on the porch of the old farmhouse with his father after a hard day in the fields. The sun was low on the horizon, the day just starting to cool off, shadows lengthening over the land. Toby rested with his broken ankle propped up on a pillow, sipping a glass of iced tea. It must run in the family, the ability to make really good iced tea, because his aunt served it just the way his mom did, in huge glasses, with lots of ice, sugar and lemon.

"Are you okay, Toby?" It was Aunt Pat, calling from inside the house.

"Yes, ma'am, thank you."

"Holler if you need anything. I'm in the kitchen fixing supper. My spaghetti okay with you?"

"If you twist my arm just right, I may be able to choke it down." Laughter from the house confirmed Pat understood the compliment.

Leaning back against a cushion, Toby looked up at the pale sky as a large flock of white wing doves flashed by on their way to roost for the night after visiting the pond. His uncle had promised the hunting would be really good this fall, and that after Toby sampled the doves cooked in the smoker and served with Aunt Pat's wild rice and vegetable casserole, he'd probably decide he had to stay with them forever just for the food.

It was a tempting thought. Although he hadn't been able to do much because of the ankle, and he knew hard work could quickly change a person's perspective on anything, Toby felt that life out here would be just fine by him.

Aunt Pat told him about their neighbors to the south across the creek that bought the old Sanderson place. The man had been some kind of executive, living the typical rat-race life in the big city, and his wife was a lawyer trying to balance the duties of motherhood with a career. Their decision to give it all up and move to the country was made for the same kinds of reasons his own mom and dad decided to volunteer for service on Oasis. A part of Toby wanted to learn hard lessons the easy way from these examples.

It would be like skipping the middle step. Why go to all that effort to make a place for yourself out in the world and then find you didn't really want to be there after all? Why not stay here, right where you would probably end up longing to be, and avoid all the trouble?

And the answer, of course, was clear and unavoidable. Each person has to come to the really important decisions in life by relying on his or her own experience. Guidance from the older people you trust is one thing, but a blueprint is quite another. Being born and raised on Oasis was in its own way the most restricting of road maps. Toby loved his parents, and knew they had chosen their future from a list of many possibilities with the intention of passing on a better life for him, but at the same time he felt cheated out of the ability to choose for himself.

Toby's thoughts were interrupted by the sound of the screen door opening. He knew it was his Aunt Pat, not just because she was the only one in the house at the moment, but also because she had a way of moving, with a quick purposefulness reminding him of his mom.

Pat walked up and refilled his glass from a huge pitcher that never seemed to be less than three-quarters full. She put the pitcher down on the small table beside his lounge, pulled another chair over closer, and sat down. Reaching out to take his hand, she asked, "Miss your mom and dad?"

The surge of emotion was almost too much, and Toby had to swallow hard to keep from losing it. His aunt seemed to realize the effect of the question, and remained silent while he took a moment to answer.

Toby gazed toward the western horizon and the setting sun. "Yes ma'am. When all this happened, I'd done some things they were upset about. Leaving them like I did was really hard because I knew they'd consider it just another foolish stunt.

"But I had to do it. It was like there was a vision or something, showing me the way. Grown-ups think kids don't consider the consequences of their actions, but that's not always true. I didn't know what would happen, just that I had to try. I made the decision to do what I thought was best in spite of what might happen."

"Would you make the same decision again?"

Toby looked at his aunt. She reminded him of his mom so much that it was hard to do without crying, but in a way it gave him strength. "I was in the hospital only a day or so when they came in."

"Hospital people?"

"From the government. And some military guys. They asked me about everything that happened, and then told me we'd do a complete debriefing later. I expect them to come driving up any day now. Anyway, this one guy seemed to be running everything, and when it was over he told me Brett had said I was a genuine hero. He said I would probably get a medal."

"You aren't answering my question."

"Sorry. Yes. I can't explain it. I'm not sure you'd believe me if I tried, but I made a difference. Most of it's probably luck, but Brett says fighter pilots often say they'd rather be lucky than good. If it's okay for him, I'll take it."

His aunt watched him with a thoughtful expression, as if considering what he'd said and how to respond. "Your Uncle Dave and I have noticed you don't talk much about what happened. But every time you do the name Brett always comes up. Is he someone special?"

"Oh, yes. He's a space command pilot and he's my best friend. I mean grown-up friend."

"What about your dad, Toby? Doesn't he qualify as your best adult friend?"

The question took Toby completely by surprise because he'd never considered comparing his dad with Brett in that way. "My dad's my dad. He's a friend, sure, but it's different with Brett."

"Why is it different?"

All these questions. Aunt Pat was like that. Toby had known her no more than a week and he already realized she could grab on to a subject like a robodog and never let go. "Parents are always judging you. Everything you do has to meet their approval. My mom and dad don't come right out and say it, but they don't have to. I know it's there, and it never lets up.

"Brett treats me more like an equal. And he's a pilot. I've decided that's what I want to be, and he's told me what I have to do. Only the best get to do what he does, and I'm going to be the best."

Aunt Pat didn't appear pleased with Toby's answer, and he was afraid this discussion was going to get more involved than he was ready for. He was about to ask for more tea when she stood up and refilled his glass. "That's very interesting, Toby, and I'd love to get into this in more detail. But that spaghetti sauce is probably needing my attention. With two hungry men to feed this gal needs to hop to it. You need anything to hold you until supper?"

"No, ma'am."

"Okay," she said over her shoulder as she went inside. "Give me about thirty minutes and then ring that bell for your Uncle Dave. He'd work out in that barn for days if I didn't insist he eat something."

Toby doubted that. His uncle could eat more than any person he'd ever seen. And no wonder. Aunt Pat was a terrific cook, and the food was always so fresh. He couldn't wait for his ankle to heal so that he could start helping out and see how they grew stuff, especially since they had adopted a "rural survivalist" lifestyle, which emphasized being self-sufficient in providing all the basic necessities of life.

Toby drank some tea, adjusted the lounge chair so it leaned back further, and closed his eyes. Being temporarily crippled had some advantages, and the ability to enjoy some quiet time was almost worth the initial discomfort.

Events immediately after the splashdown and recovery centered on receiving medical attention. Toby hadn't realized how many wounds he suffered until the excitement began to wear off and the pain took over. His ankle was the most serious, but there were enough cuts, scrapes, and bruises to make the initial days and nights after the rescue a real ordeal. During his stay in the hospital he was able to see Brett a few times, and it was easy to keep up on what was happening with him. But Brett's injuries were far more serious. When it came time for discharge, Toby asked to stay at the hospital. Neither the authorities nor the hospital personnel would even discuss it. He had no choice but to leave when they told him to.

It was one of the hardest things he had ever done. Hospitals certainly weren't his favorite places, but he felt he owed it to Brett to be there. They'd gone through a lot together, and it seemed no more than an extension of that comradeship to remain by his side through the days ahead.

But there was a reason it felt okay to leave. During the second week in the hospital, Toby was visiting Brett when a soft knock at the door interrupted their conversation. Toby turned to look and almost dropped his apple juice.

A woman dressed in the uniform of a military aviator stepped into the room. She was so beautiful that Toby could not take his eyes off of her. She nodded to Toby with a smile and walked over to the edge of the bed where Brett lay.

Toby would never forget the look on Brett's face. It was as if the sun came up in the room. The two of them spoke quietly for a moment before Brett made the introduction.

"Toby, I'd like you to meet First Lieutenant Susan Strickland, United States Fighter Command. Susan, this is Toby Williams, and he saved my life."

The rest of the visit was like a dream, and Toby would never forget it. The woman was one of the fighter pilots involved in pursuing the shuttle, and she took leave to return to the States and meet Brett. From the look of things she wouldn't be leaving anytime soon, and Toby knew that Brett was in good hands.

The debriefing sessions had been hard. He wanted to cooperate, but had no intention of discussing how and why he came to be working with the hijacker. He was able to relate the events from the perspective of a hostage, and they seemed to buy it. An extensive search of the crash site had discovered the wreckage of the shuttle and the jettisoned cargo. The identity and fate of the hijacker were unknown.

A colonel on the debriefing team called the hospital almost every day. Apparently the President himself directed that Toby be kept informed on what the government was doing. They wanted to reunite him with his parents, but that would not happen anytime soon. The initial efforts had to concentrate on assessing the damage to the space station. Engineering missions would dominate the shuttle program for the near future.

Oasis was cold and lifeless. Estimates for time to repair and return to full operation were extremely speculative at this early stage, but NASA estimated it would take a minimum of two years to establish any substantial permanent human occupation. Work on the moon colony could continue for the time being because there was sufficient stockpile of materiel to sustain construction. The addition of the Oasis evacuees to the moon colony population had allowed acceleration of the schedule because they finally had enough people to operate three eight-hour shifts.

The colonel had initially been reluctant to discuss much of anything except Toby's personal situation, but gradually softened that stance when Toby continued to ask questions.

The shuttle had been hijacked for the purpose of taking control of Oasis. The space fighter apparently was a prize offered to the Chinese government in return for providing the shuttle launch facility. NASA estimated that with the fighter as a technological model, the Chinese would develop a viable shuttle capability within the next ten years. China denied involvement with the hijacking. Diplomatic relations with the United States deteriorated overnight. China lodged a protest over the attempt by U.S. fighters to penetrate their airspace, and claimed the engagement was nothing more than a response to an outside threat.

Toby yawned and glanced at his watch. He'd never cared much for watches. Oasis had clocks everywhere, and for the most part he didn't pay much attention to what time it was. But Brett's left arm was broken just above the wrist, and since he wouldn't be wearing it for a while, he asked Toby to keep it for him until the cast came off.

Thirty minutes were about up. The aroma of the spaghetti sauce drifting over the porch from the kitchen sent Toby's appetite into high gear. The current standing joke around the farm was that since Toby couldn't do any real work, the least he could do was help Aunt Pat by ringing the chow bell. Uncle Dave had added a piece of rope so Toby could perform the task without getting up.

The sound seemed to carry forever in the still air. Toby sat up to get a better view of the barn over the porch railing, and saw his uncle come to the door and wave. He'd usually spend a few minutes out by the horse trough cleaning off the majority of the mud, dirt, and other barnyard debris before coming in for meals. There seemed to be an understanding in the family that when Uncle Dave came in the house, the farm stayed outside.

The evening had ripened into a gorgeous sunset. Toby could count on the fingers of his two hands the number of these he'd seen, and he was determined never to take the view for granted. Especially when his aunt and uncle advised him to enjoy the relatively clear air out in the country while he still could.

And what a contrast it was. Earthlings saw sunsets every day, and would consider the view of Earth from the moon to be so spectacular they'd feel the same way Toby did now. Having had the opportunity to enjoy both wasn't lost on him, and during the past week he had spent a considerable amount of his quiet time considering the four most logical possibilities with regard to his future.

The first two situations assumed being permanently reunited with his parents. Toby knew enough about why his mom and dad volunteered for duty in space to guess they would prefer he join them, whether on the moon colony or on Oasis after repairs. But his choice, based on the conviction that he was destined to be a pilot, was for their contract with NASA to be terminated and they would all live on Earth like regular people. With Oasis down, maybe NASA would need to reduce the moon colony population and offer early returns to those who wanted them.

A third possibility was to rejoin his parents now. Then with their consent and NASA approval, he could return to Earth, live with Aunt Pat and Uncle Dave, and follow his dream from there. Although parental agreement was uncertain, Toby was positive with his newly established reputation as a hero, he'd be able to generate support where it counted and have no trouble with the space agency.

And then there was the last scenario. He was perfectly positioned for it now, to live on the farm, go to school, find a way to begin flying lessons, and pursue his dream.

And although some people might consider separation from his parents unacceptable, none of them counted. For many reasons, some of which he could enumerate, but most of which he could not, Toby knew in his heart his parents would agree.

The shuffling sound of tired feet and legs attached to work boots approached the porch. Toby looked up to see the smiling face of his uncle as he stopped at the bottom of the steps up to the landing. Groaning softly, Dave bent over and struggled to remove the boots.

"Howdy, podner." His uncle always greeted Toby with a kind of exaggerated cowboy drawl. "Working hard up on this here porch today?"

Toby always played along. "Yup."

"Uh huh. Well, I hope ringing that bell wasn't no trouble, keeping you from anything important or nothing. I'm mighty obliged to you for giving me an excuse to quit working."

"You bet."

Dave got the boots off and climbed the steps. Just as he was about to walk onto the landing, Toby sat up suddenly. "Hold on there, cowboy. Appears to me you got some of that there barnyard gold splattered on them jeans. Better go clean up some more. Aunt Pat'll turn the hose to you, walking in like that."

Dave halted, looked down at his jeans, then stared at Toby with a look of feigned indignation. "Well, she might just try that. But you can mark my words. I'll scrape the stuff off, use a broom if I has to, but I'll be hog-tied 'fore I take a shower to walk in my own house."

Toby stared back, doing his best to keep from laughing. "Uh huh. Pretty big talk from a tired old barefoot farm hand."

"Who you calling barefoot, you young whippersnapper? I'll teach you to show some respect!" He dropped the boots, and was reaching down to begin tickling Toby when the voice of authority stopped them both.

"Hey! Don't you pick on him, you bully. I'll take a broom to you myself."

Dave turned and looked at Pat with a smile on his face and love in his eyes. "What happened to 'Welcome home, dear, did you have a good day at the office?'"

"You gave up the opportunity for that when we decided to work this farm. But I tell you what I can do."

"What's that?"

"Bring you a cold brew while you visit with Toby and I get supper on the table."

"In that case," chuckled Dave, "your wish is my command."

Aunt Pat turned back toward the kitchen and yelled over her shoulder. "You heard him Toby, you're my witness!"

Uncle Dave shook his head and sat down. "I can't say anything around that woman without getting in deeper. It'd take me two lifetimes to work off all I owe her."

"Two lifetimes?"

Dave smiled. "Yup. And I'd love every minute of it."

They both laughed, and Dave made himself comfortable as Pat brought the beer. "Five minutes, fellas."

They were sitting and talking quietly, enjoying the soft fading light of the day, when all of a sudden from behind the house a loud noise drowned out the conversation and Toby looked up to see a small single-engine aircraft flash by overhead.

With his mouth hanging open, Toby stared as the nose pulled up, and the airplane in one continuous motion rolled over to the left on its back and ended up banked steeply to the right. Turning to the north-west, the airplane rolled wings level and disappeared over a line of trees and out of sight.

"Holy Toledo, what was that?"

"That was an airplane, Toby. Kind of like a shuttle, but smaller."

Toby turned to look at his uncle, who wasn't being very successful in stifling a smile. "I'll tell Aunt Pat you've been mean to me. She'll believe me, you know she will, and you'll—"

Uncle Dave held up his hands in mock surrender. "Okay, anything but that." After another sip of beer, he said, "That was George Smith. He lives a few miles from here, comes by to say hello like that a couple of times a week. Owns a nice place, but doesn't work it seriously. Hard to believe, but he built that airplane right there in his workshop, and he flies it off a grass strip next to the house."

Toby was unable to speak. He had a thousand questions about what he'd just seen, but couldn't manage to get even one of them into words.

"Matter of fact," said Uncle Dave," he has a daughter about your age, maybe a year or two older. How old are you, by the way?"

Answering a question turned out to be easier. "Th-th-thirteen. And a half!"

"Hmmm. I think Kathy is probably about fifteen. Good pilot, too, from what I hear. Not legally, of course, but she's taking lessons from her dad and wants to be a military pilot."

Now Toby couldn't breathe. He swallowed hard a few times, trying to get some moisture in his mouth and find some air from somewhere. "A g-girl?"

"Yeah. You know. They're like boys, only different. She—"

"Supper's ready, men!" Aunt Pat called from the house.

"Hey, Babe?" said Uncle Dave.

"Yo!"

"Want me to set the table and eat out here? It's cooled off real nice."

"Well, hurry up, cowboy! The food's hot and ready to go."

Uncle Dave jumped up and rushed inside. Toby finally managed to restart his breathing reflex, his mind racing with the news that somewhere past those trees, an airplane, an instructor, and a girl were making his own dream for the future come true.

As Uncle Dave brought a second armload of food to the table,

Toby's brand new phone rang in his pocket. He eagerly pulled it out, wondering who was calling him for the very first time on Earth.

"Hello?"

After a short silence, a voice said, "Hi, Toby. This is Kathy, your next-door neighbor. Wanna go flying with me tomorrow?"

ACKNOWLEDGMENTS

To those familiar with the publishing industry, this page is considered part of the "front (or back) matter" that often includes the author's humble attempt to recognize the contributions of those who provided invaluable assistance along the seemingly never-ending journey from concept to reality.

As well we should, for it is my steadfast belief that few writers, if any, can in isolation bring into existence a story that works from the first word to the last without being forced by others to exit the creative fog required to complete it. The tired cliché ". . . can't see the forest for the trees" is more than apropos.

But if I were to attempt to do that here, the effort would require far too many pages, and I would undoubtedly fail to include everyone who so unselfishly gave of their time and expertise. To avoid such a *revoltin' development* (and for that term I offer acknowledgment to William Bendix in *The Life of Riley* for borrowing one of the most famous catch phrases of the 1950s), I'll make this simple.

Ann Katherine McIntosh, light of my life, you have my everlasting gratitude for your unfailing support through years of struggle to realize this dream. And to my fellow writers who read and critiqued countless pages of false starts and detours, thanks a million times over to all y'all. (For those of you who don't know, that's talkin' Texan!)

And last, but never least, to my brother, Dr. Samuel C. McIntosh, PhD in Aeronautics and Astronautics from Stanford University, my all-in-one lifelong best friend and technical adviser.

ABOUT THE AUTHOR

Following graduation from the University of Washington in Seattle with a Bachelor of Science degree in Psychology, Tosh entered the United States Air Force with the intention of serving a four-year commitment as a pilot before deciding what he really wanted to do with the remainder of his professional life. One ride in a jet trainer consigned that plan to the scrap heap.

Twenty years of flying jet fighters (including two combat tours in the F-4 Phantom II) remain the highlight of his aviation career. Another twenty years as a commercial airline and corporate pilot and current enjoyment of sport aviation in light aircraft have embedded within him a passion for sharing with others his unique perspective of what it means to be an aviator.

Publication of *Oasis* has consumed over 27 years of intermittent effort, including 12 major revisions and multiple submissions to agents, an experience that compelled him to switch genres to write an aviation thriller series about airborne murder.

Pilot Error (2011) and *Red Line* (2014) are the first two novels in the series that interweaves a life-long fascination with writing and thousands of flight hours in pursuit of one goal: to create stories that entertain and put readers up close and personal within his world of the cockpit. The third novel is in progress.

www.ingramcontent.com/pod-product-compliance
Lightning Source LLC
Chambersburg PA
CBHW020823030726
47496CB00001B/56